PARTY GIRLS DIE IN PEARLS

Party Girls Die in Pearls

AN OXFORD GIRL MYSTERY

Plum Sykes

HARPER

An Imprint of HarperCollins*Publishers*

This is a work of fiction. Names, characters, places, and incidents are products of the author's imagination or are used fictitiously and are not to be construed as real. Any resemblance to actual events, locales, organizations, or persons, living or dead, is entirely coincidental.

HarperCollins books may be purchased for educational, business, or sales promotional use. For information, please email the Special Markets Department at SPsales@harpercollins.com.

FIRST EDITION

Text design of pp. 1, 330, and 331 by Phil Beresford.
Photograph on p. 1 © Getty Images.

Library of Congress Cataloging-in-Publication Data

Names: Sykes, Plum, author
Title: Party girls die in pearls : an Oxford girl mystery / Plum Sykes.
Description: First edition. | New York : Harper, [2017]
Identifiers: LCCN 2016042149| ISBN 9780062429025 (hardback) | ISBN 9780062429049 (ebook)
Subjects: | BISAC: FICTION / Contemporary Women. | FICTION / Humorous. | FICTION / Mystery & Detective / Women Sleuths. | GSAFD: Mystery fiction.
Classification: LCC PR6119.Y54 P37 2017 | DDC 823/.92--dc23 LC record available at https://lccn.loc.gov/2016042149

17 18 19 20 21 LSC 10 9 8 7 6 5 4 3 2 1

In loving memory
Madeleine "Granny" Goad
1911–2005

PARTY GIRLS DIE IN PEARLS

CHERWELL

MONDAY, 25 OCTOBER 1985　　　　　　　　　　　　　　**10P**

Murder at Oxford College Shocks "Champagne Set"

BY URSULA FLOWERBUTTON

The girl was lying on the chaise longue when I found her that morning. She was still in her party dress. At first, I thought she was asleep. But she wasn't. She was dead. Even a girl like me—one who's read all seventy-five Agatha Christies—could never have imagined such a sinister start to her first term at Oxford. I was expecting books and ball gowns, not a dead body . . .

Full story continues overleaf

Chapter 1

The thoughts going through Ursula Flowerbutton's mind as she gazed up at the gilded, gargoyled, turreted double gate tower of Christminster College, Oxford, were—mostly—of cucumber sandwiches. She might have studied Disraeli, Gladstone, Lincoln, and de Gaulle to get through the impossible Oxbridge entrance exam, but in that moment, romantic nonsense of the fluffiest kind overpowered Ursula's intellectual capabilities. All she could think was that here she was, on her first day at Oxford University, about to commence three years of sepia-toned, *Brideshead Revisited*–style bliss.† She imagined herself poring over ancient historical manuscripts in hushed libraries by day; she'd sip hot Ovaltine while reading improving literature in her digs during the long winter evenings; there would be croquet on the college lawn on lazy summer afternoons, followed by tea and the aforementioned cucumber sandwiches—

"*Hey!*"

A sharp yell interrupted Ursula's reverie. She turned to see a rickety

---

* Oxford terms begin with 1st Week, ending in 8th Week. Freshers arrive in 0th Week, before term officially starts. Undergraduates refer to dates by week number and day, e.g., "See you Tuesday of 3rd Week" makes total sense. "See you on 29 October" does not.

† The TV version of *Brideshead Revisited*, Evelyn Waugh's classic Oxford novel, was the *Downton Abbey* of the 1980s, except everyone was secretly gay.

blue minivan, with the words "J.Y.A. Orientation Europe Ltd." emblazoned on the side, pulling away from the curb opposite the college. The source of the voice was soon revealed to be a rather exotic specimen. A girl with a voluminous, puffed-up mound of dyed-blond hair was waving desperately at Ursula. She was dressed in a green bat-winged sweater, bubblegum-pink pedal pushers, a trilby hat, and white sneakers. A heap of shiny orange suitcases surrounded her.

"Help!" came the voice again.

What a gorgeous American accent, thought Ursula, as light and frothy as an ice cream soda. Ursula was in awe. She'd never met an American before, let alone one who looked like she'd walked straight off the set of *Sixteen Candles*. The American girl's bright look made Ursula feel a little shabby. For her first day at Oxford she'd dressed in a Black Watch kilt, Fair Isle sweater, old tweed hacking jacket, and a red wool beret knitted by her grandmother.

"I'm coming!" Ursula called back, abandoning her beaten-up navy-blue Globe-Trotter suitcase and trunk on the cobblestones. She darted across the road, dodging the students on bicycles whizzing along Christminster Lane.

"Hello," Ursula said to the girl when she reached her. "Are you all right?"

"I'm totally confused," replied the American. "The traffic's all on the wrong side of the street and it's making me dizzy. I'm looking for the Christminster College campus."

"Don't worry," Ursula reassured her, indicating the gate tower across the street. "You're here."

"*That*?!" The girl's eyes widened as they traveled up-up-up the famous building. "That is not a campus. *That* is a museum."

The American then grinned, flashing immaculately straight teeth. She had chestnut-colored eyes, thick dark eyebrows, and tanned skin. With her streaky blond mane, she looked like a cross between Madonna and Brooke Shields. The girl's nose was a pretty snub, very narrow, slightly turned up at the end, just as perfect as her teeth.

"You like my nose, huh?" said the girl.

"Sorry. I didn't meant to stare," said Ursula, abashed.

"It's okay. I got it for my Sweet Sixteen. That's when everyone gets their nose jobs in New York. It's a rite of passage."

Ursula liked this girl already. She'd never met anyone as refreshingly frank. The classmates with whom she had spent most of her teenage years were the repressed results of the institutionalized timidity encouraged at English all-girls schools. The rite of passage for the majority of such creatures, Ursula included, was passing the Pony Club C Test.

"I'm Ursula, by the way," she said, introducing herself.

"I'm so happy to meet you. I'm Nancy." She surprised Ursula by giving her a huge hug, as though they were long-lost best friends.

"Let's head over," said Ursula, unfurling herself from Nancy and grabbing as many of the suitcases as she could manage.

Nancy loaded herself up with the remaining baggage, and the girls zigzagged across the street, chattering happily as they went.

"By the way, I love your outfit," said Nancy.

"Really?" asked Ursula, amazed.

"Yeah. You look really cute, kinda like . . . Beatrix Potter."

"Oh . . ." said Ursula, suddenly downcast. She had tried her absolute hardest this morning not to look like a country bumpkin. She'd clearly failed.

•

A TINY WOODEN wicket gate set within the vast, castle-like main door of the gate tower led Ursula and Nancy into an echoing, stone-flagged entrance. They dropped their luggage on the ground, gazing delightedly between the carved stone columns of the cloister just beyond into Christminster's famous Great Quad. The two girls drank in the scene before them: the immaculate half acre of lawn, mown diagonally like a green checkerboard, flagged with a discreet Please Keep Off the Grass sign; the late-morning sunshine glinting golden off the spires that topped the grand stone quadrangle buildings; a tutor, clad in a long black academic gown, scudding like a bat along the wide gravel paths around the edge of the grass.

"Wow! *Je* adoring!" exclaimed Nancy.

"It's like a dream," replied Ursula.

She felt as though she might burst with excitement. The college was even more beautiful than she remembered from her interview a year ago.*

Just then a glazed wooden door to the girls' right opened, and a boy appeared. He was tall and narrow-bodied, with a skull-like, pallid face. His gaunt look was not helped by the fact that his pale brown hair was prematurely thinning. He was wearing thick Coke-bottle glasses with horn rims and was dressed in brown cords and a dark green loden jacket that Ursula recognized as tracht. The only thing indicating that he hadn't just stepped out of "Hansel and Gretel" was the bright yellow Converse sneakers on his feet.

As he approached, Nancy nudged Ursula, declaring, "Eew. He's not my type at all. Where are all those hot, floppy-haired Eton boys† Oxford's so famous for?"

"Sshhh!" said Ursula, hoping the boy hadn't heard.

She was surprised when the boy reached them and performed a little bow. Was everyone at Christminster going to be this formal? she wondered.

"Greetings, Freshers," the boy said. He spoke with the faintest

---

* There is no Oxford University "campus." Rather, the city of Oxford makes for an informal campus, with over thirty separate colleges dotted around the town. Collectively these form the university. Each college has its own residential buildings, dining hall, chapel, libraries, grounds, etc., where students live and learn, although they can also study with other tutors in other colleges, many of whom also live in the colleges. The oldest, richest, most famous colleges—Christ Church, New College, Magdalen College, All Souls—are as grand as palaces, occupying their own mini estates within the town.

† Notorious for its poshness, Eton College is now as well known for the hotness of its schoolboys. (Recent Old Etonian, or OE, hotties include Princes William and Harry, Eddie Redmayne, Damian Lewis, Dominic West, and Tom Hiddleston.)

trace of a German accent. "Allow me to introduce myself. I am Otto Schuffenecker, Prince of Carinthia, from Austria. Second Year. History."

"Are you for real?" Nancy sounded gobsmacked.

"Absolutely." Otto smiled proudly.

(Ursula sensed that this was not the moment to mention that her A-level history course had included the study of the abolition of the Austrian nobility. There hadn't been a royal family in Austria since 1919, after the fall of Austria-Hungary.)

Otto went on to explain that, as one of the official Freshers' liaison officers, he was on hand to help new students navigate Christminster and Oxford. He seemed delighted that his first charges were to be Ursula and Nancy.

"Well, *Prince* Otto," said Nancy playfully, "inspired by your full introduction, I am Nancy Feingold, of the Saddle River, New Jersey, Feingolds, of Feingold's Gardening Tools Inc. We live really close to Manhattan—I go all the time. Anyways, I'm a sophomore at Northwestern in Evanston, Illinois, and I'm on my junior year abroad here. Or should I say my *party* year abroad?"

"Are you planning on doing *any* work while you're in Oxford?" Otto asked her with a smile.

"Sure . . . if I must!" replied Nancy. "But honestly, I've been dreaming about Pimm's, punting, and picnics all summer. My major's History. While I'm here, I plan on minoring in Earl-Catching."

Nancy exploded into giggles so contagious that Otto and Ursula soon found themselves overtaken by laughter.

Finally Otto managed to contain himself enough to tell Nancy, "Well, you're in the right place for that. Oxford's stuffed with earl types." He then turned to Ursula, asking, "And you are?"

"Ursula Flowerbutton, Modern History," was the extent of our heroine's modest introduction. Her ponies-dogs-muddy-walks-and-books upbringing in a farmhouse hidden in a country valley didn't seem exotic enough to elaborate on. But Otto raised his eyebrows quizzically, looking for more.

"Miss," stated Ursula firmly.

"Of?"

"Seldom Seen Farm, Dumbleton-under-Drybrook, Gloucester-shire," said Ursula. "It's in the Cotswolds."

"Lovely area," Otto remarked. Then he helpfully explained to Nancy, "It's the part of the English countryside that's on all the chocolate boxes. Right, girls, we'll sort out your luggage later. Follow me."

•

OTTO LED THE girls through the glazed door into the porter's lodge, a drafty little room that seemed far too small for the activity carrying on in it. From behind a worn wooden desk at the far end, the porter, a stout, officious-looking man in a bowler hat, black three-piece suit, and tie, was handing out keys to various students, one of whom had somehow managed to squeeze a bicycle into the lodge with him. Parcels and packages were piled up in heaps, and notices were pinned on various boards. A tiny window looked out onto Christminster Lane. Ursula noticed that the north wall of the room was covered with mailboxes labeled with students' names. Nancy pointed excitedly to a couple of aristocratic-sounding ones.

"'Lady India Brattenbury,'" she read aloud. "She sounds *very* fancy . . . 'Lord Wychwood.' Isn't he out of *Pride and Prejudice*?"

"That's Wickham," said Ursula. "He was a terrible cad. Ran off with Elizabeth Bennet's sister Lydia."

"Well, let's hope this lord runs off with me!" giggled Nancy.

"He's taken, I'm afraid," Otto told her. "Right, these are your pigeonholes," he explained, finding both girls' boxes. "You should check them every day for messages. Your tutor will communicate with you here. Oh, and if you want to send a note to someone in another college, leave it with the porter by nine in the morning and pigeon post will collect it and deliver."

"They deliver the mail by *pigeon* here?!" Nancy looked astonished. "I feel like I'm in *The Wizard of Oz*."

"Let me explain," said Otto. "Pigeon post is one of many archaic

Oxford traditions—it consists of college servants who ride round the city on mopeds, delivering the students' mail. Usually it only takes two days to get a message back."

"*Two days?*" Nancy was appalled. "Can't we just phone from our dorm rooms?"

Nancy's astonished expression rapidly morphed into a highly traumatized one as Otto explained that Oxford undergraduates didn't have telephones in their rooms. There were, though, two pay phones in college, which took two- or ten-pence coins.

"But no one really uses them, and if they ring, no one picks up," he added, "in case it's someone's parents."

"But what if my mom needs to speak to me?" asked Nancy. "Ursula, don't you ever want to talk to your parents?"

"I'd love to," she replied. Then she added slowly, "But they're both . . . gone."

"I'm sorry, I didn't mean—" Nancy stammered, her face registering shock and sorrow.

"It's okay," said Ursula. "Really. My grandmothers raised me. They're wonderful."

Otto curtailed the awkward moment by beckoning at the girls to follow him. The trio squeezed through the crush of students to the porter's desk.

"Deddington," he said to the bowler-hatted man when they reached his desk, "I've got Miss Flowerbutton and Miss Feingold here. Could we have their room keys please?" He then told the girls, "Not that you need to bother locking your rooms. No one ever does."

Deddington handed Otto two large keys. "Good morning. Flowerbutton. Feingold," he said abruptly. (The girls would soon learn that Deddington had never gotten used to the fact that Christminster had, finally, started accepting girls. He didn't really approve, and could rarely bring himself to use the word "Miss" when addressing the female minority in college.)

Just then, a hand clad in a bright yellow rubber washing-up glove plonked a cup of tea on Deddington's counter. Ursula turned to find a shriveled-looking woman standing beside her. She was wearing a brown polyester housecoat and old black lace-ups on her feet. Her gray hair was scraped into a tight bun.

"Thanks, love," said Deddington, taking a gulp of the tea. Then he added, "Feingold, Flowerbutton, this is my wife, Mrs. Deddington. She's the dons' scout."

"The whose what?" asked a bewildered Nancy.

"I clean for the tutors," explained Mrs. Deddington in a thin voice.

She had a mouse-like face that looked as if it were permanently etched with worry. Ursula smiled sweetly at Mrs. Deddington in an attempt to cheer her up. But the scout's expression remained dour.

"Right, try not to lose your keys, ladies," Deddington told the girls. "If you get locked out at night, ring the bell. Our son, Nicholas, is one of the night porters here. You'll see him this evening."

"Thanks, Deddington, I'll take the girls to their rooms now," said Otto, heading out. "You're on a Historians' staircase in the Gothic Buildings."

"Catch you later." Nancy waved good-bye to the porter and his wife.

"Thank you," added Ursula as she left the lodge.

The girls followed Otto back out to the gate tower, where a group of returning Christminster students had started to gather. Their ebullient greetings echoed across the quad.

"This is a huge relief," Nancy told Ursula, looking the male students up and down. "Tons of floppy-haired Eton boys."

The boys were languid and tall, Ursula observed, and noticeably scruffily dressed, with long bangs that covered half their faces. Most of the girls had super-long, super-shiny hair that they swished like show ponies' tails. Ursula and Nancy caught snatches of their conversation as they walked past.

"Jubie! Darling! *Ciao!*" squealed a girl who looked like she had modeled herself on a young Princess Diana. She had fluffy, highlighted blond hair and was wearing a lilac pleated skirt. Her pale pink–striped blouse had a high ruffled collar that was tightly buttoned around her neck.

"Tiggy! Good hols?" Jubie yelled back.

"Yar. Absolutely schizo," replied Tiggy. "How was San Trop?"

"*Wild*," said Jubie. "Completely sick."

"Is Bunter Up?"* said one of the boys.

"Not sure. Apparently Teddy's arriving tomorrow," replied another. "He's bringing Ding Dong with him."

"Yar? Great. I heard India's en route."

"Who are they?" Nancy asked Otto curiously as they headed along the gravel path on the west side of Great Lawn towards the Gothic Buildings.

"The Yars," said Otto.

"Yars?" said Nancy. "What are Yars?"

"Oh, sorry, I suppose you've never come across one. Let me explain. They're an easily identifiable English species—they all went to the same posh private schools, they still use their absurd childhood nicknames, and they always say the word 'yar' instead of 'yes.' Hence, 'Yars.'"

The Yars, Otto said, dominated the Oxford scene. They ran the Oxford Union, the magazines, the balls, the dining societies, and the drama clubs. They were Rowing Blues or drug addicts, sometimes both.

"Anyway, you two, you'll be straight in with the Yars, you'll see. They love pretty girls," said Otto.

Otto turned a sharp corner at the bottom of Great Quad. He beckoned to the girls to follow him along a narrow stone passage.

"All I can say is, thank God I'm not a Yar," he went on. "Ten percent of them are dead before the end of Oxford."

"What?!" shrieked Nancy melodramatically.

---

* "Going Up" = beginning term. "Going Down" = ending term. Not to be confused with "Sent Down" = expelled.

"Okay, maybe not ten percent. But there was that one in New College who ended up buried under her boyfriend's floorboards last term—"

"Ugghh," shuddered Nancy.

"—and the Third Year who overdosed on heroin the day before his Classics finals."

"How tragic," said Ursula, feeling unnerved.

"You know what they had in common?"

"What?" asked Nancy, a note of terror in her voice.

"They were both," concluded Otto, "very posh."

Chapter 2

The Gothic Buildings were arranged around a rather spooky little courtyard dominated by a sprawling, gnarly trunked yew tree in the center. Very *Bleak House*, thought Ursula as she looked around, noticing that the quad had four castellated turrets, one in each corner. The only dashes of color were the few pale pink autumn roses still open in the flower beds. Otto led the girls towards one of four stone archways. It had the letter *C* carved above it.

"This is your staircase," he informed Ursula and Nancy.

The girls peered curiously inside the archway. A flight of scrubbed wooden stairs led towards a window on a high landing. Two girls were standing just inside, scrutinizing a black-painted board attached to the wall on the left. The number of each room and the name of its occupant had been inscribed upon it in white italic lettering.

"Hi!" called one of the girls when she saw them. "Felicia Evenlode-Sackville. Head Girl, Roedean. Lacrosse captain, Firsts. Everyone just calls me Moo." She had the plummy Sloane Ranger accent common to the alumnae of one of England's most prestigious girls' boarding schools.

"Moo" was dressed in a navy blue regulation Roedean School tracksuit and Green Flash Dunlop sneakers. The plump blond pony-tail on the top of her head seemed to bounce in time with her words.

She had a sprinkling of freckles across her face and a healthy, sporty physique.

Moo's bumptious confidence put her in stark contrast to the other girl, who seemed too terrified to utter much more than her name, Claire Potter. Claire was a sad-faced girl, as plain as it was possible to be. She had acne-strewn skin that appeared to have the slippery consistency and pallid color of lard. She was dressed in a drab knee-length skirt, a scratchy-looking sweater, and woolly tights. Her flat feet were clad in enormous ugly brogues. She was wearing clunky spectacles, and her coarse, mousy hair was chopped short.

Ursula felt sorry for Claire Potter. She'd try and be nice to her, but she suspected she wouldn't become good friends with her. Although Claire had barely spoken a single word, Ursula, occasionally prone in the way eighteen-year-old girls are to making snap judgments based on appearance, doubted they would have much in common. Ursula couldn't really relate to short-haired girls. She just didn't understand their philosophy of life.

"Your bathroom is through there," said Otto, pointing to an open door on the left.

Ursula and Nancy stepped into the room and inspected the washing facilities. Four sinks were attached to the wall, and two whitewashed cubicles each contained a large bath. The room was icy, with the only possible relief offered by a meager fan heater installed high on the wall above the doorway.

Nancy regarded the bathroom with a look of horror. "Where are the showers?" she asked Otto.

He chuckled. "As far as I know, the only showers in Oxford are in the Randolph Hotel—oh!" He let out an excited cry. "I don't *believe* it.

"India!" he called out to a girl heading towards Staircase C. "India!"

Ursula was immediately intrigued by the new arrival. Petite and fine-boned, India had a complexion as pale as a dove's wing. She wore her dark hair in a long bob, which had been left punkily unbrushed. Ray-Ban sunglasses revealed little more of her face than sky-high cheekbones. As she drew closer, Ursula could see that the girl's lips, which were stained a dark blackberry color, were set in a full, dramatic pout. She was dressed in the Chelsea girl hipster uniform of the moment—black leather biker jacket, black Lycra miniskirt, black opaque tights, and black suede fringed pixie boots. Her hands were encased in black leather fingerless gloves. Her edgy look made Ursula regret her own tragic Beatrix Potter garb even more.

India greeted Otto with a kiss on each cheek when she reached him. She then started pinning something on one of the notice boards just inside Staircase C.

"What on earth are *you* doing Up in Freshers' Week, India?" Otto asked. "Shame on you!"

"Rehearsing. It's so annoying, I'm missing Beano's cocktail at Annabel's in London tomorrow night. Darling, don't tell a soul you've seen me here, yar?" she begged him.

"Wouldn't dream of it, sweetheart," he agreed obligingly.

India stabbed a final drawing pin in a corner of the notice. It read, "Oxford University Dramatic Society—Treasurer Required. Apply to President Dom Littleton, Magdalen College."

"Anyway, we're desperate for a treasurer, and none of the acting lot would dream of doing anything so dull. So I had the brilliant idea of putting notices in the Freshers' staircases. Saddo First Years love doing that kind of thing . . . but if no one takes this bait, maybe we can recruit someone at the Freshers' Fair on Saturday."

"I'll apply," offered Claire Potter. She spoke with a soft Welsh accent and blushed furiously as she did so.

India pushed her sunglasses up on top of her head, revealing startling violet eyes and yard-long black eyelashes. She regarded Claire Potter with the kind of disdain an eagle would reserve for an earthworm—an organism so insignificant it wasn't even worth contemplating as a meal.

"Sorry," said Otto. "Let me introduce you all. Freshers, this is Lady India Brattenbury."

"Hi." In contrast to the friendly tones she'd used with Otto, India now spoke with a clipped, cold voice.

Ursula recognized the name from the pigeonholes. Lady India was clearly Someone Very Grand. While Otto introduced each Fresher by name, India's pout became ever sulkier. Until, that is, she heard the words "Nancy Feingold."

"So *you're* the Feingold girl," she said to Nancy, her pout morphing into a welcoming smile. "I heard on the grapevine you were coming Up. Read all about the Feingold gardening-tool dynasty in *Tatler*. It's my fave mag."

"It's hardly a dynasty," insisted Nancy, looking highly amused. "It's only two generations, and that's including me and my brother!"

"Well . . . anyway, I've already thought of the most brilliant nickname for you. 'Lawnmower,'" announced India, spluttering with laughter. "Isn't that perfect?"

She didn't appear to register Nancy's rather surprised expression and carried on, "You should come to Wenty's party on Sunday night. I'll get you an invitation."

"Okay," said Nancy. "Why not?"

"It'll be sick fun. Otto's coming, aren't you?"

"Of course," he declared happily.

The other three girls were, felt Ursula, rather pointedly excluded from this conversation. But finally, fixing Ursula with a bored expression, India said, "Where were you at school?"

"St. Swerford's," said Ursula, hoping her local private school sounded a bit smarter than it really was. "On a scholarship."

When she saw India's smirk, she wished she'd never mentioned the scholarship.

"St. Whereford's?" said India. "Never heard of it."

She turned her attention to Moo, noticing her Roedean School tracksuit. "We Wycombe Abbey girls always used to beat your Roedean lot at matches."

Faster than shooting a lacrosse ball into goal, Moo retorted, "And we beat Wycombe at chess."

The uncomfortable pause that followed was eventually filled by

Claire Potter, who stuttered, "I-I-I went to the grammar school in C-C-Cardiff."

"Oh," India replied, clearly underwhelmed.

Otto looked at his watch. "Look, I must get the Freshers to their rooms or they'll never be in time for lunch in the Buttery. See you later, India?"

"Yar. Great to meet you, Lawnmower," said India.

India departed. She didn't bother saying good-bye to the other girls.

Chapter 3

The first thing Ursula did after Otto had left her to unpack in her room was to find an old photograph of her parents, taken on their wedding day, and stand it on her desk. How beautiful her mother had been, with her auburn hair cascading around her shoulders. Everyone always told Ursula she looked like her. She had been blessed with the same kind of hair—in the sunshine, it glimmered like autumn leaves, and it was so long and thick that it required almost the whole of her narrow wrist to flick it to one side. Ursula's gray eyes and china-white complexion had come from her father, though, and the freckles that were dotted across the tops of her cheeks she blamed on the rare bursts of sunshine that very occasionally reached the Gloucestershire hillsides.

Ursula's attic-like room, number 4, was perched in the turret of Staircase C. Nancy's, Room 3, was opposite, across the landing, with Claire and Moo on the floor below in 1 and 2. The décor was basic. The walls had long ago been painted an institutional yellow color, which was peeling in places to reveal fragments of old floral wallpaper underneath. Apart from the desk and its chair, the furniture consisted of a single bed, standard-issue chest of drawers, empty bookcase, armchair, and narrow closet. The original fireplace had been boxed in, and the only heat source was a meager two-bar electric fire.

So what if her room was decorated like a sanatorium and colder than an igloo? It was her new home, and Ursula adored it. After putting her room key safely in the desk drawer, she unpacked her record player from her trunk, plugged it in, put on her favorite single—A-ha's "Take on Me"—and started decorating. She draped a beloved old bedspread printed with lilacs over the bed, and put an ancient chintz cushion of her grandmother's on the armchair. Then she set about organizing her desk. Opposite the wedding photo, she laid out her stationery—pens, pencils, folders, writing paper, diary—on the right-hand side before putting a reporter's notebook in the center. She hoped she would fill it with ideas for articles for *Cherwell*,* the legendary Oxford student newspaper she longed to write for.

It didn't take Ursula long to unpack her clothes with A-ha's music to egg her on. In any case, she possessed an extremely limited wardrobe since, like most English girls, she had been dressed in the same ugly brown school uniform pretty much since she was eleven years old. She had a couple of tweed skirts, a few kilts, some Viyella blouses, several warm sweaters, and a few pairs of jeans and cords. She had one smart velvet dress that she had made herself, but her pride and joy was her one proper black-tie ball gown. It was beautiful, even if it was a hand-me-down from her grandmother, and if she was *ever* invited to an Oxford ball (please-please-please, God, let me be invited to a ball one day! she prayed), she could go. The only "trendy" things Ursula owned were her pair of Dr. Martens boots, a stripy pair of fingerless gloves, and a black satin bomber jacket, all precious birthday gifts from her groovy London godmother. Unsurprisingly, all of her clothing fit easily into the narrow wardrobe.

Ursula soon noticed a large white envelope addressed to her propped up on the mantelpiece. A mass of papers and notes fell out when she opened it. There were notices about matriculation, the Freshers' photograph, and the Freshers' Fair, which were all scheduled

---

* Launched in 1920, *Cherwell* is the only student rag that can count Graham Greene, John le Carré, and W. H. Auden among its undergrad contributors.

to take place over the next two days, Friday and Saturday. Her battels[*] for the term were to be paid immediately. A photocopied note from the captain of the Christminster women's boat team invited her to try out for the college rowing Eight. There were endless details about college meal times and a list of required dress for Formal Hall. An academic gown, Ursula realized, must be acquired that afternoon if she was going to be allowed to eat anything tonight. She also needed a mortarboard for the Freshers' photograph.

At the very bottom of the pile of information, she found a small white card embossed with the college coat of arms—a shield illustrated with a stag at the bottom, a chevron in the middle, and three fleur-de-lis above—and handwritten with the words:

DR. DAVID ERSKINE AND PROFESSOR HUGH SCARISBRICK

AT HOME

THURSDAY, 14 OCTOBER

ROOM 3, STAIRCASE B, GREAT QUAD

7 P.M.　　SHERRY

SUITS　　GOWNS

Sherry with her History tutors tonight! How thrilling, thought Ursula. Perhaps she could brainstorm with Nancy and Moo over lunch—they'd need something current to discuss with their dons. She guiltily hoped they wouldn't be obliged to hang out with Claire Potter at lunch. There was something depressing about her.

By the time Ursula had finished unpacking and wandered across the landing to Nancy's digs to see if she wanted to go to lunch, the American student's room had undergone a dramatic transformation. Her bed was now fluffed up with a squillion-tog duvet, encased in a leopard-print cover. There were matching cushions and even leopard-print pillowcases.

---

[*] "Battels" = fees for food and board.

"I brought my own bedding," said Nancy, flopping down on the newly plush bed.

The rest of the room was completely covered in clothes. As Ursula cast her eye over the sartorial chaos draped over the desk, chairs, and floor, she couldn't help feeling slightly envious. There were party dresses and glittery shoes, skintight jeans and cropped tops, piles of sports gear, roller skates, hot pants, and several varieties of sneakers. There were jewelry cases bulging with tea-bag-sized diamanté earrings, ropes of faux pearls, and armfuls of bangles. There was even, Ursula noted, a pale vanilla-colored fur coat that glistened in the way that only real mink would. Nancy had a white vanity case, now open and with crystal perfume bottles and makeup spilling out of it, that took up almost the entire surface of her desk.

Seeing Ursula looking longingly at the case, Nancy said, "You can borrow any makeup you like."

"Wow, amazing, thanks," said Ursula, who had precisely one tube of mascara and one black eyeliner to her name.

"Even with no closets and that really unhygienic twenty-thousand-year-old bathtub seven flights downstairs, I *love* this attic," sighed Nancy. "The only thing I'm stressing about is how I'm gonna store my lipstick without a refrigerator."

Ursula opened the window that overlooked Christminster Passage at the rear of the college. "It's cold enough out here," she said.

"Brrr! Freezing," said Nancy, leaning out of the window and placing her most fashionable lipstick—Estée Lauder's Russian Red—on the sill.

The girls looked down. The narrow cobbled lane below was set between high stone walls. Two male students were walking along it, pushing bicycles. Their voices echoed up towards the girls' turret.

". . . bloody good idea to get here in time for Freshers' Week. More opportunity. Before the OEs get in there with the Freshettes."

"And the Freshers' photo will be out tomorrow and then we can really get started."

"Do you remember that *minger* you snogged last time . . ."

For a split second the girls didn't know whether to be appalled or amused, but they chose the latter, collapsing into giggles.

"I hope all the boys here aren't that honest!" exclaimed Nancy, closing the window. Then she said, kindly, "Hey, I'm really sorry for asking about your mom and dad earlier."

"Don't be," Ursula replied. "I only know them from photographs. I was so young when they died. My grandmothers really are the best mum and mum. Anyway, come on, we need to get to lunch . . ."

Just then there was a rap on the door.

"A visitor! Maybe it's one of those earls I'm planning on catching," said Nancy with a wink. "Hey, come in."

A pert, bright-eyed woman wearing a floral apron and bright yellow rubber gloves bustled into the room. Despite the fact that she was lugging an industrial-sized bucket of cleaning materials, she had an exceptionally cheerful look on her face. She appeared to be in her midthirties, and had her cheaply peroxided hair half pulled back from her very made-up face with a giant glittery butterfly clip. Beneath the apron, she seemed to have a voluptuous figure. Perhaps not all cleaning ladies suffered as much as Mrs. Deddington, Ursula thought hopefully to herself.

"Good morning, Miss—?" She grabbed a list from her apron pocket and looked at it, then smiled gaily at Nancy. "Feingold. I'm Miss Blythe, your scout. But I let all the undergraduates call me Alice."

"Awesome," said Nancy.

"I'll be up here to clean your room and make your bed, miss," Alice continued, smiling. She had traces of what sounded like a Northern accent. "Every morning at ten-ish. And yours, Miss—?"

"Flowerbutton—I'm in the room across the hall," said Ursula, thrilled. This was just too grown-up for words, having a college housekeeper to look after her.

"Do you think," said Nancy, reaching for her wallet and pulling out a crisp one-pound note, "you could do some extra tidying in here today? I just can't seem to get my closet sorted."

Nancy beamed a persuasive smile at the scout. But Alice's hitherto jolly face suddenly took on a worried expression.

"I'm sorry, Miss Feingold. College servants aren't allowed to accept money from undergraduates." She sighed, gazing longingly at the one-pound note.

"Gimme a break!" said Nancy, shoving the money into Alice's apron pocket.

Their scout patted the pocket with a wink and said, "I'm ever so grateful, Miss Feingold. It'll help with . . . well, things, you know, bills and suchlike. Your room will be perfect. But don't go saying a word to the high provost now, will you?"

"Ssshhh," said Nancy. "I swear I won't."

"Nor me," said Ursula.

Suddenly there was another knock on the door. "I feel *very* popular this morning," said Nancy as she pulled it open. There on the threshold stood India Brattenbury, holding a stiff white card in her hand.

"Your golden ticket, Lawnmower," she said, handing it to Nancy. "Wenty says he's dying to meet you."

Nancy took the card and read out loud:

THE EARL OF WYCHWOOD

AT HOME FOR HIS

MICHAELMAS OPENING JAUNT

SUNDAY, 17 OCTOBER

THE OLD DRAWING ROOM, GREAT QUAD, CHRISTMINSTER

DRESS: WHITE TIE   PINK CHAMPAGNE

8 P.M.—WHENEVER   BONBONS

"A posh Oxford party, with a real earl! Oh my God!" she shrieked with delight. "My mom would be going crazy. If I could actually call her. She's a real social climber—in a cute way, if you know what I mean. Just wants the best for me. Thank you *so much*, India, this is literally my *dream*. Hey, come in."

India stepped inside the room, looking straight through Ursula, but when she saw Alice, her face brightened. "Alice, I missed you all summer," she cried, throwing her arms around the scout, much to Ursula's surprise.

"And I missed you, Lady India. Lovely to see you again." The scout beamed at her. "Righty-ho, I'll be going, don't want to disturb you ladies any longer." As she hurried from the room with her bucket, she added, "If you need anything, girls, you can always find me midmorning in the scouts' mess by the Buttery having my tea break. Oh, and the washing machines are in the Monks' Cottages. You need ten-p coins to operate them. I'll do your sheets."

"Thank you!" Nancy and Ursula chorused as she left the room.

"That woman is the best scout in college," said India. "I tell her *everything*. She treats me like a daughter. You're so lucky, Nancy, to have her. She'll do *anything* for a few quid. I mean last term for the ball she even . . ."

India whispered something into Nancy's ear so that Ursula couldn't hear. Nancy's face registered slight shock before she started giggling.

Ursula was starting to feel rather uncomfortable at this point in the proceedings. She liked Nancy so far, but the whispering had started to make her feel like she was back in the sixth form common room at St. Swerford's with the ultra-popular girls excluding her. She didn't need this at university too. She'd make her excuses and leave.

"I'm heading down to the Buttery for lunch, Nancy, if you want to join me," said Ursula.

Before Nancy could answer, India informed her, "I'm taking you to Browns for lunch. They do a real American hamburger there."

"Okay, maybe see you later," said Ursula.

"Sure!" replied Nancy.

Ursula exited onto the landing, where she found Moo and Claire Potter. It looked as though she would be having lunch with Claire, like it or not.

"We came to get you to go to the Buttery," said Moo. "Shall we get Nancy too?"

"She's going to a restaurant with India Brattenbury," said Ursula, trying not to sound envious.

Just as the three girls headed down the stairs, India's voice rang out from behind Nancy's door.

". . . and don't you dare hang out with those History beasts I met downstairs. A lezzie, a Gopper,* and a scholarship girl. Your staircase is the saddest thing I've ever seen."

* "Gopper" = from "Gopping Sloane," derogatory slang used by aristo teens to refer to their *slightly* less posh upper-middle-class contemporaries, in this case Moo.

Chapter 4

After Ursula, Moo, and Claire had forced down the tepid baked beans and rock-hard jam roly-poly on offer in the Buttery, they stopped by Walton Street Cycles to buy secondhand bicycles and then flew down High Street on them. Their destination was the university outfitter.

"Shepherd & Woodward Est. 1852," read the gold lettering above the shopfront. Inside, the store was so crowded with Freshers all trying to buy their subfusc* in time for the matriculation ceremony that Ursula lost Moo and Claire almost immediately. It was rather a relief, she felt, to be without them for a moment. Moo had talked loudly about lacrosse and skiing nonstop at lunch, and Claire, well, her self-loathing radiated from her like a contagion. After one meal with her, Ursula felt as though she had been drowned in a cloud of melancholia.

It took Ursula forever to jostle her way to the counter at the back of the shop. A harassed-looking man stood behind it. He wore a white coat and had a small badge on his lapel reading, "Mr. Hooker. Head Tailor."

"Commoner?!" he yelled at Ursula over the din of the other Freshers.

* "Subfusc" = black gowns worn for formal occasions at Oxford.

"Er, gosh, I'm not sure . . ." she said, wondering what on earth he meant.

Impatiently, Mr. Hooker gestured at two black academic gowns of different lengths hanging on the wall behind him. The longer one was labeled "Scholar"; the shorter, "Commoner."

Since Ursula hadn't had any special academic awards bestowed upon her with her entry to Oxford, she realized she would be wearing the lowliest gown on offer.

"I am definitely a commoner—"

But Mr. Hooker didn't hear her. He'd already started talking to another customer.

"A *very* good afternoon, Lord Wychwood. Nice to see you Up so early," he said, his voice taking on an unctuous tone. "How may I help you?"

Ursula glanced around to see who had taken her place. There was no other way to describe the person now standing next to her at the counter as anything other than absolutely the most perfect cucumber-sandwich-type boy Ursula had ever seen. So tall he towered over the crowd, he had a mass of messy blond hair and properly azure eyes. He was dressed in faded jeans and a cricket sweater. "Wychwood," Ursula said to herself . . . Wasn't he the earl who was throwing the party Nancy was going to with India on Sunday night? Yes. That was it.

Well, *thank goodness* she wasn't going to his party herself. The boy had dreadful manners, pushing in like that in front of a girl. There would be other cucumber sandwiches, Ursula told herself, ones of far superior quality.

"Good to see you again, Mr. Hooker," said the boy, shaking the tailor's hand and giving him a genuinely friendly smile. "I need a couple of Blues* rowing shirts, please, and shorts," he said, "on my account."

Mr. Hooker said, "Right you are, Lord Wychwood. Congratulations on your Blue."

---

* Blues are awarded for sporting prowess—the most prestigious for rowing, tennis, and cricket. Half Blues are awarded for lesser sports, including gliding.

The tailor trotted off to fetch the items, clearly having completely forgotten about Ursula's gown.

Ursula tapped Wychwood on the shoulder, saying, "Excuse me, but I was in front of you. I'm in a rush."

Wychwood glanced briefly at her. "God. Sorry. Mr. Hooker's got a terrible crush on me, you see. It's very embarrassing, but no one will get served in here till I leave."

What a ridiculous excuse, thought Ursula to herself. Wychwood was clearly as vain as he was rude. She glared furiously at him, but he didn't notice—he was already waving at someone else over Ursula's head.

There was nothing to do but await Mr. Hooker's return. Ursula turned her back to Wychwood, consoling herself with the thought that she was not just glad but *thrilled* not to have been invited to his party on Sunday. The young earl was probably a terrific snob with a dreadful character.

Mr. Hooker eventually reappeared and started painstakingly wrapping Lord Wychwood's rowing shirt and shorts in crisp white tissue paper.

"I think you've forgotten about my gown," Ursula told the tailor. "And I'd like to buy a Christminster scarf please," she added, deciding to throw financial caution to the wind and break into her meager term's allowance. The stacks of stripy woolen college scarves were irresistible. They were bound to be hideously expensive, but the chance to wear the Christminster colors, a scarlet stripe on a minty green background, was worth it.

Clearly irritated to be interrupted while serving Wychwood, Mr. Hooker grumpily snatched a gown, mortarboard, and Christminster scarf from under the counter and chucked the lot in a bag.

"Seven quid for that," he snapped.

Ursula handed over the cash, took the delicious scarf from the bag, wrapped it twice around her neck, and picked up her shopping. She was just turning to leave when she noticed India Brattenbury, sunglasses covering half her face, dashing up to the counter.

"Wenty!" she called out. Wychwood turned. As his gaze landed on India, his eyes lit up. He enveloped her in his arms, and the pair indulged in an extremely long embrace. They were obviously a couple. When they had finally unfurled from each other, India said, "I just had the most hysterical lunch with that new American girl. She's a scream. I invited her shooting."

"Good idea," said Wychwood. "There's nothing like a Yank to liven up a country weekend."

"Exactly what I thought. I'm so bored of everyone." India pouted. She then turned to Mr. Hooker and said, "Darling, can you get me a lacrosse stick? Left mine in the country."

"I'll order one in, Lady India. Should be here by the middle of next week, all right?"

"Perfect," said India, smiling at Mr. Hooker. Then she turned to Wychwood and said, "Walk me to rehearsals, baby?"

"Course I will, bunny rabbit," replied Wychwood fondly.

Hand in hand, the pair left the shop. The Fresher girls, Ursula included, mercilessly scrutinized India as she walked past them. What was so special, their expressions seemed to say, about that pout?

Chapter 5

In his new role as Freshers' liaison officer, Otto had offered to escort Ursula's staircase of Historians to the sherry party that night. He had arranged to meet Ursula, Nancy, Claire, and Moo in the porter's lodge a few minutes before seven. It was a chill, clear night, and walking from their rooms, the four girls could see desk lights glinting from the first floor of the Hawksmoor Library, which overlooked Great Quad.

Ursula felt oddly serious with her new academic gown draped over her clothes. Until this very moment, she had loved what she was wearing—her homemade maroon velvet knee-length dress with puffed sleeves and white Peter Pan collar—but next to Nancy's glitzy outfit, it seemed childishly twee. Nancy was dressed in a purple jumpsuit with a drawstring waist and such enormous sequined shoulder pads that her gown only just fit over them. Her pile of blond hair was held back on one side by an oversized silver bow, which matched her silver pumps and her generous coating of shiny eye shadow. Moo was dressed Sloane-style in a pleated skirt and a pink-and-white-spotted blouse with the collar turned up, while Claire Potter's sherry-party look consisted of a calf-length navy frock that wouldn't have looked out of place on a Sunday school teacher.

Once inside the lodge, Ursula couldn't help but notice that Deddington's place at the porter's desk had been taken by a young man.

He had a pile of accountancy textbooks stacked on the desk in front of him, the top one propped open.

"Evening, Freshers. I'm Nick Deddington, one of the night porters," he said, getting up. Ursula thought Nick looked young, early twenties at the most.

"Your dad never said you were some kind of JFK Jr. look-alike," said Nancy, flashing a flirtatious smile at him. "May I call you Deddington Jr., as an *homage*?"

The American talent for saying whatever the hell you thought, Ursula mused to herself, was one of Nancy's many attractive qualities. Nancy was right: Deddington Jr. was far dishier than his parents' ordinary looks would have led her to expect. Hair that was side-parted Kennedy-style, chocolate brown and thick, framed a chiseled, high-cheekboned face, and he was noticeably tall and athletic-looking. However, unlike Nancy, Ursula would have died before mentioning it to him. English girls just didn't do that kind of thing.

Taken aback, the young man said, "Er . . . okay . . . thank you . . . Um, ladies, remember that the college gate is locked at midnight. If you're not back by then, ring the bell and—"

"Will *you* be here at midnight?" asked Nancy, continuing to stare at Deddington Jr. with a decidedly lovelorn expression on her face. She wandered up to the counter and draped herself languidly across it.

The night porter coughed and reddened. He was thoroughly embarrassed. "Yes. On duty, miss. As I was saying, if the door's locked, ring and I'll let you in."

Deddington Jr. sat down and turned back to his books, studiously ignoring Nancy's presence. Finally, she removed herself from the porter's desk. She winked at Ursula and whispered, "British boys are *so* cute. I could literally have sex with the accent."

Ursula stifled a giggle. Meanwhile, she noticed that Claire Potter had started industriously stuffing bright yellow flyers into each pigeonhole in the lodge. Seeing Ursula looking at her curiously, Claire handed her a sheet of paper.

It stated, "Crosswords and Ice Cream Society. First Meeting Sunday, 17 October, 7 p.m. Junior Common Room, Staircase B, Great Quad."

"I decided to start my own society. Will you join?" pleaded Claire, who was suddenly much more talkative than she had been earlier. "I'm going to have a table at the Freshers' Fair on Saturday where you can sign up."

Ursula's main plan for the Freshers' Fair was to sign up for *Cherwell*. The last thing she wanted to do was sign up for Claire's crosswords club, but she knew she couldn't get out of it without seeming mean. And one thing Ursula was not was mean. She nodded a reluctant yes to poor Claire. After all, it wasn't as though she would have anything else to do on Sunday night. Nancy, peering over Ursula's shoulder at the flyer, was all enthusiasm.

"Crosswords and ice cream? How British! So eccentric! I'm there. I'll come on my way to the earl's party."

Claire managed a grateful smile, then handed Moo a flyer.

"Thanks," said Moo noncommittally.

Just then, Otto trotted into the lodge, exuding an air of brisk efficiency. He had swapped his loden jacket for an immaculate tailor-made navy blue suit and navy-and-white-spotted tie, over which his gown hung elegantly.

"Ready for a sherry hangover?" he said. The girls laughed and followed him out of the porter's lodge.

•

DR. DAVID ERSKINE'S SET of rooms was located about halfway along the eastern side of Great Quad, in Staircase B. To reach it, the four girls followed Otto through one of the many shadowy stone entrances that were dotted along each side of the quad and up a steep flight of stairs to the first-floor landing. Dr. Erskine's door was on the right-hand side, opposite one labeled "Junior Common Room."

Ursula couldn't have imagined a more heavenly place for her future History tutorials than Erskine's set. The paneling in Room 3 had been lacquered in a glossy Chinese red. Persian miniatures had been hung densely around the mother-of-pearl-framed mirror above the carved stone fireplace, which, she noticed thankfully, was roaring with flames. On the opposite side of the room, situated in front of a huge Gothic window looking onto Great Quad, was a large black lacquer desk piled high with books and papers. A huge taxidermied bird with a peacock-like tail sat proudly in the center. A backstage pass to a Smiths concert hung around the bird's neck. Gosh, thought Ursula, Dr. Erskine was cool.

"It's a great argus," Otto said, noticing Claire inspecting the creature on the desk. "It came from Borneo. Dr. Dave says it inspires his writing."

"Weird," said Claire, unimpressed.

"I think it's lovely," said Moo.

Ursula, meanwhile, noticed that the far wall of the room, lined from floor to ceiling with books, had two "secret" doors within it. One, which stood partially open, led into Dr. Erskine's bedroom. If she craned her neck a little, she could just glimpse an unmade four-poster bed and a groovy ethnic rug on the floor.

"He *lives* here?" Nancy asked Otto.

"Most of the dons live in college," he explained.

"That is *so* weird," said Nancy.

Various comfy armchairs were dotted around the room, and a large chesterfield sofa, upholstered in worn tartan, was positioned to the right of the fireplace opposite a peacock blue velvet-covered chaise longue.

"Oh!" gasped Ursula, clutching Nancy's arm with a shudder. The chaise longue appeared to hold a motionless body. But suddenly it snored.

"That's Professor Scarisbrick. Started here in 1937. He's the world's leading authority on Anglo-Saxon history. Secretly recruits for MI6," Otto told the girls in a whisper. "Gives all his tutorials lying down. Only rises if a student says something interesting. He's never got up in one of my tutes."

The sleeping don, his glasses slightly skew-whiff on his snoozing face, had thinning white hair and a hearing aid in his right ear. He was dressed in a thick brown wool dressing gown, beneath which there appeared to be a heavy tweed suit, checked woolen shirt, and a maroon-and-cream dogtooth-check bow tie. The dressing gown was slightly grubby and clearly had food stains on the lapels.

Suddenly the secret door next to the bedroom opened, and Dr. Erskine made his entrance. He was tall, with swishy caramel-colored hair and light brown eyes. Tonight he was wearing a pair of stone-washed Levi's 501s with a trendy rip on the left knee, a navy velvet smoking jacket, and a black cashmere turtleneck sweater. The finishing touch were his cream suede Gucci loafers, worn without socks, Continental-style.

"Freshers! Salaam!" he said smoothly. "Now, drinks. There's sherry for Professor Scarisbrick, but I'm assuming you lot would prefer Kamikazes . . . I try to stick to historical themes with my cocktails . . . Inspires more . . . *reading,*" he continued with a mischievous grin.

"Awesome!" said Nancy gleefully.

Ursula was perplexed; so far, her only experience of Kamikazes had been the odd mention of the suicidal Japanese pilots in books about World War II. But if a Kamikaze cocktail was some kind of educational beverage, she would, of course, try it. From a tiny refrigerator hidden in a bookcase the don produced ice, triple sec, vodka, and lime juice. While Ursula watched Dr. Erskine slosh everything into a cocktail shaker, Otto provided a running commentary on the Christminster History department.

Dr. David Erskine, he explained, was so groovy and youthful that he insisted his students address him as Dr. Dave. Only twenty-nine years old, he had climbed the greasy pole of academia with staggering speed, and was admired as much for his brain as for his belief that it was his duty to keep the myth of the bohemian, pajama-wearing don alive. To that end, he attended many of the students' grander parties and occasionally gave tutorials dressed in paisley silk nightshirts bought on "research" trips to Constantinople (as he referred to it).

Dr. Dave's specialty—the East—was as trendy as his look, and his first book, *From Constantinople to Jerusalem*, had become a must-read in political circles. According to Otto, the History don adored being on television and discussing Palestine, mainly because the makeup was so flattering. His most beautiful female students—of whom he was considered to have rather too many—were nicknamed "Dave's Babes," and it was rumored that he had "inspired" many of them with a good deal more than the partition of the Middle East.

"No one thinks he's creepy?" Nancy whispered to Otto.

"Quite the contrary," Otto told her. "He's considered one of the most glamorous dons in Oxford. Bit of a girl magnet."

As he handed around the full shot glasses, Dr. Dave reminded himself of each girl's name. The group was soon joined by four male History Freshers, all in suits and gowns. Never having socialized with a teacher before, the students didn't have a clue what to talk about and stood sipping their Kamikazes in silence.

"Guys, not like that, like this!" instructed Nancy, shooting her Kamikaze down her throat in one gulp.

Ursula followed suit. The drink was sharp and strong, and suddenly she started feeling floppy and giggly. Meanwhile, the other students glugged down their shots, resulting in a lot of hiccuping and spluttering. They looked rather shocked when Nancy held out her glass to Dr. Dave for another drink, and he happily filled it—along with everyone else's.

"May I propose a toast, Dr. Dave?" asked Nancy boldly.

The don nodded happily. "You may."

"Okay! To us!" she exclaimed, gulping her next shot down.

The other Freshers consumed their next drinks enthusiastically. After her second shot, Ursula concluded to herself that she was absolutely, completely, definitely drunker than she had ever been in her life. It was lovely. The ice was broken, and the students were soon chattering away as though they'd known each other forever.

"*Grruugggghhhh!*" The party atmosphere was shattered by a loud grunt coming from the chaise longue.

"Sherry!" mumbled Professor Scarisbrick, sounding like an ancient growling dog. "The vintage one, not the bloody cheap stuff we give the undergrads. Where's my wretched pipe?"

Without getting up, the professor fumbled around on the Persian rug below the chaise longue. He located and lit his pipe with ease, considering that his eyes remained shut.

"Professor!" yelled Dave as he took his drink over to him. "Imbibe!"

With a great deal of clawing and moaning, Scarisbrick hauled himself into a seated position and finally opened his eyes. He took the sherry and between sips glared at each student. "*Siddowwn!*" he harrumphed eventually.

The slightly tipsy, rather alarmed Freshers promptly found seats and turned their attention to the esteemed Anglo-Saxon expert.

"There is only one rule in Oxford," he barked, his deafness forcing him to speak far more loudly than he realized. "And that is to write your essay *in time for your tutorial*, when you will read it *out loud* to me or Dr. Dave, depending on which course you have selected this term. You will have one essay to write each week. You will all no doubt be wondering *how* you will get this wonderful essay written promptly—"

He stopped and pointedly eyed each of the eight students. As his pale watery gaze came to rest on Ursula, she had the sense that, were the weekly essay in question not achieved, she would be hung, drawn, and quartered by the professor, a torture about which, as a historian, she was well informed.

"Do you row, Mr. . . . ?" Professor Scarisbrick was scrutinizing a meek-looking boy with very curly black hair and a pudgy face.

"Hunt," replied the boy.

"You hunt! Gah!"

"No, I'm sorry, Professor, I mean my name is Mr. Hunt."

"So you don't hunt?"

"No. I'm from Sidcup. They don't hunt in the suburbs."

"Marvelous. Do you row?"

"Er?"

"No? Good."

The professor turned his sights on Nancy next. "Young lady, do you act?"

"I, well, sometimes . . ." Nancy started to explain.

"Sometimes should be never," ordered Scarisbrick. "All of you! The way to get your essays written in Oxford is simply to *work*. Don't do anything else. At the Freshers' Fair on Saturday, you will be seduced with invitations to scull, play hockey, write for magazines, act in plays, sing in choirs. Do not do any of it, or you will not have time to write your weekly essay. And whatever you do, *do not join the Oxford Union*."[*]

The students nodded, terrified.

"I have been known," added the professor, "to Send Down students who arrive at my tutorials without an essay."

Crumpets, thought Ursula. Being expelled for missing an essay seemed a harsh punishment, but the professor clearly meant it. She vowed to herself that she would write her essay every week, on time, come what may, if that was what it took to stay here.

"Excuse me for asking, Dr. Scarisbrick," interjected Nancy politely.

"It's *Professor* Scarisbrick," he said crossly.

"Jeez, I'm sorry, Prof, but does that rule about being Sent Down apply to the American year abroad students?"

"*Professor* Scarisbrick, please, Miss America. What is the point of having a title if no one uses it?! To answer your query, yes, the rule includes *particularly* the year abroad students, who have tended, in my forty-six-year tenure, to be the sociological group *most* likely to appear at a tutorial without an essay and therefore the *most* frequently Sent Down. Does that answer your question?"

Professor Scarisbrick did not appear to be expecting a response beyond a "yes," but he got one anyway.

---

[*] The Oxford Union is a ridiculously fabulous university debating society. Past presidents include Benazir Bhutto (1977), Hilaire Belloc (1895), and Prime Minister William Gladstone (1830), whose cabinet desk is in the Union library. *Everyone* joins.

"So how does a student get an extension?" asked Nancy.

"Extension?" guffawed Scarisbrick. "There are no extensions in Oxford."

"*No extensions?!*" Nancy was horrified.

"You've hit the proverbial on the proverbial," said Scarisbrick.

"Huh?"

"Read some bloody P. G. Wodehouse before your tutorial with me, my girl," snorted Scarisbrick before collapsing back into his prone position on the chaise longue.

"Most informative, Professor Scarisbrick, thank you," said Dr. Dave. "Now, let's get down to logistics. Tutorial times. Miss Flowerbutton?"

"Yes," said Ursula.

"I'm afraid you've drawn the short straw. You're my first tutorial. I'll see you here at nine on Monday morning."

"Excellent," said Ursula, relieved she had been allocated Dr. Dave as her first tutor rather than Scarisbrick.

Dr. Dave assigned the other students their tutorial times. Half the intake—Moo, Claire, and two of the boys—would study the Anglo-Saxon period with Professor Scarisbrick; the rest would take on the Reformation with Dr. Dave. Nancy was thrilled to learn she was in his group.

He then added, "And all of you, if you get to your tutorial and I don't answer when you knock on my door, just come straight into my rooms—you might have to get me out of bed. Whatever you do, please don't waste valuable tutorial time waiting outside like a lemon."

Chapter 6

There is *no way* I can go without you."

It was seven o'clock on Sunday evening, and Nancy had peered around the door of Ursula's room to plead with her to come along to Wentworth Wychwood's "Opening Jaunt" that night.

"How would I know what to say to an earl? I have no idea about posh British conversation. *Please* come with me," begged Nancy.

"But I haven't been invited," Ursula protested. For her, as for many English girls brought up with good manners, there was no idea more dreadful, more humiliating, than turning up uninvited to a party from which one might be turned away, even a party that one has decided one is thrilled not to have been invited to. "He doesn't even know me."

"He doesn't know me either."

"But you got an invitation."

"Look, if Wentworth Wychwood doesn't know you, he won't know that he didn't invite you. Come on, Ursula, it'll be fun . . . if we're together."

"Sorry, I can't. I promised Claire I'd go to her crosswords thing. Anyway, I don't like Wychwood much."

"I thought you said you didn't know him," Nancy said, looking confused.

"I don't."

"Well, how do you know you don't like him then?"

"He's got bad manners," said Ursula.

"Listen, no one's saying you have to be *friends* with the guy. Just keep me company. India says it's going to be a beautiful party."

Ursula couldn't help but be tempted by the thought of a white-tie party with pink champagne and bonbons. It did sound more exciting that Claire Potter's Crosswords and Ice Cream evening in the JCR. And Ursula did, after all, have Granny's lovely old ball gown in her closet. If nothing else, she reasoned, the dress deserved an outing.

•

AN HOUR AND a half later, Ursula and Nancy hovered expectantly on the threshold of the Old Drawing Room. Between screams of laughter and groans of horror, snatches of gossip floated from the throng at Wentworth Wychwood's Opening Jaunt.

. . . *Apparently Johnny Soames was so wasted he snogged the porter at Brasenose. When the provost asked him to explain himself, he said he was terribly sorry but he'd mistaken the porter for a public telephone box* . . .

. . . *I'm joining the Pooh Sticks Society. The only commitment you have to make is to show up once a term and toss a stick off Magdalen Bridge while drinking Fortnum's Afternoon blend tea. Members are called Poohsers* . . .

. . . *I can't possibly invite her to my twenty-first. She's too terribly Sloane* . . .

. . . *Anyway he was wasted and the Assassins locked him in a portaloo and rolled it down a hill and into a ditch and left him there all night* . . .

. . . *I'm starting term as I mean to go on—slightly drunk* . . .

"This place looks more like Marie Antoinette's powder room than a party venue for two Oxford boys," exclaimed Nancy, taking in the scene. "I *love* it!"

The Old Drawing Room, situated on the first floor of the Georgian wing on the west side of Great Quad, was famously the best undergraduate set in Oxford. Occupying it was a privilege traditionally accorded to the top Christminster Blue. This year, that was Wychwood—who then got to share the set with a roommate of his choice. The main room, a delicious confection of pistachio-painted paneling and swirls of gold leaf, was lit that night by candles, and the promised bonbons—pale pink ones—were piled high on glass stands dotted around on side tables. Ursula noticed two doors at the far end of the room—she guessed these led into Wentworth's and his room-mate's bedrooms. The view from the tall sash windows was spectac-ular, the full moon illuminating Great Quad as though it were an old black-and-white photograph.

The only thing that looked slightly out of place was a gloomy oil painting hanging above the elaborate marble fireplace. From a heavy mahogany frame, the stern visage of the college founder, Thomas Paget, First Marquess of Anglesey, loomed ominously over the crowd.

"This makes the Freshers' Drinks look like a bad frat party," sighed Nancy blissfully. "Thank God we're out of Freshers' Week."

Ursula agreed. "Freshers' Week"—which actually only meant Thursday, Friday, and Saturday—had been a social whirlwind ever since the History drinks. There had been a formal matriculation cer-emony to enroll the Freshers into the university on Friday morning. This had been followed by an official Freshers' photograph on Great Lawn—at which they had been informed in no uncertain terms that this was the first and last time they would *ever* set foot on the pre-cious grass of Great Quad. There had been a bop* on Friday night. A university-wide Freshers' Drinks, held in the gardens of the Oxford Union at eleven o'clock on the following morning, had mainly in-volved consuming copious amounts of a mysterious bright-blue cock-tail. The "week" had culminated in the Freshers' Fair on Saturday, at which Nancy signed up for the drama clubs and Ursula, though nursing a headache, excitedly put her name down on a (long) list of wannabe student journalists for *Cherwell*, whose first meeting would be on Monday. Now here she was at the beginning of 1st Week and Ursula's Oxford life was starting in the most unexpected way—at an extraordinarily glamorous party. One that she had not been invited

* Bop = puke-filled college disco.

to, she remembered suddenly, as she gazed upon the scene in the Old Drawing Room.

"British boys," murmured Nancy, squeezing Ursula's arm. "How come they're all so cute?"

"It must be the outfits," said Ursula.

The clothes—well, Ursula had only seen such style in her grannies' old photo albums. Here in front of her were masses of young men—Oxford men, she reminded herself happily—dressed in "white tie." The dress code—which consisted of a high-cut tailcoat, white dress shirt, elaborate gold or even jeweled studs and cuff links, a pastel-hued silk waistcoat, black trousers, shoes shiny enough to successfully powder a nose in, a stiff white collar, and a highly starched white pique bow tie—made everyone look like a movie star, according to Nancy.

"The ratio's at least four boys to one girl," declared Nancy. "I predict a high probability of successful earl-catching here."

It was true, Ursula noted, that there were very few girls in the room. Most of the Oxford colleges had only seriously started admitting women in the last ten years. They were still only a small proportion of the student body. But then, thought Ursula to herself, an eight-hundred-year-old boys club was going to take longer than average to modernize.

Ursula was curious about the twenty or so girls she did see. They glittered like exotic birds among the sea of white tie and tails. Their party dresses, each one poufier, shinier, and more extravagant than the last, were made of brightly colored taffetas, silks, velvets, or lace, and were underpinned by generous sticky-out net underskirts. A few of the most glamorous girls even had thigh-length mini ball gowns that looked like they might be from Christian Lacroix or Bruce Oldfield, famous designers whose dresses Ursula had seen in issues of *Vogue*. The young women were lavishly bedecked with diamanté bracelets, heavy paste earrings, and reams of pearls at the neck. Gone were the swishy ponytails—in their place was the curled, waved, and crimped "big hair" that was so fashionable now. Their eyes were circled with heavy eyeliner, and their mouths painted with gleaming lip gloss.

Is my dress too old-fashioned? Ursula wondered to herself. The hand-me-down 1950s number that she had found in a trunk in the attic at Seldom Seen Farm suddenly seemed far less glamorous than it had at home. Her maternal grandmother, Violette Vernon-Hay, a former famous society beauty whom Ursula had nicknamed "Vain Granny," had a few old ball gowns and pieces of Paris couture in her attics, and had allowed Ursula to choose one gown to take with her to Oxford. (Her paternal grandmother, Jane Flowerbutton, "Plain Granny," did not lend Ursula outfits. Her wardrobe mainly consisted of boilersuits in which to conduct farming activities.)

The dress was a three-quarter-length, hand-stitched copy of a Dior gown, made of now-faded lilac silk grosgrain. The bodice was beautifully boned, and made Ursula's waist look minute. A generous ruffle of soft silk net edged the top of the corset and draped over the shoulders, and the skirt and its stiff petticoats stuck out. A huge velvet bow hooked over the back of the dress and, thank goodness, covered a small tear that had been amateurishly darned. Even if the dress was old, Ursula loved the way it rustled as she walked.

"I feel super-duper underdressed," said Nancy.

"No, you look cool," Ursula reassured her.

Modern, thought Ursula, that's what she looks. Nancy's attire that night consisted of a teensy-weensy, skintight minidress made of ruched neon-yellow Lycra, fuchsia-pink suede Maud Frizon stilettos, and an enormous silver down jacket that she had thrown over the ensemble. Her hair was back-combed and hair-sprayed into her signature towering mound, so fluffy it resembled cotton candy; her eyes were boldly lined with cobalt blue kohl and matching mascara; and her mouth glistened with the Russian Red lipstick. Her tanned, bare legs added a sexy touch.

Ursula suddenly saw Wentworth Wychwood appear from the crowd. He glanced at them curiously. Oh crumbs, thought Ursula to herself, he's coming over. The embarrassment of being found out as a gate-crasher, even at a party she hadn't wanted to be invited to, was too terrible to contemplate.

As he approached, Ursula could see that the letter *W* was elaborately engraved on the shiny brass buttons of his tailcoat. Even if he was a terrible snob, so grand that even his buttons were initialed, Ursula couldn't deny that he was ridiculously good-looking.

"*You* must be Lawnmower," Wentworth said to Nancy, going straight up to her and kissing her on both cheeks. "India says you're *very* amusing."

Ursula stood shyly behind Nancy. Hopefully Wychwood wouldn't notice her.

"Is everyone here really going to refer to me as a piece of gardening equipment?" grumbled Nancy, sounding miffed.

"Most likely. Although I must say the name doesn't suit you at all—you're far more attractive than any lawnmower I've ever met. Mind you, everyone calls me Wenty, which is not an abbreviation of Wentworth. It's short for Went-Very-Wrong-Somewhere."

He laughed jovially and then, laying eyes on Ursula, suddenly stopped. Oh no! thought Ursula, *he's realized I'm a gate-crasher.* She examined a splinter in the wooden floor.

"Hi. I'm Wenty," he said finally.

Ursula slowly raised her eyes towards the boy, hoping her face didn't look as flushed as it felt.

To her surprise, he continued, "You look . . . wonderful."

"Oh . . . um . . ." Ursula didn't know what to say. At the occasional school dances she had attended while at Swerford's, the few boys present had barely noticed her, let alone paid her a compliment.

"I don't think we've met," said Wenty.

"We have, actually," she said curtly, reminding herself how rude he had been at the Shepherd & Woodward counter that day.

Wenty looked at her again, now with a flash of recognition in his eyes. "Oh, that's it, I remember now! I met you at Piggy's cocktail at Annabel's a couple of weeks ago in London."

"No," Ursula answered. "I've never been to Annabel's."

"You'll have to remind me."

"You pushed in front of me at the counter at Shepherd & Woodward last week."

Wenty looked completely blank. "Did I? Really? I don't remember."

"I'm sure you don't," she replied. Wenty was even ruder than she had thought. Not only had he pushed in front of her, he couldn't even remember doing it.

"Look, sorry, okay?" he said, trying to appease her. "What's your name?"

"I'm Ursula."

"Ursula who, exactly?"

"Ursula Flowerbutton."

"Flowerbutton. Lovely name. Unforgettable . . ."

Wenty gazed at Ursula for far longer than was strictly necessary. But Ursula was determined not to be flattered. She imagined he probably called every girl he met "wonderful" and "unforgettable."

Finally, Wenty peeled his eyes from her, saying, "Lawnmower, Unforgettable, I've already run out of champagne saucers. Come and help me find some more?"

He beckoned the girls to follow him across the landing, already swaying drunkenly as he walked. Nancy tailed him and Ursula followed reluctantly. They soon found themselves in a large, drafty bathroom with bleached wooden floors and a small window overlooking the courtyard at the back of the main quad.

A claw-footed bathtub that appeared to have been *in situ* since the '20s had been filled to the brim with icy water, and at least twenty bottles of pink Bollinger were floating around in it. A tray of dirty glasses was perched on the loo seat, and an abandoned bucket of cleaning items—washing-up gloves, J-cloths, and the like—sat on the floor next to it.

"Where on earth have our dear washer-uppers got to?" Wenty said, glancing around the bathroom. "Now . . . hmm, maybe there are some more glasses in here."

He staggered downwards to peer inside a bathroom cabinet below the sink, and seemed shocked to find it contained his own toothbrush and toothpaste rather than clean glasses. He sighed, filled the sink with water, and attempted to wash one of the dirty champagne saucers from the tray using a shriveled-looking bar of Palmolive soap and a rather grubby face flannel. There was a crunch, an "Ouch," and his left hand came out of the washbasin covered in blood.

"Oh bloody hell, forget it," Wenty said, hurriedly wrapping his hand in a face towel that had a *W* embroidered in one corner in the same shade of pale blue as his lapels. He cleaned the blood off his hand, chucked the towel on the floor, and somehow found a bandage in the bathroom cabinet.

"Do you mind?" he asked, holding out the bandage to Ursula, who soon found herself wrapping the wound. "Has anyone ever told you that you do that better than Florence Nightingale?" he said when she had finished.

"Do you flirt like this with everyone," she replied, "or just with girls who aren't your girlfriend?"

"I do adore a prude," countered Wenty.

"I am *not* a prude!" she protested.

"Okay, guys, chill," Nancy interrupted. "Let's get to the party."

With Nancy's help, Wenty managed to open a fresh bottle of champagne and slosh it into the used glasses on the tray, saying, "Don't tell anyone!"

"That's so unhygienic," Nancy told him. "Haven't you heard of mono?"

But Wenty had tuned her out. "Girls, bring more bottles of booze, will you?" he called, heading out of the bathroom.

Ursula and Nancy each grabbed a dripping champagne bottle, wiping them down with a bath towel so as not to spoil their dresses.

"He *really* likes you," Nancy whispered excitedly as they followed Wenty back across the landing.

"He's going out with India," said Ursula in a hushed voice. "He's only bothering to talk to me because I'm with you."

"I think you're being mean about someone you hardly know," said Nancy. "I dig him."

"Well, I don't," said Ursula firmly.

She had decided, though, that she was not going to let her views on her host interfere with her enjoyment of the party, making an executive decision to forget Wenty's ridiculous comments and have fun. As she passed through the gilded doorway of the Old Drawing Room into the party, which was now packed, she felt as she imagined Alice must have when she fell down the rabbit hole. A smile crept across Ursula's face.

"Oh, sorry, Nancy, do you want to leave your jacket?" asked Wychwood, turning back to the girls.

"Are you kidding me?" she replied. "This is a *Norma. Kamali. Sleeping. Bag. Coat.*"

Wenty looked blank.

Seeing his confusion, Nancy explained, "It doesn't come off. It's part of the look. This is the most aspirational jacket in New York."

"If you aspire to look like an astronaut," their host replied mischievously. Then he carried on, "Come and meet everyone—and grab a glass of champagne!"

Sipping glasses of delicious pink bubbles, the girls followed Wenty as he headed towards the center of the room carrying the tray. Guests were lounging on sofas or squashed three to a chair. Corks were popping, glasses were being filled, and tipsiness was being induced, all at a startling rate. A group had congregated around a white Steinway grand piano, on top of which a set of mixing decks had been temporarily installed. An olive-skinned boy in a white T-shirt, black jeans, and a black baseball cap with the word "BOY"[*] emblazoned in white letters across the front was DJ-ing. As Culture Club's "Do You Really Want to Hurt Me" came to an end, Madonna's "Like a Virgin" started up. He grinned at Wenty, making a thumbs-up gesture.

---

[*] Mega-groovy King's Road boutique BOY was frequented by club kids and pop stars, including Madonna. It was so groovy in there that Billy Idol worked the till.

"That's Christian. Music scholar at New," said Wenty over the music. "He's far too London-trendy to wear white tie. The other weirdo over there is my good mate Horatio Bentley. Fondly known as the 'Man in Mauve.' He's in rooms above the JCR. Studying Sanskrit. Come and meet him."

Wenty waved at an eccentric-looking figure propped comfortably against the piano. He was a squat, tubby personage. His red hair was short apart from his bangs, which he wore in a long, asymmetric style that he flicked dramatically off his forehead every now and again. Horatio was dressed in a long lilac djellaba, which, despite its voluminous folds, still strained across his considerable tummy, and his feet were clad in red velvet slippers. His neck was encased in a fat choker of tacky fake emeralds.

The girls followed Wenty over. "Divine party, darling," cooed Horatio at their host, then proceeded to kiss the young earl on the lips.

"Horatio, can you stop acting *quite* so gay *all* the time? It's getting boring," protested Wenty, wiping his mouth on the back of his hand. "How many times do I have to tell you, I am *not* a homosexual and I will *never* shag you. Darling."

"Al-aaaaas!" Horatio threw up his hands in a gesture of mock despair before turning his attention to Nancy and Ursula. His beady eyes darted quickly from one girl to the other, scrutinizing them mercilessly.

Wenty said, "Now, let me introduce you to Ursula Flowerbutton."

"Hi," said Ursula, smiling.

"And this is Nancy Feingold—"

"I know *all* about *you* already," Horatio interjected.

"You do?" said Nancy, looking rather alarmed.

"I'm the gossip columnist on *Cherwell*. It's my job to know *everything* about *everyone*. I read about you in *Tatler*. Your reputation as a beautiful American gardens heiress precedes you—"

"It's not actually gardens. It's gardening *tools*," Nancy corrected him.

"Minor detail, darling, minor detail," declared Horatio.

If he was a columnist on *Cherwell*, thought Ursula to herself, she should get to know him.

"I signed up for the newspaper at the Freshers' Fair," said Ursula. "I'm coming to the meeting on Monday."

"A girl like you will be a shining beacon of light amongst the bloodsucking cretins who staff it," Horatio said dramatically. "It'll be fun watching you fend off the tragic hacks."

"Er . . . right," replied Ursula, unnerved.

"I love your look, Horatio," said Nancy.

"That's very flattering," he said gratefully. He stroked the plastic gems at his throat. "I'm channeling Talitha Getty in Morocco—"

"Horatio, cut the crap," interrupted Wenty. "Look after these beauties very carefully while I do some waitering." He disappeared off into the crowd, filling glasses as he went.

"So, I'm curious," Nancy asked Horatio. "Who are all these people?"

"This lot?" he replied, gazing around the room. "They're known as the Champagne Set—supposedly they're Oxford's most aristocratic, social, talented, or beautiful undergraduates. But I think it's much *kinder*"—Horatio smiled wickedly—"to describe them as immature twits still obsessed with their posh public school peer groups."

"Ouch!" gasped Nancy. "That's mean."

"But true," said Horatio. "My columns are notorious—for their honesty. If that means sometimes describing my subjects in the worst possible light, so be it."

Just then, Ursula spotted a suave-looking boy crossing the room towards them. She had never seen such sophistication. His polished dark skin gleamed like a black diamond. A large gold signet ring on his left pinkie flashed in the candlelight, and his white tie looked absolutely correct, as though it had been pressed and starched to within an inch of its life. He flashed a glossy smile at Horatio as he approached.

"Who's he?" Ursula asked, trying to sound super-casual.

"Eghosa Kolokoli. Wenty's roommate. He's from Nairobi. Very snappy dresser. But don't be taken in," Horatio warned. "Eg isn't *quite* what he seems . . ."

But Horatio's warning faded into the din of the party. Ursula was mesmerized by Eg, who had suddenly transitioned to an expertly executed Michael Jackson–style moonwalk to reach Horatio and the girls.

"Eg, you're such a cliché of . . . *yourself*," sighed Horatio wearily as Eg slapped him hello on the back. "Have you met Nancy and Ursula?"

"Hello," said Eg, turning to the girls. "I'm Eghosa." He had a deep voice and a very proper English accent that sounded like something out of the 1950s. He then turned to Ursula, took her hand, and said, "Dance?"

She couldn't quite believe that a boy like this could possibly want her as his dance partner. She couldn't say yes. Her dancing was far too amateurish. She shook her head. "I'm okay, thanks," she said. "I'm sure Nancy would, though."

"Great," Nancy said, taking off her duvet jacket and flinging it on a sofa.

With that, Eg took Nancy's hand and proceeded to whirl her around the room. *Thank goodness* that's not me, Ursula told herself, as she watched the pair break into a ceroc. Luckily Nancy seemed to be some kind of Ginger Rogers. She and Eg twirled into any space they could find.

"Ah, Prince Shuffling Knickers doing his shuffling!" pronounced Horatio, pointing out Otto, who was dancing furiously by himself. "Otto!" he called out. "Come over here, you lonely saddo!"

Otto stopped suddenly. When he turned and saw his audience, he looked rather embarrassed, but still dashed over to Ursula, grabbed her hand, and brushed his lips across it, Euro-style.

"India, *Liebling!*" he said, entwining his fingers in hers.

Ursula snatched her hand back. "I'm Ursula!" How could he possibly mistake me for India? she wondered.

Otto rubbed his eyes and peered at her closely.

"Now I see. You are not India. You are Ursula. I am not wearing my glasses tonight. I never do for parties. Can't see a thing. Sincere apologies," he said, bowing almost to the floor as he did so.

"Shuffling Pants, you are such a ponce," Horatio admonished him. Ursula rather agreed. Otto's good manners, she was starting to think, were extreme even for a minor Austrian princeling.

"Shut up, Horatio," retorted Otto. "A prince always bows when he apologizes."

"Otto, all this princeling twaddle is nonsense. No one cares that you rule over a pathetic pine forest on a craggy mountain somewhere in Carinthia—"

"Oh, but I do," Nancy butted in, having just returned, breathless, from her dance. "American girls just adore a prince, even one who lives someplace no one's *ever* heard of and no one's *ever* going to go." She gave Otto a reassuring squeeze.

"Ooooh! I've spotted a gossip item," said Horatio. He moved off towards a couple snogging violently on a window seat, half draped in curtains. "See you all later."

"Thank you for sticking up for me, Nancy. You're a sweet girl," said Otto, bowing yet again.

"Oh my God, Otto," blurted Nancy. "You are so crazy posh."

"Not as posh as he is, sadly." He sighed, glancing wistfully at an extraordinarily beautiful boy standing by the fireplace.

"*Who* is *he?*" asked Nancy, gazing at the gorgeous boy, who was immaculately turned out in a spanking-new tailcoat with black satin lapels. His feet were clad in black velvet evening slippers adorned with large black satin bows, while his white tie showed off his tanned face, brown eyes, and dark, slicked-back hair to perfection. Lapis-and-diamond cuff links and studs adorned his dress shirt. If Wenty was a cucumber sandwich, Ursula thought, then this specimen—well, he was absolutely a Bendicks Bittermint,* Ursula's favorite chocolate.

The Bendicks Bittermint was talking to a boy who was his exact opposite—a portly, ruddy-faced young man dressed in grubby-looking

---

* Bendicks Bittermints, white fondant mints encased in dark chocolate, were purchased in yard-long boxes at Harrods. Pre-Diptyque candles, they were the only acceptable prezzie at grand English house parties.

tartan trousers and a threadbare claret-colored velvet smoking jacket. He reminded Ursula of a worn-out teddy bear.

"The next Duke of Dudley," said Otto.

Nancy's eyes lit up.

"Is that as good as an earl?" she asked.

"Better," replied Otto. "Would you like me to introduce you?"

"No, I think I have a better strategy," said Nancy, a determined look on her face.

"By the way, don't mention the duke thing," warned Otto. "He's very embarrassed about it."

"Watch me not mention it," she said, dashing off towards the fireplace.

It only took a few seconds for Nancy to faux trip and accidentally-on-purpose throw her third glass of champagne all over the next Duke of Dudley and his shabbily dressed friend. Shocked expressions turned to laughter as Nancy seductively patted the boys down with a napkin. Ursula looked on as Nancy flirted and joked with the Next Duke as though they were old friends already.

"Oh!" exclaimed Otto, observing the scene. It seemed he was about to say something, but then abruptly stopped himself. A sly smile spread across his face.

"What?" said Ursula. "What is it?"

But Otto didn't answer. He had already moved onto his next social opportunity, and was waving at a stunning-looking girl who was chatting nonchalantly with Christian. Her beautiful, narrow face was cloaked by two curtains of long dark glossy hair, which came almost to her waist. She was wearing a starched man's white dress shirt that barely reached to midthigh, black tights, stilettos, and not much else. An undone white bow tie hung around her neck.

"I like her take on the dress code," said Ursula.

"Isobel Floyd. She's a scene maker, always at the center of everything. Her father's the home secretary. She was brought up in Belgravia. Everyone says she was the cleverest girl at St. Paul's. She's dating Dom Littleton. He's the top stage director among the students," explained Otto, heading in Isobel's direction. "Come on, I'll introduce you."

"Sure," said Ursula. She followed Otto, feeling somewhat intimidated after the write-up Otto had given this girl.

"I see you've taken the dress code literally," Otto told Isobel as he went up to her. He kissed her on both cheeks. "Very groovy."

"It's fun, no?" drawled Isobel. "I can't face ball gowns this early in the term. I've been barefoot in Koh Samui all summer." She then drew back her curtain of hair and peered at Ursula, who had hung back shyly behind Otto. "And you are?"

"Forgive me," said Otto apologetically. "Introductions. Ursula Flowerbutton, this is Isobel Floyd. The coolest girl in Oxford."

"You're so embarrassing, Otto," groaned Isobel. She then smiled smugly, as though to indicate that yes, she probably was.

"Where's Dom? Isn't he coming?" asked Otto.

Isobel rolled her eyes, peeved. "He said he'd meet me here ages ago. But he's late as usual. God knows where he is—"

She stopped talking, her gaze now fixed on the doorway, as the very late, rather dramatic arrival of India Brattenbury captured the attention of the entire room. Her look exuded glitzy modernity. Her long white silk-satin dress, beaded from head to toe with tiny seed pearls, was cut close to her body and puddled into a pool of glistening fabric that kissed the floor. In sharp contrast, her hair had been teased into a messed-up, punky bob, and she had an extraordinary pearl tiara with a diamond star at its center perched on her head. It was probably a priceless family heirloom, Ursula guessed.

India was accompanied by a ponytailed boy wearing torn jeans, a Rolling Stones tee under a tailcoat, and pale blue John Lennon–style sunglasses. He zigzagged through the throng, arm in arm with her. Meanwhile, Horatio returned to join Ursula and Otto, kissing Isobel hello.

"My best friend," huffed Isobel, staring unhappily at India and her ponytailed companion, "and my boyfriend."

"What *could* they be doing together, I wonder?" said Horatio.

"Stop stirring, you prat," spat back Isobel. "Dom's directing India in the play this term. They were probably . . . I don't know . . . rehearsing."

"Well, she looks *rrrrr*-adiant!" trilled Horatio. Ursula could see that he was enjoying winding up Isobel about India arriving with her boyfriend. "Never have I seen a girl in pearls looking quite so groovilicious."

"God, I can't believe she's got that Chanel purse," said Isobel, enviously eyeing a miniature white satin quilted handbag hanging by a chunky gold chain from India's shoulder.

"Now now, Isobel, try and be nice," tutted Horatio.

"*Liebling*, over here," interrupted Otto, waving enthusiastically at India.

"Hi, darlings" and air kisses were exchanged as India and Dom joined the group.

"Baby," said Isobel to Dom before grabbing him by both shoulders and snogging him ravenously. No one except Ursula seemed to be the least bit embarrassed by the sight of Isobel's tongue darting its way in and out of Dom's mouth.

"Don't wait, Dom, tell Isobel *now*," said India, interrupting the PDA with a tap on Dom's shoulder. "Good friends need to be . . . honest."

"About what?" said Isobel, drawing away from her boyfriend.

Horatio nudged Ursula and chuckled, "Oh goodie. I do find a scream-up among the drama hacks terribly amusing."

Meanwhile, Isobel was looking at India suspiciously.

"Shouldn't we tell Henry Forsyth first?" said Dom to India. "I mean it *was* his role—"

He stopped, seeing that a goth-looking boy with straggly, shoulder-length black hair and a month's worth of beard growth had strolled up. In his tailcoat he looked like a teenage Dracula. Despite being only about five feet four inches tall, he had presence.

"The Rodent arriveth," whispered Horatio mischievously to Ursula. "Let the spat commence."

"The Rodent?" repeated Ursula.

"My pet name for Henry Forsyth. Fitting, isn't it?"

"No!" But Ursula couldn't help giggling.

On tiptoes, Henry Forsyth craned his neck to peck Isobel on both cheeks.

"Henry, something's going on," she hissed at the bearded boy. She couldn't hide the agitation in her voice. "Something about your role."

He stood back, regarded Isobel's distressed face, and said, somewhat melodramatically, "Isobel's angry; and the heavens themselves / Do strike at my injustice."

Otto looked quizzically at Henry.

"*The Winter's Tale.* I've been speaking in semi-intermittent iambic pentameter since the summer," he explained. "The Method. Preparation for taking on the Prince of Denmark."

"Pretentious twat," whispered Horatio to Ursula. She stifled a laugh.

"Please, Dom. Tell him." India nudged Dom so hard he almost fell onto Henry.

"Dom?" was all Henry said.

"Er, well, yeah, Henry, mate," replied Dom nervously. "Look, mate, I want to be mega-radical with the Michaelmas production of *Hamlet.* I mean, yeah, any old public school toff can play *Hamlet,* mate. But Ophelia is a much bigger challenge for an Old Etonian like you. It will be so modern. India's completely right about that."

"India! What the—?" Henry gagged. "Am I to conclude that she is directing the director? Ugh. How pathetic."

"Haven't you heard about gender-blind casting? It's so *moderne,*" India interjected. She smiled charmingly at Henry. "I mean, you as Hamlet—snoresville. You as Ophelia? Now *that* will make waves."

Henry Forsyth seethed. Gosh, he would have made a good Hamlet, Ursula thought. Finally, he announced, "I have not invited every agent in London—contacts I have been building up in the theater world since I played Julius Caesar in F Block* at school—to watch me nancy about in a dress in three weeks' time. *I* am playing Hamlet, as we agreed last term."

"Henry darling, listen, I *adore* you. You're a *star*, absolutely," India cooed. "But we've got to be relevant, otherwise everyone will carry on thinking Oxford drama is a stuffy old boys club. The problem is, everyone's seen Hamlet played by a man, it's not exactly *original*. So that's why, when Dom and I . . . *analyzed* the play . . . together a couple of days ago, Dom switched the casting and he . . . suggested that *I* play Hamlet now."

"You?!" Henry exploded.

"It's the in thing now at drama school to reverse the sexes in the classic roles," she replied coolly.

"Sounds idiotic."

By this point, some of the other guests at the party had realized India, Dom, and Henry were putting on a not-to-be-missed show, and a circle of spectators was forming around them.

"It's going to be thrilling for everyone," India continued, "particularly you, Isobel."

"Really," Isobel deadpanned, looking about as thrilled as Anne Boleyn heading for the executioner's block.

"Isobel, sweetheart, you are my bestest friend *in the world*. I honestly couldn't wish for a better understudy, and you will *definitely* get to play Hamlet as I'm *obviously* going to be 'ill' on the Saturday night of 3rd Week. It's my shooting party at Brattenbury Tower that weekend. So you get to be Hamlet."

"Shooting weekend? What shooting weekend?" muttered Otto crossly to Ursula and Horatio. "She hasn't invited *me*. Outrageous. After she came to our wild boar shoot at the *Schloss* and drank all our peach schnapps and didn't leave any tips for the staff."

---

* Year groups at Eton are referred to by letter, from F to B. F Block is for the youngest boys, aged around thirteen.

"Are you surprised?" Horatio asked Otto, eyebrows raised. "Rich girls are always *by far* the cheapest."

Meanwhile, Ursula couldn't help but notice a radical change in Isobel's expression. A smug smile was suddenly dancing around her lips; she now resembled Marie Antoinette when confronted with a huge slice of cake.

". . . well. Oh," Isobel was saying, "I mean, I agree, we have to modernize. Oxford can't carry on putting on *The Importance of Being Earnest* every two minutes. It's so bourgeois."

"Mate," Dom said to his girlfriend, "I'm so glad you're on board. Come on, Henry, how about it? How about Ophelia?"

Henry stared him down, unmoved. Finally he hissed, "You've forgotten one tiny little detail, Dom. India is a bit of posh totty who couldn't act her way out of a local village hall."

There were a few gasps from the group that had assembled and then a deathly silence fell, with all eyes on India. She smiled at Henry, rather seductively, and then, as if by magic, her face transformed. The bloom drained from her cheeks and her skin took on a ghastly pallor. Slowly, she raised one arm and pointed behind Henry's head, as though terrified of something. She took a deep breath and began, in a whisper:

> Angels and ministers of grace defend us!
> Be thou a spirit of health or goblin damned,
> Bring with thee airs from heaven, or blasts from hell . . .

She was pointing, Ursula and the rest of the room now realized, at the gloomy portrait of Thomas Paget hanging over the fireplace. Her voice trembled, as though the ghost of Hamlet's father was standing before her—

> Be thy intents wicked or charitable,
> Thou comest in such a questionable shape
> That I will speak to thee . . .

"I think this one can act her way out of a village hall and all the way to Broadway," murmured Nancy, who had sidled up to Otto, Ursula, and Horatio during India's speech, still flushed after her run-in with Next Duke.

"She *is* Hamlet," said Ursula, amazed.

At this point, India fell to her knees beneath the painting, and an utterly convincing tear rolled down her cheek as she finally ended Hamlet's soliloquy.

There was an astonished silence; then Wenty, rushing over, cried out "Bravo! Bravo!" and the room erupted into applause. India got up and smiled seductively at Wenty, who kissed her enthusiastically on the lips. Meanwhile, with a look of cold envy in his eyes, Henry Forsyth looked hard at India and said, "You deserve *Macbeth*."

India looked shocked. Henry stormed across to the other side of the room, the champagne in his glass splish-sploshing angrily from side to side. In a far corner, a little group soon huddled round him to commiserate.

"Spoilsport," concluded Lady India, regaining her composure. "He's easily pretty enough to play Ophelia."

•

LATER THAT NIGHT, as Ursula, Horatio, and Nancy hung out on the huge sofa beside the fireplace, the talk was of India.

"*Quel* performance," said Horatio drolly. "Much better than the deathly drawing room drivel Oxford University Dramatic Society usually bores everyone to tears with."

"She's really a brilliant actress," Nancy said. "I'm surprised she hasn't got an agent already."

"Oh, but she has, darling, she has," replied Horatio. "The same one as Rupert Everett, apparently."

He got up to go.

"Well, toodle-pips, all," he said. "It's been fun. But I've got about six more drinks parties to get to tonight."

"Bye!" said Nancy.

"See you at the *Cherwell* meeting," added Ursula.

As soon as Horatio had departed, Wenty took his place in an arm-chair opposite the girls and India perched on his lap, draping her arms languorously around his neck. Occasionally she stroked his cheek, her immaculately lacquered nails, painted as dark as oxblood, lingering around his lips. Ursula squirmed with embarrassment when Wenty started kissing India's fingers.

She was starting to feel her head swim. The drama of the party had exhausted her, and her nine a.m. tutorial, followed by the all-important *Cherwell* meeting, for which, it was dawning on her, she did not have one single idea for an interesting article, or even an idea for an uninteresting one, loomed at the back of her mind. Meanwhile, Isobel, Wenty, India, Nancy, and everyone else were carrying on drinking as though they would be lying in until noon tomorrow.

"Enjoying your first Oxford party?" India asked Nancy.

"It's awesome," she replied. "Actually, I've even fallen in lust already."

"What?" cried India. "Who with?"

"The next Duke of Dudley."

India winced. "Really?" she said, looking amazed. "You do know the Dudley country place doesn't have central heating yet?"

Nancy's face lit up. "He has a country house? With no central heating? How . . . eccentric! How romantic!" she said. "On top of that, he's the hottest boy I've ever laid eyes on. Makes Rob Lowe look homely."

"You *must* be love-struck," laughed Wenty.

Ursula's room beckoned. She stood up, put down her glass, and turned to go.

"Sneaking out?" said Wenty. He jumped up off the sofa and grabbed her by the wrist. "Don't leave just yet, Unforgettable."

Before she could say a word, India, fuming, had torn his hand from Ursula's wrist. "Wenty. That's. *It.*"

With that, India released his hand, grabbed a glass of champagne, and dashed towards the door of the Old Drawing Room. Clutching a fresh bottle, Wenty followed in hot pursuit, calling out, "My darling! Don't go! Champagne?"

"My star," yelled Dom chasing after them. "Wait!"

"My boyfriend," shrieked Isobel, scooting after Dom.

"My part!" raged Henry Forsyth, stamping furiously after everyone.

"Should we go after them too?" asked Nancy, wobbling dizzily as she got up from the sofa. She was very, very drunk.

"I think the party's over," said Ursula. "Let's go to our staircase."

"What about stopping by Claire Potter's Crosswords and Ice Cream Society meeting?" giggled Nancy.

Oh no, thought Ursula guiltily. They'd forgotten about poor Claire's club. "I think it'll be finished by now," she said, looking at her watch. It was a few minutes before midnight. "Let's go."

But Nancy had collapsed back on the sofa. Ursula tried to pull her up by her arm, but Nancy just giggled and asked for more champagne.

"Need a hand?" Eg had appeared out of nowhere.

"I think so!" said Ursula gratefully.

With his help, Ursula guided Nancy through the party, grabbing her duvet coat en route. As they reached the door, Ursula noticed a boy lying across the threshold. He appeared to have fallen asleep, his head propped up against the doorframe, but as Ursula and Nancy tried to step over him, he jerked awake and grabbed at Ursula's ankle.

"Hey, gorgeousness, sleep with me," he slurred.

"What? Ugh! No!" yelped Ursula, yanking her leg away from him.

"How about you, beautiful? Sleep with me?" the boy said to Nancy.

"That sounds *so* romantic in your British accent," said Nancy woozily, stopping with one leg on either side of him.

"Just ignore Duncan," said Eg. "He propositions everyone when he's drunk. Even me."

But Nancy was oblivious. She slumped down on top of the boy and started French-kissing him. Ursula turned to Eg, shocked.

"I think we're in for a long wait," he said, shaking his head and smiling. Ursula couldn't help grinning back at him, despite her friend's predicament.

"Nancy. Nancy!" she said. "What about the next Duke of Dudley?"

Nancy managed to break off her snog for long enough to utter, "Who?"

Chapter 7

The possibility of being labeled a lemon by Dr. Dave was, Ursula concluded, as she hovered uncertainly on the icy landing outside his rooms exactly ten minutes before the scheduled start of her tutorial, far more sinister than that of seeing her tutor in his pajamas. If he did not answer the door at nine, she was determined, as per his instructions, to go straight inside, regardless of any pajama-related embarrassment that might ensue.

The minutes ticked by painfully slowly. Ursula let out a yawn so long and rumbling that, had anyone heard it, they might have mistaken it for a wolf's howl. The truth was, she was shattered after Wenty's party last night. Despite her vow to be in bed by midnight, she had only been able to prize Nancy from Duncan's drunken clutches at around one a.m. Thank goodness Eg had hung around, chatting with her and keeping her entertained. By the time Ursula finally fell asleep—a state further delayed, she surmised, by the combination of the bone-chilling cold in her turret and the boardlike sensation of her mattress—it was almost two in the morning.

God, it was cold on Dr. Dave's landing. Even in one of her warm kilts, a duffel coat, and her new college scarf, Ursula felt goose bumps appearing under her clothes. She checked her watch. Still only eight minutes to nine! She decided she would occupy herself by opening the surprisingly large number of envelopes she had found in her pi-

geonhole that morning. The first missive, a grand invitation printed
on a stiff cream card, was unexpected. It was as smart as the kind of
thing a countess would send out for her debutante daughter's coming-
out ball, and read:

THE PERQUISITORS

REQUEST THE PLEASURE OF YOUR COMPANY FOR

BUCKS FIZZ

MONDAY, 1ST WEEK

AT THE MONKS' UNDERCROFT, MAGDALEN COLLEGE

R.S.V.P. THE HON. RUPERT BINGHAM,   8 P.M.

MAGDALEN   SMART

Who were the Perquisitors? wondered Ursula. She didn't know
anyone called the Honorable Rupert Bingham. She must have received the invitation by mistake. But then she noticed that her name
was written in dark blue ink on the top right-hand corner of the invitation. It *was* meant for her. Ursula wasn't sure whether to feel excited
or creeped out. Were the Perquisitors one of Oxford's notorious secret societies? And how did the Perquisitors know her? It didn't matter, she thought. She couldn't possibly go anyway. It would be most
odd to go to a party you'd been invited to by someone you'd never
met. She'd had her ball-gown-wearing moment at Wenty's party. It
had been wonderful, but tonight would be books and Ovaltine.

A feeling of increasing confusion enveloped Ursula as she opened
the other envelopes. It seemed that she'd been invited to a different
party—by boys she didn't know—almost every night that week. And
not just any old party—they were strictly black-tie affairs. Wednesday
night had been reserved for a party being thrown by a society called
the Gridiron Club.* Meanwhile, four boys named Kit, Angus, Jamie,
and Tony had invited Ursula to join them on the Friday for cocktails

---

* The Gridiron Club, an all-male dining society, was founded in 1884. Past members
include John le Carré and David Cameron. The rule book runs to ten pages.

at a place called Vincent's. Who on earth were Kit, Angus, Jamie, and Tony? And what was Vincent's?

Just then, Ursula heard footsteps coming from the floor above her and looked round to see Horatio wandering down the stairs, a vision in mauves. He was dressed in a lavender-colored velvet jacket, which was thrown over a violet gingham shirt and purple Prince of Wales–check tweed trousers.

"Morning, Horatio," Ursula called out.

"Ciao, petal," he replied, coming up to her and kissing her once on each cheek. He tugged at her scarf. "A tip. College scarves are *terribly* passé. Burn it at once. They're for Japanese tourists."

"Really?" said Ursula, contemplating the tragedy of burning such an item. Even if it was horribly gauche, she thought to herself, it was far too expensive to discard. And it was the coziest thing in the world.

Horatio suddenly noticed the invitations in Ursula's hand. "Good haul!" he congratulated her. "Looks like you'll be in a ball gown every night this week."

"Horatio, I can't go to all these parties. I'll have far too much studying to do after my tutorial. In any case, I don't know any of these people, and I've no idea how they know me."

"Let me explain. Remember the Freshers' photograph you did on Friday on Great Lawn?"

"What's that got to do with it?" asked Ursula.

"On the Friday night of every 0th Week, as soon as the Freshers' photographs have been developed, Dave Brooks's darkroom on Market Street is crammed with Hooray Henrys[*] going through each college photo looking for pretty Freshers. They circle the best-looking ones, get the girls' names off the photo, and send them invitations to their societies and parties."

"A beauty contest?" said Ursula, affronted.

"In polite British society, it's known as a cattle market!" hooted Horatio, bellowing with laughter.

---

[*] "Hooray Henrys" = Sloane Ranger boys. Term often abbreviated to "Hoorays."

"But what about the girls who aren't picked? They must feel so left out," she said.

"It's very depressing for the plain Janes," he agreed, exhaling a long sigh. "The selection process is so sexist it's probably illegal. But no one cares about all that crap. The parties are *great* fun. You must go to the Perquisitors' tonight."

Ursula couldn't help but feel her interest piqued. Despite the Hooray Henrys' truly wicked selection methods, she was secretly flattered to have been "picked" by them—it was nice to be considered one of the pretty girls. Still, she told herself, she wouldn't go to the parties. How could you call yourself a modern girl if you didn't stand up to chauvinists? Ursula was going to stand up for feminism. She'd stand up for the plain Janes. Perhaps she could write an article about that for *Cherwell*—the inalienable right of the plain Jane to attend *any* Hooray Henry party she wished.

Ursula suddenly felt horrible about how she'd treated Claire Potter. She'd cruelly dismissed her as a potential friend because she was so dowdy. She'd written her off as a plain Jane just as cavalierly as the Hoorays would. Ursula vowed to make an effort with Claire. She was probably fascinating, regardless of her sad short hair.

"I'm definitely not going," she told Horatio. "I want to do some reading tonight."

"Well, I'll be there, so if you change your mind—come!" he exclaimed. "Don't forget, it's the *Cherwell* meeting at twelve today. I'm going down to the offices now to sort everything out. Toodle-oo!"

As the clock on the gate tower chimed nine, she stuffed the cards into her satchel and knocked on Dr. Dave's thick oak door.

No answer.

Two minutes passed, then three, four. No sign of Dr. Dave. Not being a lemon, Ursula reminded herself, was crucial if she were to make a good impression. The heavy door groaned as she gingerly pushed it open. Inside, Dr. Dave's rooms were quiet as the grave, and the only light was a white sliver of sharp morning sunshine that curled around one of the curtains. Ursula could vaguely make out the familiar outlines of Dr. Dave's armchairs, sofa, and the chaise longue opposite. The silhouette of the great argus loomed ominously in the half darkness.

"Oh!" Ursula gasped, suddenly noticing a large, person-shaped mound on the chaise longue. Surely Dr. Dave hadn't slept there? How embarrassing, she thought.

Perhaps if I noisily open the curtains, Ursula decided, he'll wake up of his own accord. That would avoid a mountain of awkwardness. The thought of disturbing the author of *From Constantinople to Jerusalem* from a snooze on his own sofa was simply too dreadful. She went over to the window and flapped the drapes unnecessarily wildly as she drew them back. Light flooded the room, picking up the gleaming red lacquer of the walls and glinting here and there off Dr. Dave's Eastern trinkets. Ursula could now see that a thick Turkish blanket was pulled up over the sleeping figure.

But the mound was still motionless.

"Dr. Dave?" she said brightly. "Good morning?"

Silence.

Ursula sighed. In the daylight she could see that a pool of fabric was spilling onto the floor from beneath the Turkish blanket at one end of the chaise longue. As she looked more closely, she realized that the fabric was white satin, beaded with pearls. There was no mistaking the fabric or the gown—it had to be the extraordinary dress that India had been wearing at Wenty's party last night. But why was *she* asleep *here*, in Dr. Dave's rooms?

Ursula tiptoed closer to the sleeping girl. It must have been freezing in here last night—India had pulled the Turkish blanket up so high over her body that only the top part of the back of her head was visible. A hand was peeking out from beneath the blanket and grazing the floor. It appeared to be clutching a champagne saucer.

Ursula cleared her throat. "Erm . . . hello?"

Nothing.

"Excuse me, Lady India?"

The girl didn't stir. Ursula stole closer. There wasn't a sound, a sigh, a movement coming from her.

Ursula could hardly breathe as she rushed around to the far side of the chaise longue. Now she was behind it, she could see India's face. The Turkish blanket was drawn right up to her chin. Her eyes were closed, as though she were taking a nap. But this was not a peaceful sleep. India's cheeks were colorless, her complexion dulled to the chalky pallor of stale pastry.

At that moment Ursula was enveloped by fear as the sickening thought dawned that there might be no life in the girl before her. India's once-crimson lips, still posed in their customary haughty pout, were now the bluish hue of a nasty bruise.

Stop being a lemon, Ursula chided herself. There was no time to waste. She must get help, and fast. As dire as the situation seemed, perhaps India could be revived. Ursula turned and rapped as violently as she could on Dr. Dave's bedroom door, shouting his name. He must be in there, she thought, pulling the door open. But she was greeted by the sight of an empty, unmade bed. On the side table next to it was the Chanel purse that India had been carrying last night. Ursula dashed out of the little bedroom and threw open the door to the bathroom. Empty. The room smelled noticeably lemony and fresh. She spotted a large bottle of Eau Sauvage cologne on the side of the sink. The lid was off.

Ursula rushed from Dr. Dave's rooms and out onto the landing. The JCR! she thought, seeing the door was ajar, and sped into the room opposite. Immediately she saw that there was someone in an armchair at the far end. She rushed over.

There was Otto Schuffenecker, sitting bolt upright in a worn wingback chair, still in his tails and white tie from the night before. He was fast asleep. Two glasses and an empty bottle had been kicked over and were lying on the floor next to him.

"Otto!" Ursula yelled desperately.

He didn't stir. Please, God, don't let Otto be dead, she prayed. That would be too Agatha Christie for words. She shook the boy by his left arm, as violently as she dared, shouting, "Otto. Otto! Wake up!"

"Ah, India darling, *mein Liebling,* you are soooooggghhh sveee-ee-et," he grunted, grabbing Ursula's waist and burying his head in her kilt.

"Ugh! Otto, *get off,*" she screamed, whacking him with her notepad.

"Aggghh!" squealed Otto. "Wenty! More champagne."

"Otto. Wenty's party finished hours ago."

Otto screwed up his eyes and squinted at her. "Where's India?" He looked around the room. "Where am I?"

"You're in the JCR."

"*No!*" shuddered Otto. "How uncool. Please never tell anyone you've seen me here, or I'll be sacked from the Gridiron Club—"

"Gridiron Club?" Ursula butted in. "Was it you who—?" But before Otto could answer, she had refocused on the current emergency. "Otto, I think something terrible has happened. It's India. She's . . . unconscious," Ursula stammered, unable to articulate her worst fear.

"What?" cried Otto, virtually jumping out of his tailcoat. "But . . . last night . . . we were so, she was so . . . ." He seemed terribly confused.

"She was so what?" asked Ursula.

"Sexy," he said, arching one eyebrow provocatively.

"Otto, what on earth are you talking about? Come with me, quick."

Ursula grabbed his arm and heaved him from the chair, dragging him towards Dr. Dave's rooms. As they left the JCR, Ursula noticed a pile of blank crossword puzzles stacked neatly on a table near the windows, as well as a cluster of little round tubs filled with melted ice cream. It looked like only two pots had been eaten. Poor Claire. It didn't look as though her event had been a big success. She'd make it up to her for not going. Maybe she'd invite her for a chocolate digestive in her room or something.

"Ah, it's so nice to hold your hand," Otto cooed as he stumbled behind Ursula. "I think I love you as much as I love India."

"Otto, you're still drunk," she reprimanded him, opening Dr. Dave's door. "Look," she whispered desolately as they reached India. Otto walked round to the back of the chaise longue. When he saw India's face, he finally appeared to sober up.

"Christ!" he said. "I must feel the pulse on her neck. If there is any pulse, I will give her the kiss of life . . ."

He gingerly turned the blanket down from Lady India's chin. As he did so, he let out a bloodcurdling screech, leaping away from the girl like a grasshopper who'd met up with a five-thousand-volt electric fence.

"What is it?!" gasped Ursula, still on the opposite side of the chaise longue. She rushed around it.

Ashen, speechless, Otto pointed at India's neck. The scene before them was ghastly.

India had a bloody slash wound extending from one side of her neck to the other. A crimson river had oozed down her collarbone and onto her décolletage, where it had coagulated. The top part of the pearl-encrusted gown was soaked with blood. Ursula felt herself almost freeze with shock. The girl had been attacked with no mercy. A monstrous crime had been committed.

"Oh my God," Ursula cried. "No! It can't be! India! India!"

She started shaking the girl, hoping, praying, that she would miraculously take a breath. But India was cold, stiff with rigor, unresponsive.

"Let me try," said Otto.

"There's no point. She's gone," Ursula told him.

"I must try something, anything," he insisted.

Otto leaned awkwardly over the chaise longue, put his lips on India's mouth, and blew air into the girl's lungs as hard as he could, over and over, but it was to no avail. Eventually, he sat on the floor, head in hands. It was hopeless. India was gone.

Ursula sat down opposite him, took his hand, and felt him squeeze it hard. The only thing to do now was to get help.

"Do you think you can manage to fetch the porter?" Ursula asked him gently.

"Er . . ." But Otto couldn't say more—his face turned a vile shade of green, and he vomited violently on the Persian rug.

"Ooops," he said, looking at Ursula, mortified.

"Poor Otto," said Ursula, patting his back comfortingly. "Go and get Deddington. I'll wait here."

He nodded numbly, but got up and rushed down the stairs. When the thud of his feet finally faded, Ursula was alone with India's body, feeling totally dumbfounded. Poor India—killed. But by *whom*? *Why*? Was there a murderer on the loose in Christminster? Ursula felt her spine crawl with fear.

The seconds seemed to tick by terribly slowly. Ursula carefully replaced the blanket over India's body, making sure to cover the terrible neck wound, as if restoring some semblance of peace to the dead girl. It was then that Ursula noticed that the champagne saucer, still clutched in India's stiff left hand, was broken. Ursula crouched down on the floor to get a closer look: the stem of the glass was intact, but half of the saucer part of the glass was missing.

Ursula's observations were suddenly interrupted by the sound of footsteps and a voice. She quickly jumped up from the floor and looked around to see Dr. Dave breezily entering the room, holding a stack of history books. He shut the door behind him and acknowledged Ursula, nodding his head to her. He then opened the book on the top of the pile and quoted from it dramatically.

"'Blood defileth the land, and the land cannot be cleansed of the blood that is shed therein, but by the blood of him that shed it,'" he read aloud.

"Blood?!" she interjected, desperate to explain about the blood situation on the chaise longue. "Dr. Dave—"

But he continued: "Blood indeed! Blood for blood! That was how Ludlow—a Fifth Monarchy fanatic—saw the world. Now, your essay question for the week, Miss Flowerbutton."

"Dr. Dave, erm, I think, well—that's India Brattenbury," said Ursula, gesturing at the body under the blanket.

"A not unusual occurrence," he replied with a sly grin, and prodded India's leg. Ignoring the fact that she didn't respond, Dr. Dave motioned to Ursula to sit in an armchair, impatient to start the tutorial.

"But—" she started.

"Just listen please, Miss Flowerbutton," he said. "Your moment to speak will come. Now, the Scottish Covenanters. After the Reformation, there is little doubt—"

Dr. Dave stopped abruptly and wrinkled his nose. Like a dog following a scent, he soon found himself staring at Otto's pile of puke.

"If India parked that custard on my Persian rug—"

A rap at the door interrupted his flow. Dr. Dave sighed. His eyes zipped to the top of their sockets and seemed to stick there—such was his annoyance. "Come in," he called.

Ursula jumped up from the armchair to see Deddington entering the room.

"Deddington? Something urgent? I'm in a tutorial with Miss Flowerbutton."

"Yes, very sorry to interrupt you, Dr. Erskine, but it has been brought to my attention that Lady India Brattenbury may be on your chaise longue."

"Standard procedure," replied Dr. Dave. "Most mornings there's a student asleep on my chaise longue. They're usually able to snooze through the first two tutorials of the morning if they got really drunk the night before. Anyway, since you've interrupted me, Deddington, can you make yourself useful and get my scout up here early to remove that?"

Dr. Dave pointed at the yellowing, stinking pile of sick on the floor. It was too complicated at this point, Ursula felt, to explain that Otto Schuffenecker was to blame and not India.

"Absolutely, Dr. Erskine," agreed Deddington. "But Lady India—"

Just then Otto burst in.

Dr. Dave's face turned puce with annoyance. "Otto, if you are here to tell me that your next essay is going to be late, come back never!" he snapped.

"It's India," said Otto, looking shaken.

"I am well aware that India Brattenbury is asleep on my chaise longue," Dr. Dave barked.

"But she's not asleep!" screeched Otto.

"Well, it doesn't take a doctorate in Aristotelian syllogistic logic from Oxford University to see that the girl's plainly not awake. Which leads me to deduce that the only other thing she could possibly be is asleep," said the tutor.

"Or . . . *dead*," howled Otto, collapsing on the tartan sofa and shaking uncontrollably.

"Otto, you are clearly under the influence of a hallucinogenic drug!" barked Dr. Dave. "Right, Miss Flowerbutton," he continued, ignoring Otto's shivering frame. "After the Reformation, the Scottish—"

"Dr. Dave," said Ursula, desperate. "*Please* listen!"

Profoundly fed up by this point, he growled, "What is it now, Miss Flowerbutton?"

"I'm afraid Otto's right," she said, her voice barely more than a whisper. "India's dead."

Finally, Dr. Dave directed his gaze back towards the chaise longue, walked over to the mound, and put his hand on India's back, as though to check her breathing. When he got no response, he walked around to the back of the sofa and looked at India's face. Slowly, he lifted the Turkish rug from the girl's neck. Shocked, he clutched at his forehead. "My God! Deddington, go and inform the high provost of the situation."

The porter dashed out of the room while Ursula, Otto, and Dr. Dave stood in appalled silence.

Finally, Dr. Dave said, "Right. Try to remain calm. Ursula, despite the tragic circumstances of our tutorial today, your priority is writing your first essay this week. You may not be able to imagine it now, but work will take your mind off this frightful discovery you have made. So let's not waste these few minutes of uninterrupted tutorial time before the high provost arrives. Why don't you start with S. A. Burrell's

article in the *Scottish Historical Review*. Volume forty-three. Burrell
wrote a very famous piece in 1964 called "The Apocalyptic Vision of
the Early Covenanters." Tell me why his argument's wrong. I'll look
forward to hearing you read out your essay this time next week."

Ursula took a deep breath. She did need to calm down, or she'd be
no help to anyone, least of all herself. Deciding not to admit that she
had no idea what an "Early Covenanter" might be, she scribbled the
title of the article on her notepad. As she did so, she heard Dr. Dave
utter the most awful retching sound. Ursula looked up. Dr. Dave had
parked his own custard next to Otto's.

Alas, she thought wistfully. Today hasn't been very *Brideshead Revisited* at all.

Chapter 8

Ten minutes or so after Julius Scrope, the high provost, was alerted to the grisly situation, he appeared in Dr. Dave's rooms, with Deddington at his side. Ursula observed that High Provost Scrope, a Christminster alumnus who had famously made his fortune as a corporate raider, was dressed today as though he were attending a city board meeting. His slicked-back hair, dapper pinstripe suit, and silvery tie were far flashier attire than was required in the world of academia.

Eyeing Ursula and Otto suspiciously, he took in the scene and summed up the situation as a "Nasty, nasty, er . . . accident" before asking Deddington to call an ambulance.

"Right, sir. Please send my condolences to His Lordship," said Deddington, leaving the room.

"I will," replied Scrope. He then turned to Dr. Dave, saying regretfully, "I'll have the unhappy task of informing the girl's father this morning." Then, as though thinking aloud, he added, "God knows what this means for the legacy."

"What?" asked Dr. Dave suddenly.

"Oh. Oh, nothing. Nothing whatsoever," replied Scrope curtly.

"How could anyone call this an accident?" Ursula whispered to Otto while Scrope ushered Dr. Dave to a far corner of the room, where they now consulted in low voices. "I'm going to say something." She steeled herself. "Excuse me for interrupting, High Provost, but . . . perhaps we should call the police? I mean, in case it's not 'an accident'—"

"Miss—?"

"Flowerbutton," Ursula informed him.

"As I was saying, Miss Flowerbutton. This is clearly a tragic . . . ahem . . . accident and that is the way the authorities will no doubt see it. Now, thank you for your help, but I do suggest that this environment is not suitable for undergraduates and perhaps you and Mr. . . . ?"

"Prince," said Otto.

"Mr. Prince, thank you, should be getting on with your academic work. And, don't say anything to anyone about the sad circumstances this morning, eh? There is a vast fortune at stake and the press mustn't get a whisper of this. We must respect the . . . er . . . privacy of the Brattenbury family at this tragic time."

The two undergraduates nodded, as they were clearly expected to, and exited the room. At the bottom of the staircase, they stood and looked at each other, both in some kind of shock.

"God," said Otto. "Mister!"

"Otto!" scolded Ursula. "What are we going to do?"

The two of them stood in silence for a few moments, as though in mourning. Then Otto said, "You know what you were asking me earlier?"

"What?" asked Ursula.

"About the Gridiron Club. I nominated you as a Potential Babe when we were deciding which girls to invite to the party."

"God, Otto, you are so shallow!" she admonished him. "This is not the moment to be thinking about parties."

He looked thoroughly embarrassed. "Sorry, you're completely right. It must be the shock of everything." Then he said, hopefully, "You will come, though?"

•

CHERWELL, EST. 1920 read the shiny brass plaque positioned on the white-rendered wall of an old Tudor cottage in the city center. Underneath, someone had stuck a Post-it note on which they had scrawled the words "Editorial meeting—third floor." Ursula rested her bicycle against a pile of others propped along the wall, locked it, and pushed open a tiny, creaky medieval door studded with enormous iron nails. It led into a wonkily cobbled courtyard with a rickety staircase on the left. She headed up and soon found herself at *Cherwell* HQ—an unnecessarily formal description for a couple of cramped attic rooms, a loo, and a corridor piled with old copies of the student newspaper.

Ursula hadn't known what to do with herself that morning. On the one hand, anxiety and fear overwhelmed her, as her mind kept flashing back to the sight of India's bloody, wounded neck. On the other, she found herself behaving in incredibly ordinary ways. It felt peculiar, almost surreal, to be buying a midmorning Kit Kat from the vending machine in Kitchen Quad. She watched with a sort of dazed amazement as other students chatted, argued, and smoked as though it was a perfectly average Monday morning. Death, Ursula realized, did not interrupt the humdrum business of life, or the eating of Kit Kats.

As she munched on her chocolate, Ursula wondered what her grannies would do in her situation. Vain Granny would certainly have taken to her boudoir for at least a week. But Plain Granny would have remained unbowed. As she had told Ursula throughout her childhood, in difficult situations the only thing to do was Keep Going. (This advice was regularly interchanged with "Kick On," a phrase Plain Granny would screech loudly at complete strangers on the hunting field.) Ursula *would* Keep Going. However unsettled she felt, she must stick to her original plans for Monday, like the *Cherwell* meeting she'd signed up for. She needed something, anything, to help distract her, even temporarily, from the horrific scene that morning.

Determined to be as professional as possible, Ursula had brought her old school satchel, in which she had carefully arranged a yellow legal pad, a reporter's notebook, and several pens and newly sharpened pencils. Her heart beating fast with anticipation, she squeezed her way along the corridor towards the sound of voices coming from one of the attic rooms. She peered shyly round the doorway, and took in her first glimpse of the *Cherwell* offices. The main editorial room, with its low, sloping ceilings, cracked magnolia paint, and institutional-looking, tatty blue carpet, was shabbier than Ursula had expected. But she could just glimpse the sparkling Oxford rooftops from two cobweb-covered dormer windows that looked out north over the city.

Along one side of the room a beaten-up collection of desks and tables, piled with the detritus of student journalism, had been pushed against the wall. Bliss, she sighed to herself as she took in the sight of the surfaces overflowing with stacks of black-and-white photographs, old magazines, newspapers, rough layouts, pencil sharpenings, empty crisp packets, stained tea mugs, and Coca-Cola cans. A couple of prehistoric-looking typewriters peeked out from under the mess. To Ursula, it was a paradise of creative chaos.

A gaggle of students—Second and Third Year writers and editors, Ursula assumed, and mainly boys, she couldn't help noticing with a frisson of excitement—was grouped round a large layout table in the center of the room. They were leafing through back issues of the newspaper, gossiping like mad while consuming cigarettes and mugs of tea at a rate of knots. She spotted Horatio, legs crossed, perched on a high stool with a smoldering Sobranie cigarette (purple, naturally) in one hand and *Interview* magazine in the other. As Ursula wandered in, he looked up and blew her an extravagant kiss. Oh God, she thought, Horatio doesn't know yet. He's been here all morning, and no one's told him what happened to India.

Over the next few minutes, a dozen or so wannabe Fresher journalists arrived and drifted hesitantly to the farthest corner of the room, where they clustered in a nervous huddle. Ursula smiled shyly at the other students as she wandered over. No one smiled back: there was an atmosphere of unspoken but intense competition.

Eventually, an auburn-headed boy with the lanky proportions of a stick insect stood up. He had a black hardback notebook in one hand and an unlit cigarette in the other. Dressed in drainpipe jeans and a maroon sweatshirt with the words "Lincoln College" emblazoned across the front, he also wore clunky Clark Kent–style glasses and had a layer of soft, pale pink fluff on his chin, as though he had not quite developed real stubble yet. The students around the table quieted down as he began to speak.

"Hello. Right. Yup. Er. Well . . ." He scratched his head, as though he had forgotten what he was going to say. "Er, yup, what I mean is, I'm Jago Summers and, erm . . . I'm the editor . . . of *Cherwell* . . . this term. Yup."

He lit the cigarette and inhaled deeply, as though pondering his next move. The group waited expectantly. Jago took another drag. By his third drag of the Marlboro Red, he was ready to continue.

"Right, yup, yup! Sorry. Freshers," he said, aiming a long gaze at the group of wannabe writers in the corner, "first of all, let me warn you, many of you will be disappointed today. Not for one reason, but many. We are generous with our allocation of misery here."

The Freshers giggled, but more out of fear than real amusement.

"Er, yup, so your first problem: there is a strict hierarchy here at *Cherwell*. Even though, well, I really hate hierarchies, they're completely anachronistic, but, er, I mean, that's sort of the way it is, right?"

"Apparently his nickname is Vague-o," whispered a Fresher behind Ursula. The group stifled their chuckles.

". . . so, it's like, each section has an editor, and each section has, like, a deputy section editor, and under them, feature writers, leader writers, copy editors, subeditors. And, I mean, it's really hard, but no one gets to write for a section until they have written for news. By which I mean, forget about writing about anything glamorous like arts or movies until you have cut your teeth on local news issues, and local news issues include such intriguing matters as the allocation of, like, public toilets on Cornmarket or the fate of the rotting beams in the ceiling of Wadham's Great Hall. Woodward and Bernstein did not start out with Watergate as their first story."

Ursula noticed two Fresher students pick up their bags and attempt to slip out of the meeting unnoticed. Jago waved one stick insect arm at them. "I totally get it if the whole hierarchy thing's getting to you," he called after them as they left. Then to everyone else, he added, "Sad, really sad. Right, the next disappointment I would like to announce is that not all of you will get to write something every issue. Anyone else want to leave?"

He glared at the group of deflated Freshers. No one moved a muscle.

"Okay, awesome. The next tragedy is that even if you are lucky enough to be commissioned and actually write something, it will probably be killed."

Ursula and the other Freshers, severely intimidated by now, didn't dare ask what he meant by "killed." But their mystified faces prompted Jago to pick up a sheet of text off the layout table, scrumple it into a ball, and aim it correctly at the bin.

"Oh, right," gulped Ursula.

"In fact, it will take most of you an average of four or five attempts at stories before one gets run," said Jago.

"Harsh," murmured the Fresher standing beside Ursula.

"Right, let's allocate some stories," the editor continued. "Usual procedure is that anyone who's interested in writing something, just put your hand up."

A scruffy young man dressed in baggy shorts and a sweatshirt that read "Hertford College Ultimate Frisbee" on the front and "Fear the Deer" on the back grabbed a piece of chalk and headed over to the large blackboard propped in the corner of the room.

"Everyone, this is Michael, our managing editor," said Jago.

"Yeah," said Michael while frantically leafing through a notebook for article ideas. He then scribbled a list of upcoming stories on the blackboard. Ursula scanned the list for something she might be able to volunteer for. Among many other topics, she read:

—Trinity students steal boat club megaphone to shout abuse at Japanese tourists

—Ancient Philosophy don at Pembroke resigns to become plumber

—Emperor Hirohito's grandson seen doing own washing on first day at Merton College after bodyguard shows him how to use machine

—First woman fellow elected at All Souls after 545 years

As Jago read each idea out loud, pretty much every hand in the room went up. I don't stand a chance, thought Ursula. Only one idea was allocated to a Fresher—the story of a cat who had given birth to three kittens in the Jesus College organ.

"Right, don't worry if you didn't get a story," said Jago as he came to the end of the list. "There'll be other chances. If you did get a story, congratulations. You may come and use the typewriters here in the office at any time. There's only one rule. The deadline for all stories is ten o'clock on Sunday mornings, we go to print on Sunday afternoon, publish on Mondays. Anyone who misses the deadline gets fired. Meanwhile, keep an eye out for stories. Sometimes things that don't seem like news turn into a great story. Do your trawls . . ."

"What are trawls?" asked a ballsy Fresher.

"Sorry," said Jago. "A trawl is fishing for information. Everyone needs to make at least three visits a week to someone important in their college or the university societies to talk to them, get the gossip—"

"And speaking of gossip," interrupted Horatio, "proper gossip comes straight to me. I'm Horatio Bentley and I'm writing the gossip column—John Evelyn's Diary.* So if you hear any tales of backstabbing, debauchery, misdemeanors, drunkenness, inappropriate sex— well, you can find me in the Bodleian Library most mornings or in my rooms at Christminster College at tea times. Right now the hunt is on for Pushy Fresher of the Week. If you have any suggestions for

---

* *Cherwell's* longest-running column, named after diarist John Evelyn (1620–1706), makes Page Six look kind.

candidates for the most odious and offensive First Year in the university, be so kind as to let me know."

"Thanks, Horatio," said Jago. "Right—"

He was interrupted by the arrival of a breathless girl wearing a CND T-shirt and cutoff denim shorts and tights. She had turquoise hair and a ring through her nose.

"Late again, Karen," huffed Jago. "Everyone, this is Karen Porter, our news editor."

"Jago, I've got something," said Karen, ignoring his irritation. "There's a rumor that a male undergraduate died this morning at Christminster. Some kind of accident."

"What? Who?" cried Horatio.

"No names yet," replied Karen.

"Shit," said Jago. "The story's yours."

Should she say something? Ursula wondered. She knew the high provost had forbidden her and Otto from talking about India's death, but clearly, everyone was going to know about it sooner or later. If she was going to be a *Cherwell* writer, she could hardly hold back information that might be crucial to a story. In the name of Truth, of Proper Journalism, of Full Disclosure (and a teensy bit for the sake of Personal Ambition, if she was being totally honest), she must make Jago aware of Karen Porter's mistake. If Woodward and Bernstein hadn't stuck up for The Truth, well . . . it didn't bear thinking about. Gingerly, Ursula raised her hand.

No one noticed.

"Excuse me," she said.

Jago looked at her quizzically. "Yup?"

"Well, it's just, I think I may have some information relevant to the Christminster story."

Karen Porter frowned. *I don't need help from some Fresher,* her expression seemed to say. If Jago sensed her displeasure, he chose to ignore it.

"Go on," he said, his full attention now focused on Ursula.

"Well, the dead undergraduate, in fact, it was a girl."

"How do you know?" asked Karen with a scowl.

"I found the body."

There was a shocked silence. Ursula soon realized that twenty or so faces were staring at her expectantly. But she knew she shouldn't say much more now.

"Great scoop," said Jago. "Right, er, what's your name?"

"Ursula Flowerbutton."

"I like it. Good name for a writer. Ursula, I'm reallocating the story to you."

"But it's Karen's story . . ." Ursula started to say. She'd only wanted to help the news editor, not snatch her scoop.

"You're at Christminster. It makes sense for you to do this story, Ursula. Karen's got plenty else to do, haven't you." It wasn't a question.

Karen smiled a little too brightly. "Yeah, loads," she replied.

"Okay, thanks, everyone, I look forward to receiving your copy at the end of 1st Week," said Jago, dismissing the meeting. "Ursula, Horatio, wait behind please."

As the other students were leaving, Horatio dashed up to Ursula. "Someone died in college? Who?"

"It's India." Ursula could hardly bear to say what she knew she had to. "She's dead."

Horatio whitened. He gulped, unable to speak.

Jago shut the office door after the last of the students and editors had left.

"Did you say India?" he asked. "India Brattenbury is dead? That pretty, posh, actressy girl? What happened to her?"

Ursula could barely hold back tears as she told Jago and Horatio about finding India's lifeless body on the chaise longue, the slit across her throat.

Horatio shook his head in disbelief. "Oh God," he whispered sadly.

"I don't think it was an accident," said Ursula.

"You're saying this is a murder?!" said Jago, almost hyperventilating with glee. "Ursula, this could be *huge* for *Cherwell*. You and I need to have a meeting. Why don't we meet tonight? Somewhere private. Somewhere like . . . my rooms. Come to Magdalen at six. My room's in the cloisters."

Horatio lit another cigarette, took a long drag, and regained his composure. He then pursed his lips, cocked his head to one side, and stared dubiously at Jago, who ignored him, saying, "We can discuss the piece. The tone. Your reporting skills. How to cover a police investigation . . . that sort of thing."

"I'll be there," said Ursula.

"I think you may well need a chaperone," suggested Horatio, raising one eyebrow archly.

"Horatio, don't even think about nicking this story off Ursula," Jago informed him. "It's hers. Officially."

"No need to worry about that, I'd much rather stick to the party reporting. Crime's not my style—not enough champagne or gossip on offer. I was just thinking that Ursula may need a companion at her meeting with you tonight," said Horatio.

Jago crossed his arms. "Sometimes I wish you'd naff off and stop interfering, you old queen."

"I take enormous offense at that homophobic slur," retorted Horatio. "I am *not* an old queen. I'm a young one."

Chapter 9

*B*rideshead, bonbons, cucumber sandwiches—and now a murder. Ursula's sepia-hued fantasy of Oxford had been dramatically interrupted by India's death. After bidding farewell to Horatio and Jago, she sped back to Christminster on her bicycle, her brain buzzing with questions. For now, the *Cherwell* assignment had done the trick—her fearful mood was, if not dissipated, edging to the back of her mind for the moment. Although she had intended to spend the afternoon in the library, she was soon diverted from her plan: the sight of an ambulance parked at an acute angle on the apron in front of Christminster called for immediate investigation. She threw her bicycle against the college railings, grabbed her satchel, and dashed into the gate tower.

A small group of somber-looking students stood gazing at the ambulance and talking to each other in low tones. Ursula caught snatches of their conversation.

"... *Apparently it's a Second Year* . . ."

". . . *Some kind of accident* . . . *Wentworth Wychwood's Opening Jaunt* . . ."

". . . *Blood all over the walls* . . ."

The group suddenly fell silent as Julius Scrope, accompanied by two paramedics, came into view. Head down, he was marching determinedly along the cloister towards the gate tower, his heels clicking against the stone flags, the medics barely able to keep up with his snappy pace.

". . . I am afraid, High Provost," Ursula heard one of them saying, as they came closer, "we will need to alert the police *now*. We have delayed far too long this morning already—"

"There's no need for the police, surely?" Scrope looked agitated. "The, ahem . . . disruption to undergraduates. Work. Police crawling all over the college—not conducive to academic studies. The dons would never allow it. I think it would be more . . . civilized to take her straight to hospital."

"No can do, sir," said the other paramedic, rather too gleefully, thought Ursula, as he and his colleague followed Scrope under the cloister.

The provost stopped beneath the gate tower. It was only then that he noticed the small audience of undergraduates gathered there, who were clearly enjoying the proceedings immensely. He glowered at them.

"I presume you are all en route to lectures or the library," said Scrope.

The group rapidly dispersed, while Ursula, from her spot in the shadows, slipped unnoticed into the porter's lodge, conveniently forgetting to completely close the door. Feigning an unnaturally keen interest in the hockey fixtures on the notice board, she listened as the negotiations between the high provost and the paramedics became more fraught.

"'No. Can. Do,'" huffed Scrope. "Meaning what? Just get the girl to hospital."

"Problem with that, sir," Ursula heard one of the paramedics say, "is that we can only take a body to hospital if it's still alive—"

"Not that we can *officially* say she's dead," interrupted his partner.

"What?!" snapped Scrope.

"Only the police can officially declare someone dead."

"Well, if you can't declare her dead, surely that means she is, in theory, alive," insisted Scrope, "in which case you can take her to hospital."

"Oh no, sir, I'm not saying she's *alive*, I'm just saying we can't formally declare her dead. But she clearly is dead, to all intents and purposes. Which means we can't take her to hospital."

Scrope snorted like a frustrated stallion.

"Even if the victim had been decapitated, it's still the case that the police surgeon is the only one who can *officially* declare her dead," the paramedic continued. "Now if you'll excuse me, High Provost, I'm going to radio the police from the ambulance."

The door to the porter's lodge received an irritated kick from Scrope, and its two-hundred-year-old hinges creaked in protest as he stormed inside.

"Bloody red tape. Deddington, in about ten minutes the college is going to be crawling with coppers. Keep them under control, would you? And keep the press *out*," he blustered, red-faced. "Lord Brattenbury is expected to arrive fairly soon. Poor man. Send him straight to the mansion when he arrives."

"Yes, High Provost," Deddington replied.

As Scrope turned to go, his eyes lighted on Ursula and he scrutinized her for a long, uncomfortable moment. Ursula prayed he wasn't going to accuse her of student journalism, punishable by some kind of ancient Oxford torture, and was relieved when he finally just said, "You're the one who found her, aren't you?"

She nodded.

"Are you all right?" barked Scrope, not seeming particularly concerned.

There was a killer on the loose. Nothing was "all right," Ursula thought to herself. Still, the last thing she was going to do was admit to Scrope—or herself—how terrified she really was. "I'm fine," she said.

"Jolly good. Don't disappear off anywhere."

"I won't," she promised.

•

NOTHING COULD HAVE prepared Ursula for the task that lay ahead. Not only had she never written a newspaper article, she'd never been mixed up in a murder, either. She knew that if she was going to write something decent for *Cherwell*, she'd need to get a scoop that no one else had. She would cover the police investigation from the minute it started, but in the meantime, she needed to understand as much as she could about the girl India had been.

Ursula hoped desperately that Nancy was in her room. Perhaps Nancy's recollections of her lunch with India a few days ago might give her a clue about where to start. As she dashed along the west side of Great Lawn towards the Gothic Buildings, Ursula glanced up towards the windows of the Old Drawing Room. The curtains were closed, even though it was past one o'clock already. Crumbs, she thought, maybe Wenty doesn't know yet. She prayed she wouldn't run into him now.

She took the steep stairs of the Gothic Buildings two at a time. When she reached the top and was standing outside Nancy's door, she was completely out of breath.

"Nancy!" puffed Ursula, rapping on the door.

She waited a few seconds and knocked again. Finally, Nancy's voice could be heard uttering a muffled "Hey?"

"It's me, Ursula," she said from the other side of the door.

"Come in, it's open."

Ursula opened the door and stepped inside. Nancy's extensive evening wardrobe was still strewn around the room, and her desk was now submerged under an avalanche of writing materials. The surrounding floor was covered in scrunched-up balls of paper. Gosh, thought Ursula, American girls were much more studious than English ones. It looked as if Nancy had been working all night, even *before* she'd had her first tutorial.

Nancy was still in bed, her hair distributed wildly across the leopard-print pillowcase upon which she was lying facedown.

"Ow," she croaked. "My head."

Gingerly, the American turned her face towards Ursula. Nancy's eyes were covered by a quilted madras-check sleep mask on which her initials had been monogrammed in an elaborate copperplate script. The breast pocket of her light blue cotton Brooks Brothers nightshirt displayed the same monogram, as did, Ursula noticed, a pair of slippers that had been tossed beside the bed. (An infinitely more exciting way of identifying your clothes, thought Ursula, than the standard-issue Cash's nametapes that Plain Granny had sewn inside her uniform throughout her school days.)

Without removing the sleep mask, Nancy sat up, wincing as she propped herself against the cold bars of her iron bedstead. "I feel like an extra in *Annie*," she complained, slowly pushing up the mask until it was perched like an Alice band on top of her head. With her mascara from the night before still smudged around her eyes, unkempt hair, and several pillow marks indented on her cheek, she looked like an accidental version of Cyndi Lauper.* She rubbed her eyes, blinked a few times, and yawned. Suddenly she sat bolt upright and exclaimed, "Oh my God, I overslept! What time is it?! Have I missed my tutorial?"

"It's almost one thirty," said Ursula.

"Phew," sighed Nancy. "My tutorial's at two. How was yours? Utterly terrifying?"

"Well, um . . ." Unsure exactly how to explain just how frightening her tutorial and entire morning had been, Ursula let her voice trail off.

"Oh Jesus," said Nancy, rubbing her temples. "I had way too much to drink last night. But, wow, what a party! I don't know how I'm going to cope with Dr. Dave. My brain feels like one great big pink champagne bubble."

She tumbled out of bed, flopped down in the hard wooden chair at her desk, and started fumbling beneath the piles of papers there. Finally she retrieved a packet of Camel Lights and a glossy red matchbox with the word "AREA" splashed across it. Nancy offered Ursula a cigarette, but she shook her head. She was secretly desperate to

---

* Cyndi Lauper, of "Girls Just Want to Have Fun" fame, was to Madonna what Meghan Trainor is to Taylor Swift.

try one, but St. Swerford's punishments for smoking had been harsh enough to prevent her ever even contemplating it. Seeing Nancy blowing curls of smoke as proficiently as a 1940s movie star made Ursula feel unbelievably square.

"I've been writing all night," Nancy said, casting her eyes over the chaotic desk. "Letters of Love. To Next Duke. Here," she continued, handing Ursula a piece of fuchsia-pink paper. In extravagant, curly-wurly letters written in silver glitter pen were the words:

Hi Next Duke!

How are you? Can you ever forgive my totally gross American behavior last night? First off, I was so drunk that despite our awesome conversation, I cannot remember your Christian name. Secondly, sorry for spilling champagne all over your coat. As all the JYAs were warned at our orientation last week in London, we must try to be "civilized" now that we are in Oxford. I guess I failed!!!

The only way I can make it up to you is to come and get your gorgeous coat and have it dry-cleaned.

R.S.V.P., please.

xxx

Nancy Feingold

(Room 3, Staircase C, Christminster)

"It's a very . . . *original* love letter," said Ursula, handing it back, though she couldn't quite see the romance in it.

Nancy winked as she folded the letter and put it in an envelope with "F.A.O. The Next Duke of Dudley, Merton College" written on the front in the same glittery ink.

Discarding her nightshirt, Nancy pulled on a pair of drainpipe Gloria Vanderbilt jeans, added an oversized yellow sweatshirt, slipped her bare feet into high-top sneakers, and threw a stonewashed, shoulder-padded denim jacket over the whole ensemble.

"You look really fashionable," Ursula complimented her, envying the ease of the wonderful American outfit. Her own collection of kilts and cardies really did seem outdated, she thought, looking down at her own clothes.

Nancy must have sensed Ursula's sartorial discomfort. "Hey, I had an idea for you," she said sweetly. "I mean, you're so cute, so pretty. You've got legs like Jerry Hall . . . but no one can see them. Why don't we cut your kilts short? Make them into mini kilts. That would be *so cool*. Everything has to be mini now to look trendy."

"Oooh . . ." Ursula smiled at the idea. Shortened, her kilts would be much more fashionable than they were now. But it would take her forever to hem them, with all the pleats. "But I just don't have time for all that sewing—"

Ursula was interrupted by the unmistakable tones of Alice the scout calling from outside Nancy's room, "Are you in there, girls?"

"Here!" replied Nancy.

Alice put her head round the door.

"I was just passing," she said, "and I wanted to check you're both all right. Dreadful news, isn't it?"

"What is?" asked Nancy curiously.

Alice's face fell.

"Hey, come in," Nancy urged her.

"She doesn't know yet," Ursula told the scout as she came into the room.

"Oh, oh, I see. Oh dear." Alice looked on the verge of tears.

"What's going on?" Nancy asked.

"Don't worry, I'll explain everything," said Ursula.

"Thank you, Miss Flowerbutton," Alice replied gratefully. "I'll leave you now." Just as she was closing the door, she added, "Do take care, girls, won't you, round college? And I don't mean to seem nosy, but did I just hear one of you talking about kilts needing to be taken up? I take in sewing. I could have them done by tomorrow morning."

"That would be great," said Ursula. "Thanks!"

"All right, I'll take them from your room," said Alice, disappearing.

After the scout had gone, Nancy asked, "What's happened?"

"Oh, Nancy, it's awful," said Ursula, sitting down on the bed. "I went into Dr. Dave's rooms this morning for my tutorial. He wasn't there, but India was lying on his chaise longue. She was dead."

"Dead?" Nancy stared at Ursula, completely shocked.

"I think she was murdered."

"Murdered?" Nancy gasped, her face turning pale. She took a long drag of her cigarette.

"Her neck . . . I don't know how to describe it . . ." The horror of the scene came back to Ursula. "Her neck had been . . . slashed. The blood had dripped down her dress."

"But—? I can't believe it. And . . . I thought she was studying English, not History. Why would she be in Dr. Dave's rooms anyway?"

"I don't know. But we've got to find out. I went to the *Cherwell* meeting this morning, and somehow . . . well . . . I've got to write an article about the murder. By Sunday morning. I don't know where to begin."

"Come on," said Nancy, grabbing a miniature Louis Vuitton rucksack into which she put a notebook, pens, and the letter to Next Duke. "We've got the perfect excuse to go back to Dr. Dave's rooms. My tutorial's in twenty minutes."

The girls clattered down the staircase. At the bottom they came upon Mrs. Deddington and Alice with a mountain of sheets at their feet. Ursula noticed her kilts piled next to them. But work seemed to be the last thing on their minds. They were discussing something intently in whispers. When Mrs. Deddington noticed the girls, she gave them a wary glance and tapped Alice smartly on the shoulder. Both scouts abruptly stopped talking.

"Hello again, girls," said Alice.

"Just helping out with a little bit of extra laundry this morning," said Mrs. Deddington. She started gathering up the dirty sheets.

"Are you okay?" she asked Ursula. "I hear you were the one who found her."

Ursula nodded gratefully. "I'll be fine," she said. "Poor India."

"It's a great shame," said Alice. "She was a lovely girl, wasn't she, Mrs. D.?"

Mrs. Deddington didn't say anything. A sour expression momentarily clouded her face.

"You didn't like her?" said Nancy.

"I didn't really know her. Like Alice says, I am sure she was very nice," protested Mrs. Deddington. But her brittle smile was unconvincing. "I better get on," she said, and scuttled off with a large armful of laundry.

As Ursula and Nancy headed out into the courtyard of the Gothic Buildings, Ursula noticed the afternoon light was now starting to bathe the stone walls in mellow amber rays.

"Can you tell me about your lunch last Thursday with India?" asked Ursula as they walked along.

"Sure," Nancy said. "So, it was, like, totally awesome for me to be hanging out with this super-cool English girl. We walked to this cute little brasserie called Browns on Woodstock Road. Anyway, we get there, she walks straight in past the line of people waiting—who all looked kinda irritated—and asks the maître d' to take us to her favorite table."

Once Nancy and India had been seated at the best table in the restaurant, Nancy recalled, India had ordered a hamburger for her, saying, "Wouldn't want you getting homesick."

"It was like the smallest, most pathetic hamburger I'd ever seen. I could have eaten twelve, literally," Nancy said. "Anyway, then she asked me if I wanted to join her shooting party in a few weekends' time at her dad's country place."

Ursula fished her reporter's notebook from her satchel and, as they walked, scribbled some notes:

—Otto had mentioned shooting weekend. Annoyed he hadn't been invited.
—Why would India invite Nancy, whom she only had met that day, and exclude old friend Otto?

Nancy continued with her account of the lunch. "So I said to India that I *loved* to shoot, I used to spend hours at the range with my father in New Jersey. Anyway, India was totally freaked when I said this. She was like, 'Girls don't shoot in England. We just load.' So I asked her, hadn't she ever heard of Betty Friedan? She said, 'Who?'"

The upshot was that, despite the thorough lecture Nancy had proceeded to give India on the subject of gender equality in the modern world, India deemed this information completely irrelevant to the politics of an English shooting weekend, telling Nancy that she hadn't been in England long enough to realize that even though the UK had Mrs. Thatcher and punks, things weren't as modern as they seemed. Shooting weekends at "Bratters," her ancestral home in the Derbyshire Dales, were run as though it was 1925.

Still, Nancy had become extremely excited when India informed her that shooting parties had a dress code all of their own. The American girl loved the idea of dressing in tweed plus fours and green Wellington boots during the day and changing into a black-tie party dress for dinner.

"It sounded like *Falcon Crest*,* only classy," Nancy told Ursula.

India had invited nine "guns"—the boys—and nine girls. The tenth gun would be her father, Lord Brattenbury, the tenth girl India herself.

"What about her mother?" asked Ursula.

Nancy pondered for a moment. Then she said, "You know, I don't think she mentioned her mom . . ." Nancy frowned, trying to recall the exact conversation. "No, I'm sure she didn't . . ."

"So if she'd invited nine girls and only nine boys because her father was going to be the tenth gun and India was the tenth girl," interrupted Ursula, "that must mean, for some reason, her mother wasn't going to be there. Did she say exactly who she'd invited?"

"Oh, yes, she was very clear that it was going to be a weekend for the Champagne Set. She said Wenty and Eg were definitely going, and Dom Littleton . . . and I *think* she mentioned Dr. Dave."

---

* *Falcon Crest*, which aired from 1981 to 1990, revolved around a feuding wine-growing family in the Napa Valley. Also known as *"Dallas* with grapes."

While they headed towards the porter's lodge, Nancy peered over Ursula's shoulder as she scrawled:

—India invited don to shoot. Why? Same don in whose rooms then found dead.

"That is *so* creepola," said Nancy.

"I know. And why invite an Oxford don and not Otto, who was her friend?"

Nancy shook her head. "I wonder who's going to play Hamlet now?" she asked.

"Her understudy, I suppose . . ."

Ursula broke off. She and Nancy looked at each other as they walked. They seemed to be thinking the same thing.

"You don't think . . . Isobel . . . ? No *way*," said Nancy slowly.

"She couldn't have," Ursula agreed. "They were best friends."

Still, she found herself adding a grim note to her pad:

—Could Isobel <u>really</u> have killed India over the Hamlet role?

—Or what about Henry Forsyth? Could <u>he</u> have done it?

The girls had reached the gate tower. Deddington was standing underneath it talking to a smart-looking man dressed in a navy suit and a camel coat.

". . . the entire college is saddened, Lord Brattenbury," Deddington was saying.

"Oh my God, India's dad!" gasped Nancy to Ursula.

"The high provost awaits you in his mansion," said Deddington, pointing to the far end of Great Quad.

"Thank you, Mr. Deddington," said Lord Brattenbury. "Are the police here yet?"

"Just one junior officer so far. Apparently the senior detective's delayed. Something about a stolen Blues boat."

"God almighty. There's a life lost and the police are tending to a boat. Oxford! Will you come and tell me the minute the detective arrives?"

Deddington nodded and went inside. Lord Brattenbury rushed past the girls with barely a glance at them. His face looked pinched, tragic.

They dashed into the porter's lodge.

"Ah, Feingold," said Deddington. "Delivery just arrived for you."

"Oh?" said Nancy.

"You'll find it on the apron in front of college. Wouldn't fit into the lodge. Here," he added, handing her a key.

"Ursula, quick," said Nancy, glancing at her watch.

She put her letter for Next Duke into the pigeon post sack on Deddington's desk, and the girls grabbed their mail from their pigeon-holes and sped out of the gate tower. The ambulance had now gone. In its place stood a glossy scarlet moped with a black leather seat and a white basket attached to the handlebars. The word "Spree"* was written in loopy white writing on the side. Nancy emitted a whoop of joy.

"My Spree!" she squealed, delighted, jumping astride the adorable little motorbike. Her mom, it transpired, had shipped Nancy's favored mode of transport from Northwestern to Oxford. "I never could really see myself on a bicycle. Look, Ursula, you can fit on the back."

"It's gorgeous," she said.

The huge college clock slowly chimed twice. "I'm gonna be late for the tutorial," shrieked Nancy, jumping off the moped. "Come on!"

---

* Honda Spree = "It" motorbike for 1980s American college kids.

Chapter 10

As the girls walked speedily towards Dr. Dave's staircase, Ursula opened a couple of the envelopes she had found in her pigeonhole. One of them contained an invitation to afternoon tea that day at four o'clock in the junior common room. The host, Ben Braithwaite (Second Year, Engineering), the president of the JCR committee, had invited the Freshers to meet their "College Parents." Ursula showed it to Nancy.

"An Oxford Mom and Dad? Cute! And 'afternoon tea.' How retro," she sighed happily. "This place is more like the Ritz than school."

Ursula had survived a very long time without parents, and wasn't sure now was the moment to acquire a mother and father. Still, an invitation to tea was hard to resist. Four o'clock tea by the fire at Seldom Seen Farm—hot buttered crumpets, Plain Granny's homemade scones with jam and clotted cream, Victoria sponge cake—had been Ursula's childhood treat, as cozy as it was scrumptious. Surely an Oxford tea would be just as comforting. And it would give her a good excuse to scope out the JCR unobserved. Ursula had a hunch that the room, which was right next to Dr. Dave's set, might hold a clue to what had happened to India.

"Let's go to the tea together," she said, following Nancy into Dr. Dave's staircase. After that, she vowed to herself, she *would* go the library.

As the girls climbed the stairs, they could hear the sound of squabbling voices drifting down from the landing above them.

"I'm sorry, sir. You can't go in there."

"But these are my rooms. I'm due to give a tutorial in about thirty seconds."

"Your rooms are a crime scene. You'll have to wait for the detective inspector to arrive."

On the first-floor landing, the girls found a uniformed police constable who looked about their own age barring entry to an irate Dr. Dave.

"I shall be bereft without my Montblanc. May I at least get it from inside?" pleaded the don.

"Your what?"

"My fountain pen."

"No one can be allowed into the crime scene. Might disturb evidence. I can lend you a Bic," the constable offered, a film of nervous perspiration starting to dampen his face.

"Thank you, but . . . no. I have never written a word of my manuscripts with a Bic and I am not about to start now. I do hope that, despite the tragic circumstances of last night," continued Dr. Dave, "the inspector will understand that I do need access to my rooms as soon as is humanly possible. I need somewhere to give my tutorials, and volume two of *From Constantinople to Jerusalem*, the sequel to my first bestselling tome on the Middle East, is due to be handed in to my publishers at the end of the month. I can only write sitting at my black lacquer desk with the great argus watching over me. . . ."

The constable maintained his position across the doorway, arms crossed. "The DI will be here shortly," he said, his expression set. Then, noticing Nancy and Ursula standing there, he blushed furiously, as though he had never seen such pretty girls in his life.

"Hello, Officer. I'm here for my tutorial," said Nancy. "And good morning, Dr. Dave."

"Good *afternoon*, Miss Feingold," was his curt reply. Nancy reddened. "I'm afraid we will be conducting our first tutorial . . ." He trailed off, looking around for a suitable perch, before his eyes alighted on the dust-laden window seat below the landing window. ". . . here." He beckoned her to sit. "Now," he began, "the Scottish Covenanter—"

But he got no further before the policeman, seemingly concerned by Ursula's presence, interrupted.

"And may I ask what reason you have to be here, miss?" he said to her. "This is a potential crime scene."

It wasn't a good idea, Ursula presumed, to admit she was writing about India's murder for *Cherwell*. So she said, "I thought I could help the police with their inquiries."

The constable looked unimpressed. "And how would you be proposing to do that, miss?"

"I'm not sure . . . but I was the one who found the victim."

The constable started. "Did you say *you* found her?" he asked, sounding amazed.

"Yes," said Ursula.

"You were the first person on the scene?"

"Yes."

"You're sure of that?"

"Yes."

The constable narrowed his eyes at her suspiciously. "Miss—?"

"Flowerbutton," Ursula informed him.

"Right, Miss Flowerbutton. You must remain here until the detective inspector arrives. You are a Person of Interest."

"I am?" remarked Ursula hopefully. Perhaps this would give her unlimited license to skulk around the police investigation—how perfect for her article. "I'll stay as long as you need me," she said, planting herself on the staircase leading up to the next floor. Bother, she thought, if only she'd been to the library already, she could have checked out her book and started reading about the Early Covenanters while she was waiting for the DI.

"May I continue, Officer, with my tutorial now?" groaned Dr. Dave from the window seat where he and Nancy were seated, patiently waiting.

The constable nodded.

"Well, Miss Feingold. An eventful morning, soon to be made only more so by the introduction of Scottish religious fanaticism into your life. Your task this week is to familiarize yourself with an article entitled 'The Apocalyptic Vision of the Early Covenanters' and tell me why the author is wrong."

"Tell you . . . sorry . . . who's what?" said Nancy. She looked puzzled.

"Why the author is wrong," repeated Dr. Dave.

"O-kaaaaay . . . I guess." For the first time, Ursula detected a chink in Nancy's armor of self-confidence.

"You'll find the college library very useful. The librarian up there, Olive—I mean, Ms. Brookethorpe—will help you find the literature. She's the prim-looking one, with a nice bottom—"

Dr. Dave's description of Ms. Brookethorpe was interrupted by the sound of footsteps clattering up towards them. The constable rushed to the top of the staircase. When he saw who the footsteps belonged to, he hurriedly stood to attention.

"Detective Inspector Trott!" he said, greeting the man who soon appeared on the landing.

In his midthirties, Ursula guessed, Trott was a beady-eyed, clean-shaven man with a muscular jaw and black hair cropped so close to his skull that you could see the veins pulsing in his temples. He was wearing a Barbour jacket over an unremarkable navy suit, white shirt, and shiny red tie. His face conveyed only unemotional professionalism, giving nothing away.

"Show me," was all DI Trott said in reply to the constable, flashing a cursory glance in the direction of Ursula, Nancy, and their tutor.

"She's in here," said the constable, opening the door to Dr. Dave's rooms.

He had barely put his toe over the threshold before Trott snapped,

"Wait outside please, Constable! Only one person at a time until we have gathered all the evidence."

A tense silence settled on the party on the landing. As the minutes ticked slowly by, Ursula dreaded to think what Trott was witnessing inside. When the inspector eventually reappeared, he was stern-faced.

"Constable. Radio the station and tell them I need scene of crime officers, forensic scientists, a police photographer, the exhibits officer, the police surgeon," he ordered. "They better tell the Home Office pathologist to bring his murder bag with him."

Trott now turned his attention to Ursula and Nancy with a searing glare. "Who are these two?"

"Miss Flowerbutton discovered the body," replied the constable, pointing at Ursula. "Miss Feingold is one of Dr. Erskine's students. She's been having a tutorial."

"Right. Keep Miss Flowerbutton here. I'll question her myself later."

"I'll wait with you," Nancy offered.

"Thanks," said Ursula gratefully.

Trott then opened the door to the JCR, peered inside, and said, "This'll have to do as a temporary incident room for now. Constable, anyone who arrives comes straight in here please. No one is to enter the crime scene until they've reported to me."

•

THAT AFTERNOON, URSULA and Nancy perched, seemingly unnoticed, at the top of the flight of stairs above Dr. Dave's rooms as the full force of the Thames Valley Police swung into action. The landing and JCR were soon populated by a collection of investigative personnel, each of whom would disappear into Dr. Dave's rooms one at a time, only to reappear a few minutes later carrying various miscellaneous items, which would then be discussed with DI Trott, now installed in the JCR. Ursula surreptitiously scribbled notes constantly, while Nancy consumed cigarette after cigarette.

Dr. Dave, who had somehow managed to continue with his tutorial schedule from the window seat, became more agitated as each object was transported. The sight of an officer emerging from his rooms while swaying beneath the weight of his beloved great argus was too much.

"Young man, young man!" he called out. "Is there really any compelling reason to remove poor Panoptes?"

"Eh?" mumbled the officer.

"Argos Panoptes was the all-seeing giant of Greek mythology," said Dr. Dave. "I named the great argus you have in your arms after him. Does he really need to be moved?"

"Evidence," replied the officer curtly, before adding, "Let's hope he really is all-seeing."

Before Dr. Dave could protest, the officer had staggered away down the stairs under the weight of the taxidermied bird.

"God knows how I will finish the book without Panoptes," sighed Dr. Dave, bereft.

Every now and again a local officer of some description—traffic warden, social worker, county councillor, transport policeman— would appear on the landing. When the constable asked them the purpose of their visit, they universally offered a variation on the phrase "just popping in to have a look." They were, Ursula observed, behaving as though they were here to greet a newborn baby, not inspect a freshly murdered corpse.

By midafternoon, DI Trott reappeared from the JCR and consulted in a low voice with the constable, though Ursula could only catch snatches of the conversation.

". . . why you kept *her* hanging around directly outside the crime scene . . . did they teach you nothing in training, constable? . . ." His voice rose with irritation. Trott was giving the young policeman a serious ticking-off.

"But I thought you said to keep the prime suspect here—" whimpered the constable.

"Ssshhhttt! I didn't mean *right here* . . . Anyway, it's too late now. I need to get on."

I'm the prime suspect? said Ursula to herself. She felt utterly confused—and petrified.

"I'm ready for you, Miss Flowerbutton," said Trott.

"See you later, at the JCR tea?" said Nancy, giving Ursula a comforting hug before she left. "And then let's go to that party tonight together, the Acquisitors—"

"Perquisitors," Ursula corrected her as she followed Trott into the JCR. "I can't."

Chapter 11

You didn't mean it, did you?" asked Ursula, worried, as she walked alongside Trott into the JCR.

"Mean what, miss?" said Trott, striding towards the far end of the room.

"That thing you said about me being the prime suspect?"

"Standard procedure, miss. The person who finds the body is always the prime suspect."

"But why?"

"It's your alibi. Let's just imagine you killed your friend—"

"She wasn't my friend."

"I see," said Trott. He looked at Ursula warily.

"I mean, I don't mean that I hated her. What I mean is she wasn't my friend because I didn't really know her." Ursula felt panicked.

"Right. Well, to return to your earlier question, let's just imagine you *did* kill this girl who you *say* isn't your friend. The easiest thing is to say that you found her. It gives you an excuse to be in the room where the body is, and accounts for any of your fingerprints that might be found. So that's why you're officially the prime suspect. Only you're not meant to know that you are," he grumbled. "That young constable, I don't know. Now, if you could wait until I start my interview before you speak again please."

Ursula had been too frantic to notice much about the JCR this morning. But now, as she talked with Trott, she tried to take in every detail. She didn't want to miss a clue, if there was one.

It had probably been a very grand room once, thought Ursula. Now, it had the gloomy air of an abandoned nursery. The oak paneling, once polished to a conker-like shine, no doubt, was scarred by years of student life. The two tall Gothic revival stone windows at the front of the room had a pretty view of the immaculate Great Lawn, but cobwebs drooped grubbily in their arches. A fly buzzed hungrily over the remains of Claire Potter's Crosswords and Ice Cream meeting, which still filled the table beneath the windows. Ursula hadn't paid attention this morning, but she now saw that two chairs were pulled up to the far end of the table and that a pink plastic spoon had been left inside one of two empty ice cream tubs there.

Trott and Ursula reached the far end of the room, where various officers were attempting to set up the temporary incident room the DI had demanded.

"Sir," barked a woman officer, as Trott and Ursula headed past her. She was in the process of turning the tatty billiard table in the center of the room into a makeshift exhibits area.

The far end of the room was dominated by a huge, bulky television set positioned in one corner and surrounded by a semicircle of ugly brown and beige sofas and armchairs with stuffing poking out here and there. They were now occupied by six or seven police employees. Behind the television, shelves were piled high with books, videocassettes, and old boxes of Scrabble and Monopoly.

"Right. Sit down, Miss Flowerbutton," Trott finally said, gesturing towards two chairs drawn up on either side of a red Formica-topped table in the corner opposite the television set.

They took their seats, and DI Trott opened a brand-new blue-backed A4-sized notebook, picked up a pen, and pressed PLAY on the tape recorder that had been set up on the table.

"Now, tell me, how did you come upon this body this morning?" he asked.

"Well, it all started because I didn't want to be a lemon," said Ursula. "You see, Dr. Dave has very, very strict rules. . . ."

Ursula tried to remember everything from the absolute beginning. She told Trott about Dr. Dave encouraging students to enter his rooms if he didn't answer a knock, finding India on the chaise longue, the dreadful realization that she was not breathing, discovering Otto asleep in the JCR.

"He was in that chair," added Ursula, pointing to the wingback chair in the middle of the room.

"Constable!" yelled Trott to no one in particular.

Four officers simultaneously sprang to their feet from the TV corner.

"That chair's evidence. Get it photographed, take fiber samples, and bag it up," ordered Trott. "And don't touch it."

Trott turned his attention back to Ursula.

"Right, miss, you were saying a young man was in here?"

"Yes, Otto Schuffenecker. It was Otto who realized India was definitely dead."

"Someone track down an Otto Schuffenecker and interview him today," Trott barked at his team. "How did he know she was dead?"

Ursula recounted to Trott the grim moment when Otto had turned back the blanket covering India, the sight of her neck, the blood on her white gown, his attempt to resuscitate her.

"Then I asked him to run and get the porter, Deddington. And I stayed with India . . ."

As a single tear finally rolled down Ursula's cheek as she recounted the sight of the lifeless girl, Trott offered a tissue, but his expression remained unchanged, emotionless. He transcribed Ursula's story methodically, with the air of a man who was writing a polite thank-you note for a particularly uninspiring Christmas gift. Every few minutes another member of his team would come and interrupt him with a question, but he seemed to possess a remarkable ability to delegate detailed tasks without ever losing the thread of the story Ursula was telling him.

"Why are there so many people here?" she asked, noticing that the stream of police personnel coming in and out of the room was ever increasing. She needed to fully understand the police investigation if she was going to be able to report on it properly in her article.

"Murders aren't solved by two friendly bobbies these days, miss. It's not like you see on TV. There will be at least a hundred people on this over the next forty-eight hours. Before the evidence disappears."

"Really?" said Ursula, her faith in Hercule Poirot brutally shattered.

"Yup. Although most of us in the force are well aware that it's more than likely to be an utter waste of police time and resources."

"Why?" asked Ursula.

"Murders are often the least interesting crimes to solve. Most of them are straightforward domestics. It's usually The Husband or The Boyfriend. Look close to home, I always say. Look close to home. Now, you were saying that you stayed in the room while this"—Trott looked down at his notes—"Mr. Schuffenecker—"

"Prince," Ursula corrected him.

"Eh?" The DI frowned.

"It's Prince Otto Schuffenecker. He's an Austrian royal—at least he would have been if they hadn't abolished them after the First World War. He gets very offended if anyone calls him mister."

"Right, er . . . thank you. So you were saying, this prince fellow, he's gone down to the lodge to alert the porter?

"Yes, and—"

But Trott's attention had been diverted. "Hello, Doc!" he exclaimed, signaling to a very tall white-haired gentleman who had just entered the JCR.

"Who's that?" asked Ursula.

"Home Office pathologist," replied Trott. "Dr. Euan Rathdonelly. Everyone just calls him Doc."

Despite his advancing years, Doc, who was dressed in an immaculate Prince of Wales–check suit, strode energetically across the room towards Ursula and Trott. He possessed the sort of pink-cheeked vigor and beaming demeanor of the jolly headmaster Ursula had so adored at pre-prep school. His elegance was marred only by an ungainly black duffel bag weighing down his left shoulder.

"Marvelous murder you've got here!" declared Doc gaily, sounding like a cheerfully excited father who's just watched his child in their school pantomime. "I had a quick peek. Hope you don't mind."

"All right to get on?" asked Trott, shaking Doc's hand warmly.

"Right away," the pathologist replied.

He plonked the duffel bag on the floor, unzipped it, and retrieved a pair of Wellington boots, a large leather apron, and some black rubber gloves. By the time he had put the items on over his Savile Row suit and lit a cigar, he looked, thought Ursula, like an upmarket butcher. Next he rifled around in the duffel and retrieved swabs, tweezers, and a few plastic bags, revealing the sharp blade of a scalpel glinting from inside the holdall. Ursula gulped.

"Right, miss, you stayed in the room while your friend went down to the porter's lodge. Correct?" Trott continued.

"Yes," replied Ursula. "And while I was waiting, that's when Dr. Dave arrived. He was due to give me my first tutorial on—"

She stopped, noticing from the corner of one eye that an officer was clearing away the remains of Claire Potter's tragic Crosswords and Ice Cream party. Ursula jumped up from her chair and dashed across the room towards the table beneath the Gothic windows.

"Wait!" she gasped. "Don't move a thing!"

A rather surprised-looking officer froze, a pot of melted ice cream in one hand and a black trash bag in the other. "Sir?"

"Miss, I'd appreciate it if we could continue with your statement," responded Trott, impatiently checking his watch.

"But—the ice cream—it's a *clue*," said Ursula.

An agitated Trott harrumphed, "Cool it, Nancy Drew." (Ursula was secretly flattered by Trott's remark. After all, when it came to girl detectives, Nancy Drew was her heroine.)

"Trott, just a minute," Doc said, bounding over to where Ursula was standing. "If there's a clue in the ice cream, I would like to know what it is."

Trott's usually stony face twitched very slightly with irritation, and he looked at Ursula coldly. Then he turned to his tape recorder and stated for the record, "Interview temporarily suspended. Witness believes there is something of significance in . . . ice cream."

Frowning, he turned off the tape recorder and headed over to the table beneath the Gothic windows. He indicated to the officer that he should return the pot of melted ice cream to its former position.

Ursula seized the moment.

"It's not exactly *in* the ice cream, this clue," she stammered excitedly, "but, look, if you sit down here . . ."

She slid into one of the two chairs that had been drawn up to the table, with the two empty tubs of ice cream in front of them. From the corner of her eye, she saw Trott raise an eyebrow skeptically.

". . . you can see that someone sat here while they were eating ice cream," she continued, pointing out the two pots on the left-hand side of the table, which were, indeed, scraped clean. Each tub would have contained enough ice cream for one person. The pink plastic spoon that Ursula had noticed earlier was still resting inside one of them. "But no one touched the pots at the other end of the table, they're full of melted ice cream—"

Trott rapped his fingers impatiently on the tabletop, but, undaunted, Ursula continued.

"You see, Claire Potter—a Fresher—held her first Crosswords and Ice Cream Society party in here last night. But it looks like only one other person came, because Claire sat here, with that person, and, well, they ate one small pot of ice cream each."

Trott sighed. "Shall we get back to the interview now, miss?"

"Sorry. I'm not being clear," said Ursula. "If you were sitting here last night, eating ice cream, perhaps all alone, waiting for someone, or perhaps with someone . . . well, anyway, *look!*"

From her seat, she pointed through the tall Gothic windows and out towards the lawn of Great Quad below.

Trott reluctantly squatted beside her. "Nice view," he said curtly.

"Whoever was here could see exactly who was coming and going across Great Quad all evening."

"In the dark?" said Trott.

"It was a full moon last night," she said. "Beautiful and bright. India was at a party in the Old Drawing Room—I know because I saw her there—which is almost directly across the quad from here. At some point she must have crossed it to get to Dr. Dave's rooms. Whoever was sitting in these chairs might have seen her."

Trott looked at Doc and jerked his head to him. They moved off for a moment and conferred in low voices.

Within minutes, an officer was dispatched to track down and interview Claire Potter, and the police photographer was summoned from Dr. Dave's rooms to the JCR. After the photographer had snapped photographs of the table, chairs, and ice cream tubs, Doc used a pair of tweezers to place the used tubs and single plastic spoon in clear bags and label them. Officers started delicately dusting the table and chairs with powder for fingerprints. A cigar wedged into the side of his mouth, Doc then headed off into Dr. Dave's rooms to examine India's body.

"I think you'd better tell me all about this party," Trott said to Ursula.

"Of course," she said. "It was *lovely*. It was Wenty's party. Lord Wentworth Wychwood. He's a Second Year. Rowing Blue. That's why he has the Old Drawing Room, it's a privilege for Blues. He's terribly pleased with himself, being an earl and Blue—you can imagine, Inspector."

Trott concurred. "I know the type."

"Anyway, the party was, I suppose, a sort of first-night-of-term thing, everyone in white tie and ball gowns."

"Very nice," commented Trott tartly.

"Yes, Detective, it *was* heavenly, I mean, there were pink *bon-bons* and matching pink champagne. My American classmate Nancy thought it was *very* unhygienic that Wenty—that's Lord Wychwood's nickname—used dirty champagne saucers because his washer-uppers had disappeared. Nancy's from New York, so she's terrified of mono."

"You say this, er"—Trott looked down at his notes—"Lord Wychwood served alcohol in champagne saucers?"

"Yes," said Ursula.

"*Only* saucers, not flutes? Or wineglasses?" asked Trott.

"Saucers. I'm sure of it. Wenty is far too much of a snob to use flutes."

Trott beckoned an officer over. "Track down a Lord Wentworth Wychwood for interview. He's a Second Year here. Person of Interest."

"Yes, sir," said the officer, dashing off.

"Oh, you don't think—Wenty?!" Ursula gasped, the horrible image of India's bloody neck zooming back into her mind. "He was in love with India, he wouldn't want to . . ."

"So Wenty was Lady India's boyfriend?" continued the DI. "Oh dear me . . . that makes him a Person of Great Interest."

Ursula's mind suddenly flashed back to Trott's earlier comment. What had he said? "Look close to home. It's usually the husband or the boyfriend." But Wenty? Ursula suddenly found herself feeling defensive.

"I don't think he'd ever harm her. Wenty genuinely cared about India."

"How do you know?"

"When she got upset about something—" here Ursula paused. Instinct told her it wouldn't be wise to elaborate on India's reaction to hearing Wentworth call another girl Unforgettable. "—and ran out of the party, he chased after her."

As Trott scribbled his notes, Ursula noticed the door to the JCR being slowly pushed open. First, a very large bottom came into view, then an enormous tea trolley containing a huge, steaming tea urn and piles of cups and saucers. The owner of the significant bottom, a pudgy boy dressed in cheap bleached jeans, an anorak, and an old pair of grubby sneakers, dragged the trolley all the way into the room. He was followed by a group of six students clutching clipboards, posters, drawing pins, and various lists.

". . . you see, this is why I am *not* happy about First Years holding events in here. What a mess!" the pudgy boy was complaining loudly, seeing the table still covered in pots of melted ice cream. "And guess who gets to clear up? Yours truly, the JCR president."

"Your committee will help," volunteered a girl dressed in a tie-dyed tunic and clogs, with a ring through her nose and long, matted blond dreadlocks. She grabbed a bin bag from the bottom of the trolley and started chucking the pots into it.

An officer dashed forward. "Excuse me, miss, please don't touch those."

Seeing his uniform, the girl backed away from the table and twisted a dreadlock nervously. Trott stood and strode over to the interlopers, saying, "I'm afraid you can't come in here."

The pudgy boy drew himself up to his full height, summoning all the courage he could muster.

"Sorry, I think there's been a misunderstanding. I'm Ben Braithwaite, JCR president," he said, then paused, as though waiting for some kind of recognition of his authority from Trott. None was forthcoming.

"Anyway, I—well, we—the JCR committee, have this room booked from four till six for the Freshers' Tea," Ben went on, trying to sound as official as he could.

"I'm Detective Inspector Trott. Thames Valley Police Criminal Investigation Department. Unfortunately, a homicide has taken place in college today. We're using this space as a temporary incident room."

Ben and his committee looked appalled.

"So it's true? A *murder*? In college? I thought it was just people starting silly rumors," said Ben.

"I'm heading up the inquiry," replied Trott.

"Oh. What a shock." Ben seemed stunned for a moment, then

looked at his watch. "Problem is, eighty Freshers are due to arrive here in . . . gosh . . . less than five minutes . . . to meet their College Parents. Detective, I'm afraid there's not much I can do about that now."

"Detective Inspector," added the dreadlocked girl with a pleading look, "it is *crucial* for the *welfare* of the Freshers that they each have a College Mother and Father."

Trott raised his eyebrows and sighed. "All right, get on with it," he huffed. "I'm going to clear our lot out of here. We need to get a proper incident room set up down at the station anyway."

Ben nodded gratefully and reached down to the bottom tier of the tea trolley, from where he procured a plate piled high with dry-looking cookies.

"Custard cream, Detective?"

For the first time, Ursula detected the glimpse of a smile on Trott's face.

"Don't mind if I do," he said, gobbling one down. "And I'll have a cup of tea while you're at it."

Ben hurriedly produced one, and after a few gulps, looking satisfied, Trott told Ursula, "Right, Miss Flowerbutton. I'm going to suspend my interview with you for now. I'll want to talk to you again, most likely. Don't leave Oxford without letting me know."

Thank goodness, she thought to herself. The interview session had been surprisingly tiring. She still had so much to do today: she needed to get to the library after the tea and find the article Dr. Dave had assigned, get to Jago's room by six for her editorial meeting with him, and then back to her room and spend the evening reading, as planned.

While the JCR committee prepared for the tea party, Ursula perched on one of the windowsills overlooking Great Quad. Her mind was whirring, and she hastily jotted a few notes on her pad:

—India crossed Great Quad last night. Her white dress and tiara would have been hard to miss in the moonlight. If Claire

Potter and her mysterious ice-cream-eating companion had seen her, could they have followed India into Dr. Dave's rooms? —But why would Claire Potter, or her unknown friend, have any interest in disposing of India Brattenbury—

Ursula suddenly stopped writing. The tiara! What on earth had happened to the tiara?

Chapter 12

The clank of cheap teacups interrupted Ursula's cogitations. She looked up from her notebook. The police team had started to relocate from the JCR, but she had to speak to Trott before he left. She speedily weaved her way through the bewildered-looking Freshers who were gradually filling the room and helping themselves to cups of tea.

"Excuse me, Detective Inspector," Ursula said, spotting him by the door. "There's something I forgot to tell you. India was wearing a tiara at the party—pearls and diamonds, I think it was some sort of family heirloom—but it wasn't with her this morning when I found her."

"Hmmmm," Trott mused. "We'll investigate."

After he left, Ursula joined a group of Freshers clustered around a trestle table where the tea urn had been set up along with plates of custard cream biscuits and a few packets of malted milks. She grabbed a cup, sighing wistfully to herself as she sipped the overstewed PG Tips. The JCR tea wasn't exactly the comforting gateaux fest she'd been hoping for. Still, she hadn't eaten since breakfast and was starving. She devoured a cookie.

While the tea got under way, Ben Braithwaite and the dreadlocked girl pinned an elaborate family tree on the JCR notice board. Maybe, Ursula mused, it would be fun to have a mother and father for a change. Having said that, her friends at St. Swerford's had only ever mentioned their own parents with an agonized roll of the eyes and pretense at vomiting.

Ursula wandered over to the family tree to learn her fate, and saw that the dreadlocked girl was now pinning up a garish orange poster on the board next to it. In large, black lettering it screamed:

STRESS?! ANXIETY? DEPRESSION?
SPEAK TO YOUR WELFARE OFFICER

Beneath the words were grainy black-and-white headshots of the girl along with Ben Braithwaite and the rest of the JCR committee. Already, Ursula noticed, the welfare officers were hungrily prowling the room, as though each was hoping to be the first to land a Fresher who was suffering from Stress! Anxiety! or Depression!

The Freshers did not seem to have been afflicted by the aforementioned psychological conditions. Rather, they had been struck by a highly contagious case of Murder in the Dark. The news of India's death had clearly spread rapidly through the college already. The Freshers were jittery, but the death had also added a frisson of excitement to things. The possibility that any one of the students standing in the JCR at that moment could be next had brought a heightened sense of drama to their first week at Oxford. The questions that usually dominated these events—Where did you go to school? What subject are you studying? Did you take a gap year?—were replaced by darker gossip. As Ursula scanned the family tree for her name, she overheard ever more hysterical outbursts among the Freshers around her.

. . . *I heard a Third Year say she was queen of the Yars. Must have been a lefty who did it . . .*

. . . *thirty-five stab wounds, she was unrecognizable, apparently . . .*

. . . *strangled. A homeless drunk broke into the don's rooms looking for port and throttled her with baler twine . . .*

Ursula turned her attention back to the family tree, an extraordinarily detailed diagram of College Mothers, Fathers, Sons, Daughters, and even Grandparents. It took Ursula ages to find her name, positioned next to those of her siblings. She had two "brothers"—Paul Davies, Medicine, and Matt Owen, Geography. Her "sister" was Claire Potter.

Ursula traced the line upwards to her parents. Her "father," it turned out, was Ben Braithwaite, the JCR president. He seemed perfectly nice, if a bit officious. Finally her finger landed on the name of her "mother"—someone named Jocasta Wright.

The dreadlocked girl, who had now finished putting up her welfare sheet, looked over at Ursula and said, *"Man!* I'm your mum!"

Jocasta Wright then enveloped her in an enormous hug, nearly suffocating her. She reeked so strongly of joss sticks that Ursula sneezed violently.

"Sorry!" she said, extricating herself from Jocasta and her tie-dyed tunic.

"No, don't be. I don't want you to be sorry for anything. That's like a total waste of head space. I'm here for you, man. Great, man," Jocasta said in a low, languorous voice.

"Thank you," said Ursula sincerely.

"No, man, don't thank me. It's my *duty* to be here for you. My College Mum . . ." Jocasta broke off and looked wistful. "She was, yeah, totally uninterested. I met her at the tea and never saw her again. But I'm going to be a *proper* mother to you, I promise."

What did that entail? Ursula wondered.

"So, right, any probs, I'm here. I'm chairperson of the OSSTDAC—sorry, that stands for the Oxford Student Sexually Transmitted Diseases Advisory Committee—so any worries on that front, honestly, you can talk to me. In confidence. Herpes, VD, AIDS, contraception, abortion, family planning clinics . . . Personally, I prefer the coil to the Pill . . ."

As Jocasta listed the various diseases and unwanted outcomes of sex that might afflict her during her time at Christminster, Ursula wondered what her student "mother" would think if she admitted—

which Ursula had no intention of doing—that she was a virgin, and a very innocent one at that.

The nearest Ursula had come to sex was a French kiss with her second cousin Reggie Vernon-Hay in the attic at Seldom Seen Farm one Christmas. The snog had occurred more out of Ursula's sense of desperation than any real attraction. After all, she had reached the age of fifteen and never kissed a boy. This was not out of reluctance, but rather a supply issue. Boys were thin on the ground if you attended an all-girls school and lived on a remote farm with elderly relatives. Snogging Reggie was, for Ursula, the only way she was going to pass the vital First Kiss milestone before she turned sixteen. Otherwise, she feared, she would be doomed to end up like one of Jane Austen's lonely spinster characters, crocheting doilies in an ivy-strangled cottage.

Despite Ursula concluding, post-snog, that the experience of touching tongues with a boy was only marginally less revolting than that of swallowing the lumpy school mashed potatoes that were served with most of Swerford's horrid school dinners, she was excited that she had *finally* snogged someone. Even if it was her cousin, which was sort of incesty, it still counted.

When it came to sex, Plain Granny (a Catholic, strict) had attempted to instill into her granddaughter the belief that sex before marriage was a sin. Vain Granny (Church of England, lapsed) espoused a different view. Her motto—"Don't have sex before breakfast, you never know whom you might meet at lunch"—was oft repeated in front of her granddaughter.

The result of this eccentric sex education was that Ursula felt free to settle herself somewhere between her grandmothers' extremes. If she fell in love, she'd have sex, but she wouldn't have sex just to rid herself of her virginity, and she certainly wouldn't get married just to have sex. Marriage was a very long way off—and would happen only after her career as a writer had been established. It was 1985, after all, not 1935. Ideally, the falling in love would happen in Oxford and Ursula's virginity would soon be happily in the past.

". . . and we offer free packs of condoms to every student, male or female," Jocasta was saying. "Personally, I find Durex the most reliable, and pleasurable, with *loads* of K-Y . . ."

Ursula felt herself reddening.

"It's nothing to be embarrassed about, just come and ask me for them, I could get some now for you—"

Luckily for Ursula, who felt as though her face was now the color of beetroot, Jocasta was stopped in her condom-sharing tracks by Claire Potter, now heading towards them with Ben Braithwaite. She pointed at Ursula and said, "There she is."

"My second daughter," said Ben, greeting Ursula with a handshake. "Hello."

"Hi," said Ursula, relieved to be rescued from Jocasta, and realizing that now was the moment to make up for her mean attitude to Claire. "Look, I'm really sorry I didn't make it to your crosswords event," she told her.

"That's okay. We all had a *really, really* great time, just like I told that policeman when he came to talk to me earlier," she said with a wink.

What was that supposed to mean? Ursula wondered. She noticed that Claire had put on makeup for the tea, a thick layer of orangey foundation that only half disguised her acne and a violet-colored metallic lip gloss. Something seemed different about her. She seemed almost cheerful today. Almost.

"Did you get your reading list yet?" Claire asked.

"Dr. Dave didn't exactly give us a list. He only asked us to read one article."

"Professor Scarisbrick read out a list of fifteen books on Anglo-Saxon history I have to get through by next week. Luckily I learned speed-reading at school," Claire said with a slightly smug smile.

Ursula felt vaguely disconcerted. Why was one tutor assigning fifteen books and another just one article?

"If you have any questions about your tutorials, or any problems," began Ben, "think of talking to me as just like talking to one of your parents. . . ."

Ursula nodded vaguely. She never told anyone her parents were gone unless it came up directly.

". . . if you need a chat, *anytime*, just come to my room—"

"I'd *love* to," said Claire, fluttering mascara-clogged eyelashes at him.

Jocasta pursed her lips disapprovingly at Ben, who coughed and cleared his throat. "Sorry, not *my* room—that wouldn't be appropriate—come and find me, er . . . here in the JCR. I'm always around."

"Okay," said Ursula, unable to imagine confiding in Ben about anything personal.

"And don't forget, you'll be allocated moral tutors by the end of the week," added Jocasta. "So there are plenty of people to talk to if, you know, you're suffering from Stress, Anxiety, or Depression, Sexually Transmitted Diseases—"

"Hi, Moo," interrupted Ursula, saved by the sight of her fellow historian bounding up to them. The ponytailed blonde had traded her Roedean gear for a dark green tracksuit that bore the name of the college and a pair of crossed oars printed in scarlet on the front. In her left hand she had a clipboard and pen, and in her right, an enormous wooden oar.

"Hi, all. I'm recruiting for the Freshers' boat. Ursula, you'd make a good Seven with those long legs and arms of yours."

"But I've never rowed," protested Ursula. Her daddy longlegs proportions had made sport a misery for her at school. She had liked riding and that was it. She had absolutely no intention of joining any kind of team while at Oxford.

"Hardly anyone's rowed before they come to Oxford," said Moo. "The Second Years are going to teach us. Apparently it's really pretty down on the river in the mornings."

An image of sunrise on the water popped into Ursula's head then, and suddenly the rowing thing seemed irresistibly romantic in a way that netball and lacrosse never had.

"I'll give it a try," she said.

"If you're doing it, I'll do it too," said Claire, grabbing the clipboard from Moo and scribbling her name at the top of the list. "Since we're sisters now."

Chapter 13

Parents, sisters, moral tutors, condoms, boats—Ursula suddenly felt overwhelmed. Perhaps it was from being an only child and growing up in such a remote place, but she liked—no, needed—to be alone at times. The silence of the library beckoned alluringly. Perhaps she could escape before her "brothers" appeared.

Ursula managed to slip out of the JCR unnoticed and onto the landing. Dr. Dave's pile of books was still on the dusty window seat, but he was gone. The constable was nowhere to be seen, and the door to Dave's set was closed, though semi-audible voices were coming from behind it. Ursula stood as close to the door as she could and put her ear to it.

". . . looks like it's the jugular . . . but there isn't enough blood . . . ask the Coroner to order a postmortem . . ."

Doc's Scottish accent was unmistakable. What had he been saying? Something about the jugular and blood. No, "there isn't enough blood." What did that mean? Not enough blood for what, exactly?

So intent was Ursula's concentration that when Nancy's face appeared beside hers, she jumped, her heart pounding.

"You scared me!" gasped Ursula. India's murder had set her on edge far more than she had realized.

"What are you doing?" said Nancy. "What about the tea party?"

"Ssshhh," said Ursula. "They're all in there, listen."

Nancy put her ear to the door.

". . . time of death?" ("That's Detective Trott's voice," whispered Ursula.)

"When was the victim last seen alive?" ("That's Doc, he's the forensic pathologist," Ursula told Nancy.)

"Maybe midnight," said Trott. "We need to speak to everyone who was at the party to establish exactly who saw her last."

"And what time was she found?" Doc asked.

"Nine in the morning."

"Then the time of death was sometime between midnight and nine in the morning," said Doc.

"Doesn't the hypostasis help?" asked Trott.

"Detective Trott, you know as well as I do that too much has been claimed for the usefulness of hypostasis as an indicator of time of death. It's too variable."

"What on earth are they talking about?" Ursula whispered to Nancy.

"Hypostasis," she answered. "When the blood stops circulating, gravity pulls it down to the lowest part of the body. The skin looks bluish-red."

Ursula was impressed. "How do you know that?"

"My older brother Frank's a med student, Yale. He's a super-geek. He's got some *horrible* stories."

Just then the doorknob turned, and the girls hastily retreated to the window seat and watched as DI Trott walked out together with a female police officer. The two of them were talking so intently that they didn't notice Ursula and Nancy.

"WPC Barwell, can you arrange for Lord Brattenbury to come down to the morgue later and formally identify the body?" Trott was saying in a low voice. "I don't want the father seeing her like that."

"Yes, sir, I'll make arrangements," replied the other officer before they both disappeared down the stairs.

"This is so sad," said Nancy.

"I know," said Ursula.

She checked her watch. It was already half past five. Where had the day gone?

"Nancy, I'm so sorry, I must go."

"What about the JCR tea?" asked Nancy. "I need you with me for moral support."

"I really have to get to Jago's." Ursula was growing desperate about fitting everything in. "I can't be late for the editor of *Cherwell*."

Suddenly Nancy squealed. She and Ursula watched as two paramedics emerged from Dr. Dave's rooms carrying a stretcher weighed down by a full body bag. Doc followed behind, closed the door after him, and then looked around. He immediately spotted Nancy and Ursula.

"Ah. Sherlock Holmes," he said, eyeing Ursula. "We meet again. Listen, you shouldn't be hanging around here. Nor should your friend." Doc glowered at Nancy. "This is a crime scene."

"Sorry—" Ursula started to say.

"Oops!" The paramedic at the far end of the stretcher stumbled slightly as he reached the staircase.

To Ursula's horror, a mottled, bluish-looking foot suddenly lolled out from the bottom of the bag. A brown luggage tag was tied tightly around the big toe with a piece of string. India's name was scrawled on it in black capital letters.

"Ugghh-ggggh! I feel like we're in *Frankenstein*," groaned Nancy, nonetheless transfixed by the ghoulish sight.

Doc hastily dashed to the end of the stretcher, stuffed India's foot back in the body bag, and zipped it up. He said to the paramedics, "Can you accompany the victim to the mortuary? Then get hold of the coroner and ask him to order an autopsy. I need to get her on the slab." About to head down the stairs, he looked back at Ursula and Nancy and said, "Girls, scarper!"

As soon as the paramedics were out of sight, Nancy turned to Ursula and said, "That toe. I think it's important."

"How?" replied Ursula.

"It's got hypostasis. That suggests India's left foot was the lowest point of her body at the moment she died."

"Right . . ." said Ursula, not quite sure of the significance of Nancy's conclusions. "Look, I've got to go." She made a move towards the stairs.

"Maybe I don't feel like your fancy British tea after all," Nancy said, following her. "I need a drink. Come to the Buttery Bar after your meeting with Jago?"

"I can't," said Ursula. "I'm sorry. I've got to go to the library as soon as I get back."

"You, my friend," Nancy complained, "can be a real downer sometimes."

Chapter 14

Ursula, yup, er . . . hi," stuttered Jago as he opened the door to his room just after six that evening. "Come in."

Barefoot and dressed in jeans and a T-shirt, he held a poster for *Raging Bull* and a packet of Blu-Tack in his hand. His room—a rather poky, north-facing space at the back of Magdalen's grand cloisters—was still in a state of disarray. "Sorry about the mess," he gulped. "Haven't had time to unpack and sort anything yet."

Jago stuck the Robert De Niro poster in the middle of the far wall. Ursula noticed the single bed was covered with more posters, for films like *American Gigolo, Alien, Scarface,* and *E.T.* A small sofa was heaped with several boxes of duty-free Marlboro Reds, a half-unpacked suitcase, and that day's newspapers. Ursula glanced at the headlines, realizing she hadn't looked at the news for days. The *Daily Mail* headline screamed, BRITISH TELECOM DITCHES RED PHONE BOX. The *Times* was more serious: REAGAN AND GORBACHEV TO END COLD WAR.

"Hang on, let me move all this crap," said Jago, clearing a space on the sofa so Ursula could sit.

"Thanks," she said, taking her notebook and a pen from her satchel.

"Drink?" Jago offered.

"I'd love a cup of tea," she said.

"My kettle's broken, sorry," he replied. "Glass of wine?"

"Okay," said Ursula.

Jago somehow located a wine box among the mess, and squirted white wine into two paper cups. "Here," he said, handing one to Ursula. "Now, let's get down to business."

Jago planted himself on the sofa next to her, so close that his knee touched her left thigh. She moved a little to her right, to try and make space. Then he moved a little to his right, until his knee was squashed against her leg again.

"What's the latest?" Jago asked Ursula, polishing off his cup of wine in two swigs and helping himself to another.

"They're ordering an autopsy. They just took India's body from college."

"How do you know?" he asked. "You know we can't make any mistakes in this story. It's got to be spot-on."

"I saw them removing the body. It was horrible," she told him. "India's left foot fell out of the body bag. It had hypostasis in it."

"Really?"

"I saw it with my own eyes," she replied, taking a sip of the wine. It was warm and horribly vinegary.

"Didn't you say earlier that when you found India she was lying on Dr. Dave's chaise longue?" asked Jago.

"Yes. Why?"

"So, the hypostasis is in her left foot . . . meaning that was the lowest point of her body when she died."

Nancy had said exactly the same thing, thought Ursula. Jago continued hypothesizing.

"The fact that the blood coagulated in her foot means that she died *exactly* where you found her, because when you are sitting or lying on a chaise longue your feet are usually the lowest point of your body."

Ursula noticed that Jago's right hand was now resting on her left knee. As subtly as she could, she slid out from underneath it. "I don't quite follow."

"What I mean is, we can conclude, from the foot situation, that

India died *on* the chaise longue," he said, sounding convinced and moving his hand back to her knee.

Ursula boldly lifted it off and put it back in Jago's lap. "She was murdered lying down?"

"Maybe . . . If she died *on* the chaise longue, it must mean that either she was already lying on it when her throat was cut, or she was standing close to it when she was attacked and fell back onto it," said Jago.

Ursula sensed that The Hand was now resting along the back of the sofa behind her head. She wished Jago weren't quite as friendly as this.

"I think she was already on the chaise longue," said Ursula. "It makes more sense."

"How can you be so confident?"

"There was the stem of a broken champagne glass still in her hand when I found her," Ursula replied. "Surely she would have dropped it if she'd fallen backwards onto the chaise longue?"

"Which makes me ask, how did India end up with a broken champagne glass in her hand in the first place?" asked Jago.

Ursula winced. She felt The Hand touch the back of her head. She decided to ignore it, saying, "It didn't look as though there'd been any violence or disturbance in the room. So, if there was no fight, if India was killed when she was lying on the chaise longue, maybe she knew her killer. Whoever it was came into the room—perhaps she was lying there waiting for them, she knew them so well and trusted them so much that she didn't even get up."

"Perhaps," Jago posited, "she was expecting some kind of romantic rendezvous."

"In Dr. Dave's rooms? And that still doesn't explain the broken champagne glass."

"Maybe she thought she was somewhere else, maybe she was too drunk to know that she'd gone to the wrong room," he suggested.

"Wait!" said Ursula. "What if it *wasn't* the wrong room—"

Ursula stopped talking. From behind, she could feel The Hand twisting a lock of her hair.

"What is it?" asked Jago, looking surprised.

"I've got to go," Ursula jumped up, yanking her hair from his hand at the same time. "I've got someone to meet . . . um, *very* urgently," she said, trying to sound convincing. A drink in the bar with Nancy suddenly seemed like an excellent idea.

"But we haven't talked about police procedure yet. The protocol of covering a murder investigation."

"Oh, yes, right," stuttered Ursula. "Any tips?"

"First off, when you write about the police investigation, get two or three verifications of every fact, every statement. Don't take anything the force says at face value. Having said that, my advice is pretty irrelevant—the police won't tell you anything useful anyway. You're going to have to figure out what happened to India by yourself."

"You're saying I've got to *solve* the murder?" Ursula said, surprised.

"Well, it would be a pretty boring piece if you didn't, wouldn't it? Ursula, unless you get the scoop and figure out who murdered India, your story gets killed."

Jago might seem vague on the surface, but underneath the laid-back posturing, the boy was ruthless, she thought to herself.

"Won't be a problem," she said, trying to sound as confident as possible, while simultaneously wondering how on earth she was going solve a murder, write a lead article for *Cherwell*, *and* complete her essay on the mysterious Early Covenanters all in under a week. She really *did* need to get to the library tonight.

Just as she was leaving, Jago said, "Look . . . er . . . Ursula, I'd like to see you again . . ."

"Sure, at the *Cherwell* office," she replied in her firmest tones. Surely The Hand would stay where it should if they weren't alone for their next meeting.

"Well, no actually." Jago suddenly sounded awkward. "Er . . . there's this cocktail thing at Vincent's on Friday. Why don't we go . . . together?"

Was Jago asking her on a date? Ursula wondered, feeling perturbed.

"Er . . ." she hesitated. How awkward. It seemed a little inappropriate, professionally speaking, to go on some kind of date with her editor. But if she said no, would Jago be so humiliated he wouldn't even consider running her story?

"No strings attached," he said, apparently sensing Ursula's reticence. "Just, you know, as friends . . . colleagues."

"Friends," said Ursula, thoroughly relieved. "Great."

It would be interesting to have someone like Jago as a new friend, thought Ursula. A cocktail at the mysterious Vincent's sounded fun. As long as The Hand wouldn't be revisiting The Knee.

Chapter 15

Twenty minutes later, Ursula was relieved to find Nancy perched on a high wooden stool at the bar in the Buttery, a large, slightly dank half cellar located in the old Kitchen Quad just to the east of the porter's lodge. The presence of two police officers, seated in a corner drinking orange juice and observing the scene like a couple of Stasi operatives, made for an edgy atmosphere.

"Hey, I thought you were going to the library," said Nancy when she saw Ursula.

"I'm en route," she said, taking the stool next to her friend. "I'm going just as soon as I've had a shandy."

"How was Jago?" Nancy inquired.

"Interesting." She decided not to say anything about The Hand for now.

Just then, Otto ambled in. He wandered up to the bar and leaned against it, slumping his head in his hands. Ursula noticed the policemen nudge each other and start whispering when they saw him.

"Otto, are you all right?" Ursula asked.

"Er . . . God . . . ugh," Otto grunted. "Bit hungover. I've spent the afternoon in the Eagle and Child trying to forget what happened last night. Didn't work."

"Drink?" offered Nancy.

Otto shook his head. "Maybe later."

"Okay, so one Jell-O shot for me please," Nancy asked the barman. "And a shandy."

"Thanks," Ursula said.

Ursula noticed that Nancy's hands were shaking slightly. She seemed jittery.

"Are you okay?" she asked.

"I've just never seen a real live dead foot before," Nancy replied. "And . . . the fact that it was India's too, I mean, it's all so strange. I feel afraid, Ursula. There are police wandering all over college. They're everywhere."

"They're here to protect us." Ursula tried to sound reassuring.

"Maybe we should all carry rape whistles," said Nancy nervously. "If someone tries to attack us, at least we'd have that."

The barman placed the girls' drinks on the bar. The fizzy shandy perked Ursula up and took away the taste of Jago's nasty white wine.

"No one else will be attacked," said Otto suddenly. A film of perspiration was starting to appear on his face. He looked drained.

"You don't know that, Otto," chided Nancy. "Anything could happen. We need to protect ourselves." She guzzled her Jell-O shot in one swallow. "Another please?" she asked the barman.

"But . . . sorry . . . I mean . . ." Otto stuttered and wiped his forehead with a handkerchief.

"You mean what, Otto?" Ursula asked him firmly.

"I mean, yes, get the rape whistles. Keep safe."

Just then, Ursula spotted Horatio sauntering into the bar. He had, naturally, changed for the evening and was now clad in a floor-length violet velvet silk kaftan.

"Great dress, Horatio," said Nancy when she saw him.

"Thank you, darling," he said, kissing the girls twice on each cheek and then looking curiously at Otto. "God, you look like you've just been vomited from a sewer. Are you quite all right, Otto?"

"I have never known a day of such ghastliness," the prince replied, looking ever more pale.

"You'll get through this," Horatio said kindly. "I know you and India were great friends. You must be devastated." He leaned against the bar and ordered two neat whiskeys, handed one to Otto, who didn't touch it, and downed the other himself.

A few moments later, one of the officers in the corner walked purposefully over to the group at the bar. He singled out Otto, saying, "My colleague and I have reason to believe that you are one Otto Schuffenecker."

Otto looked startled. "I am," he said in a whimper.

"We've been looking for you all afternoon. You're wanted down at the police station."

"What! Why?" Otto was panicking.

"You're needed for an interview and fingerprints."

Otto reluctantly nodded his agreement. Without saying another word, the officer took him by the arm and marched him swiftly towards the door.

"Oh my *God!*" Nancy looked as though she were on the verge of weeping. "Otto! *No!* What about the Perquisitors' party tonight? I need you as my walker!"

But Otto didn't get a chance to reply. As he was walked up the stairs, Eghosa was descending them, dressed in fencing kit and carrying a foil. Eg looked askance at the police officer and his charge as they passed him.

"Ursula, now you've *got* to come to the party with me tonight," Nancy begged her. "Next Duke might be there. Or some other duke type. Ursula, you *cannot* let such a fabulous social opportunity pass me by."

"I already told you, I can't go," she replied. "I'm sorry, but we don't even know these Perquisitor people, and I've got to start my reading in the library."

"Hey," Nancy soothed her. "Stop stressing. Dr. Dave's only given us one little article. It'll take five minutes to read."

"You really should go to the party," Horatio urged Ursula. *"Every-one* will be there. You'll get some marvelous material for your article."

This remark caught her attention. She knew that she desperately needed material, especially after her recent conversation with Jago. She felt her resolve softening.

"Maybe I could come for a *tiny* bit, then go study straight after-wards," said Ursula, grateful that the Hawksmoor Library stayed open all night. She'd still have plenty of time to start her reading.

"Told you you'd be in a ball gown every night!" quipped Horatio.

"The same one, unfortunately," laughed Ursula.

"I'll lend you a party dress," Nancy said. "I've got pretty much the entire Bloomingdale's evening wear department in my room."

"That's so kind of you," said Ursula, suddenly delighted about the prospect of another ball-gown-wearing moment, particularly if the ball gown was from a New York department store. Visions of a croissant-munching Audrey Hepburn in *Breakfast at Tiffany's,* dressed in sunglasses and a Little Black Dress, came to mind. Per-haps Nancy could magically turn Ursula into a New York party girl for the night.

Eghosa came up to the bar and greeted Horatio and the girls. "Mind if I join you?"

In his fencing regalia, he looked dazzling, Ursula thought. He put his mask and sharp-looking foil on the bar and took a stool next to her. She couldn't help staring at the sword—could it cut a throat?

"Just a Perrier please," said Eg to the barman.

Ursula could see that his mood today was very different from last night. Gone was the suave, amusing disco dancer, and in his place was a troubled young man.

"Are you all right?" asked Ursula shyly.

"It's not me I'm worried about. It's Wenty. He's in a bad way. The police have been in and out of our rooms all day. Wenty's freaking out."

"Everyone in Oxford is terrified," said Nancy.

Eg looked at the girls with concern in his eyes. "Don't go anywhere alone, either of you. Always have someone with you, especially at night."

"Maybe we should all walk together to the Perquisitors' party tonight?" suggested Ursula.

"I'd love to spend the evening with you . . ." Eg said. He caught Ursula's eye and she felt a flutter of excitement. "I mean, I'd love to spend the evening with *all* of you . . . but, actually, I'm going to give it a miss," he continued. "I said to Wenty I'd stay in tonight. Keep him company. We'll probably play vingt-et-un and get drunk."

Eg finished his Perrier, settled his tab, and got up to leave. As he departed, he said, "Remember what I said. Go everywhere in a pair."

Once he was out of earshot, Horatio said, "No wonder everyone calls him Saint Eghosa."

"Such a great guy," agreed Nancy. "Looking out for Wenty like that."

"And us," said Ursula. "He's right. We should stick together. It's safer."

Suddenly a voice from behind the girls bellowed, "Ciao!"

The trio turned to find Moo had entered the Buttery with her oar and a grinning Claire Potter in tow. Ursula wasn't sure why, but Claire's newly cheerful demeanor unnerved her. How could she be so uncharacteristically merry on such a dreadful day? Did she know something? What *had* happened in the JCR last night? Ursula was determined to prize the information out of her.

"Heard you were in here! Hiding from your new parents already?" hooted Moo, jogging from one foot to the other. "Nancy, I need you."

"For?"

"The Freshers' boat. We're recruiting a coxswain."

"A who?" Nancy looked befuddled.

"The cox steers the boat. I need someone short and light. There's no rowing involved, you just have to have a loud voice to shout at everyone."

"I can sure as hell yell," she demonstrated accommodatingly.

"You're in," said Moo. "Training starts tomorrow morning. The team is meeting in the porter's lodge to run down to the river."

Moo turned and jogged away, Claire following. Just as Moo reached the door of the Buttery, she looked back at them and added, "See you at six a.m.!"

Chapter 16

The Bloomingdale's evening wear department, a.k.a. Nancy's closet, was not, Ursula soon discovered, in the business of supplying simple, low-key *Breakfast at Tiffany's*–style cocktail frocks. Nancy, who had quickly swathed herself in a second skin of thigh-length, ruched gold lamé for the Perquisitors' party, offered Ursula a succession of ultra-trendy dresses to try.

"This would look *genius* with your hair," Nancy insisted, holding up a stretchy bright orange creation that looked more like a swimming costume than a party dress.

"A *bit* bright for me, maybe?" responded Ursula, dismissing the dress as kindly as she could.

"Or what about this?" Nancy went on, pulling a green satin Vivienne Westwood–inspired puff-ball dress from the closet.

"I *love* it," Ursula gasped.

But before she could try it on, Nancy was stopping her, saying, "No, wait, I have a *way* better idea. This one."

Ursula was soon happily adorned in a scarlet taffeta strapless mini-dress printed with huge black polka dots. The tiny frock was held in place by what felt like suction around her chest, and frothed out into heavenly, miniature layers of thigh-length frills. Ursula had seen pictures of these super-fashionable "ra-ra" dresses in Vain Granny's *Vogues*, but had never imagined she'd actually get to wear one.

"I think fur would work with that," Nancy said, handing her a fake-fur crimson stole. Ursula wrapped the deliciously soft fabric around her shoulders as Nancy clipped glitzy faux-ruby-and-diamond earrings onto her ears. A matching necklace and bracelet soon followed. They completed the outfit with silver fishnet tights and a pair of red suede pumps, which were far too small. Ursula dashed back to her room to find her old plain black court shoes, hoping no one would notice her feet.

"Okay, makeup," said Nancy when Ursula had returned. She opened her vanity case, which contained a palette of cheek and eye colors. Nancy applied emerald green eye shadow to Ursula's lids, matching mascara to her lashes, and shimmery metallic blusher to her cheeks. She then insisted on sizzling Ursula's hair with a pair of boiling-hot, high-tech American crimping irons. By the end of the terrifying process, Ursula's tresses resembled spun sugar.

Since there was no full-length mirror in either girl's room, Ursula could only review her look in thirds by standing on a chair and looking at various sections of her body in the mirror over Nancy's sink. She adored the dress portion of the outfit, but the makeup and jewelry was far glitzier than she was used to.

"I look like David Bowie," she protested.

"Stop!" Nancy insisted. "You look amazing. You look cooler than Sue Ellen in *Dallas*."[*]

Finally, the girls were ready to go. As Ursula put her satchel over her shoulder, Nancy cried, "*No!*"

"What is it?"

---

[*] The ultimate TV representation of '80s fashion, *Dallas* (1978–1991) was a high-glam soap about the Ewings, a backstabbing Texan oil family. Typical looks included sequin-encrusted mohair sweaters, leopard-print cleavage-revealing dresses, and silver knit batwing dresses. Having languished for decades in the depths of uncoolness, such items are now desperately trendy again.

"That bag. You *cannot* accessorize a mini ra-ra dress with a high school satchel. Here, borrow this," Nancy said, offering Ursula a minuscule red velvet clutch.

"I can't fit my notebook in there."

"You really need your work things?"

"Yes," Ursula stated firmly.

Because, she vowed to herself, after the *teensiest* stop at the Perquisitors' party, she was absolutely definitely, really and truly, honestly going to the library.

•

"IS IT NORMAL in Oxford to throw a cocktail party in a dungeon?" Nancy asked a little later as they picked their way down the steep flight of stone steps beneath Magdalen College Chapel that accessed the Monks' Undercroft.

"I guess so," Ursula laughed, surveying the scene.

Despite being inhabited that night by a student DJ spinning poppy records by Wham! and Duran Duran, and sixty or so beautiful young Oxford undergrads in black tie, the place felt eerie to Ursula. Dripping cathedral candles lit the vaulted fifteenth-century crypt, and it was chilly enough down there that, even with the borrowed stole, Ursula's arms immediately prickled with goose bumps.

She and Nancy soon found the bar, where they ordered two glasses of Bucks Fizz. Slightly desperately, they sipped their drinks as they scanned the room for a familiar face.

"Oh my God," whispered Nancy suddenly. "I cannot believe *she's* here!"

"Who?"

"The 'best friend' . . . I can't remember her name." Nancy indicated someone on the other side of the room. "I mean, shouldn't she be in mourning?"

Ursula spotted Isobel Floyd huddled in a distant corner, surrounded by a group of boys. Looking like a groovier Little Lord Fauntleroy, she wore dark purple velvet knickerbockers with bows at the knees and a matching jacket with "leg-o-mutton" sleeves. A lacy blouse peeked out from underneath the jacket.

"Oh, poor thing, I think she's crying," Ursula said. "Look, someone's just given her their handkerchief."

"I guess she is really upset about India," Nancy conceded.

"I think not." The familiar voice came from behind them.

Horatio Bentley had arrived, to Ursula's and Nancy's relief.

"Horatio! Help! We don't know anyone," wailed Nancy.

"Don't worry, I'll introduce you to the Perquisitors," he assured her.

"What the hell is a Perquisitor anyway?" Nancy asked.

"It means the original owner of an estate—from the Latin *'perquisitum,'* for purchaser. My personal translation is 'white-tie wankers.' Ha-ha-ha-ha-ha!" Horatio's belly jiggled beneath his kaftan as he laughed. "Crikey . . . *brilliant* idea for a weekly column. Jago would love it." He retrieved a small Moleskine notebook from a pocket and scribbled "White-Tie Wankers" on a blank page.

"So they're kind of like a high school clique?" said Nancy.

"I suppose. The difference is that this clique, like most cliques in Oxford, is not bound by ties of friendship but by disdain for other people. You too, girls, will soon join a clique and spend your evenings laughing at the people you hung out with during Freshers' Week."

"Which ones are the members?" asked Ursula.

Horatio pointed out four boys across the room, each one floppier-haired than the last.

"Rupert Bingham, Tom Higginbottom-Jones—fondly known as Wobbly Wobbly-Bottom to his friends—Alexander Fitzwilliam-Hughes, and Lucian Peake. Between them their families own half of the British Isles. Anyway, they ponce about in dinner jackets all term, providing reams of gossip for *Cherwell.* Among the mantelpiece-conscious, the Perquisitors' stiffie[*] is considered the ultimate invitation

---

[*] "Stiffie" = Sloane speak for invitation, derived from the fact that smart invites were once hand-engraved on exceptionally thick, stiff card.

this week. Personally, I say the thicker the card, the more boring the party. Hmmm . . . that would be a *truly* cruel opening for my article about tonight . . ."

Horatio frantically scribbled the line in his notebook, a mischievous grin on his face. "By the way, Ursula, very fashionable outfit tonight."

"Thank you," she said. The red polka-dot dress was turning out to be great fun—she had felt herself attracting admiring glances from a couple of boys as they sauntered up to the bar. "It's Nancy's."

"Looks like it," replied Horatio. Ursula wasn't entirely sure whether to take this as a compliment.

Rupert Bingham, a sandy-haired boy with a smooth, shiny face, waved to Horatio and came over to greet him. Ursula noticed the boy's eyes hungrily devouring the sight of Nancy in her gold lamé, before he directed an equally lascivious look at her in the polka-dot dress.

After Horatio had introduced him to the girls, Rupert pleaded, "Now, Horatio, you *will* give the party a nice write-up in your column, won't you?"

"I'll try, but I can't promise, Roo darling." Horatio's tone was puckish. "After all, that wouldn't be fair on all the parties I've slagged off, would it?"

While the others chatted, Ursula's gaze wandered and she soon spotted Dom Littleton mingling with friends. Despite the low lighting he was wearing his blue-lensed sunglasses. She watched, intrigued, as he sauntered up to Isobel, who pointedly turned her back on him and carried on talking to another boy. What was she so furious about? wondered Ursula. Horatio had been right when he'd encouraged her to come to the party earlier. She could definitely pick up some material here.

"Horatio, I think I need your help with the story," she said as soon as Rupert Bingham departed. "Jago says the police won't tell student journalists anything. Have you got *any* ideas about who might have wanted India out of the way?"

"Whodunit?" Horatio raised one eyebrow. "India was . . ." He paused, as though searching for the right words. "Complicated. Spoiled. Difficult. Deceitful—"

"How?" asked Ursula.

"Well, I'm not suggesting that what she did was so deceitful that the Deceived in Question would have wished to cut her milky throat, but frankly, India didn't care who she trod on."

At this point Horatio pointedly directed his gaze at Isobel, whose fury seemed to have miraculously dissipated. She was now talking intently with Dom Littleton, the hint of a smile on her face.

"Isobel? She did something to Isobel?" asked Ursula. "But they were best friends."

"So?" said Horatio. "Don't you have best friends you are violently jealous of?"

Ursula shook her head. Plain Granny had seen to that. Jealousy was simply not allowed at Seldom Seen Farm.

"Hey, I know *exactly* what you mean," said Nancy. "Literally *all* my friends at Northwestern are totally jealous of me."

"I can only imagine!" guffawed Horatio. Then he continued, "Call me conceited, but I wrote a *terrifically* witty column about India and Isobel last term. It was called 'Les Soeurs Uglies,' the thesis of which was that India and Isobel were so competitive and envious of each other that they were just like Cinderella's ugly stepsisters—cleverly in disguise as best friends and great beauties."

"Horatio, are you saying that Isobel killed her bestie?" said Nancy, amazed.

"All I am saying is that Oxford is a very intense place. Rivalries get out of hand here. If you offend other people for too long, you generally exit this place with an assortment of meat cleavers through your back."

"But what did India do to Isobel that was so awful?" Ursula was desperate to follow this lead. She knew she was onto something.

"All I know is that at the end of last term, Dom decided to direct *Hamlet*. Henry Forsyth was set to play the title role. Isobel was to be Ophelia. Then the next minute, everything changed. Dom suddenly gave India the Ophelia role, and Isobel was demoted to her under-study. Everyone knows that Isobel is an even better actress than India was. It was bizarre."

"So India stole her best friend's role last term?" Ursula clarified.

"Horrid, isn't it?" said Horatio. "Then, at Wenty's party, we all find out that Dom has gone barmy and given Henry Forsyth's Hamlet role to India. The next thing we know, Girl-Hamlet is dead. Ah!" he said abruptly. "We were *just* talking about you!"

Isobel Floyd had arrived at the bar. She gave Horatio a smooch on each cheek.

"Dreadful about India," he said.

"It's just so sad. Losing my greatest pal," Isobel agreed. She visibly paled as she added, "It's terrifying, to think there's some madman on the loose killing beautiful undergraduates. Makes me feel sick. I mean, I could be next." She shuddered. "Anyway, I've got a scoop for you, Horatio. *Darling.*"

He raised his eyebrows. "Pray tell."

"I've agreed—with a very, very heavy heart, of course—to take on the Hamlet role—"

"You must be scared stiff!" Horatio blurted out. "Your pretty throat could be next!"

Isobel whacked him hard on the arm. He looked sheepish.

"For *God's sake*, Horatio," she huffed. "Anyway, as I was saying, I'll be taking on Hamlet. Obvs . . . in India's honor. We're going to dedicate the show to her. You won't forget to mention that in your article, will you, about the dedication? I know she'd want the show to go on, as they say on Broadway. She was such a great friend, truly my best friend in the world."

Nancy nudged Ursula and hissed into her ear, "The subplot thickens."

"Of course I will, Isobel," said Horatio with a coy smile. "Any other Good Works you would like mentioned in my scoop?"

Isabel looked slightly confused. Then she said, "Yar, you mean, like, the well I dug in Bangladesh on my gap year?"

Horatio spluttered with laughter and Isobel reddened, realizing she'd been played.

"You're hateful, Horatio," she snarled. Then she suddenly burst into tears. "I'm so-ooo-rrr-rreeeee-ggghhh—" She hiccuped, wiping her eyes on her frilly cuff. "It's just, India, she was my soul . . . ugggh-hhh . . . mate. I just hope they find the murderer soon."

"You may be able to help with that," Horatio told her.

"What?!" she snapped, hurriedly sniveling her tears away. "Why do you think *I* know anything about the murder?"

"Ursula's trying to solve the case for *Cherwell*. Just tell her anything you know, it could really help."

"Gosh, yes, of course, *anything* I can do. Anything." Isobel turned to Ursula and smiled sweetly. "Let's go up into the quad so we can talk privately."

•

THANK GOODNESS SHE had her notebook and pen in her satchel, thought Ursula as she followed Isobel up the stairs and out into Magdalen's main quad. Isobel led her towards the cloisters and sat on a stone bench under the eaves, huddling her knees to her chest.

"You know everyone calls him 'Horrid' Bentley. Horrid by name, horrid by nature," said Isobel, lighting a cigarette. She offered the packet to Ursula. "Want one?"

Ursula was about to say she didn't smoke, but then thought better of it. She needed to bond with this girl. She took a cigarette from the packet of Marlboro Reds and twirled it in her fingers, delaying the moment she would have to attempt to light it.

"He's terribly cruel about people in his column. When he wrote about India he called her the 'Hereditary Husky.'* She wouldn't have

---

* A shapeless, quilted green shooting coat, the Husky was key Sloane kit. The only person who looks good in one is the Queen.

been seen *dead* in a Husky. Oh God, I don't mean *dead* dead. I meant, metaphorically dead. But—ugh! Now she is dead."

Isobel dropped her head into her hands. She seemed genuinely upset.

"Have you got any idea who might have done this to India?" asked Ursula gently.

"Why would *I* know anything? I mean, of course I don't!" Isobel dragged needily on her cigarette.

"You were her best friend. Did she tell you about anything—*anything*—that was worrying her?"

"Honestly, her life was great. I mean, she was going to play Hamlet. It was her dream."

"Is it true," Ursula ventured, somewhat timidly, "that she stole the role of Ophelia from you last term?"

"Did Horrid tell you that? God, he's a stirrer. She got the part because she was . . ." Isobel hesitated. ". . . better suited to the role. It was all very professional. I was fine with understudying. Really."

Not very convincingly said, Ursula thought to herself. But she played along, asking, "Do you mind if I write this down?"

"Of course not. I wouldn't want this to come out wrong in *Cherwell*. Scribble away."

Ursula retrieved her notebook and pen and turned to a fresh page. "Where did you go after Wenty's party?"

"Why?"

"India was killed sometime between leaving Wenty's party and nine in the morning when I found her. I'm trying to figure out if anyone saw anything after the party, before she went to Dr. Dave's rooms."

"I went to bed. My room's in the Monks' Cottages. I'm right above the laundry. India and Otto are on a staircase near mine."

"Were you alone?"

Isobel took a moment to answer. Eventually, she said, "I went to my room alone. I went to bed alone."

"Dom didn't stay over?"

"He had tech rehearsals for *Hamlet* with the lighting crew at eight a.m. the next day. He decided to come back here to Magdalen, get a good night's sleep."

"Did you see India between leaving the party and getting to your room?"

Isobel paused. She looked long and hard at Ursula. A sad expression clouded her face.

"I suppose there's no point in pretending. They were having a row. India and Wenty."

"What about?" asked Ursula.

"You," declared Isobel.

"*Me*?!" exclaimed Ursula.

"India stormed out of the party, don't you remember?"

Ursula recalled India's abrupt exit from the room, and Wenty chasing after her.

"Well, Wenty ran out after her, and then Dom went after them both, and of course I went after Dom."

"And Henry Forsyth went after you all, as far as I remember," added Ursula.

"Henry was desperate. He said to me, when we were outside Wenty's room, that his 'career' would never recover after what India had done. As if he has a career as an actor ahead! Horatio's nickname for him is the Rodent. Very fair, everyone thinks." Isobel snickered. Then, suddenly looking frightened, she grabbed Ursula's arm. "God. You don't think Henry did it?"

"Do you?"

"He's such a wimp. I can't imagine him murdering someone. But he had a motive, I suppose."

"Where did Henry go when he left Wenty's staircase?"

Isobel released Ursula's arm and pursed her lips. "I think he hung around, but I wasn't paying much attention," she said. "I was too distracted by the argument. We'd all chased down the staircase after Wenty and India, and there they were in the middle of Great Quad—on the *grass*—and India was screaming at Wenty."

"Why?" said Ursula.

"She was in a fury because she'd heard him call you Unforgettable. She was yelling at him that Unforgettable was his pet name for *her*. I heard her say, 'There's only one Unforgettable in your life, and that's *me*.'"

"What did Wenty say to that?"

"He told her, 'Forgive me, my darling. It was only some random Fresher. It wasn't serious.'"

"Oh," said Ursula. She was rather offended to be labeled a "random Fresher," but this just confirmed her doubts about Wenty's character: the boy was clearly just as superficial as she suspected.

Isobel went on to explain that India, in a rage, had refused to accept Wenty's apology, and had accused him of being a terrible flirt.

"She was convinced that Wenty—" Isobel stopped abruptly. She seemed reluctant to go on.

"Convinced of what?" Ursula pressed her.

"That he was . . ." Isobel paused. She seemed uncharacteristically unsure of herself.

"That he was what?" urged Ursula.

"Sleeping around."

"Who with?"

"Oh, um . . . God knows! Anyway, then Wenty started accusing *her* of being the flirt. So she said, 'I can't help it if everyone flirts with me!' Then she laughed. Wenty was fuming. He started talking about Dr. Dave, accusing India of seducing him."

"She seduced a *tutor*?" Ursula was properly shocked.

"Look, Dr. Dave has affairs with lots of students. Everyone knows."

Otto had mentioned something about the don having dalliances with his students, Ursula remembered, but she had thought he was exaggerating.

"But why did Wenty think Dr. Dave and India were having an affair?" asked Ursula.

"They did have a *tiny* fling, almost a year ago. Dr. Dave spent a couple of weeks at Bratters over the Christmas holidays when India was a Fresher. *Supposedly* he'd gone there to write. But there was more poetry going on in the rose bedroom with India than politics being written in the study. Dave's very . . . attractive, isn't he?"

"But he's a tutor!" exclaimed Ursula.

"I know. I mean, I'd never—" Isobel started. "Anyway, Dave and India were infatuated with each other for a bit. But it was over in a few weeks. India told me all about it. They stayed friends. India saw Dr. Dave as a *confidant*. Maybe Wenty was suspicious that there was still something going on. I mean, India was still always in and out of Dave's rooms, having endless long chats with him. Anyway, last night Wenty threatened to report Dr. Dave to the high provost, for sexual harassment."

Maybe he should have, thought Ursula to herself. But she didn't say anything. Isobel was in full flow: "India went mental. The only civilized thing about the scream-up was the way Wenty kept filling India's glass with champagne! Then the night porter came out and hollered at them to get off the grass, and I saw India run off towards Dr. Dave's staircase, probably to warn him about Wenty's threat. She was very loyal to Dave."

"It all sounds terribly complicated," said Ursula.

"It is. When I heard that India had been found dead in Dr. Dave's rooms, I couldn't believe it. There's *no way* he did it."

"How can you be so sure?" asked Ursula.

"Er . . . well, I don't know. I just don't think Dr. Dave would do that kind of thing."

Isobel looked away from Ursula suddenly. She lit another cigarette and inhaled deeply. Ursula dashed off some thoughts on her notepad:

—Could Dr. Dave have killed India? Had the affair with her been secretly reignited, as Wenty suspected?
—But the don was sick when he saw India's corpse. Surely a cold-blooded killer wouldn't vomit at sight of own victim?

"What about Wenty? Where did he go when the night porter told everyone to leave?" Ursula asked.

"Must have gone back to the party, I imagine. I wasn't really paying attention," Isobel told her.

Nor, unfortunately, was Ursula. She couldn't remember whether she'd seen Wenty at the party again or not.

"Anyway, this morning I woke up late," Isobel went on. She faltered as she added, "I couldn't believe it when my scout told me what had happened. Do you want a light?"

Ursula had completely forgotten that she still had an unlit cigarette in her left hand. She couldn't admit now that she didn't smoke, so she put the cigarette between her lips and took a tiny, terrified drag to light it from Isobel's gold Zippo. It was disgusting. She coughed and spluttered. The cigarette went out.

If only I wasn't so square, wished Ursula, I'd have learned to smoke at school like normal girls do. She made a note to herself to practice smoking in private before attempting it again in the presence of someone as cool as Isobel Floyd.

"It's a crap lighter," lied Isobel, kindly saving her from further embarrassment. "Look, I have to go, I've got rehearsals early tomorrow in the Burton Rooms. If you need anything else, just come and find me there. By the way," she added as she dashed off across the quad, "that's a really cool dress."

Chapter 17

Just as Ursula was about to return to Christminster—and the library she hadn't yet laid eyes on—she noticed a group of revelers entering the quad from the Monks' Undercroft. Nancy's gold dress shimmered in the moonlight.

"Yawn. Yawn. Ya-aaaa-awn!" Horatio's bellow was unmistakable. "That party was as stiff as the invitation. Ursula!" he called. "We're all going back to Dom's room."

"Coming?" asked Nancy.

Perhaps there'd be more "material" at Dom's gathering, Ursula reasoned. She'd go for half an hour and then absolutely, definitely go to the library. "Sure," she said, following the group up a steep staircase to a smoke-filled room on the third floor of the cloisters.

Dom Littleton's room was easily large enough to accommodate a core group of ten or fifteen friends. Ursula was surprised to see Henry Forsyth in the room. He didn't seem pleased to be there—he looked as though he was about to punch someone. Dom's quarters weren't exactly luxurious: the only places to sit were the bed, a couple of hard chairs, the two window seats, or a few grubby-looking cushions on the floor. His halfhearted attempt at decoration had consisted of draping the wall above his bed with an exotic hanging picturing the elephant-headed Indian god Ganesha. One corner was falling down.

Ursula couldn't quite understand the attraction of Dom's room. Nancy, however, could.

"A bong!" she cried happily, kicking off her heels and plonking herself down on a cushion next to their host, who was already sitting cross-legged on the floor sucking on an enormous plastic tube full of smoke.

Ursula watched as Dom closed his eyes, exhaled a long plume of white smoke, and then passed the peculiar contraption to Nancy. Ursula had never seen a bong before, but it was pretty clear what was going on. She had never touched drugs herself, and seeing Nancy giggling madly in a smoky haze didn't make her any more inclined to try them.

Ursula didn't really like the atmosphere in the room—everyone seemed focused on getting to the bong, the drugs. But she was here now and among India's friends. There might be clues to be uncovered, especially about the victim's last few hours.

Ursula sat down gingerly on the other side of Dom, very uncomfortably as it turned out. Her dress was so short that the only way to sit on the floor was with her knees pulled up awkwardly next to her.

"Sorry, man, the bong's going anticlockwise," Dom drawled to her.

"That's okay," she replied, relieved.

"Did I see you talking to Isobel earlier?" he asked, filling a cigarette paper with loose tobacco.

"Yes, I'm writing an article about India for *Cherwell*. Isobel answered a few questions."

"Turning detective?" Dom said, looking at her with surprise.

"Sort of," she replied.

He fished a black substance out of a plastic bag and started crumbling it on top of the tobacco, rolled up the spliff, and lit it.

"Smoke?" he offered. Ursula shook her head.

"So I guess you know all about India's infatuation with Dr. Dave."

"Isobel seems to think India and the tutor had a fling, but ages ago," said Ursula.

"Yeah, man. Bet Isobel didn't tell you about *her* one-night stand with Wenty, though," Dom cackled, seeming completely stoned.

Ursula gasped. "No, she didn't. What do you mean?"

"I followed India and Wenty out of the party. Isobel and Henry did too. We all saw the major slanging match between Wenty and India. First, India accuses Wenty of being a terrible flirt—"

"—which he clearly is," interjected Ursula.

"There's no argument there. But then, Wenty accuses India of still being involved with Dr. Dave. She denies it, and then accuses Wenty of sleeping with her 'best friend,' Isobel. My girlfriend! Wenty denied it, but India didn't believe him. She went nuts," Dom recalled. "That's when she ran off towards Dr. Dave's rooms."

"Dom, do *you* think Wenty and Isobel ever—"

"Course they did. New College ball behind the Pimm's tent this past summer. Everyone knew. Except India."

"But Dom, weren't *you* upset?" Ursula couldn't quite believe how laid-back he seemed to be about his girlfriend's extracurricular exploits.

"Man, do you dig *Siddhartha*? I read it on my gap year in Nepal. I renounced all personal possessions, just like Siddhartha. Isobel doesn't belong to me. If she shags some idiot toff, that's her spiritual journey, man. When things go pear-shaped, I just say, '*Om*.'* Then nothing freaks me.

"O-o-o-o-m-m-m-mmm . . ." chanted Dom, dragging deeply on the joint. He closed his eyes, crossed his legs, put his hands together in prayer, and sat there like a yogi, meditating.

His drug-induced trance didn't look like it was ending anytime soon. Ursula got up, amazed at how edited Isobel's version of the Great Quad row had been, and made her way over to Henry Forsyth, who was on the other side of the room nosing through Dom's record collection. Perhaps he could confirm Dom's version of events.

"You a Run-D.M.C. fan?" said Henry when he saw Ursula. He was

---

* The holy word "*Om*" saves Siddhartha from his own suicide in Hermann Hesse's 1922 Buddhist novel. Required reading among Oxford students in the 1980s, the book was seen as an antidote to the Thatcherite "Yuppie" decade.

holding a single with the title "It's Like That" emblazoned across the front. "I dig hip-hop."

"Me too," lied Ursula, deciding now was not the moment to admit that she was more of a sheet music kind of girl than a hip-hop fan.

Henry put the single on the record player and carefully lifted the needle onto the vinyl. Run started rapping and an athletic-looking boy dressed all in black except for a white baseball cap, white sneakers, and an enormous gold chain round his neck suddenly broke into break dancing mode. A little group, the most vocal of whom was Nancy, was soon cheering and clapping him on as he spun on his hips and shoulders.

"He should be on the stage," declared Henry, admiring the boy's moves.

"I hear *you're* a brilliant actor," said Ursula.

Henry smiled for just a moment. "To misquote Oscar Wilde, 'To lose your Hamlet role to a girl once may be regarded as a misfortune, but to lose it twice looks like carelessness.' No doubt you've heard about the scandal over my role?"

"Well, I was at Wenty's party last night," Ursula replied. "I saw the whole thing."

"Quite a performance, wasn't it?" grumbled Henry. "Although the drama in Great Quad after the party was truly worthy of an Oscar . . . and then the murder! God. Sunday night was like some kind of Alfred Hitchcock movie come to life."

"Why do you think Dom gave India your role?" Ursula asked him.

Henry looked at her suspiciously. "Why are you so interested?"

"I'm investigating what happened to India for *Cherwell*."

"Press. I see," he said sternly. Henry looked so fierce that Ursula wondered if she had blown her chance of getting him to open up. She should never have mentioned *Cherwell*!

"I wouldn't mention your name, I promise," she said hurriedly. "I'm just trying to find out a bit of background. That's all."

"You misunderstand," replied Henry. "I'll only help you if you *do* mention my name."

"Er . . . okay," said Ursula.

"I want *my* Hamlet role back," he declared, his face hardening. "I wouldn't be in Dom Littleton's godforsaken room tonight unless I thought I could persuade him to get rid of Isobel. The publicity will help."

"I *completely* understand," said Ursula. She'd play along with Henry. "It all sounds *very* unfair," she added with a sympathetic smile.

"It was absurd. What happened was *ab-solutely ab-surd*," Henry complained. "I've been building up to *Hamlet* since F Block. Dom and I did some *awesome* productions in our second year here. *Equus* was the hottest ticket in Oxford last summer. Took all my clothes off—huge audiences! Dom and I had it all planned. We'd take on *Hamlet*. He'd direct. I'd star. We'd invite all the agents. Dom and I agreed on everything. Naturally, I wanted Isobel Floyd as my Ophelia. She's the best actress in Oxford. And the most beautiful. Only problem was India Brattenbury thought that *she* was the best actress in Oxford . . . It's such a pathetic cliché. They all want to be Ophelia, don't they?"

"I suppose so," said Ursula.

"India didn't give a flying you-know-what about her best friend. All she cared about was herself. One minute Isobel was going to be Ophelia, the next minute India had the role. She seduced Dom—"

"What?" said Ursula. Had she heard Henry correctly? "Did you say *India* seduced *Dom*?"

"Course! That's how she got Isobel's role. The only talent involved was hers for shagging. Everyone in Oxford knows that India was pretty selfish, but stealing your best friend's role *and* sleeping with her boyfriend—that's a double betrayal."

Gosh, Ursula thought. This all made Louis XV's love life seem positively boring. "Do you mind if I make some notes?" she asked Henry.

"Go ahead," he replied.

Ursula jotted in her notebook:

—Isobel: one-night stand with Wenty while dating Dom
—Dom: infatuated with India while dating Isobel

—India: dating Wenty, sleeping with Dom, confiding in Dr. Dave
—Wenty: dating India, up to no good with Isobel

"Anyway, I should have seen the whole Hamlet thing coming, I suppose," continued Henry. "When India arrived on Thursday night with Dom at Wenty's party and they told me that *she* was going to be Hamlet—! God! I thought he'd really lost it. India had brainwashed him. The whole thing was utterly humiliating. I could have killed her. Tragically, I didn't get the chance."

Henry laughed at his own horrid joke then his face lapsed into a cold, sullen expression.

"Anyway, I couldn't believe it when Wenty and India started rowing in Great Quad and he suddenly accused her of shagging some tutor!"

"Apparently the affair with the tutor was over a while ago," Ursula explained.

"Really? It was bad enough that India was stringing Wenty along as her boyfriend while she was bonking Dom. If she'd been at it with a tutor as well . . . Christ! No wonder Isobel and Dom started having a massive barney."

Ursula was surprised. "Isobel never mentioned that she argued with Dom that night," she said. "He didn't either. Isobel said that she and Dom agreed to spend the night apart because he had rehearsals early the next morning."

Henry let out a hollow laugh. "Isn't it amazing what people choose to forget when it suits them?"

"What happened with the two of them?" asked Ursula.

"Look, I'll try and get this right, but it's complicated. I was standing at the edge of Great Quad, with Isobel and Dom. When India accused Wenty of cheating on her with Isobel, Dom didn't really seem to react. It was as though he didn't care. But when Wenty accused India of sleeping with Dom, Isobel went bonkers on him."

"Even though she'd slept with Wenty?" Ursula was incredulous at the story. From her virginal point of view, Oxford seemed to be in a state of permanent orgy.

"I know. Talk about double standards. Isobel whacked Dom on the head with her evening bag and announced she would be spending the night alone."

"What did Dom do?" asked Ursula.

"He just said, 'Om,' which really annoyed Isobel. She stomped off towards the Monks' Cottages, furious."

Ursula couldn't believe that she'd been so naive. Isobel's version of events—that the row between Wenty and India had been over Dr. Dave—was only a tiny portion of the truth. Horatio hadn't invented the rumor about India stealing her friend's role. Things were far messier than even he could have imagined. No wonder Isobel had had her back turned to Dom at the beginning of the Perquisitors' party tonight—she was furious with him for cheating on her with India. Ursula wondered if giving Isobel the Hamlet role had been Dom's way of trying to make up with her. Perhaps Isobel was even more ambitious than her late friend had been. She could conveniently forget her boyfriend's indiscretions if it meant being the star of the show. Jago was right: every story needed to be verified two or three times over.

"So then Dom pushed off back to Magdalen—"

"Are you sure?" said Ursula.

Henry hesitated. Pondered for a moment. "Well, I'm just *assuming* he came back here . . . Maybe he did, maybe he didn't. You don't think . . . Dom would have wanted to hurt India, do you?"

Ursula shrugged her shoulders. "Who knows. What happened after that?"

"It was all over pretty quickly. The night porter appeared from the gate tower and told everyone to leave. We all scattered, to God knows where . . . You will remember to mention my name in the article, won't you?"

"Absolutely." Ursula said with a smile.

"And please do feel free to suggest that I'd make a far better Hamlet than Isobel," added Henry.

"Sure," said Ursula, crossing her fingers as they said good-bye.

She looked at her watch. It was almost midnight already. A perfect moment to depart for the library, à la Cinderella. She found Horatio and Nancy sharing a cigarette in a corner. After updating them on the various love affairs India was embroiled in before she died, she told them she was going.

"No way! Why? It's early!" complained Nancy, puffing smoke into the air. "And you're not allowed to go anywhere by yourself, remember?"

"I'm just . . . tired," said Ursula. "I'll be fine on my own."

"I'll walk you back, Ursula," said Horatio. "Can't have you being murdered while you're reporting on a murder now, can we? Although that would make a *marvelous* diary item."

Ursula poked him in the ribs. "That is so mean!" she cried. "But I'll take you up on the offer. Let's go."

As they left the party he added, "By the way, I do envy you this story. There's going to be enough revolting gossip in it to fill the entire men's public urinals on Cornmarket."

Chapter 18

E xcuse me," Ursula whispered as quietly as she could. The midnight hush in the Hawksmoor Library was so still, so soft, she felt wretched marring it even for a moment. The only sound in the room was the occasional turning of a page.

A prim-looking woman in her late twenties was seated behind the librarian's counter, reading intently. "Olive Brookethorpe, Ms., Librarian," read the badge pinned to her dress. The Laura Ashley number was navy and printed with lilac flowers, with frills at the neck and the cuffs, and Ms. Brookethorpe's smooth shoulder-length dark hair was held back by a matching navy velvet Alice band.

The librarian momentarily glanced up from her work, peered disapprovingly at Ursula's ra-ra dress, lifted her forefinger to her lips, and pointed to a large sign on the desk. It read, "Silence Please." With that, she snapped her head back down and continued scribbling.

Ursula wasn't quite sure where to start. A lone graduate student, who looked Lilliputian against the vast room with its domed ceiling, was sitting at a desk, poring over a pile of manuscripts. Perhaps she could help.

Ursula tiptoed, as quietly as she could, towards the student, who, she soon saw, was clad in a tattersall nightie and huddled under a knitted blanket. Fuzzy pink slippers covered her feet, and her hair, an uncontrollable frizz of mouse brown, tumbled out of a tortoiseshell comb on the side of her head. She looked up when she heard Ursula approach.

"Don't tell me you're trying to borrow a book," she said in a low voice.

Ursula nodded.

"Alas!" whispered the girl.

Without raising her voice, she introduced herself as Flora White, a Classics scholar. The problem with book borrowing, she explained, was that Ms. Brookethorpe was notorious in college for her desire to create as hostile an atmosphere as possible in the Hawksmoor Library.

"As gatekeeper of some of the rarest manuscripts in the world, she sees it as her duty to be extremely unhelpful. After all, she can only protect the books from the *revolting* vandal-like paws of undergraduates if no one borrows any of them, and the way to ensure no one borrows the first editions or ancient folios is to make the—theoretical—borrowing process as arduous as possible," explained Flora. "Photo ID, signed letters from tutors, university seconders—there's always one more impossible-to-find document that Ms. Brookethorpe requires."

"Why is she like that?" asked Ursula.

"The less time Brookethorpe spends collecting books from the secure stacks in the tunnels underneath college, the more time she has to recatalogue fragments of the thirteenth-century Bible that was written and illustrated by the order of Augustinian monks who first taught at Christminster," Flora told her. "She's here every night working on it. If she ever finishes the recataloguing, she'll be made a fellow. But she never will. Everyone knows that. It's pathetic . . . Look, the protocol is, you fill out a request slip and leave it on the librarian's desk, and then she's obliged to serve you."

Flora turned back to her work. "Sorry, major thesis crisis," she said apologetically. "Two days to finish thirty thousand words on the moral significance—or not—of Virgil's *Aeneid*."

Ursula thanked her and tiptoed back towards the librarian's counter.

"Sorry to interrupt," she said, sotto voce. "I'd like to fill out a request slip."

"Bodleian card please," hissed Ms. Brookethorpe.

She could barely hide her disappointment when Ursula produced the university library card with her photograph on it from her satchel. The librarian took it and disappeared into a small office behind the desk, from which Ursula could hear the sound of a photocopier whirring. After ten long minutes Ms. Brookethorpe reappeared and handed the card back to Ursula, as well as a slip entitled "Hawksmoor Library—Request Form."

She thanked the librarian and scribbled "'The Apocalyptic Vision of the Early Covenanters,' Scottish Historical Review, Volume 43, April 1964, S. A. Burrell" on the request form and handed it back to her. Brookethorpe scrutinized the request form, beady-eyed, and then declared, "That doesn't mean anything to me." Impatiently, she rolled her eyes heavenward.

"It's an article, from the *Scottish Historical Review*," explained Ursula.

"I am well aware that you seek an article from the *Scottish Historical Review*, Miss Flowerbutton." In a deeply offended tone, she then addressed Ursula with the following monologue:

"If you are to borrow from this esteemed library, you must inform me of the shelf number and pressmark of the volume you require. The title and author are not enough. Then, you must fill out each of these"—she handed Ursula a white form, a pink form, a green form, and a blue form—"with all the information about the book, and leave it in the box on the librarian's desk. The pressmarks can be found in the catalogues at the other end of the library." Ms. Brookethorpe pointed towards the most distant part of the room.

Ursula set off. A monolithic statue of Thomas Paget, seated on a throne with a tower of books on one side and a sword and shield on the other, was prominently positioned in the center of the room. As she traipsed the considerable length of the gallery, she allowed her gaze to drift towards the arched, double-height windows that over-looked Great Quad.

The north side of the room was lined with ornate bookcases. Over each section, the subject of the books below was indicated in Latin, inscribed in grand gilt lettering. Ursula passed "Theologia," "Historia Antiqua," "Historia Orientalis," and "Philosophica," all the while painfully aware of the click of her heels echoing on the black and white marble flags as she progressed along the gallery.

She finally found herself confronted by the three massive oak chests that contained the Hawksmoor Library catalogue. Within each were hundreds of cards containing the details of every book belonging to the college, organized alphabetically. Ursula quickly located the Bi–Bu section, wrote down the pressmark and shelf number of the article on the various forms, and headed back to the librarian's desk, where she held out the forms to Ms. Brookethorpe.

"All forms must be left in the librarian's box," Ms. Brookethorpe ordered officiously, pointing to a completely empty brown leather box on her desk. Ursula put the forms inside.

"How long does it take to get a book?" she asked.

Ms. Brookethorpe gave her a stern look and then regarded her watch.

"It's almost half past midnight. As such, Nighttime Lending Rules apply. We are *very* understaffed. Depending on where your volume is located in the stacks, which contain over a hundred thousand items, well, there really is no predicting how long it could take to bring a book to you," she concluded with a smile. She cocked her head to one side, as if to say, *Surely* that *will put you off.*

When Ursula replied, "I'll wait," Ms. Brookethorpe huffed, looking irritated.

Ursula found a seat at the desk closest to the librarian's counter and started unpacking her satchel. She watched from the corner of her eye as Ms. Brookethorpe sat herself down again and continued working.

Eventually, the librarian peered casually in the box, as though she had no recollection of Ursula's recent request. With a look of surprise on her face, she removed the slip and read through it, terribly slowly, before disappearing into the office again.

While Ursula waited, her head resting drowsily on one elbow propped on the desk, her gaze alighted on the window, and thence Great Quad below. However trying the acquisition of the *Scottish Historical Review* article was proving to be, the moonlit scene more than made up for it. It looked so mysterious out there, the gables and turrets casting elongated shadows across the lawn. The college grounds were quiet, as though they had fallen into a deep sleep.[*]

Suddenly, Ursula sat bolt upright, alert, and rushed over to the window, pressing her face against the glass. A woman—she was sure it was a woman; she could make out the bottom of a knee-length skirt—was walking, head down, across the lawn. She appeared to have a bottle of champagne in one hand.

Wait. No. *It can't be,* said Ursula to herself.

But it was. How could she not recognize the silhouette of that frumpy calf-length A-line skirt, the outline of hair cut unflatteringly short, the impression of glasses . . . Claire? Claire Potter was roaming the college at almost one in the morning, walking on the sacred, forbidden grass of Great Quad with a bottle of champagne in her hand? She hadn't seemed that type at all. Ursula watched as she headed in the direction of the Monks' Cottages, soon disappearing into the passage leading to them. What was she doing going down there? . . . Wasn't that where India's rooms were? Who would want to go there alone in the dark, the day after a murder? Why wasn't she scared?

Just then, Ursula heard the squeak of Ms. Brookethorpe's pumps, and looked round to see the librarian walking—as slowly as someone

---

[*] Pubs and bars closed at eleven p.m. in England in the 1980s. It was impossible to buy a drink after that, except in a nightclub. By midnight, the grounds of Oxford colleges were deserted; the drinking carrying on in students' rooms.

with two functioning legs could possibly manage—towards a locked bookcase nearby with the words "Historia Caledonia" inscribed above it. She took a large brass key from her pocket, unlocked the door to the case, and retrieved a weighty leather-bound volume, which she brought over to Ursula's desk and wordlessly plonked in front of her with a heavy thud.

"Thank you," whispered Ursula, picking up the book and rising to leave.

Ms. Brookethorpe wrestled back the tome and slapped it back onto the desk. She tapped the spine of the book and pointed to a label, which read "Confined to the Library" in threatening black letters.

"You do realize this volume cannot be removed from the Hawksmoor Library?"

"Why?" asked Ursula.

"It is signed by the great historian S. A. Burrell, which makes it far too valuable to be taken to an undergraduate's room. It is priceless and cannot be replaced," the librarian explained victoriously.

Ursula sat back down, opened her satchel, took out her notepad and pen, and opened the *Scottish Historical Review* at the contents page. Her heart sank as she noted that the "article" began on page 146 and ended on page 402.

"No pens!" Ms. Brookethorpe rebuked her, snatching Ursula's from her hand. "You may have this back when you leave. Readers are strictly forbidden from using ink in the Hawksmoor Library. Pencils only. 2B. You may collect one from the porter's lodge and the cost will be added to your battels."

This woman wanted her to lose the will to live, or at the very least the will to read, thought Ursula. She dug around and found a pencil in her satchel.

Ms. Brookethorpe conceded that point with a wilted sneer and slunk back to her desk.

Ursula looked at her watch. It was already after one in the morning! She turned to page 146 and read the first sentence of the article:

In the spring of 1639 Dr. Walter Balcanqual, soon to be Dean of Durham for his services as amanuensis and pamphleteer on behalf of King Charles I, remarked the astonishing arrogance of the Scottish Covenanting leaders in their various petitions and manifestos . . .

Who was Dr. Walter Balcanqual? wondered Ursula. What was an "amanuensis"?

She examined the footnote at the bottom of the page, hoping it might help. "See 'Queries of D. Balcanq. to the King as to the Declaration' (Wodrow MSS., Folio LXVI, No. 34 (1639?)," she read. Clarity did not envelop Ursula, even a tiny bit. She scanned the next lines:

In 1643 while the Solemn League and Covenant was under negotiation with England, the poet Drummond of Hawthornden pointed out the seeming absurdity of Covenanting aspirations.

The lengthy footnote to this sentence read, "William Drummond of Hawthornden, 'SKIAMAXIA: or a Defence of a Petition Tendered to the Lords of the Council in Scotland,' in *Works*, 1711."

It took her at least forty-five minutes to get through the first few paragraphs of the article. The reading for her essay was going to be much more involved than she'd imagined when Dr. Dave had asked her to read "one short article."

She stared dejectedly out of the window, exhaustion starting to overcome her. How bizarre: there was the ungainly silhouette of Claire Potter again. This time, she was crossing the lawn of Great Quad in the other direction, *from* the Monks' Passage, the bottle of champagne still in her hand. When Claire reached the west side of the lawn, she disappeared towards the Gothic Buildings.

Ursula checked her watch again. Almost two a.m. As her tired eyes lingered on the moonlit quad, her brain suddenly sprang into life. What if . . . ? she wondered. What if Ms. Brookethorpe had been here late last night, working on her fragmented-Bible project? Would she have seen anything? Something? Someone? Out there, either going to or leaving Dr. Dave's staircase? Could she have seen the murderer?

Ursula took off her high heels and padded softly over to the librarian's desk.

"I was wondering . . ." she started.

Ms. Brookethorpe's head shot up in irritation. "What is it?"

Hmmm, thought Ursula, it might not be the best approach to dive straight in and ask if the librarian had seen Lady India's killer last night.

"Er . . . well, I'm kind of stuck."

Ms. Brookethorpe regarded her suspiciously. "Stuck?"

"Some of the language in the article . . . I mean, do you know what an amanuensis is?"

"It's the Latin for a scribe. Secretary."

"Gosh, you're clever," said Ursula.

For the first time, she saw Ms. Brookethorpe look the tiniest bit pleased.

"Oh, well, no . . ." she started, embarrassed. "I've got a doctorate in Middle English. University of Monmouthshire."

"Do you really work here all night on the Bible fragments?" asked Ursula.

Ms. Brookethorpe nodded. "It's my passion."

"So, you're here every night?" Ursula was getting closer.

"Mostly. Oh, except Sundays. I sing in the college choir every Sunday evening."

Drat, thought Ursula. The one night Brookethorpe wasn't here was last night.

"But choir traditionally never takes place on the Sunday of 1st Week, so I came up here as usual."

"Really?" said Ursula, trying not to let her excitement show. "It's a terrific view from here over the quad at night."

"I'm usually too busy working to notice it. Although last night . . . frightful row out there. Couldn't concentrate at all. Terrible what hap-

pened to that poor girl. Unthinkable. In such a wonderful place . . ."
Suddenly, Ms. Brookethorpe seemed to want to chat.

"I know," agreed Ursula. "Did you see anyone out there you didn't
recognize last night, after the row? Anything . . . unusual?"

"I've been racking my brains about that. Wondering, did I see
something? Hear anything? Could I help the police? All I know is,
well, there was a jolly good shouting match out there, *on the grass*.
We all heard who was in love with whom. You know, usual student
nonsense."

"Well, thank you for your help with the Latin word," said Ursula.
"I'm going to read now—"

"But what was odd," interjected Ms. Brookethorpe, "now I come
to think of it . . ."

Ursula turned back to her. "What?"

"Well, it was just . . . Oh, it's probably nothing."

"It might not be nothing."

"I suppose at the time I didn't think anything of it. But a few minutes after the night porter had sent everyone home, I saw someone.
Alone. Heading towards the Monks' Cottages. It must have been, oh,
half past midnight or so by then."

Surely it hadn't been Claire Potter the librarian had seen? But then,
it could have been Claire. After all, she'd been right next to the scene of
the crime for part of the evening. She could have seen India approach-
ing Dr. Dave's staircase, followed her into his rooms, and attacked her.
But why, after that, would she have gone to the Monks' Cottages rather
than the Gothic Buildings, where her own room was located? What
was in the Monks' Cottages that so interested her? And why would
she be going back tonight? Ursula wondered what Claire's motive for
murder would have been anyway. Even if she'd been upset that India
had branded her a "lezzie," was that a reason to slit someone's throat?
This wasn't *Carrie.* Or was it? wondered Ursula, with a slight shiver.

---

* In *Carrie*, Brian De Palma's 1976 high school horror movie, the bullied outcast
takes revenge on her class by killing them all at their prom. *Glee*, get lost.

"Was it a girl you saw?" she asked.

Brookethorpe let out a bitter little laugh.

"A girl prowling the college grounds at night? I don't think so."

"You think it was a man?"

"I know it was a man. I know the cut of that jacket. The swoop of that . . ." Here Ms. Brookethorpe looked away, wistfully. ". . . that hair. In the full moon, I could see David—sorry, I mean Dr. Erskine—down there as though it were broad daylight."

"Dr. Dave?" gasped Ursula. "How can you be sure it was him?"

"I just know. But don't say a thing to anyone," the librarian begged her.

"No, of course I won't. But how peculiar that he was out there at that time," said Ursula.

"Well . . . perhaps it wasn't him. I don't want to cause any trouble. No, I must have made a mistake—I'm sure of it now. Please forget what I said about Dr. Dave. Promise me," she added, desperately clutching Ursula's hands, "and I'll let you take a duplicate copy of the Scottish Historical Review up to your room overnight."

Chapter 19

How could she ever forget, Ursula wondered to herself as she wearily descended the library stairs, that Ms. Brookethorpe had been so utterly convinced—and then so unconvincingly unconvinced—that she had seen Dr. Dave in Great Quad last night? Clutching the *Scottish Historical Review* under one arm, Ursula felt vaguely guilty that she had accepted Ms. Brookthorpe's clear bribe to forget her tale, but getting the extra time to study the impenetrable text was an offer too advantageous to turn down.

"It's a bit late for the library, isn't it?" A male voice echoed up the stairwell.

Ursula started, afraid.

"Who's there?!" she gasped, peering into the shadows at the bottom of the stairs.

"It's me, Eg."

"What are *you* doing here?" Ursula asked fearfully. Hadn't Eg said he was spending the night taking care of Wenty? If so, why on earth was he wandering around college at half past two in the morning?

"Wenty's fallen asleep—finally. I wanted some air, so I took a stroll round Great Quad. I saw you in the window of the library. I thought I'd wait and see you safely back to your room."

"Thank you," said Ursula uneasily, coming around the bend in the staircase to speak to him face-to-face. She wasn't sure whether to be grateful for or suspicious of Eg's gallantry. What if he was lying? What if *he* was the killer, and had been waiting for her . . . ?

There was an awkward silence while Eg drank in the novel sight of Ursula in Nancy's party dress.

"Wow," he said admiringly. "You look more beautiful than . . . a Christmas tree."

Ursula just smiled shyly, flattered.

"Look, I didn't mean to freak you out. Come on, I'll walk you back. We don't want another fatality tonight, do we?"

"You think the killer's here, in the college? That's really horrible," said Ursula as they set off.

"We just need to stay safe."

As they walked under the gate tower, Ursula glanced through the window of the lodge and saw two uniformed police officers inside, talking to the night porter.

"What are they doing here so late?" she asked Eg.

"I bet they'll be here twenty-four hours a day for the next few days. Hey—Ursula, where are you going?" he said, as she opened the door to the lodge.

Ursula turned and winked at the boy. "Just checking my pigeon-hole . . ." she said with a coy smile.

"There won't be anything in it now."

But Ursula ignored him and went inside, Eg following reluctantly. The pigeonhole was of course empty, but she grabbed a piece of paper and pretended to write a note while she listened to the police officers' conversation with the night porter.

". . . you're saying you didn't see anyone . . . unexpected that night?" asked one officer.

"I don't think so," replied Nicholas Deddington. "Everything was as usual."

"When you say 'as usual,' sir, can you explain *exactly* what you mean by that?" the other officer said.

"The main entrance is locked at midnight. Anyone arriving after that rings and I let them in."

Just then Nick became aware of Ursula and Eg. "I've got a parcel for you, Ursula," he said. "Wouldn't fit in your pigeonhole. Here."

She thanked him and took the parcel, which had been wrapped in brown paper and tied with string, and stamped with the Dumbleton-under-Drybrook postmark. "Grannies!" cried Ursula. "A parcel from Granny and Granny," she told Eg. She couldn't wait to get back to her room and open it.

A few minutes later, as they made their way along the west side of Great Quad towards the passage leading to the Gothic Buildings, Ursula said, "You know India and Wenty had the most dreadful row out here last night, before she died."

"Wenty told me the whole story tonight over cards," Eg recalled.

"Do you know if he came straight back to the Old Drawing Room after the argument?" asked Ursula. "I don't remember seeing him again after he'd gone after India, do you?"

"Is it true you're writing this up for *Cherwell*?" Eg asked.

She nodded.

"I'm not going to be much help, I'm afraid. I was hanging out with Christian DJ-ing for most of the night, so I didn't notice where Wenty was. There were so many people coming in and out."

"True," said Ursula. "What time did you get to bed?"

"Two, three maybe . . ."

"Was Wenty there when you went to bed?"

"Wait—you don't think he did it? Come on!"

"I'm not saying that. I'm just trying to establish where everyone was last night."

"Look, I was so knackered by the time I got to bed that I can barely remember my head touching the pillow. But when I woke up the next morning, very late, around midday, Wenty was still asleep in his room. We had a cig together in the Old Drawing Room. Of course, we had no idea that something terrible had happened to India."

"What did you talk about?"

"Oh, mainly what an awesome party it had been. You know, the usual rubbish. Wenty bragging about how cool he was, that sort of thing."

At this, Ursula sighed. Wenty was just as conceited as he seemed.

"Did he say anything about the argument he'd had with India?"

"He only mentioned it in passing. Wenty and India had so many fights that I didn't take much notice at the time. He seemed pretty chilled actually. He was extremely happy that the washer-uppers had come back and cleaned up. When I went to bed the Old Drawing Room was trashed, but when we got up, it was immaculate."

As Ursula's staircase came into view, she noticed someone was emerging from the entrance, though she could only make out the silhouette of a caped figure. Eg must have seen the same person because he grabbed her by the waist and drew her swiftly into a flower bed against the wall of the Gothic Buildings.

"Ouch!" yelped Ursula as a thorny rosebush pricked her legs.

The figure approached and peered at the flower bed.

"Ursula! Daughter! I've been worried about you. Where have you been?"

It was Jocasta. Ursula's mind was playing tricks on her. She had mistaken the floaty tunic she was wearing for a far more sinister cloak.

"What are you *doing*?" Jocasta asked, squinting at her for a moment before spotting Eg's arm around Ursula's waist.

"Okay. Right. Sorry, man. I can see I'm interrupting something private," Jocasta said apologetically. "Am I an overprotective parent or what?"

"No," protested Ursula, removing herself and her grannies' parcel from Eg and the flower bed. "You're not interrupting anything. Honestly."

"I thought you were the murderer," Eg explained as he followed Ursula back onto the path, "so I grabbed Ursula and we hid in the rosebushes."

Dubious of his explantaion, Jocasta raised one eyebrow at the pair.

"Look, guys, it's *fine*. Just make sure you're being safe," she said in an understanding tone. "Have you got condoms—"

"It's not like that," Eg tried to explain. "We're not . . ."

But Jocasta was already forcing one into Ursula's hand. "The instructions are on the packet," she said, soon wafting away along the Gothic passage and leaving Eg and Ursula to whatever she imagined they wanted to be left to do. Mortified, Ursula shoved the condom into the front pocket of her satchel, hoping it was too dark for Eg to see.

"Right, I'll leave you here," he said. "Unless . . . would you like me to . . . um, well . . . escort you up the stairs?" He looked longingly at her, and she felt a flutter of excitement inside.

"No, honestly, I'll be fine from here." She smiled, trying to regain her composure. "Good night, and thank you for walking me back."

Ursula had only taken a few paces when she heard Eg's voice again. She flinched, on edge. What did he want now? It was so late.

"Anytime. In fact, I was wondering . . . would you let me . . . well, erm, maybe . . . take you out to dinner?"

Phew, thought Ursula to herself. If Eg was asking her on a date, the indications were that he wasn't about to kill her now before she went to bed. Her relief that she was not about to have her throat slit was soon replaced by the ecstatic realization that Eghosa Kolokoli— the dishiest disco dancer known, as far as she was concerned, to womankind—was asking *her* to have dinner with him.

"Dinner," Ursula repeated. The state of disbelief brought on by the word almost paralyzed her with delight.

"At Chez Romain? On Turl Street?" asked Eg. "It's French. Very nice—"

Before he could continue Ursula blurted out, "I'd love to."

Chapter 20

Ursula was desperate for bed, but the intense excitement of being asked on her very first date set her mind whirring. As she started to ascend the staircase, her brain bubbled over with delicious dinner-date-type questions: What would she wear? What would she and Eg talk about? Would they kiss?

She had no idea how on earth she'd get to sleep tonight after so much drama, but she'd have to try. In less than four hours' time, she had pledged to be in the porter's lodge to jog down to the river for her first coaching session with the Christminster rowing squad. She'd save her dear grandmothers' parcel as a treat for tomorrow.

Only—what was that? Ursula thought she heard a strange sound coming from the landing above her. She stood stock-still and listened. The sound came again. Ursula's heart thudded like a ticking stopwatch. Silently, she removed her shoes and inched, as quietly as she could, up the last few steps. Now it was clear the sound was a human cry, something like "Whhh-aaa-yyyy," followed by hiccuping and loud sobs.

Ursula tiptoed up onto the landing between her and Nancy's rooms. The sobs were becoming more intense, and were definitely coming from her friend's room. Was Nancy having some kind of crisis? Perhaps she was terribly homesick for New Jersey? Suddenly the sobbing turned into a gurgling, choking sound. Ursula froze. Was her friend being strangled? Was there a killer on the loose in college, as Eg thought?

Ursula didn't hesitate another moment. Heart pumping, breath suddenly short, she threw down her satchel, parcel, and the *Scottish Historical Review* and flung open the door to Nancy's room, ready to take on an attacker.

The sight that met Ursula was bizarre. The column of light coming from the landing behind her illuminated a shadowy figure writhing madly on the floor while Nancy cowered on the bed, brandishing a hockey stick.

"Ursula!" she screamed. "Thank God you're here. He's gone crazy."

Now you never know where things will lead in life. Being prep school leapfrog champion had seemed, to Ursula, to be one of those achievements that was not going to add up to much. Until now. Reptile-style, Ursula leapt upon the writhing form, squashed the flailing arms under her knees, and pushed its head to the floor.

The room was deathly quiet for a long moment. Then Nancy shrieked, "I think you've killed him. Oh my God."

The body beneath Ursula squirmed. Then it said, "I am *not* dead," sounding irritated. "But I wish I was dead. I deserve to die."

Ursula instantly recognized the Germanic inflection. Otto. He started sobbing violently, almost toppling Ursula. She stayed put, not sure whether it was safe to release her captive. What had he done to make Nancy so afraid?

"Nancy, what happened?" gasped Ursula.

"He just burst in here, like, going crazy, hysterical, saying, saying— that—that—Oh Ggg-o-ugh-o-od."

Now Nancy was blubbing. She wept as though the Trevi Fountain had sprung a leak.

"That he—he—*hiccup*—he—*hiccup*—thinks—said—but no! It can't be."

She collapsed on her leopard-print pillowcase, mumbling unintelligibly, while Otto squirmed beneath Ursula. He managed to crick his neck about halfway round so that she could see a bloodshot left eye, and croaked, "I know who killed India."

Ursula slowly released her prisoner from her grip. After he'd wobbled uncertainly to his feet—he was definitely drunk, she thought—Otto brushed down his velvet smoking jacket and tuxedo trousers, and stood sheepishly, hanging his head.

"Otto, did you just say that you know who killed India?" asked Ursula slowly.

"Yes," he rasped.

"But how?"

"How?" wailed Otto, gulping back tears. "How do I know? Because . . . i-i-i-it was . . . I think . . . it w-w-was . . . *me*."

Ursula just looked at him, stunned, while Nancy elaborated: "He's turned into some kind of lunatic. I thought he was going to kill me when he showed up in here, drunk and raging. Here, Ursula, tie him up," she added, chucking her a yellow silk taffeta sash belonging to a ball gown.

Otto offered Ursula his hands, which she tied in embarrassed silence, knotting the sash three times before finishing with a huge bow. He sank dejectedly into the chair by Nancy's desk, looking like a very strange birthday gift, buried his head in the yellow bow, and awkwardly blew his nose into it.

"Noooo! That's Bill Blass demi-couture," Nancy objected.

The misfortunes of Nancy's party frocks were not uppermost in Ursula's mind. Oddly calm, she looked hard at Otto and said, "Try and remember exactly what happened."

"I lied," he told her. "I lied to the police. When they questioned me today, they asked me when I last saw India. They were taking my fingerprints, my blood. How could I tell them the truth? I said I hadn't seen India after she left the party. I told them I'd fallen asleep in the JCR, that I hadn't seen her up there. None of it's true! I thought I could pretend. But I can't. I had to tell someone. That's the trouble with being a devout Roman Catholic. You need to confess. I thought Nancy was the right person to hear me out."

"Why?" Nancy looked amazed.

"You're from America. You have so many murderers there. You understand them."

"I *so* do not!" retorted Nancy crossly.

"Just tell us what *really* happened, Otto," Ursula pressed him. "The truth."

"It all started with Wenty. I knew that he wasn't serious about India, that she was just another conquest to him."

"Wenty doesn't seem like your average douche bag," protested Nancy. "He was just charming at his party. And *boy*, is he hot."

"The good-looking ones are *always* the worst," Ursula said. She wasn't at all surprised to hear that Otto thought Wenty was a player.

Otto continued, "But *I* was serious about India."

"*You* and India?" said Ursula, astonished.

"When she and I were Freshers, well . . . we . . . she was my First Love. There was this one fine autumn day, our first term. We took a picnic down to the boathouse and took a punt out on the river."

Otto's eyes slightly glazed over, as if he were back on the waters of the Isis with India, not trapped in a dorm room in makeshift handcuffs.

"We drifted lazily along. We drank port and ate wild boar pâté that I'd brought back from the *Schloss*. I told her I'd shot the very boar we were eating. It wasn't true, but she was impressed—she loved to shoot, and that's when she invited me to Bratters, shooting. I felt . . . elated. An invitation to a prestigious English estate! I knew my father would be proud."

"Austrian parents sound *so weird*," Nancy said in an aside to Ursula.

Oblivious to her comment, Otto continued, "There was a romantic moment. We floated beneath a weeping willow tree, and we kissed, touched tongues—"

"Eew! More than we need to know!" objected Nancy.

"That kiss," said Otto, closing his eyes, "was the most significant snog of my existence. It tasted *very* much of the wild boar. Perfection."

Nancy's face wrinkled with distaste. Ursula, meanwhile, hung on Otto's every word for a clue.

"But that happiness I felt, our love—"

"She was in love with you as well?" asked Nancy skeptically.

Ignoring the question, he continued, "She told me everything. I was always there for her. I always hoped, one day, that we'd kiss again, especially after I skillfully shot a woodcock on that shooting weekend at Bratters. But she grew distracted. There were many admirers. She was some kind of Zuleika Dobson.* Only . . . uuu-gguu-uuh," he gulped, "she is dead and her lovers are not!"

Tears squirted from his eyes.

"Otto, try and calm down. You need to tell us exactly what happened on Sunday night," Ursula said.

"Something happened before that. It was last Thursday," he sniveled. "India came to my room—our rooms are both in the Monks' Cottages. Hers is—was—next door to mine. When we got our room assignments at the beginning of this term, I thought it was a sign . . . that we were meant to be together . . . Anyway, she was very upset. She said to me, did I know anything about Wenty and another girl? Had he cheated on her? Well, everyone had been gossiping that Wenty had got off with Isobel last term at the New College ball. I couldn't *not* tell her what I'd heard—"

"Did you think it was true?" Ursula interrupted.

Otto hesitated. "I don't know why anyone would say something like that if it wasn't true."

"But, to be clear, you never *actually* saw Isobel and Wenty make out?" Nancy pressed him.

"Er . . . I suppose . . . not . . . with my own eyes."

"So how did India react when you told her this rumor about Wenty and Isobel?" said Ursula.

"She was infuriated. I don't know what she meant, but India said, 'She'll see,' and stormed out of my room."

---

* To prove their love for the beauty of the title, every male undergraduate commits suicide in Max Beerbohm's novel *Zuleika Dobson* (1911). Imagine *Gone Girl* in Edwardian costume.

Nancy turned to Ursula and said, "Do you think India showed up at Wenty's party with Dom just to spite Isobel?"

"Yes, and I think she'd been sleeping with him for ages," replied Ursula. "I think this all goes way back to the summer, when India stole Isobel's role as Ophelia. But perhaps India had decided it was time Isobel knew about her involvement with Dom. Otto, go on please."

"From the moment she arrived at Wenty's party, looking so stunning, on Dom's arm, I could tell it was over with Wenty."

"How did you know?" asked Ursula.

"It was in her eyes. Behind the sparkle, I don't know, there was something . . . hurt. I knew India very well, you see. And then, later, Wenty came back after she stormed out of the party and asked for my help—"

"Your help? How?" asked Ursula.

"Wenty returned to the party in the Old Drawing Room sometime after midnight. He told me that he needed to speak to me 'privately.' We retreated to the bathroom across the landing from his set. It was just me, Wenty, and a couple of scouts who were washing up. He was pretty drunk," Otto went on. "We all were that night. Wenty said that he and India had had an enormous row in the quad, and that he thought she had gone to find Dr. Dave. He wanted me to go up and see, bring her back. So I told him I would. But I didn't mean it."

"What?" said Ursula, confused.

"I sensed an opportunity," said Otto slowly, looking ashamed.

"What sort of opportunity?" she asked curiously. Surely he didn't mean he sensed an opportunity to kill India?

"It was my opportunity to have India. For myself—ugh-ugh-uggggg—" Otto's breathing sped up and he started to sound hysterical, screeching, "I double-crossed Wenty! He thought I was his friend! He *was* my friend! But I wanted her too much! I didn't care about him!"

For once, Ursula actually felt sorry for Wenty. His "friend" wasn't exactly loyal.

"Otto, take a chill pill," ordered Nancy. "What happened next?"

"I took a bottle of champagne from the bathtub, two more glasses.

I had one acid tab in my pocket. I swallowed half. Kept the other half for India," Otto told them, gradually calming down. "I was drunk, excited, tripping. I knew it was over between Wenty and India. It was my turn. When I reached Dr. Dave's staircase, I called out for India. I heard a voice above me. Suddenly, there she was in front of me, a vision. A slightly blurry vision, I admit—I refuse to wear my glasses to black-tie parties. That white gown she was wearing, the pearls gleaming in her tiara . . . she looked marvelous. I think she had come out onto the landing, I can't remember exactly, but I said to her, 'Liebling, you are the most exquisite girl I have ever seen,' and I took her hand. It was very romantic, gentle. I poured her a glass of champagne and put the half tab in it—"

"Did you tell her about the acid?" asked Ursula.

Otto looked hurt. "Do I look like the kind of sleaze-bucket who spikes an innocent girl's drink?"

Ursula didn't say anything. Whether or not Otto had told India she was about to consume half an acid tab didn't really matter in the great scheme of things. The end result was that, by this point in the chain of events, India was under the influence of drugs as well as the alcohol she had consumed at Wenty's party.

"Did you see anyone else on Dr. Dave's staircase?" asked Nancy.

"I don't remember seeing anyone else at all," said Otto. "We went into the room almost immediately. We started kissing. She kissed me as though she had never been kissed before. We ended up on the sofa, and at one point I fell off it, my passion was so great. But it didn't hurt. I felt as though I was floating, in a lilac cloud. I told her I loved her, that she was my one and only true *Liebling*. She said—even with my poor recall I can remember this as if it happened a minute ago—she said that she had never felt like this, ever. The joy I felt! I had waited so long for this! I sensed an invitation to her next shooting weekend would soon be forthcoming! And then I—*ach mein Gott*! I must have killed her after that."

"Otto, no, you can't have—" Nancy started.

But he interrupted her, saying, "I can't remember anything after that. My brain must have blocked it out. The act. The horror. I just remember waking up in the JCR and thinking Ursula was my *Liebling*."

"Otto, are you sure you're not imagining things?" she protested. "You were horrified when I showed you her body. You were so shocked you were sick—"

"Of course I was! I couldn't believe what I had done."

"There was no blood on your clothes. How could you have killed her like that and not had any blood on you?"

"I have proof. Physical proof."

"You do?" said Nancy, looking uneasy.

"Undo my trousers!" ordered Otto.

"Oh Jesus, he's totally lost it," Nancy bawled at Ursula.

Otto started fumbling awkwardly with his flies, despite his silken handcuffs, and his trousers fell to the floor, revealing a bony, pale pair of legs. He was wearing white underpants.

"Look!" he said, gesturing at a huge purple splodge of a bruise on his hip. "You can't deny it. The fall from the sofa did this. It all happened. I did it. I was with her all night. I was the only person up there. I would have seen something if someone else had done it. Or heard something. It was, maybe, a terrible accident."

The girls stared at the bruise, speechless. There was no denying Otto's physical evidence. And, when she really thought about it, Ursula felt that his behavior on Monday morning, after seeing India's body, had been pretty peculiar, veering from one emotional extreme to the other.

"I need to tell the police the truth. And then they can hang me. With my *Liebling* gone, I couldn't care less about dying. Bring me to the noose."

"Otto, the death penalty was abolished here twenty years ago," Ursula reminded him.

"How inconvenient," he wailed. "Regardless, first thing, I'm turning myself in."

"Otto, don't do any such thing," Ursula ordered the boy.

"You can help me?" he said, sounding desperate.

"I don't know yet. Just go to your room, get some sleep, and don't say another word to anyone. *Especially* not the police."

•

IT WAS AROUND three in the morning by the time Ursula finally shut the door to her room, switched on the bedside lamp, and sat on the bed. She was exhausted, but sleep seemed impossible after Otto's confession. Perhaps unwrapping the parcel from her grannies would calm her nerves. She smiled as she examined the contents: a bar of Kendal Mint Cake from Plain Granny, a bottle of Yves Saint Laurent Rive Gauche perfume from Vain Granny, and two letters, one from each of them. News from the farm! How comforting the idea of home seemed now. Ursula lay back on her pillows and began to read Plain Granny's letter.

Dearest Ursula—

In haste as sheep are out—miss you dreadfully. Without you house feels like a roly-poly pudding without the jam filling. Your old teddy bear Huggle very forlorn sitting on your bed all alone. Farm busy as ever, although chickens have stopped laying in protest at your departure. Making mountains of jam, blackberries this year are . . .

But Ursula was asleep, still in her party dress, dreaming of Seldom Seen Farm.

Chapter 21

Someone was hammering on Ursula's door. It was a brutal awakening from the heavenly jam-roly-poly-and-teddy-bears dream she was right in the middle of. Ursula sat bolt upright on her bed. The room was pitch black. The hammering intensified. It sounded as though someone was trying to bash her door down. There was nothing for it. Petrified, Ursula leapt from her bed and yanked her door open, simultaneously managing to hide behind it as she wondered who this could be.

Light from the landing illuminated something protruding into the room. Ursula heard the squeak of sneakered feet crossing the threshold. As her eyes adjusted to the light, she realized that the object in silhouette was a large wooden oar. It prodded the bed, as though searching for someone. Suddenly the most bizarre thing happened. The sound of singing filled the room:

> *Oh, what a beautiful morning,*
> *Oh, what a beautiful day.*
> *Get yourself down to the ri-ver,*
> *Or Christminster's boat rows away!*

"Moo!" said Ursula crossly, recognizing her voice. "I thought I was about to get bonked on the head."

"That's the idea. Got you out of bed pretty damn quick, didn't it? Fifteen minutes till the Freshers' Eight meets in the porter's lodge to run down to the river." Moo, perky as hell and already in her college tracksuit and sneakers, regarded the polka-dot dress Ursula was still wearing from last night. "Super nightie."

Ursula rubbed a sleepy bug from her left eye and looked at her alarm clock: 5:45 a.m. already. "I'll be there," she said.

"Good-o," said Moo, jogging energetically across the landing to Nancy's digs, where the door bashing started all over again.

Ursula shut the door. As she dressed in her college tracksuit, she reviewed Otto's peculiar account of Sunday night. The facts certainly added up to a nasty outcome for him: Ursula had, after all, found him passed out in the room next door to one that had contained India's corpse, and he had freely admitted that he had spent most of the night in Dr. Dave's rooms with India after he had left Wenty's party and hadn't seen anyone else up there that night.

But, Ursula asked herself, how could Otto be so convinced that he had killed India if he couldn't remember actually doing it? If it was in fact possible to forget that you had just murdered a very close friend, which Ursula seriously doubted, there was the question of the influence of drugs and alcohol. Although Ursula had no personal experience of acid, she had heard that it made the user feel as though he or she was hallucinating, not homicidal. Was Otto's whole story in fact a nightmarish vision?

And what about India? Even if Otto had spiked her glass of champagne with half an acid tablet, would she really, after the famous row with Wenty, have suddenly become infatuated with someone else? Her love life was complicated enough.

Still, against all the odds, it appeared that Otto and India *had* spent the night in each other's arms. Otto had the bruise to prove it. But that still didn't convince Ursula his tale of murder was completely reliable. That perfect slit that Ursula had witnessed on India's throat didn't quite gel with Otto's belief that he had killed her accidentally. It had been neat, clean, the work of someone who was careful and calculating, rather than the drunken mistake of a minor Austrian princeling. But why would Otto lie? If he was lying, was he protecting someone? If so, who?

Ursula wrapped her cozy college scarf tightly around her neck. It would be freezing outside this early, and even colder down on the water. She quickly glanced in the mirror. Her eyes were still daubed with the eye shadow and mascara from last night, and her crimped hair had turned into a mad-looking bird's nest. With time running short, she hurriedly wove it into two scruffy plaits and stepped out onto the landing. Despite having had only a couple of hours sleep, her excitement about her first Oxford rowing session energized her. Sunrise on the river would be magical.

"Hey!" Nancy was already outside Ursula's room waiting for her.

"Wow," Ursula exclaimed as she took in her friend's rowing costume. There really was no other way to describe the outfit as anything other than a costume, she thought.

"Thank you," said Nancy proudly. "I was really worried about looking appropriate."

Nancy's "appropriate" rowing costume consisted of the following: a dark green blazer with red grosgrain trim and the Christminster coat of arms embroidered on the breast pocket, a starched white button-down shirt, a striped college tie, and a dark green pleated gymslip skirt. Her knee-high socks were, of course, knitted in college colors, and her feet were clad in white puffy high-top sneakers. She looked like a St. Trinian's girl who'd got lost in a hip-hop video.

The girls clattered down the staircase and across Great Quad towards the porter's lodge. It was just starting to get light, but the day was disappointingly gray. Portentous iron-black clouds were gathering above, and Ursula could already feel fat drops of rain plopping onto her cheeks.

"I *cannot* believe what happened last night," said Nancy as the girls walked. "Otto seemed so nice when we met him that first morning. But on *America's Most Wanted* it's always the cute, quiet ones who turn out to be homicidal maniacs."

"We need to keep our options open. I think that Otto *thinks* that he killed India, but I'm not certain he did," said Ursula, elaborating on her doubts about Otto's tale.

Suddenly the rain droplets became a downpour, and they sprinted as fast as they could to the shelter of the gate tower. From the other direction, Mrs. Deddington, head down against the weather, was dashing with a tray of tea from the Kitchen Quad. By the time she was under cover, her brown frock was limp and the two cups of tea and pile of Marmite on toast on the tray were spotted with rain and had lost any allure they might once have had.

"What a waste," sighed the scout, heading into the porter's lodge.

"Oh no, Marmite's *always* delicious . . . Mmmm," Ursula volunteered.

She and Nancy followed the Marmite's aroma, and Mrs. Deddington, inside. There they found Alice, dusting industriously while chatting to Deddington and his son, who were swapping shifts. Mrs. Deddington placed the tray on the porter's counter.

"*What* is *that* stuff?" asked Nancy, contorting her face at the sight of the dark brown substance on the toast.

"Only the most scrummy thing in the entire world," said Ursula. "You have to try it."

"Miss Feingold, if you come down to the scouts' mess at five o'clock, I'm sure Mrs. Deddington will make you some Marmite on toast to try, won't you, Linda? Miss Flowerbutton, come along as well," said Alice.

Mrs. Deddington put her hands on her hips and huffed.

"Come on, Linda," Alice cajoled her. "It's nice to have the students down for tea sometimes. We all need cheering up, don't we, after yesterday."

"True," she sighed. "But only for five minutes, mind. I'm busy today."

"See you later, Mum," said Nick, gulping down his tea. He pecked his mother on the cheek, picked up his bag of textbooks in one hand, a wilted piece of toast in the other, and disappeared. Deddington, meanwhile, took up his position behind the desk, nodded hello to the girls, and tucked into his toast.

"I'll drop your kilts off in your room this morning," Alice told Ursula. "They look lovely now they're short."

"Oh, thank you!" Ursula was delighted. "I can wear one on my date tonight—"

"Date! *Date*?" interrupted Nancy. "What? Who?"

"Shhhh!" said Ursula. "I'll tell you later."

The Freshers' Eight—which, apart from Ursula, included Moo, Claire Potter, and five other young women who had arrived in dribs and drabs over the last few minutes—was finally gathered in its entirety. A Second Year girl soon appeared and started barking at them officiously.

"Right! My name is Eleanor! Thompson! I am the president of the Christminster Boat Club!" shouted the girl, who was dressed in skin-tight cycling shorts and a college tracksuit top. Her hair was scraped into a tight bun, revealing a stern, plain face, and her muscular thighs, Ursula noted, bulged intimidatingly, like two prize marrows at a country fete.

"Remember! You're a team! From now on," Eleanor continued, "everyone needs to pull their weight. Literally. If one of you pulls her oar at the wrong time, you're *all* in the water. It's down to your cox to tell you when to pull. Make sure you listen to her. Respect her."

The team nodded obediently. Then Eleanor asked, "Which one of you is the cox anyway?"

No one said anything. Ursula looked round. Nancy was staring dejectedly at her empty pigeonhole. Ursula nudged her.

"Nancy," she hissed, "you're needed."

"Nothing from Next Duke," her friend said, disconsolate. She turned from her pigeonhole to Eleanor. "I'm Nancy, the Freshers' cox. Hey."

"I might have known," said Eleanor, scrutinizing Nancy's outfit disapprovingly. "Right, Coach is meeting us down at the boathouse. Let's go."

Just as the girls jogged out of the college gates, a bellowing crack of thunder delivered another torrent of rain. Pelted by the harsh weather, Ursula and Nancy jogged behind Claire Potter down Christminster Lane. Ursula hoped she could speak to Claire after the rowing session. She *must* know something about that doomed Sunday night. Perhaps from her seat close to the window, maybe eating ice cream, she had seen India dashing from Great Lawn towards the JCR staircase. Or could she have heard Otto professing his undying devotion to his *Liebling* on the landing outside the JCR? Might Claire have seen Dr. Dave in the quad, as Ms. Brookethorpe said she had? And what about Claire's companion? Ursula knew that two ice creams had been consumed that night, and unless Claire had been extremely hungry, Ursula had to assume that someone else had eaten the second tub. But who? And had he or she seen anything? And, finally, what on earth had Claire been doing prowling Great Quad at one a.m. last night?

The girls reached the corner of Christminster Lane, where they turned and jogged down High Street, past the spires of Magdalen College Tower.

"So who's this mysterious date with?" panted Nancy as they jogged.

"Eg," Ursula told her. "Can you believe it, he's asked me out for dinner." She still could not quite believe it herself.

"Oh my God, he is *so hot*. Do you have a crush on him?"

Before Ursula had a chance to answer, Eleanor Thompson shouted from behind them. "Stop gabbing, you two, and get a move on!"

Ursula watched with awe as Nancy sprinted forward and easily overtook the rest of the Freshers' Eight. She was a superb runner and now seemed oblivious to the drenching she and the other Freshers were experiencing. Ursula's own tracksuit was soaked through, and her plaits soon resembled two drowned worms. Her feet squelched in her Green Flash. Her toes were becoming numb. But she refused to let her enthusiasm be dampened. As she followed the team along a track by the river, Ursula found herself captivated by its (very) damp charm. Rain droplets bounced brightly off the water. The fingerlike fronds of drooping ash and weeping willow trees swept the surface.

When the girls jogged past a herd of Highland cattle grazing the riverbank, Ursula felt as though she'd stepped into a scene from a picture postcard.

Thank goodness! she thought, winded, as the white-painted boathouses at last came into view. The girls trotted over a footbridge and finally caught their breath in front of the largest boathouse on the river's edge. On this section of river, the widest part, it was already rush hour. Sculls were powering smoothly up towards the Head of the River, coaches were yelling instructions at different teams, and rowers were warming up on the quayside.

The boathouse's huge wooden doors were already flung open, and a fit-looking group of male rowers expertly hoisted one of the many boats stored there above their heads. Ignoring the pelting rain, they marched it out of the boathouse like a troop of soldiers and effortlessly deposited the boat in the water. "Your carriage awaits, ladies!" called one of them. Ursula had never seen so many dishy, well-built boys in her life.

Minutes later, she found herself seated at the front of the boat, the handle of a huge oar hovering above her knees. Moo was seated immediately behind her. The rest of the girls filled the other six rowing spots in the boat, and Nancy sat facing them from the bow. Her right hand rested on the rudder control. Her left hand gripped a loudspeaker. Even though her usually bouffant hair now resembled a wilted pancake, Nancy looked thrilled with her new role.

"Your coach today," yelled Eleanor Thompson from the bank, "is Wentworth Wychwood. He's a top rowing Blue. Please pay attention to his instructions. You'll learn a lot from him."

Wenty? Oh no, thought Ursula. She couldn't imagine anyone she'd less like to be bossed around by in a boat than Wentworth Wychwood.

He soon appeared, sensibly dressed with a waterproof jacket over his Blues tracksuit, his hair covered by a thick black woolen hat. Though he looked worn and tired, Ursula couldn't help admitting to herself, grudgingly, that he was terribly handsome all the same.

"Morning, ladies," said Wenty, flashing his beautiful smile at the Freshers, who responded, Ursula included, with a Group Swoon.

"Coach, before we start, I have a really important question," Nancy said, her voice reverberating loudly through the loudspeaker.

"Yes, Nancy," replied Wychwood.

"It's about Next Duke. The Dudley one?"

"Nancy, please concentrate on coxing," Wenty said, looking amused. "Ladies, please lift your oars so they are flat above the water."

The boat wobbled unevenly as the girls gingerly moved their oars.

"I'm just wondering," continued Nancy, "is he, you know . . . coming over to your rooms again soon?"

"Doubt it," replied Wenty. "He hardly ever leaves Merton. Except to go to chapel. He's a recluse. The only reason he came on Sunday was because he's had a crush on India since childhood . . ." Wenty suddenly stopped talking and seemed desperately sad. Ursula couldn't help but feel sorry for him. After a few seconds, he managed to pull himself together and said, "Right, that's enough small talk. Ladies, turn your oar at a right angle to the water."

Wenty expertly instructed the girls how to dip their oars in the water and pull them forward. Nancy was soon shouting *"Pull!"* at the top of her lungs through the loudspeaker. Timidly at first, the Freshers' Eight dragged their oars through the water every time she made the command. Rowing was much more difficult than Ursula had imagined, and mostly the boat bobbed along like an ungainly bath toy. But the very occasional feeling of gliding that the girls achieved, even in the driving rain, was bliss. While she was out there on the water, Ursula felt energized and peaceful. But as soon as the crew returned to the boathouse, she was back on her mission, and cornered Claire Potter immediately.

"Hi, Claire," she said. "Did you enjoy it?"

"Not really," the other girl answered as she dried her hair with an old towel. "Ugh. I'm soaked."

"Claire, may I talk to you? About what happened on Sunday night?"

"What about it?" she retorted, suddenly blushing bright red. She held the damp towel to her face as if to cool down her cheeks.

"I'm trying to find out what India did after she left the party."

"What's it got to do with you? The police are all over college investigating. Why not leave it up to them?"

"Of course the police are investigating. But, it's just, I'm supposed to be writing an article about it all for *Cherwell*."

"Why would I know anything about what happened to India?" Claire said defensively.

Ursula was getting the distinct feeling that the girl had no interest in being even the slightest bit helpful to her, even after her apology. Still, she persisted.

"Claire, your Crosswords and Ice Cream party was almost next door to the room India died in. Did you see anything? Hear anyone?"

"I was very . . . er . . . occupied . . ." Claire hesitated. ". . . with the . . . um, function that night."

Why was she lying? Ursula wondered. After all, one of the few concrete facts Ursula knew about the night in question was that only two tubs of ice cream had been eaten at the Crosswords and Ice Cream party. It was most likely that Claire had had only one guest, and that was only if she hadn't eaten the two tubs of ice cream herself.

Claire now looked extraordinarily embarrassed. *That's it!* Ursula deduced. Claire was lying because she was ashamed that her club had been such a flop. It would be cruel to confront the poor girl with her lies now, and anyway, Ursula might squirrel more information out of her by playing along.

"How long did all your friends stay in the JCR?" she asked, trying to sound casual.

"Er . . . I'm not sure," Claire stammered.

"Did they leave before midnight? After?" Ursula went on.

"It's hard to say when you're . . . occupied."

What on earth was Claire talking about? It was inconceivable that she hadn't heard anything from the JCR during Otto and India's tryst.

After all, her virtually deserted party would have been extremely quiet. How could she have heard absolutely nothing?

"Unforgettable, hello," Wenty suddenly interrupted them.

Ursula looked at him with amazement. How on earth could he call her Unforgettable now, after everything that had happened? Perhaps sensing her discomfort, he cleared his throat and said, "Sorry, I mean Ursula. I'm a mess . . . with everything that's happened." He sounded sincere. "Look, I'd like to talk to you. Privately. Would you allow me to . . ." Wenty's voice trailed off and he stood looking at Ursula searchingly. A rather intense moment was abruptly curtailed by Claire Potter.

"I know when I'm not wanted," she said, stomping off.

"Claire, wait . . ." Ursula called after her unconvincingly. But her teammate didn't look back.

"Allow you to?" replied Ursula slowly to Wenty, returning her attention to him.

Wenty didn't answer her immediately. He just let his clear blue eyes linger on hers for what seemed like forever. Ursula felt slightly giddy. Eventually, he said, "To buy you a . . . fry-up?"

Ursula looked away from the boy and chided herself before she answered him. She did not need to start going all giddy on someone like Wenty. He was exactly the sort of boy to be avoided in Oxford. She already had a date for dinner tonight. She didn't need a breakfast date as well.

"Sorry, no, I have plans," she announced, feeling *very* pleased with herself. Turning down Wenty was immensely satisfying.

"Plans for breakfast? Don't be ridiculous."

"I am not being ridiculous!" Ursula retorted.

Wenty persisted, saying, "Look, I just want to talk to you, about India, sooner rather than later."

"Oh," said Ursula, feeling humiliated. Wenty had not been asking her on a date after all.

"I've heard you're writing something for *Cherwell*," he continued. "I think we can help each other. Breakfast? Please?"

Chapter 22

I t was with some trepidation that Ursula followed Wenty under an awning displaying the words "Since 1654" and through the tiny front door of the Queen's Lane Coffee House. Even if her rendezvous with him was strictly business, she had never experienced anything quite as intimate as an unaccompanied fry-up with a boy before.

The little café was a welcome, warm respite from the rainy street. The interior was spartan—dark brown chairs and tables, plain oak beams and ancient-looking plastered walls. Portraits of the café's previous undergraduate clientele—which apparently included Samuel Pepys and Lawrence of Arabia—were hung in nooks and corners, manna to tourists. The only clue that it wasn't still 1654 inside the coffeehouse was the speckled yellow linoleum tile floor. The place was already crammed with students tucking into enormous cooked breakfasts of eggs, bacon, sausages, baked beans, and piles of fried white bread. Ursula was ravenous after the rowing session.

"Do you mind if we sit over there?" asked Wenty. "Easier to talk about . . . well, everything."

He led her towards a rickety round table in a far corner, away from the crowd. Ursula hesitated for a moment, thinking the situation looked far too secluded and romantic for a breakfast that was strictly business. Wenty noticed her reluctance.

"Don't worry, no one's going to think there's anything going on, Flowerbutton," he said.

"Okay," said Ursula, sitting down and noticing a pink plastic rose in a vase on the table. "I just don't want anyone thinking we're on, well, some kind of . . . breakfast date. It would be really unprofessional, for the article and everything."

"Flowerbutton, I wouldn't ask you on a date if you paid me. You're adorable, but you're far too prim for me." Wenty smiled and took a seat, looking very amused by his insult.

"Wenty," Ursula exclaimed, "you're so full of yourself! And I am *not* prim."

"All right, square."

"Ughhhhhhh!" Ursula groaned. He was impossible. "Can we change the subject please?"

"Sorry. You must be freezing. Here."

Wenty jumped up, took off his waterproof jacket, removed his dry sweatshirt, and tucked it around Ursula's sodden shoulders. He was impossible, but perhaps the boy had a smidgen of gentlemanliness in his soul, she thought, hugging the sweatshirt round herself for warmth. A smidgen.

"You look like you need a hot chocolate," he suggested.

"And that fry-up please," she said. "I'm starving."

"Flowerbutton," declared Wenty, "you're a one-off."

"What?"

"Of all the beautiful girls I have invited to breakfast here, not *one* has *ever* ordered the fry-up."

How predictable, thought Ursula. I am only one of *many* girls to have spent a rainy morning in a cozy corner of Queen's Lane Coffee House with Wentworth Wychwood. That smidgen of goodness this boy possessed was probably such a small amount that it was almost negligible.

A waiter approached. After Wenty had ordered two full English breakfasts, he said to Ursula, "India loathed coming here. She'd always order marmalade on toast, not touch it, and then complain to the waiter that it was cold. She was so contrary, but, at the same time no one knew how kind she was underneath all her bravado. She used to visit her old nanny in her little cottage in Brattenbury every time she went home. Adored her. India even put up with my dreadful piano playing. I'm hopeless, but she pretended I was good."

"That's sweet," said Ursula.

"She had her difficult side, of course. People thought she was spoiled, arrogant. But I understood why she behaved the way she did."

At this, Ursula's ears pricked up. "What do you mean?"

"Her mother ran off to a squat in Clapham to be a heroin addict with some cockney artist when India was three. Died a few years later. Tragic. India was raised by her nanny until Lord Brattenbury packed her off to boarding school when she was seven. India was the most insecure, most messed-up girl I ever met . . . I was crazy about her . . . She *made* you crazy."

Ursula nodded, but didn't feel any more enlightened. What did Wenty mean, India made him crazy? Crazy enough to kill her? Out of jealousy? If he was so infatuated with her, though, why had he slept with Isobel? And what about all the other girls who everyone claimed Wenty was chasing behind India's back?

Just then, the waiter returned with a large tray and set two full platters on the table. Ursula and Wenty tucked in, both famished. Ursula sipped at the delicious hot chocolate. Wenty took a gulp of his coffee, and then, looking sadly at Ursula, he said, "Have you got any idea what happened to India? Do you know *anything*, Flowerbutton?"

"Not much," replied Ursula. She obviously wasn't going to tell him about Otto's bizarre outburst the previous night. Or the information she'd gleaned from Isobel. "But I think you might be able to help, Wenty. You're one of the last people who spoke to or saw India that night. I need you to tell me everything you know."

He produced a sodden packet of Marlboro Reds and a plastic lighter from his back pocket.

"It's my fault that she's dead, you know," he said, lighting the first of many cigarettes. "I might as well have done it."

"What?" said Ursula, trying not to look too shocked. Was she about to hear a second confession, of sorts?

Wenty rubbed one side of his head, the cigarette almost singeing his hair. "Flowerbutton, if I hadn't called you Unforgettable that night, India would still be alive today. She was very insecure. Got easily jealous . . . you saw her. She was furious with me. Probably had every right to be." Wenty stopped talking for a moment, an embarrassed expression on his face. "I wasn't a very good boyfriend."

"Really," said Ursula, deadpan. His admission was hardly a surprise to her.

"Someone told her—God knows who, I could murder them—that I'd shagged Isobel Floyd. Of course, I told India I hadn't. I mean, Isobel was her best friend, for God's sake, what kind of person would do that?"

Had Otto been lying, wondered Ursula, when he had told India that Wenty had been up to no good with Isobel? Had he just used it to try and steal India away for himself?

"Why would someone say that about you and Isobel if it wasn't true?" asked Ursula, munching on her fried bread.

Wenty looked sheepish. "It wasn't *exactly* not true."

"I see."

"Look, I shagged Isobel, okay. Behind the Pimm's tent, New College ball. We were both blotto, so if you ask me it doesn't count. I couldn't tell India the truth, but I wasn't a very good liar. She knew. It was obvious. And then when she heard me call you Unforgettable at the party, that was it. She went nuts on me in Great Quad. I begged her to forgive me. You know, I loved her more than anything. I'd never have cheated on her if I'd been sober, never! But instead of forgiving me, she wanted to punish me. She was still at it with Dr. Dave, I'm sure of it."

"Really?" asked Ursula. Everyone had said the affair with Dave had been over for a long time, but perhaps Wenty was onto something.

"Revolting ponce. India was always up in his rooms having 'long talks.' I mean, please! If she wasn't still in love with him, why did she go to his rooms on Sunday night?"

"I don't know. No one does yet. What happened when you went back to the party after the row in Great Quad?" asked Ursula.

"I was worried about India . . . angry . . . jealous. I went back into the Old Drawing Room and found Otto. We went to the bathroom for a private chat and I asked him to go after India and tell her that I was sorry about Isobel. I couldn't bear to let a bit of extracurricular activity part us forever. I thought I'd marry India, one day." A tear rolled slowly down Wenty's cheek. "Sorry," he said, brushing it away. "Anyway, Otto said he knew India felt the same way about me, and then he went off to retrieve her. But he never came back. After an hour or so, I started getting concerned. I decided to go over to the staircase myself."

That was odd, thought Ursula. Ms. Brookethorpe hadn't said anything about seeing Wenty crossing Great Quad that night. She had only mentioned spotting Dr. Dave walking towards the Monks' Cottages.

"Did you see anyone in Great Quad as you walked over?"

"No," said Wenty. "But I was so furious I probably wouldn't have noticed if the entire Household Cavalry had been on parade. I just wanted to get to India before . . ." He trailed off, his face grim.

"Before what?" asked Ursula.

"Oh . . . nothing. It's pointless now. I was too late anyway."

What did he mean? she wondered. Had he somehow known that India was in danger? Was he too late to save her life? Was she already dead by the time he reached Dr. Dave's rooms? Did this mean that Otto had, in fact, done her in?

"Are you saying, Wenty, that India was already dead by the time you reached Dr. Dave's rooms?"

"Dead? Ha! God, no." He laughed bitterly. "When I got to the staircase, India was alive and kicking . . . or should I say alive and shagging?"

"You saw her with—"

"I didn't need to," he interrupted. "I could hear them at it. Laughing, giggling, screaming. They were bonking so hard I could hear everything from the bottom of the staircase. That feeling I'd had for a while, that she was shagging someone behind my back—I was right."

The whole thing was far worse than Wenty realized, thought Ursula. She dreaded to think about what would happen when he discovered, which he inevitably would, that India had not been with Dr. Dave that night, but with Wenty's "loyal" friend Otto.

"What did you do?" asked Ursula.

"I . . . er . . . didn't want to go up . . . It would have been too humiliating," Wenty said, then hesitated for a moment. "So I went back to my rooms. Went to bed. Didn't wake up till midday on Monday."

If Wenty hadn't gone up the stairs, as he said, he couldn't possibly have killed India. But was he telling the truth? A nasty sense of doubt crept over Ursula. Ms. Brookethorpe didn't seem to have noticed Wenty going back across the quad to his rooms. Could she really have missed him twice?

"Look, sorry," he continued, glancing at his watch. "I've got to get to a lecture. We could carry this on later. Why don't you . . . come up to my rooms . . . after dinner?"

Ursula frowned at the boy. He seemed unable to resist flirting, whatever the circumstances. After her experience with Jago, the last thing she was going to do was go to Wenty's rooms alone, at night. She wasn't interested in becoming one of his many conquests.

"I can't," said Ursula. She couldn't resist adding, "You see, I'm busy tonight. I've got a date. I'm going for dinner at Chez Romain."

"Ooh, la-di-da! Chez *Romance*, don't you mean? You've only been in Oxford a few days and already you're going to the couples' restaurant."

"The couples' restaurant?"

"It's so expensive that after one dinner there, you're officially a couple with whoever took you. It's much too extravagant for a casual date. Anyway, who are you going with?"

"Eg, as a matter of fact," replied Ursula.

"Eg?" Wenty chortled.

The idea of Eg and Ursula on a date prompted tears, this time of laughter, to flow from Wenty's eyes. Ursula had no idea what was so funny.

Chapter 23

By the time Ursula arrived back at college that morning, soaked and freezing, she was desperate to change into something warm and dry before starting her day properly. The freshly shortened mini kilts beckoned. But her attention was soon distracted from her sartorial musings by the sight of Ben Braithwaite, looking like a frightened weasel, being shepherded out of college by two police officers. Ursula smiled at him as reassuringly as she could, but Ben, clearly paralyzed with terror, did not respond. How on earth was he connected to India's death? she wondered.

En route to her room, she headed to the porter's lodge to check her pigeonhole. As she approached, she could hear Deddington's voice. He sounded irate.

"As I've already explained, college isn't open to the public this morning, sir."

Ursula slipped into the lodge, where she saw the porter talking to a man dressed in a long black overcoat and holding a scruffy briefcase. He was unshaven and had lank, greasy hair.

"Come on, just a quick walk around?" said the man, taking out a ten-pound note.

"Impossible." Deddington pushed the note back into the man's pocket. "There's police all over college. No one's allowed in unless they're a member of the university."

Ursula took her time opening the one note she found in her pigeonhole while continuing to eavesdrop on the conversation between Deddington and the strange man.

"This was Lady India Brattenbury's college? You can confirm that at least?" the man persisted.

"No idea, sorry," Deddington said, shaking his head. "Now, do I need to show you out? Or should I ask the police to do that?"

"I'll find my own way." With that, the man speedily exited the lodge, eyeing Ursula furiously as he did so.

"What was all that about?" she asked the porter.

"*Daily Mail*. Neil Thistleton, he said his name was. Snooping around. Don't speak to him if you see him around town. Gutter journalist," he grumbled.

"I won't," Ursula promised.

She turned her attention back to the note in her hand. The photocopied sheet was from Eleanor Thompson and it read:

Freshers' Eight meet again 6 a.m., Saturday, porter's lodge.

Alas, thought Ursula. Friday was the night of the Vincent's cocktail party. Getting up for six a.m. after an evening out wasn't exactly her idea of fun. But if she were ever to make the boat team, she didn't have much choice. Despite all his faults, Wenty's excellent coaching had inspired her to go for it, rowing-wise. She wanted to impress him and make the team next term.

Her plan for today was to spend the morning in the library, attacking "The Apocalyptic Vision of the Early Covenanters" with renewed vigor, and the afternoon gathering more material for her article. She needed to think how to approach Dr. Dave. Was there a polite way to ask your don about the details of a love affair with his student?

As she made her way to her staircase from the lodge, Ursula suddenly heard agitated voices coming from the direction of the provost's lodgings, the Georgian mansion situated in the southwest corner of

Great Quad. She drew close to the building and noticed the front door was just ajar.

". . . I'm afraid it's not good news, High Provost."

Ursula stopped outside the house. The dry tones of DI Trott were unmistakable. He continued, "We believe the girl was murdered—"

"—but you can't be sure? That it was murder?" Ursula now heard High Provost Scrope's alarmed voice.

"We're ninety-nine percent certain that Lady India died at someone else's hands. The autopsy is due to take place later this morning at the John Radcliffe Hospital, and I have no doubt that the procedure will confirm the suspicions of the police force. Now, I have some questions for you, High Provost."

"Rather busy this morning, I'm afraid. I'm chairing a meeting of the fund-raising committee shortly. Could you come back another time? It would be so unfortunate if any members of the committee were to see a police officer here."

"This won't take long," Ursula heard Trott say.

Suddenly she noticed a woman peering at her through a large sash window on the ground floor of the house. Her face was powdered and lipsticked, and her hair coiffed into a twirl resembling a Walnut Whip. She was wearing a royal blue suit and a pale yellow blouse with a huge pussycat bow tied at the neck. She appeared to have modeled herself on Margaret Thatcher. She was sitting at an old-fashioned mahogany desk, neatly arranged with various documents. That must be Scrope's secretary, Mrs. Gifford-Pennant, thought Ursula, noting the typewriter and telephone on the woman's desk.

"Wouldn't have thought a college as wealthy as Christminster needs a fund-raising committee." Trott sounded surprised.

"It does if we are to remain the richest college in Oxford," Scrope told him curtly.

"Perhaps we could start with that," Trott replied. "I understand that generations of Brattenburys have attended Christminster and that the family has pledged a considerable endowment to the college."

"Mrs. Gifford-Pennant!" called out Scrope. "Please show this gentleman into the drawing room. And cancel the fund-raising meeting."

Ursula watched from outside as the secretary hurriedly jumped up from her seat and disappeared from the room. Next, Ursula heard footsteps in the hall. Seconds later, Mrs. Gifford-Pennant's meringue-like coiffure and powdered nose appeared around the slightly open front door of the provost's house. She squinted at Ursula suspiciously and abruptly slammed the door.

●

WHAT DID THE Brattenbury family have to do with the Christminster College finances? Was this endowment somehow connected to India's death? Ursula wondered as she clambered up the steep stairs to her room a few minutes later. When she reached it, Alice was inside, cleaning.

"You look like you need a mustard bath," the scout said when she saw the girl's bedraggled state.

"No time," Ursula told her. "I've got to get to the library."

"Well, I'll leave you to it then," said Alice, ducking out of the room, which, Ursula noticed, was now immaculate.

As soon as she was alone, Ursula removed her damp tracksuit and changed into a black turtleneck sweater, a red tartan now-mini kilt, and gray woolly tights. She laced up her Dr. Martens boots and threw on the bomber jacket that her groovy godmother had given her, hoping she looked much less Beatrix Potter–like than she had a few days before.

Ursula grabbed the duplicate volume of the *Scottish Historical Review* and put it into her satchel, noticing that her desk had been neatly reorganized by Alice. A large red cardboard folder containing her handwritten notes for the *Cherwell* article and her reporter's notebook had been placed in the center. She opened the notebook and added her thoughts from her breakfast with Wenty:

—If Wenty thought he heard India and Dr. Dave "shagging" (not knowing India was actually with Otto), could he have been angry enough to return to Dr. Dave's staircase later that night and kill his girlfriend?

Ursula tore off her new notes and left them inside the folder. Then she put her notepad in her satchel and dashed out, but not before picking up Vain Granny's letter too—she'd read it later when she needed a break from the Scottish Covenanters.

It was almost ten by the time she reached the library, where Ms. Brookethorpe, who was restacking shelves of ancient manuscripts, acknowledged her with a faint nod of the head. Nancy was already seated, frantically chewing the end of her pencil and sighing loudly as she pored over the master volume of the *Scottish Historical Review*.

"I need help. What does this mean?" she whispered as Ursula settled herself at the next desk. Nancy pointed at a passage on page 157, which began:

In "Doctrine, Discipline, Regiment, and Policie" the Scottish Kirk "had the applause of forraine Divines" and was "in all points agreeable unto the Word" until the crown had begun its policy of episcopal subversion.

"It's about the dispute," Ursula started to say, "between the English and Scottish over Rome—"

Before she had a chance to go on, Ursula realized the shadow of Ms. Brookethorpe was looming over them.

"Silence in this reading room is nonnegotiable," said the librarian grandly.

"Sorry," Nancy apologized.

Ms. Brookethorpe nodded her acknowledgment and then, to Ursula's surprise, said to her in a low voice, "Can you come into the office please? I need to . . . check something . . . on your library card."

Ursula followed her into the small office behind the librarian's desk, a room that was humble in comparison to the rest of the Hawksmoor

Library. A large photocopier dominated it, and rows of box files lined the shelves on the walls. In one corner was a tiny, rather grubby butler's sink, next to which a kettle, a box of Yorkshire tea bags, and a pint of long-life UHT milk stood on the Formica countertop. Ursula started to hand over her library card, but the librarian gestured for her to put it away. She flicked the kettle on, and then stood stiffly facing Ursula, looking distinctly uncomfortable.

"I hear you're writing about the murder for *Cherwell*," she said nervously. "You mustn't mention me by name in your article. No one can know that I told you what I did. Dr. Erskine has a lot of . . . Well, I suppose you could say . . . he has a lot of influence over the History department in the university. I wouldn't want anything to jeopardize my work with the Bible fragments."

"I completely understand," said Ursula as sympathetically as she could. "All my sources are anonymous." (She imagined this must be how professional journalists reassured their sources.) "I'll never mention your name, I swear."

Ms. Brookethorpe poured the boiling water from the kettle onto a tea bag in a mug and slowly stirred the brew as she spoke.

"Thank you, that's a relief. Now, I imagine you'll be wanting to get back to those Apocalyptic Covenanters."

"Yes," said Ursula. "But there's just one thing I wanted to check first. About the night of the murder."

"Oh?" The librarian looked anxious.

"Are you *sure* you saw Dr. Dave crossing Great Quad that night?"

"I've already told you what I saw. So far the police haven't asked to speak to me and I'm hoping it will stay that way. I don't want to be caught up in all this."

"Did you see anyone else?"

"You really mean it when you say no one will know that I have spoken to you?"

"I absolutely promise," Ursula reassured her.

"All right then. I *suppose* I did see someone else," the librarian said finally.

"Why didn't you mention them before? When I spoke to you last night?" asked Ursula, a little annoyed.

"It was late . . . I . . . I don't know . . ." Ms. Brookethorpe was hesitant. "I must have forgotten. I didn't think a couple of undergraduates skulking around college was important."

"Two?" asked Ursula. "Together?"

"No, they weren't together. I can't be completely sure of the exact time, but about an hour after I noticed Dr. Erskine walking towards the Monks' Cottages, someone ran across the lawn towards the JCR staircase from the direction of the Old Drawing Room."

If everyone was telling her the truth, thought Ursula, it must have been Otto who had run past.

"Are you sure the person was running?"

"Yes. I remember thinking it quite odd that he was in such a hurry at that hour. It must have been almost one a.m."

"He?"

"It was definitely a man—I could see the silhouette of a tailcoat in the moonlight. I don't know who it was, though, I'm afraid."

"Did he return to the Old Drawing Room?"

"I don't think so. The only other person I saw that night was another man coming across from the Old Drawing Room to the JCR. Another undergraduate in tails, this one with fair hair. It was around two a.m. by then."

"How do you know?"

"I remember thinking how sleepy I suddenly felt and checking my watch. Bible fragments make you lose track of time, you know."

It seemed as though Wenty had been telling the truth. Ursula felt relieved.

"How long do you think it was until the fair-haired boy returned to the Old Drawing Room?"

"Neither of them returned to the Old Drawing Room," said Ms. Brookethorpe.

"Are you sure?" Ursula pressed her.

"The only thing I saw after that was someone heading from the entrance of the JCR staircase towards the gate tower. It was definitely the same student."

She must be mistaken, Ursula told herself. Wenty had returned to his room after visiting Dr. Dave's staircase.

"How can you be sure?" she asked.

"When I left and went down to the lodge, I said good night to the porter—Deddington's boy—and left through the main entrance onto Christminster Lane. I saw someone riding away from college on a bicycle. I remember because I was amused to see him swaying from side to side along the lane. He must have been rather drunk."

"And you say you know for sure that it was the same person who had crossed the lawn a few minutes earlier?"

"Oh, yes. I'm very good on hair, as you know. It was the blond one. Wentworth Wychwood."

●

. . . though there be new out-casts betwixt Christ and Scotland, I hope that the end of it will be, that Christ and Scotland shall yet weep in one another's arms . . .

It was hopeless. The impact of the Scottish Reformation on the religious scene in the seventeenth century just couldn't hold Ursula's attention in the way that India's murder could. She couldn't concentrate at all, so she took out Vain Granny's letter and read it.

Dearest Ursula,

I do hope you wear the Yves St. Laurent scent every day. It's irresistible to young men—it smells of Paris. I am sure you are having a marvelous time, but please do not spend too much time in the library studying or you will turn into one of those ghastly bluestockings. Look at what's happened to that poor woman Mrs. Thatcher. Went to Oxford, became prime minister, closed the coal mines, and is now the most hated person in the country! Do spare yourself that fate by going to as many parties as you can,

flirting like mad, drinking masses of champagne, and missing at
least half of your tutorials. Meeting your first few husbands while
young and beautiful is imperative.

Your most loving,
Grandmama Violette

P.S. More ball gowns in attic if required.

Grandmama! Ursula sighed. She did miss her a lot. What a character Violette was. She put the letter in her satchel and turned back
to the Early Covenanters, rereading the impenetrable paragraph, but
her mind drifted. It was no good. She pulled out her reporter's notebook and jotted down more notes:

—Either Brookethorpe is lying, or Wenty is. But why would
Brookethorpe lie? Why would she make up a story about an
undergraduate cycling out of college in the middle of the night?
She wouldn't. But then, why would Wentworth lie? Why would
he have said he'd gone back to the Old Drawing Room when in
fact he'd left Christminster?
—Trott said, "It's usually the husband or the boyfriend." If
Wenty is lying, is it because he was somehow involved in the
murder? But if he had killed his girlfriend, would he really have
cycled off out of the college straight afterwards, presumably
covered in blood?

Ursula's analysis of her investigation was interrupted by Nancy's
manicured hand depositing a note on the open page of her book. The
scrawled writing read:

I'm freaking out. I cannot understand any of this stuff. I don't know why
they accepted me. I am not smart enough for Oxford. They're gonna find
me out soon and send me back. I'm gonna be like a return at Saks.
By the way, you look super-duper cute today in that mini.

Ursula scribbled a message back and handed it to her.

Glad you approve of outfit. Let's visit Dr. Dave later? He could help with Covenanters.

P.S. I overheard Trott earlier. The autopsy's happening this morning.

Ursula saw Nancy's eyes widening as she read the last sentence. "What are we waiting for?" she demanded, springing up from her desk. "Come on!"

Chapter 24

This is a *really* pretty place to be dead," said Nancy, gazing admiringly at the classical stone facade of the Radcliffe Infirmary as they alighted from the Spree, having sped along the Woodstock Road to the hospital. Ursula had to agree that the hospital did look more like an ambassadorial residence than a medical center. Elegant stone pillars and wrought-iron gates separated it from the road, and a fountain featuring a stone figure of Triton bubbled in the center of the front lawn. The ambulances parked outside looked almost incongruous.

"Nancy, we could get into *terrible* trouble," Ursula warned her as they made their way through the main gates. "How on earth are we going to persuade them to let us inside?"

"Hey, I've talked my way into Danceteria every Thursday night in New York since I was fourteen. This'll be a breeze," her friend replied.

Did they Send Down students for gate-crashing autopsies? Ursula wondered. And did she really have the stomach to witness a human dissection, anyway? She started imagining all sorts of gruesome sights.

Nancy marched boldly past the fountain and straight up the steps to the main entrance. Ursula had no choice but to follow. Inside, a matron and a junior nurse dressed in matching blue uniforms, white aprons, and stiff little white hats were sipping cups of tea at the front desk. Ursula was extremely surprised to see that they were talking with the creepy man who had been in the porter's lodge earlier.

"Oh my God," she whispered to Nancy. "That's the *Daily Mail* journalist again. Don't say a thing to him, okay?"

Nancy nodded.

"I heard that Lady So-and-So was always going to come to a sorry end," the younger nurse was telling him. "The mother was a drug addict . . ."

Excited, Neil Thistleton scribbled violently on his notepad.

Suddenly spotting the two interlopers, Matron nudged the younger nurse. She scolded her, "That'll do, Jean." Turning to Thistleton she said, "I'm sorry, sir, but you will have to leave now."

"Look, I know the autopsy's going on in there—" replied Thistleton.

"It's time to go," Matron cut him off.

Ursula glanced around at the grim institutional interior of the hospital. The long corridor beyond the nurses' station, painted a drab green, stretched on seemingly forever. Stretchers and wheelchairs were abandoned at intervals along it. Scruffy signs hanging from the ceiling announced, with false jollity, the name of each ward— "Primrose Ward," "Daffodil Ward."

Nancy and Ursula approached the desk. Before either girl could say a thing, the matron barked, "Visiting hours don't start till four!" She then turned back to Thistleton, saying, "We can't have the general public wandering around the hospital. Please be on your way."

The journalist turned on his heel, irritated. As he did so, his beady gaze landed on Ursula.

"You were there, this morning, at Christminster," he said, eyeing her coldly.

Ursula felt cornered, but managed to say, "I think you've made a mistake."

"No. I know about you. You're the one who found her, aren't you?"

How on earth did he know? Ursula was staggered.

"It's true, isn't it?" he badgered.

"I have no idea what you're talking about," she replied, turning her attention to Matron. "Excuse me—"

"Visiting hours don't start till four," the nurse snapped again.

"We're not visiting a patient," Nancy told her, leaning on the counter. "We are here to observe Dr. Rathdonelly's autopsy today. For our . . . ahem . . . dissertations." Nancy was a superb liar, thought Ursula to herself.

"Oh, you're medical students. Right, well, that's different," said Matron, suddenly smiling. "Go straight down to the end of the main corridor, turn left, third right. Look for the black double doors with opaque glass. There aren't any signs to the mortuary. There are surgical overalls hanging on the pegs before you go in. Use those."

"Wait! *You two* are going to Lady India's autopsy?!" protested Thistleton. "Why can't I 'observe'?"

Matron smiled superciliously at the journalist. "Observing a dissection is a privilege limited to members of the university," she informed him.

"But—!"

"Please leave now, sir."

"Bloody privilege," Thistleton cursed as he finally left.

•

THE GIRLS NERVOUSLY approached the morgue via a long corridor. They could soon hear the sound of Doc's distinctive Scottish tones echoing from the other end of the passage.

". . . are you writing this down? I know Trott wants my report *ASAP*. My first conclusion, on examination of the neck injury, is that the murder weapon was most likely the missing portion of the broken champagne saucer found clutched in the victim's hand . . ."

The double doors to the morgue swung back and forth as a stream of visitors—technicians, nurses, and police officers—rushed in and out. The girls took green surgical overalls off the pegs outside the morgue and put them on over their clothes. To Ursula's amazement, no one took the least bit of notice of her or Nancy as they changed. They carried on listening to Doc's analysis while they did so.

". . . On inspection, I have found a small shard of glass measuring three millimeters by one millimeter lodged inside the left edge of the slash wound. Its slightly curved character leads me to believe that it is a tiny piece of the aforementioned missing portion of the broken champagne saucer found in the victim's left hand at the scene."

"Killed with her own champagne saucer," said Nancy. "That's horrible."

"I know," Ursula agreed.

Three junior doctors in white coats strolled into the morgue, and Nancy quickly tagged along behind them, Ursula on her heels.[*] Once inside the room, the girls hung back close to the door, trying to be discreet.

The morgue was glittering in its brightness. Everything was white, shiny, glaring—white tiles on the floor, white tiles on the walls, dazzling steel benches, steel sinks and taps on hoses. A set of X-rays was illuminated on a light box on the far side of the room.

"Ugh!" Ursula gasped suddenly.

Close by, on a small dissection table, sat a pair of hands, *just* hands, nothing else attached. A technician, wearing rubber gloves, picked one hand up and gently lifted one finger, pressed it onto a pad of ink, and then pressed the same finger onto a sheet of paper, producing a print. Ursula recognized the dark red polish on the nails. The hands belonged to India.[†]

Ursula's eyes soon came to rest on the porcelain slab in the center of the room. There lay India, naked, blueish white, only she didn't look much like India anymore. Her chest had been cut open in a Y-

---

[*] Before the advent of DNA testing in the late 1980s, autopsies were much more casual affairs than they are now. Since there were no DNA samples to contaminate, police, hospital staff, and medical students would come and go fairly freely from the morgue.

[†] Until the late 1980s in Britain, it was accepted practice to sever a victim's hands in order to take a perfect fingerprint. The families never knew.

shape, from the side of each shoulder to her abdomen. Her organs had been placed in clear plastic tubs, arranged neatly on a metal trolley, and variously labeled "Stomach Tub," "Liver Tub," and so on. Her scalp and a section of her skull had been removed to retrieve her brain, which had been placed on another small table near her head. Of course, she had no hands. Had Ursula attempted to imagine a scene of such sterile horror, she couldn't have.

"Ee-ee-e-ew—this is terrible," wailed Nancy into her ear.

"I just can't believe it," Ursula said sadly.

She was amazed by how crowded the room was. There was a uniformed policeman with a Dictaphone recording Doc's every word. A medical secretary stood next to him, scribbling down the report in shorthand. Various doctors and medical students in white coats looked on, transfixed. Lab technicians dashed around cleaning large knives and saws that wouldn't have looked out of place in a butcher's. Nurses wandered in and out, replenishing the staff with instant coffee. In death, as in life, India attracted quite an audience.

At the center of the scene was Doc, rubber-booted, gloved, and covered in a green operating gown and cap. In one hand he wielded an elongated pair of tweezers, in the other a steel ruler. His chomped on a cigar jammed in one corner of his mouth in the manner of a man relaxing at his club rather than dissecting another human being. Everyone listened intently as he went on, cigar in situ, saying, "For the record, please state that I am defining the wound as a 'slash' wound of the type typically produced by the exquisitely sharp edge of a piece of broken glass. The slash is twelve and a half centimeters long. It is longer than it is deep, and the wound is deeper on the *left* side of the neck than the *right*."

"So the attacker was right-handed," whispered Nancy.

"I guess," Ursula whispered back.

"Which rules almost everyone in as a potential suspect," Nancy said regretfully, her voice hushed.

Doc went on. "The depth of the wound is twenty millimeters. The wound is straight-edged, which leads me to assume that the chin was raised during the attack. This stretching of the skin leads to a clean wound, rather than the jagged cut seen when a weapon is drawn over loose skin."

"What sort of person lifts someone's chin to kill them?" Nancy asked quietly. "That's *so* weird."

"I can't imagine." Ursula shuddered.

"The jugular vein has been severed, causing the pooling of blood that was seen at the scene of the crime, and consistent with venous bleeding," Doc continued. "However, I must caution that the severing of the jugular vein was *not* the cause of death. There was not enough blood loss for that."

Ursula got out her reporter's notebook, which she hoped could pass for a medical student's, and started taking notes. She'd never get the details right otherwise.

"On *close* examination, it is apparent that the jugular vein was divided during the attack. There is a hole—measuring half a centimeter—that left the wound open to the environment. This leads me to conclude that, since the victim could not and did not die as a result of blood loss, that an air embolism is the official cause of death. An air embolism is caused by aspiration into a cut jugular vein while standing or sitting with the neck at a higher level than the thorax. It literally sucks air from the outside into the vein. The air remains in the right side of the heart. Death is usually immediate."

"Do you think the killer just meant to wound her?" asked Nancy, her tone still low.

"Maybe," Ursula replied.

"This is a peculiar case," continued Doc. "Often when someone is stabbed in the neck they don't die immediately. They're still capable of moving. They struggle. This girl didn't. There are no defense wounds on her arms or hands. No contusions. There was no blood anywhere else apart from on her neck and dress. The room was undisturbed with no sign of a fight. She was attacked in the exact position she was found, with her upper body slightly raised on the upper part of the chaise longue. The hypostasis in her left foot confirms this."

"I knew it!" said Nancy triumphantly.

A medic tapped her on the shoulder. "Sssshhhhhh!" he scolded.

"Sorry," Nancy apologized. Then, seemingly out of the blue, more quietly, she said, "Hey, what are you gonna wear on your date tonight?"

"Er . . . I'm not really thinking about it right now," murmured Ursula, trying to concentrate on her note taking. "Maybe I'll just wear this." She looked down at her mini kilt, which was definitely trendy enough for a date.

"You cannot wear a woolen skirt, however short it is, on a romantic dinner date!" Nancy told her, highly indignant. "I'll lend you something. I've got the perfect dress. You'll die when you see it."

Ursula smiled, looking forward to wearing one of Nancy's party dresses again. "If you're sure," she said gratefully.

Meanwhile, Doc was still pondering India's murder out loud. "Now, why would a girl lie on a chaise longue and allow her throat to be slit without defending herself? Did she know her attacker extremely well? So well that when he came up behind her she had no reason to suspect any ill intent? How did the murderer manage to break a glass without alerting his victim to the fact that she was in imminent danger? Was the glass perhaps already broken when the murderer arrived on the scene? Did India break the glass herself? Luckily, I have no need to answer such questions. My job is purely to define the cause of death for the courts. My conclusion is that the girl died as a result of an air embolism."

A technician rushed up with a note in his hand. "Doc, the bloods are here," he said. "The victim had extremely high levels of alcohol in her blood. No indication of any narcotics. The stomach contents show that she hadn't eaten for at least ten or twelve hours before the attack took place. The alcohol would have been absorbed into her bloodstream much more quickly than if she had eaten. She would have felt highly intoxicated."

Ursula nudged Nancy. "No drugs. Wow. Looks like Otto didn't give her that half tab of acid."

"But why would he lie about that?"

"No idea," said Ursula softly. "I think he's covering something up. I don't know what, and I don't know why. But I just don't believe India would have spent the night in his arms without chemical help."

"But she was 'highly intoxicated,'" Nancy reminded her.

"True. But was she intoxicated *enough* to feel as though she was in lust with Otto?"

"I see what you mean. I'd have to drink the entire Champagne region dry before I even kissed the guy on the cheek," Nancy conceded.

Doc was finishing up, replacing his instruments and untying his gown. A nurse took it from him, and he handed her his used gloves. He suddenly stopped and jokingly whacked the side of his own head.

"Oops—forgot something," he said. He removed the cigar from the corner of his mouth and addressed the medical secretary. "Add this to the report: The fingerprints on the glass were smudged, so they're not much use. But there was a tiny trace of sodium dimethyl-dithiocarbamate on that shard of glass."

"Sodium dimethyl-whatty?" repeated Ursula, attempting to scrawl down the name of the chemical as best she could

"I haven't a clue," said Nancy. "But I know someone who would."

"Who?" asked Ursula.

"My brother, Frank. I told you, he's doing medicine. He knows all this kind of stuff. I'll call him as soon as we get back."

"Call him?!" Ursula was shocked. "You can't *telephone* America from a college pay phone. You'd need at least forty or fifty ten-p coins. Send him a telegram instead."

"Okay, sure," said Nancy. "Fingers crossed he can help."

"Right, inform the family that the funeral can go ahead on Thursday," Doc told the uniformed policeman. Then he said to a junior doctor, "Put everything back in and sew her up."

"Yes, Doc," said the young man, moving to retrieve the organs from the tubs.

Then Doc suddenly changed his mind, saying, "On second thought, I'll keep her brain for the collection in my office. I've never had an aristocrat's brain before.* It'll be fascinating for lectures."

With that, he plopped Lady India's brain into a large jar of formaldehyde and gazed lovingly at the spongy-looking object as it sank to the bottom. "Beautiful girl, beautiful brain," he said cheerfully, before adding, "ugly death."

Clutching his trophy, Doc bade a jaunty farewell to the staff. Just as he was about to push open the swing doors, he caught sight of Ursula and Nancy. He stopped. Oh dear, thought Ursula to herself, we're in deep trouble now.

"Ah, Holmes and Watson, isn't it?" he said with a friendly tone.

"We prefer Cagney and Lacey,"† replied Nancy. "More modern."

"Quite right. Didn't realize you two were medics. Keep up the good work. We need more women doctors."

"We sure do," replied Nancy, flashing a confident smile at the pathologist.

"Well," he said, "I hope this morning kept you entertained."

"It was awesome, Doc," Nancy told him sincerely. "But you've given me a phobia of champagne glasses. Almost makes me never want to go to another cocktail party again. *Almost.*"

---

* As pathologists couldn't take a DNA sample from a body part in 1985, if they suspected that a case might be reopened during the next thirty years, they were legally obliged to preserve the relevant body part. Until the late 1980s, pathologists kept many victims' brains and organs on their office shelves, "just in case."

† *Cagney & Lacey* (1982–88) was the first "feminist" buddy cop show. Worried that the female detective characters were too aggressive, CBS canceled the show in 1983. Furious fans staged a letter-writing campaign, forcing the network to reverse its decision. The show won fourteen Emmys.

Chapter 25

The sight of Horatio Bentley holding court beneath the gate tower that afternoon was a soothing antidote to the bleak hours spent in the morgue that day. While Nancy popped into the lodge to check for a missive from Next Duke, Ursula listened with amusement as he assigned various gossipy stories to a couple of student hacks.

". . . I heard the Corpus Christi sherry party was a *huge* embarrassment," he said, grinning gleefully. "One of the Latin scholars drank all the sherry before the guests arrived. A dry night was had by all. Gillian, you can write that up?"

"Sure," a girl agreed, scribbling details on a notepad.

"Bobby, can you take on an item about Harry Bladon? He's been censured by the Keble JCR committee. The entire college is incensed by his hogging of the college pay phone."

"Who's he telephoning?" asked Bobby, an eager-looking boy.

"Seccies. The rumor is that he's so intellectually insecure he won't ask female undergraduates out. Thinks secretarial college students are easier to talk to. Pathetic dweeb."

"No problem," replied Bobby.

"*Au revoir*, hackettes!" cooed Horatio to the two writers as they dashed off after their stories. "And *bonsoir*, beauty," he added, noticing Ursula. "How's your day going?"

"Rather gothic, actually," she replied. Then, dropping her voice, she continued, "We've been at India's autopsy."

"How grisly," he gasped. "What did you discover—"

Before Ursula could answer, she was interrupted by a shriek from Nancy.

"Guys. I don't believe it. A note from Next Duke!" Nancy was as pink and quivery as an overwhipped Angel Delight. "Listen."

Dear Miss Feingold (if you must insist on using my title, I'll insist on using yours),

"*So* witty!" she giggled. "I dig funny guys. Oh my God, wait until you hear this."

Her voice going up an octave every few lines, she read on:

I was touched to receive your note and your extraordinarily generous offer to dry-clean my jacket. I cannot accept. Were the garment in question to be cleaned every time someone spilled a glass of champagne or vomited on it, it would spend so much time at Jeeves that I would never actually get to wear the tatty old thing.

"Next Duke's *so* self-deprecating. I mean, did you *ever* see a better-dressed guy? How hot," Nancy continued, enraptured.

But Ursula's mind was back at the hospital.

"If India didn't have any narcotics in her blood, that means that Otto didn't give her any. Doesn't it?" she asked out loud.

"What are you on about?" Horatio looked thoroughly confused.

"Sorry. Otto told us he spiked India's drink with LSD, but the autopsy results contradict that."

"Oh my God, listen to this!" squeaked Nancy, utterly engrossed in Next Duke's letter.

As a token of my appreciation of your offer, may I invite you to join me—

Ursula interrupted her friend. "So if he didn't give the LSD to India, what did he do with it? Perhaps he gave it to someone else? But who? Maybe he didn't give it to anyone at all. Perhaps it's still in the pocket of his tailcoat. And if it is, then—"

But Nancy wasn't listening. She went on,

—for a picnic breakfast at sunrise on Port Meadow this Saturday?

"Hang on a momento," exclaimed Horatio. "Am I to believe that Paddington is asking you on some kind of date?"

"Paddington?" Nancy looked puzzled.

"Everyone calls him that. He looks so like an orphaned teddy bear."

"He does not!" she retorted. "Next Duke is the most beautiful boy I have ever wanted to make out with. And the poshest."

"I feel a diary item coming on," said Horatio. "This is actual *news*. Algernon Dalkeith has *never* been on a date since he started at Merton two years ago, despite the attentions of many wannabe duchesses."

"Who?" asked Nancy, flummoxed.

"Sorry. Until he inherits the dukedom, the eldest son of a duke bears a different name and title to his father, the current Duke of Dudley. Next Duke's real name is Algernon, Marquess of Dalkeith," Horatio explained.

"Next Duke's *way* easier," countered Nancy.

"What a shame you can't go on the sunrise date with him," Ursula commented.

"What do you mean I can't go?"

"Rowing squad. We meet on Saturday again at six, remember?"

Nancy's face fell. "My parents would *literally* stop paying for college if I turned down a date with the next Duke of Dudley. This is a *major* social opportunity for me."

"Ursula, can't you make an excuse for her?" asked Horatio. "For the sake of the Feingold clan. For the sake of *Cherwell*. This is going to be a marvelous John Evelyn story."

"I guess. Just this once," she said reluctantly.

"Thank you, Ursula. I'll pay you back, I promise. Okay, I'm gonna go compose a poetic reply. See you at four thirty—I'm psyched to try Marmite with Mrs. Deddington."

With that, Nancy dashed off in the direction of her room, clutching Next Duke's note tightly to her chest.

"I'm going to try and pin down Otto," Ursula told Horatio. Her essay would just have to wait until after her dinner with Eg.

"Good luck, sweetie," he said. "I'm off to the cinema. *Another Country*'s[*] showing again. It'll be even better the sixth time."

Having bid Horatio good-bye, Ursula set off towards Monks' Cottages. She'd started to feel convinced—she wasn't quite sure why; it was just a sense she had—that if she could learn the whereabouts of the missing half of the acid tablet, she might be one step closer to figuring out what had really happened on Sunday night.

Monks' Cottages had a far cozier feel than any of the quadrangles Ursula had so far seen in Oxford. It could be accessed by a narrow passageway on the eastern side of Great Quad, and consisted of a collection of low higgledy-piggledy stone dwellings built around a tiny grassy courtyard with a cobbled path running around the edge. There was an ancient well in the middle, overshadowed by an old apple tree, and the borders were filled with autumnal seed heads. She did hope she would be billeted here in her second year.

Ursula could hear the washing machines turning over on the ground floor of Staircase A, and noticed a couple of students wandering out of the student laundry lugging their washing. Otto's

---

[*] *Another Country* (1984) starred '80s pretty boys Rupert Everett, Colin Firth, and Cary Elwes as boarding school pupils tangled in a web of homosexuality and spying. Shot like a Ralph Lauren ad, the film was as chic as it was camp.

rooms, she knew, were in Staircase D, where India's had been as well.

A chill enveloped Ursula as soon as she stepped inside the arched entrance. India's name was, of course, still on the board listing the staircase's occupants—she had been in Room 3. Otto was in Room 4. Both rooms were on the second floor.

Ursula headed up the staircase towards Otto's room, praying that he would be in this afternoon. As she reached the top of the stairs, the first thing that caught her eye was the blue-and-white police tape across the front of India's room. "Crime Scene Do Not Enter," read the words on it. Next, she spotted a hunched heap on the floor outside the door to Otto's room. As she drew closer, it became apparent that the heap was human. Arms hugging its legs, head buried in its knees, the heap was hiding its face. Whoever it was, Ursula thought to herself, was in a pathetic state.

"Erm . . . hello?" she said softly.

The heap responded by burying its head even deeper in the folds of its clothes. It was then that Ursula clocked the clunky brogues and thick maroon tights protruding from the bottom of a particularly unappealing gray flannel skirt. There was only one person in college who dressed like a geography teacher. Ursula knew instantly that the heap before her was none other than Claire Potter.

"Claire?" she asked. "Are you okay?"

"*Fine,*" grunted the heap, sounding annoyed.

Claire Potter momentarily lifted her head and looked at Ursula. Her face was red and blotchy, her eyelids swollen. Submerged in the inflated puffiness of her complexion, her eyes appeared to have shrunk to the size of two tiny currants.

Ursula was concerned. "Claire, what's happened?"

"Nothing. That's what. *Nothing!*" came the angry reply.

"Nothing?"

"He's ignoring me. Pretending nothing happened."

"Who? Do you want to talk about it?" Ursula asked, sitting down next to her. She noticed the other girl was clutching a pen and paper in one hand.

"No," retorted Claire, and started frantically scribbling on the notepaper. Ursula looked over the girl's shoulder as she wrote.

> *Prince Otto Schuffenecker,*
> *You are informed that your membership of the Christminster College Crosswords and Ice Cream Society has been revoked, nulled, voided, and canceled.*
>
> > *Claire Potter*
> > *President*
> > *Christminster College Crosswords and Ice Cream Society*

Tears spurting from her already swollen eyes, Claire heaved herself up from the floor and pinned her note to Otto's door.

"I never even invited him in the first place!"

"Invited him to what?"

"My Crosswords and Ice Cream club."

"Did he come?"

"Yes."

"But that's *so* strange," Ursula said. Why would Otto have claimed he spent Sunday night locked in an embrace with India if he was at Claire's crosswords club?

"What, that someone like *that* would want to be with someone like *me*? Is that what you're saying is 'so strange'?" Claire asked bitterly.

"No, no, of course not," said Ursula, trying to calm the girl, although, if she was brutally honest, she did think it odd that Otto would have chosen to spend the evening after Wenty's party with Claire rather than India. "Just tell me what happened."

Claire shook her head. "I can't."

"Why?" asked Ursula.

"It's too embarrassing. I just want to forget about it." She turned and started to walk back downstairs.

"Claire, wait. This could be really important. I need to find out who killed India. It's scary, not knowing who did it. Having a murderer wandering around Oxford. Or even in Christminster."

Claire looked spooked and paused at the top of the stairs. "I couldn't tell the police what really happened," she croaked. "I lied to them in my interview. What's going to happen to me?" Her voice rose higher with panic.

"Listen, I think you can help solve this case. No one will know what you say to me. But you've got to start being truthful with someone."

"I know," Claire said, hanging her head. "But not here. I don't want to run into *him*." She beckoned to Ursula to follow her.

A few minutes later she found herself in the student laundry at the bottom of the neighboring staircase, watching Claire angrily unload a large tumble dryer full of clothes.

"I'll fold," offered Ursula when she saw Claire flick the iron on.

"Thanks. Look, you can't tell *anyone*," the girl entreated, laying out an ugly salmon pink nightdress on the ironing board. It looked like the kind of thing a great-aunt living in a retirement home would wear.

"You have my word," Ursula promised, shaking out a pair of jeans.

"I'd spent ages getting everything ready for the club. I was wearing a lovely white dress, my old confirmation dress. I had photocopied tons of crosswords from the *Times* newspaper. I had quite a few little tubs of ice cream already dished out for the guests. I put everything on the big table in front of the window in the JCR. It looked really nice. I thought everyone was really going to enjoy themselves, only . . ." Claire bit her trembling lip. She hiccuped. "Only, ugh, well, the thing is . . . no one c-c-c-a-aaaame."

A fat tear rolled the length of her nose, and perched there, wobbling as she spoke.

"I thought you said the club was really busy when we talked at the boathouse yesterday," said Ursula.

"That wasn't *exactly* true," Claire admitted, tapping a finger on the metal base of the iron to test its heat. "I mean, *I* was busy, but the party wasn't."

Ursula frowned. "How?"

"Like I said, no one showed up. I tried to stay cheerful, you know, trying a couple of the crosswords by myself, but after a couple of hours I just felt like such a loser," Claire moaned, pressing the hot iron onto the nightdress. "The ice cream was melting, it was such a waste. But I felt as though I had to stay all evening, in case someone showed up. So I sat at that big table in front of the window and watched to see if anyone would come. After ages and ages of nothing, there was that big argument in Great Quad at midnight. And then I saw India dashing towards the JCR staircase. I was so excited that someone was finally coming to the party! I went to the door, opened it a crack, and listened. I heard someone coming up the stairs, peeked round the door, and sure enough, there was India. I think she was quite drunk because she was stumbling a bit. Her dress was so long that she kept tripping on the hem as she walked, and she was steadying herself against the wall of the staircase. She didn't even notice when her tiara fell off while she was on the landing . . ."

So that's what happened to the tiara, thought Ursula to herself. But that didn't tell her where it was now.

"India didn't notice me. But then no one ever does. When she got to the landing, she didn't turn left to come into the JCR. She went and knocked on Dr. Dave's door."

"Did he answer?"

"No. She knocked a couple of times, but no one came. Then she turned the handle of the door and went in. I heard her call out 'pudding' once she was inside the room."

"'Pudding'? You're sure?"

"Yes. I was weirded out. What was India doing calling a don 'pudding' in the middle of the night?!"

"Did anyone answer her?"

"I don't think so. I mean, I didn't hear Dr. Dave's voice. Just hers. Anyway, he'd already gone."

"You saw him leave the room?"

"No, I didn't, but it was so strange. A few minutes after India had gone into his rooms, I sat back down at the table by the window, and I looked out over Great Quad, and there he was, walking along the path. It looked like he was heading from the Kitchen Quad towards Monks' Cottages."

Ursula racked her brain. Hadn't Ms. Brookethorpe said something similar? About seeing Dr. Dave out in the quad after the argument? Why had he gone outside at that particular moment?

"Did you notice him go down the staircase that night?" she asked Claire.

"That's the weirdest thing. I didn't hear anyone go *down* that night, they only came *up*."

"They?"

Claire looked away.

"This is the embarrassing bit," she mumbled, sounding ashamed. "I was sitting back in the JCR, and then—it must have been about half an hour, or more, after India had gone into Dr. Dave's rooms—I heard footsteps on the staircase again. This time I was determined to recruit a club member. I put on a big smile and went and stood out on the landing. And then, this is really bad . . ." Claire's voice faltered.

"What happened?" Ursula asked her.

"It just looked so pretty, I couldn't help it."

Ursula had no idea what Claire was talking about but tried to look encouraging, hoping the girl would continue.

"I picked up India's tiara. I was going to give it back to her the next morning. But it was so lovely and I thought I'd just try it on for a moment. I'd just put it on my head when Otto appeared. He was carrying a bottle of champagne and two glasses. He saw me! *He* saw *me*. And he said all these really nice things to me."

At this memory, Claire wept copiously, so much so that snot started dribbling from her nose onto her top lip. She wiped at it, unsuccessfully, with the back of her hand.

"Like what?" asked Ursula, wondering, again, where the tiara had ended up.

"He said I was the m-m-most—uu-ggg-hh—exquisite girl he had ever seen."

"Are you *sure*?" Ursula pressed her. Hadn't Otto said he had told India she was "exquisite"?

"Of course I'm sure. No one's ever said anything like that to me before. I'll never forget it. Then he took my hand, and we went into the JCR. We each ate a melted ice cream. He poured champagne for both of us, and once I'd finished it . . . I don't know, it was all so romantic . . . I fell in love with him! I thought he was in love with me. We kissed. It's the first time I've kissed a boy. It felt as though we were floating, in a lilac cloud."

"Claire, have you ever heard of LSD?"

"What does that stand for?"

"Don't worry about it," said Ursula. Poor Claire. She didn't have a clue what had happened to her. "What did you do with Otto?"

"Oh, it was marvelous. We didn't do any crosswords. But we ate ice cream together."

"You're saying Otto ate a tub of ice cream?"

"Yes. He had the chocolate chip."

Finally, the identity of the mystery ice cream eater had been revealed—Otto—and the fate of the other half tab of acid. Ursula knew Otto's story had been messy, that he had been trying to cover something up—and it was this. He'd spent the night on Sunday not, as he must have wished, entwined with India, but tangled up with Claire Potter on the JCR sofa, and he was thoroughly embarrassed about it. Unless, of course, Claire was making the whole story up. But how would Claire know all the details Otto had mentioned if she were lying? She seemed sincere enough. Ursula had to believe that Claire was the honest Welsh lass she appeared to be.

"So how did the night end?"

"He fell off the sofa. I helped him get up and put him in the wing-backed chair. He said all these lovely German-y words to me. Like 'libb-ling,' something like that. Then he passed out. So I went to my room. Now he's acting like nothing happened. He walked straight past me in the porter's lodge the next day. Didn't even say hello, let alone 'libb-ling.'"

"I am so sorry," said Ursula, sensing the other girl's deep pain and disappointment. "Men can be awful."

"I just want to die," sniveled Claire. "I've been a fool, haven't I? Why would someone like him want someone like me? I'm just some Welsh turnip."

"Don't talk like that, Claire. Perhaps you both just . . . made a mistake," Ursula told her, wondering how Otto would react when confronted with the error he had made. "Claire, did you visit Otto late on Monday night?"

"How do you know?!" she gasped, mortified.

"I saw you, from the library window."

"I went to his rooms, but he wasn't there."

That was certainly true, thought Ursula. He had been bawling his eyes out in Nancy's room at the time.

"Then he ignored me again this morning at breakfast. So I decided to take my revenge."

"Revenge?" said Ursula, feeling alarmed.

"You saw the note. I'm banning him from the crossword club. Hopefully that'll hurt him as much as he's hurt me."

With that, Claire flicked off the iron, grabbed her pile of clothes and put them in a basket, and started to head out of the laundry room.

"Claire, wait," Ursula called out. "What did you do with the tiara?"

"I was going to get it back to Lady India, honestly. But then, when it turned out she was dead . . . I was so terrified . . . I hid it. I couldn't tell the police I had the tiara, could I? They might have thought I'd killed her for it . . . and if my parents found out I'd stolen something—a tiara belonging to a murder victim—my dad would go mad. I wouldn't be allowed to stay at Oxford. I don't know what to do with the tiara now. It's still in my knicker drawer."

"Oh, right." Ursula was rather surprised by this news.

"Don't say a thing," begged Claire. "And thanks for listening."

With that, Claire stomped out of the laundry. Ursula sat for a few moments, still astonished by the story she'd heard. She tried to order her thoughts by writing them down in her reporter's notebook.

—It's not impossible to imagine that while on LSD Otto could have mistaken Claire in her white confirmation dress for India, particularly as she had India's tiara on.

—Cannot quite believe that Claire thought it was good idea to hide India's tiara with knickers.

Ursula decided to go back up to Otto's room and leave him a note asking him to come and find her this afternoon in the library. When she reached his door, she noticed that Claire's note had gone. Otto must be inside. Before she knocked she couldn't resist trying the handle of India's room opposite, police tape or no police tape. Unsurprisingly, the room was locked. Ursula crossed back to Otto's side of the landing, knocked on his door, and called out his name.

"Enter," a voice called out weakly from inside.

Ursula pushed open the door. Otto's room was small, untidy but cozy, whitewashed, with medieval oak beams in the ceiling. Two tiny dormer windows on the far side of the room overlooked the Monks' Garden. Otto was standing, face like a tomb, in the middle of the room, dressed in black trousers and a black frock coat embellished with elaborate gold frogging.

"For the funeral. It's on Thursday, at the church at Bratters. I just heard," he said gloomily when he saw Ursula. "I shall turn myself in to the police immediately afterwards. My only question is whether it is appropriate to wear the Austro-Hungarian imperial sash at a wake." He held up a ravishing strip of red-and-white brocade against the coat. "What do you think?"

"I don't think you're going to be turning yourself in when I tell you my news. Or should I call it *your* news?" said Ursula.

Otto threw down the sash on his unmade bed and grasped her by the shoulders. "Tell me," he said.

"Otto, you can't remember killing Lady India because you didn't do it."

"How can you be so sure? I have done many things I can't actually recall doing. When I was fourteen I was found drunk in the schnapps cellar at the *Schloss* dancing the polka with a chicken at three in the morning. I was wearing nothing but shooting socks. I don't remember a thing about it. That doesn't mean I didn't do it."

"Otto, you weren't with India on Sunday night. You were with someone else."

"What?"

"You were snogging a Fresher all night."

Otto's face brightened.

"I knew it was you!" he cried. "When I awoke that morning and there you were, standing before me. Your kilt felt so familiar against my cheek. *Liebling*!"

He grabbed Ursula by the waist and started nuzzling her shoulder.

"Ugh!" she said, pulling away.

"You have gone off me already?" He looked terribly upset.

"I was never on you in the first place. I wasn't the Fresher you were with that night. It was someone much more . . . interesting."

"Ah! You mean Lawnmower! The Dollar Princess. Yes, she would be wonderful for the *Schloss*. She could fund the rethatching of the medieval barns."

"Otto, the girl in question is a lovely Fresher named Claire Potter."

"I know no one of that name."

"But you do, Otto."

"I do?" He looked blank.

"She was at the History drinks with us. She's on my staircase."

"Describe her."

"Okay. She's quite pale. Dark brown hair—"

"She sounds just like India," he interrupted. "No wonder I mistook her for my true *Liebling*."

"Anyway, dark brown hair, cut very short. Glasses. She usually dresses in woolen skirts and brogues."

Otto frowned. "I hope you're not talking about who I think you're talking about."

"She's very upset. Says you keep ignoring her."

"Don't be absurd!" he exclaimed. "Even without my glasses I would never exchange saliva with a girl like that one. I would rather have killed my darling India than kissed that toadlet. She is not rich. She is not from a great family."

"Otto, how can you be such a terrible snob?"

"She is not beautiful," he continued. "In fact she is the ugliest specimen of Fresher I've ever had the misfortune to set eyes on. I have never knowingly spoken to her, so I can't tell you definitively that she is not even interesting, but I suspect, were I to converse with her, which I hope never to, that I would swiftly be proved right. I expect she is as dull as the color of her hair."

"Otto, I'm afraid you've done a whole lot more than converse with her. She's so upset about it all that she's banned you from her Crosswords and Ice Cream Society."

"That note! On my door. I couldn't understand it."

"Look, find your tailcoat. The one you were wearing on Sunday evening."

"Why?" he asked, opening his wardrobe and retrieving it.

"You'll see."

Ursula took the tailcoat from Otto and put her hand into the right-hand pocket. She was sure that what she was looking for would be there. She grasped something small and hard, took out her hand, and showed Otto what was in it: a small pink plastic ice cream spoon.

"You didn't do it, Otto. The night India was murdered, you were eating melted ice cream and snogging Claire Potter."

Chapter 26

"Yeee-uuuuggg-cccchhhhh!"

Nancy had just bitten into her first ever slice of hot buttered Marmite on toast. Her expression was one of pure agony, though she somehow swallowed what was in her mouth.

"Sorry!" she said. "People really eat this for fun here?"

"Most of the students wolf it down," said Mrs. Deddington sniffily.

"Honestly?!" replied Nancy, sounding astonished. "Give me peanut-butter-and-jelly sandwiches any day."

"I *adore* Marmite on toast," Ursula told them, taking a thick slice from the plate. "Mmmmm!" she sighed, munching away. "Delicious."

"Nancy, I'll make you a cup of tea to wash away the taste," said Mrs. Deddington, flicking the kettle on.

The scouts' mess, located in the original college kitchen next to the Buttery Bar, was a rather dark, spartan room, imbued with a very British air of thrift. A pine dresser was stacked with basic blue-and-white-striped crockery, and a few threadbare armchairs were arranged beside a mean-looking gas fire. Scouts took their meals on schoolroom chairs set around the two wooden tables arranged at one end of the room.

"*Iced* tea?" Nancy asked, looking hopeful.

Pouring the boiling water into the truly enormous sixteen-cup teapot, Mrs. Deddington looked very confused.

"Okay, maybe not. Hot tea it is!" said Nancy, trying to sound pleased.

"Give it two minutes to brew," said Mrs. Deddington. "Here, sit in the warm." She beckoned the girls towards the armchairs, rubbing her hands together in front of the stove. "Damp today, wasn't it? Autumn's really here now. But it'll be clear tonight. There'll be a frost in the morning."

"I can't believe you guys think *that* is a heater," Nancy commented, looking at the stove's little flame. "In America we'd call that a cigarette lighter."

Just then, Alice bustled merrily in, dumped her cleaning stuff, took off her rubber gloves, and said, "How about a cuppa, Linda?"

"Just made," said Mrs. Deddington, pouring four cups of tea.

She handed a steaming cup to each of the girls and another to Alice, who leaned against the sideboard as she sipped.

"Do you want to travel up to poor Lady India's funeral with us on Thursday?" Mrs. Deddington asked her. "We're driving."

"I don't think I'm invited," said Alice, looking heartbroken.

"Don't be silly, you must come," insisted Mrs. Deddington. "Everyone knew you were Lady India's favorite scout. It would be remarked upon if you weren't there."

"I suppose, yes, I would like to pay my respects. Say good-bye." Ursula thought she saw Alice's eyes well up a little. Poor thing, she thought, she must be just as devastated as India's friends. "India was a really . . . *special* girl."

"Terrible really, something like that happening here. On the grounds," Mrs. Deddington tutted. "The police seem to be spending all their time in the high provost's lodgings. Why they aren't speaking to *every* student who was at that party of Lord Wychwood's, I'll never know."

"Do you think the killer was someone who was at the party?" asked Ursula.

"I'm talking out of turn. I wouldn't know anything . . . about the party . . ." Mrs. Deddington hesitated as she spoke, as though she was slightly unsure of herself. Ursula noticed her direct a particularly sharp look at Alice, who tried to avoid catching her eye. "See, I wasn't here . . . in Christminster on Sunday night. Can't miss my weekly dose of *Dallas!*"

That was an odd thing to say, thought Ursula—that she wasn't in college on Sunday night. Surely Mrs. Deddington was never in college at night.

"Good episode this week, wasn't it?" said Alice.

"Er . . . yes, one of my favorites," agreed Mrs. Deddington. "Anyway, Alice, let us take you with us to the funeral. I wouldn't have it any other way."

"I suppose, yes, we all need to say good-bye to the dear girl. A proper farewell." Alice looked downcast.

"At least that's settled," said Mrs. Deddington. "Now, more tea, girls?"

Chapter 27

O tto and *Claire Potter*?! *No. Way*," cried Nancy, amazed.

"I know—but don't tell anyone, I promised Claire I'd keep it all a secret," said Ursula, doing up the pale pink satin buttons on the front of the navy velvet coatdress that Nancy had lent for her date with Eg. It was slim-fitting, and Ursula loved its extravagant satin sailor collar. "But Otto can't deny it. I found a plastic ice cream spoon in his tailcoat pocket, exactly like the ones Claire had out that night. She feels like he's ignoring her, but the truth is he can't remember anything about it."

"No wonder she's gutted," said Nancy. Then, admiring Ursula's appearance, she added, "This look is *great* for a date. You don't look slutty, but you don't look completely unavailable. That dress says, '*Maybe* I'll make out with you, but no blow jobs tonight.'"

Ursula tried her hardest not to look too shocked. Her goal was for tonight to conclude with a proper kiss that didn't resemble disgusting school food. She couldn't contemplate anything more complicated.

She had promised to accompany Nancy to see Dr. Dave before heading off to meet Eg at the restaurant. As they made their way from the Gothic Buildings to his staircase, Nancy said, "I'm seriously hoping Dr. Dave's in right now. There is literally no way I am going to be able to produce a sentence, let alone an essay, if he doesn't explain that article to me. I read and reread the first section again and again, and I *still* can't figure out one word of it."

When they reached Dr. Dave's landing, a male student emerged from his rooms, clutching a heap of history texts.

"Looks like he's in," said Nancy, relieved, and knocked on the door.

"Come in," came the reply.

Ursula followed Nancy into Dr. Dave's rooms, which were arranged almost exactly as they had been the first time they had visited for the sherry party. The only thing missing was the great argus. As she took in the familiar sight of the chaise longue to the left of the fireplace, the memory of India's corpse lying there came back to Ursula as vividly as though the girl were still there now.

The evening was starting to close in, and the room seemed dark and slightly claustrophobic. Dr. Dave was not in his usual ebullient form. He was gazing Byronically out of the window over Great Quad, as if lost in thought. Yes, thought Ursula, seeing him in profile, his hair *did* have an undeniably languid swoop to it. Perhaps Ms. Brookethorpe *had* seen him that night, very late, walking towards the Monks' Cottages.

The girls stood there awkwardly, not quite knowing what to do. Suddenly Dr. Dave spun around.

"Forgive me, ladies," he said. "I'm shattered. I've spent half the afternoon being interrogated by that nincompoop Trott in a miserable room at the police station. The twit was trying to get me to confess to India's murder, based on nothing. It was like being persecuted by Oliver Cromwell. Anyway, what can I do for you?"

"It's about the article," said Nancy hesitantly.

"Marvelous analysis of the Scottish Covenanters, isn't it?" Dr. Dave brightened at the thought of it.

Suddenly, Nancy's face started to crumple. To Ursula's and Dr. Dave's utter amazement, she began shedding tears by the gallon.

"Boyfriend problems?" the tutor asked tentatively.

"No, academic ones," Nancy sniffed.

"Here." Dr. Dave offered her the blue silk handkerchief from his top pocket. "Don't tell me bloody Brookethorpe wouldn't lend you the *Historical Review*."

"It's not th-th-that," stuttered Nancy, blowing her nose into the hanky. "I-I-I c-can't understand why you guys let me into Oxford in the first place. I wanna drop out. I'm too dumb. Northwestern was so much easier. I can't understand a word of that article you want me to write about. I mean, what is a forraine?"

"There is a very useful book in the Hawksmoor Library. The *Dictionary of the Older Scottish Tongue to 1700*. If you were to look up the word 'forraine' in it, you would discover that it means nothing more complicated than 'foreigner.' Someone like you, in fact."

"Oh," said Nancy, dabbing her eyes and looking relieved by the simplicity of the answer.

"Gin fizz, Miss Feingold?" offered the don. "When a student comes to me with a crisis of confidence, I say start on the booze. Restores the spirit far more quickly than anything else. Miss Flowerbutton? Drink?"

The girls nodded. Dr. Dave went to his fridge, put ice cubes, sloe gin, sugar syrup, and soda water into a cocktail shaker and shook it violently. He then poured out the fizzy red cocktail and handed each of the girls a glass. Ursula thought the drink was delicious—sharp and tangy and very alcoholic. The tutor drained his in one gulp and immediately poured himself another. Drawing himself up, he then pronounced, "As the great Marcus Aurelius said, 'If you are distressed by anything external, the pain is not due to the thing itself but to your own estimate of it, and this you have the power to revoke at any moment.'"

"That's so deep," said Nancy, cheering up a little.

"Miss Feingold, we dons have a tendency to suggest to students that the world is square. Christ, it's freezing in here."

"Uh?" said Nancy, looking confused again.

Dr. Dave took a match from the mantelpiece, struck it, and lit the fire. Flames began to flicker about the kindling and newspaper underneath the logs.

"The onus is on you, the student," he continued, "to convince us that the world is round. Or hexagonal. Or triangular."

"What? I don't get it!" Nancy said.

"Metaphorically speaking. I asked you to tell me in your essay why S. A. Burrell was wrong about the Scottish Covenanters. Have you asked yourself whether I am wrong to ask you if he is wrong?"

Nancy slowly shook her head. Meanwhile, Dr. Dave, having drained his second glass of fizz, was already most of the way through his third.

"Perhaps I am. The truth is, there is *nothing* wrong with Mr. Burrell's paper. It's a seminal work," Dr. Dave said wistfully. "It's the kind of thing I hope to write myself one day."

"Really?" Nancy looked incredulous.

The don nodded. "Yes . . ." He regarded himself broodingly in the mirror, where he saw a lock of hair had fallen over his forehead and rearranged his swoop to best advantage. "No undergraduate ever understands the work here until their final exams. The whole point of Oxford is to learn how to win an argument. To be so brilliant that you can convince me that the world is a rhombus, or that Cromwell was England's great liberator. In the meantime, just read, read, read. Start with that Scottish dictionary I mentioned."

"Okay," said Nancy.

"If you have any more problems, Miss Feingold, please let me know. What you are experiencing is a common occurrence. As a moral tutor I frequently find myself ministering to troubled undergraduates—"

"—like poor India?" interrupted Ursula, trying to sound as innocent as she could. It was the perfect moment to change the subject.

Dr. Dave nodded and lit a cigarette.

"Ah, India. She had beauty, talent—and troubles." He sighed, exhaling elaborate smoke rings. He plopped down onto the sofa next to Nancy.

"Did she confide in you?" asked Ursula.

"Oh, yes, absolutely," he said. "We became quite, er . . ." He coughed and looked faintly embarrassed. "Yes . . . we were jolly . . .

friendly! Mmm . . . I spent a lovely Christmas at Brattenbury Tower last year. Working on my new book."

"Did India let you get *any* work done?" said Nancy, directing a suggestive wink in his direction.

"*Much* less than I had hoped." Dr. Dave smiled cheekily.

"I'm not surprised," said Nancy.

Dr. Dave shrugged his shoulders casually, as if to say, *No one is.* He didn't seem the faintest bit perturbed by Nancy's hints that he'd been having an affair with a student. In fact, thought Ursula, he seemed pleased, almost flattered by it. She decided the moment was right to dig a little deeper.

"Was that why India was here on Sunday night?" asked Ursula.

"Rather curious, aren't you?" he said, topping up everyone's glass, including his own.

"Actually, I'm writing up the story for *Cherwell*," she explained. "It's so important to get the facts straight, isn't it?"

Dr. Dave regarded her for a moment. Finally he said, "I see. An amateur sleuth with journalistic ambitions. Hmmm . . . I like to encourage young writers. I'll try and help you."

"Thanks. Can we go back to what happened on Sunday night?"

"God knows why she was here that night," sighed Dr. Dave, sounding frustrated. "She had absolutely no reason to come here. No reason at all. If she hadn't, she might still be alive."

"But you were such *good friends*," said Nancy suggestively.

"Ah, but the . . . *friendship*, so to speak, was over," he replied. "I'd told her not to come up here. I couldn't allow her to visit me in college anymore."

"Why?" asked Ursula.

"My fiancée." Dr. Dave smiled gaily.

"*Fiancée*?!" repeated Ursula, staggered by this new piece of information. "You're engaged?"

"It's fairly new. We got engaged in Venice in September. Any close friendships with the girls here—well, all that had to stop. Naturally I told India about Fiammetta—"

"When?" interjected Ursula.

"As soon as India came up this term. She was upset. Blubbed a bit. But she didn't take much notice of what I'd said—she still kept appearing in my rooms last week, wanting advice, chats."

It was no wonder, Ursula thought to herself, that Wenty thought India and Dr. Dave were secretly still seeing each other. Dr. Dave peered at the fire. The flames seemed to be disappearing. He picked up a pair of bellows and puffed at the kindling a few times until it relit.

"India was in love with you?" Nancy asked.

"I don't think so," said Dr. Dave. "But she certainly liked to confide in me. I finally told her—this must have been on Saturday—that she must never, ever come to my rooms again."

"So why *did* she come up here then, on Sunday night?" asked Ursula.

"I've no idea." Dr. Dave shook his head. "I wasn't here."

That's not what Brookethorpe had told her, thought Ursula. Or Claire Potter, for that matter. Both had said that they'd seen Dr. Dave heading towards the Monks' Cottages, just after India had entered the JCR staircase. Surely they couldn't both have been lying?

"Where were you?"

"I was at home."

"Home?" Ursula was surprised. She'd always assumed that Dr. Dave lived in college full-time—at least that's what Otto had said.

"Fiammetta and I bought a house on Cranham Terrace a few months ago. The pretty corner one with the wisteria. I only stay overnight in college when I absolutely have to these days. I was late in here the next morning, as you know, Ursula."

She couldn't deny it. Dr. Dave had certainly not been in his rooms when she had found the body. He hadn't arrived until well after nine in the morning, and so must have spent Sunday night elsewhere. What time had he actually left college? Ursula wondered. Long before India came to his rooms, as he said? Or after the argument took place on Great Quad, per Ms. Brookethorpe and Claire's accounts? The existence of a fiancée further complicated things: Could Fiammetta have been a motive for Dr. Dave to have gotten rid of the girl who was almost stalking him? Or perhaps Fiammetta had found out about India and been driven to attack her fiancé's former fling herself?

The fire was starting to smoke slightly. Dr. Dave puffed at it more fiercely with the bellows and more smoke swirled back into the room. The atmosphere was soon clogged enough for girls and don to be coughing. Dr. Dave dashed over to the window and opened it.

"I think the chimney might be blocked," Ursula volunteered.

"Oh piffle." Dr. Dave covered his nose and mouth with a handkerchief, stood next to the fireplace, and somehow managed to reach his free arm up into the chimney breast without catching fire or choking to death.

"Definitely something stuck up here," he said, pulling at something inside it.

He retrieved his hand, which was holding what looked like a scrunched-up towel.

"Odd," he said, examining it. He unfolded the fabric and almost jumped out of his skin, letting out a yelp of fear at the same time.

"Uuggghh-aaahhh!" he shouted.

Dr. Dave flung the towel to the floor, where it landed in a heap. Ursula saw what had frightened him so much: the towel was caked in dark red dried blood. And on one of its corners, she spotted a familiar motif—an embroidered blue *W*.

Chapter 28

A swanky mixture of potted palms, mirrored paneling, and Parisian toile-covered walls, the dining room at Chez Romain, the famous French restaurant on Turl Street, was the most glamorous—and romantic—place Ursula had ever been. She sat comfortably on a dark green leather banquette at a table laid with an immaculate white linen cloth. Eg, sitting opposite her, was dressed in a crisp pale blue shirt and a sports jacket. He looked as striking as ever. A candle and a vase containing a red rose only upped the romantic ante. Ursula was in, she thought happily, for a major kissing session later on tonight.

"Wine list, sir?" asked a waiter wearing a white tuxedo.

"No, no, thank you," said Eg. "Just a 7Up please."

"A glass of champagne for *mademoiselle*?" asked the waiter in a terrible fake French accent.

Ursula smiled. "Lovely," she said.

Hopefully, she thought to herself, a glass of bubbly would settle her nerves after the discovery of Wenty's bloody towel in the chimney. After he'd contacted the police, Dr. Dave had warned Ursula and Nancy not to mention the towel incident to anyone for the moment, and they'd agreed. That night, Ursula wanted to forget all about murder and enjoy herself with Eg. And anyway, he was so close to Wenty that he was the last person who needed to know about the latest discovery.

The drinks soon arrived on a little silver tray. Ursula took a long swig from her glass.

"Delicious!" she said.

"Good," said Eg, glugging at his 7Up.

"Why don't you have a glass of champagne?" she suggested. "It's *so* scrummy."

"I don't drink," he told her.

"Really?" Ursula asked, rather concerned. How on earth was Eg going to get around to the snogging marathon later without a little bit of alcohol to help things along?

"It's against my religion," he explained.

"Right," she said, trying not to sound too surprised.

"You look very pretty tonight, Ursula," he told her.

Though flattered, she wasn't quite sure what to say. She just tried to smile. Luckily, the moment was interrupted by the return of the faux French waiter.

"Menu?" he said, handing Eg and Ursula a pair of enormous leatherbound volumes.

Ursula opened hers and was so entranced by the array of dishes on offer that she had no idea how she was going to choose between the various delicacies. She noticed that her menu didn't include any prices and hoped she didn't choose anything expensive by mistake.

The waiter hovered impatiently over them as they perused the menus. Finally he said, "*Mademoiselle?*"

"Er . . . I'm not quite ready, sorry," replied Ursula, hoping Eg would order first. If he ordered a starter, she would too. "It *all* looks so delicious."

"*Monsieur?*"

"The melon balls to start, and then the duck *à l'orange*," said Eg. He snapped the menu shut and handed it back to the waiter. "Ready, Ursula?"

"Yes," she said. "May I please start with the prawn cocktail, followed by the salmon *en croûte?*" She hoped her choice would seem ultra-sophisticated.

"*Merci,*" said the waiter. He dashed off to place the order.

Now that the two of them were left alone, Ursula wondered what on earth they would talk about. They had at least two hours of dinner and chitchat to get through before the kissing fest would begin. It seemed a torturously long time to wait.

"I'm so glad you could come tonight, Ursula," said Eg. "Even with everything that's going on in college."

"It's nice to forget about it all for a bit," she replied. "This is a lovely restaurant. Have you been here a lot?"

"No, actually. Never." Eg sounded embarrassed.

"Why did you choose it then?" Ursula found herself giggling. How odd, she thought, to invite a girl on a date to a serious French restaurant that you'd never tried.

Eg looked tense. "Er . . . well, I . . ." he stuttered. "Apparently, this is where you take girls on dates."

He looked round the room, and Ursula followed his gaze, noticing that almost every table was occupied by a loved-up pair, most of them holding hands or staring longingly into each other's eyes.

"Where else have you taken girls on dates before, then?" she asked.

Eg looked deeply uncomfortable. It was most odd that the smoothest, most sophisticated boy Ursula had ever come across seemed to be allergic to any conversation related to going out with a girl.

"Well . . . the thing is . . . I guess, nowhere really," he mumbled.

"Nowhere—?" started Ursula.

"*Mademoiselle. Monsieur,*" the head waiter interrupted.

He was trailed by two younger-looking waiters, each bearing a huge platter covered with an enormous, gleaming silver cloche. The platters were set down in front of Ursula and Eg, and the silver domes simultaneously and flamboyantly removed.

Ursula could barely hide her disappointment when she saw her starter. The cloche had hidden an eggcup-sized glass containing no more than two teaspoonfuls of prawns and Marie Rose sauce. How on earth was she going to make this last?!

"So this is what they call *nouvelle cuisine?*" Eg chuckled as he looked at his platter. Positioned in the center were four melon balls no larger than marbles. "Perhaps I should have taken you for a kebab."

Ursula was just about to dig her spoon into the minuscule portion of prawn cocktail when she heard Eg clear his throat several times. She looked up to find that Eg had his eyes shut tight and his hands clasped in prayer over his plate.

"O Lord," he began, "who has multiplied loaves and fishes, and converted water to wine, O Lord come to our table, as guest and giver, to dine. Amen."

He paused for a few moments, then popped his eyes open. "Sorry," he said.

"Don't be," replied Ursula. "It's lovely to say grace sometimes."

"It's just a bad habit really," joked Eg, plopping a melon ball into his mouth. "Dad says grace at every meal."

"Wow, he must be *very* religious."

"He has to be. He's the bishop of Nairobi. Very strict Anglican."

The last thing Ursula had expected was to discover that someone as suave as Eg was a vicar's son.

"My mother was a Sunday school teacher," he went on. "She met my dad in church. What do your parents do, Ursula?"

Now it was her turn to feel anxious.

"My father, he was . . ." Ursula trailed off for a moment, remembering her father's handsome smile in that treasured wedding photo. "He was a doctor. Mummy was a musician."

"Was?" said Eg slowly, kindly.

"They died when I was six. An accident."

"I'm sorry," he replied sympathetically. "I'd never have imagined anything like that in your background. You're always so cheerful."

"I have so much to be cheerful about," Ursula reassured him. "I was raised by my two grandmothers. They each lost a child, but they are the strongest women I know. They always told me Mummy and Dad wouldn't want me to be sad, they'd want me to enjoy life. So that's what I try and do. I miss my parents every day, but I know they are watching over me, all the time, from heaven."

Ursula couldn't quite believe it when Eg teared up. He dabbed at his eyes with his napkin.

"Oh, Eg, don't be sorry for me," she insisted. "I'm lucky. My grannies are amazing. They love me so much."

"Crikey, look at me," he replied, blowing his nose. "I am the biggest wimp. I cried all the way through *E.T.*"

The trio of waiters soon arrived with the next course. Ursula's salmon *en croûte* was the size of a goldfish, she noted sadly when the next cloche came off, while Eg's duck *à l'orange* was barely bigger than a chick.

"Do you miss Nairobi?" asked Ursula, taking a teeny-tiny bite in an attempt to make her food last.

"It's nice to have a bit of freedom, actually," said Eg. "In Nairobi, I certainly wouldn't be taking a nice English girl out for dinner."

"Really? Why not?"

"Well, actually, I wouldn't be able to take *any* girl for dinner. Kenya's really old-fashioned still. The bishop's son is supposed to marry a good religious girl from our tribe."

Ursula felt confused. If Eg's romantic destiny lay with a girl in Nairobi, why had he invited *her* on a date?

After the main course had been cleared, a waiter wheeled the most extraordinary trolley of puddings up to their table. There were meringues, tarte tatins, gateaux, trifles, crème brûlée—all in enormous quantities. Thank goodness, thought Ursula—her tummy was still rumbling.

As they tucked into dishes heaped with two or three puddings each, Eg said, "But . . . I'm not sure that's for me. When I saw you at Wenty's party—this exquisite English girl—I thought, I've *got* to ask you out for dinner. Even if it's forbidden."

"Forbidden?" She was starting to feel alarmed.

"Look, I'll admit something to you. This is the first date I've been on in Oxford," he said, looking absolutely mortified.

Was this why Wenty had laughed so hard when Ursula had told him that Eg had invited her for dinner?

"Okay," she said. "My turn to admit something. It's my first date too!"

They burst out laughing together. Eg scooped up his last spoonful of pudding. "Come on, let's get out of here."

A little later, as they were walking back to college, Eg put his arm around Ursula's shoulders and pulled her in towards him. They wandered happily along Broad Street, past the cafés and tourist shops, and then turned into Christminster Lane. The only thing that dampened Ursula's mood was the sight of a police car departing from outside the college gates. She tried her hardest not to think about India's murder. She wanted to keep romance uppermost in her mind.

When they reached the landing outside her bedroom, Eg turned Ursula towards him, a hand on each of her shoulders, and said, "Ursula, you are . . ." he looked lingeringly at her lips. ". . . very special."

Finally, thought Ursula, kissing time. She closed her eyes expectantly. Absolutely nothing occurred. Patience, she told herself. She waited a little longer. She felt Eg remove his hands from her shoulders. Then she heard footsteps on the stairs.

Ursula pinged her eyes open. Eg was halfway down the staircase.

"Good night, lovely Ursula," he said, half turning back towards her. "God bless you."

Chapter 29

The temperature in this bathroom is *literally* a violation of my basic human rights. I still don't get why Northwestern has en suites and Oxford basically has horse stables with bathtubs in them."

Nancy, bellowing her complaints from the bathtub in the cubicle next to Ursula's, was not particularly enjoying the bracing draft circulating in the communal bathroom at the bottom of the girls' staircase in the Gothic Buildings at eight o'clock that Wednesday morning.

"Nancy, *no one* turns the heating on in England in October. You just put on another sweater," Ursula told her.

"In the bath?" replied Nancy. "Anyway, how was it?"

"What?" Ursula replied, knowing perfectly well what Nancy was referring to.

"Your romantic dinner. Did you make out?"

This was *so* embarrassing. "I suppose . . . well . . . no," she admitted.

"Why not?"

"I have no idea," said Ursula. "Instead of kissing me at the end of the night, he blessed me!"

"Oh my God, that is *so* creepola." Nancy sounded horrified. "You need to be careful. He might be one of those gross Moonies."*

---

* The Reverend Sun Myung Moon's controversial Unification Church, nicknamed the Moonies, became a huge cult in the 1980s. It brainwashed thousands of virtual strangers into marrying one another at mass weddings.

Just then, Ursula heard the pay phone ringing in the corridor outside for the first time since she had arrived in Oxford.

"It's way too cold to go answer it," called Nancy from her cubicle.

"Otto told us never to answer the pay phone anyway, in case it's
someone's parents," agreed Ursula.

Finally, the ringing stopped. But a few seconds later, it began again.

"Maybe we should get it," said Ursula.

"Rather you get fatal pneumonia than me, darling," replied Nancy.

Ursula got out of her bath, wrapped a towel tightly around her,
and opened the door to her cubicle. Suddenly the ringing stopped.

"Drat," said Ursula. Goose bumps were starting to appear on her
forearms.

A few moments later, a bleary-eyed Claire Potter entered the bathroom, still dressed in her nightgown.

"There's someone wants to talk to you," she said to Ursula. "On
the pay phone. Says it's urgent." Then she nudged Ursula and whispered into her ear, "I can't go to the police about the tiara. I'm too
scared. Anyway, no one is ever going to think of looking in *my* knicker
drawer for anything."

"Claire," said Ursula, her voice low, "you can't get away with keeping it there forever. I better answer that call."

Who on earth would be telephoning so early? she wondered, hoping Granny and Granny were all right. As she stepped from the bathroom into the Gothic corridor, with its archway open to the quad, a
brutal wind snapped against her naked legs and feet.

Ursula shivered as she picked up the handset that Claire had left
hanging off the hook.

"Hello?" she said curiously.

"Unforgettable! Is that you?"

"Wenty?" said Ursula, surprised to hear his voice. Why on earth
was he on the telephone at this hour? "I've told you a million times
not to call me that."

"Okay, sorry, Flowerbutton. Look, there's no time to explain. I'm
at Oxford police station. I was arrested late last night."

"Oh no!" Ursula gasped. Even though she'd known this was going to happen as soon as she'd seen the *W* on that bloody towel, she still felt shocked. That must have been why that police car was leaving college when she and Eg returned from dinner.

"This is the last call I'm allowed today," Wenty continued. "I've spoken to my parents and a lawyer, but I thought maybe you might know something—anything—that could help me get out of here. Because of that *Cherwell* story you're writing."

"What were you arrested for?"

"On suspicion of murder."

Ursula was silent. She didn't know what to say. Even if Wenty was one of the most aggravating people she had ever met, being arrested for murder was a fate Ursula wouldn't wish on anyone.

"Look, I didn't do it. You know that, don't you?" Wenty sounded desperate. "But they're saying they've got new evidence against me since Monday when they first interviewed me in my rooms."

"What kind of evidence?" she asked, although she knew exactly what he was going to say.

"It's a hand towel. Someone found it hidden in Dr. Dave's rooms. It's one of the old Wychwood family ones. Got the bloody *W* on it. 'Bloody' being the operative word." He laughed weakly. "It's covered in blood. The police are saying they tested it last night. Found my blood on it. And India's. They're saying it's proof I was in Dr. Dave's rooms that night. They've shown it to me. It's my towel. There's no getting away from it."

"I know," said Ursula.

"What?" said Wenty. "How do you know?"

"I was in Dr. Dave's rooms when he found it. How did it get there?"

"You don't mean to say you think—"

"I'm not saying I think anything," said Ursula. "Just tell me how it got there."

"I don't know, do I? That's why I'm ringing you!" he wailed.

"But it's yours. How can you not know?"

"I told you, I didn't go into Dr. Dave's rooms that night. God knows how it got there. You've got to believe me. Someone else put it there, and that someone is trying to frame me. I cut my hand when I was trying to wash up a champagne glass during the party. I wrapped my hand in the towel, remember?"

"Yes, yes, I do," replied Ursula, thinking back to the moment when Wenty had tried to wash up the champagne saucers. It had seemed funny at the time.

"That's why my blood's on it. I think I left it on the floor in the bathroom. Someone used that towel when they killed India—to clean up. You've got to find out who hid the towel in Dr. Dave's rooms. That person is India's killer, not me."

The problem with Wenty's story, Ursula mused, was that he wasn't quite the plain, honest cucumber sandwich he would like to be taken for. If Ms. Brookethorpe had been right about seeing him cycling away from college in the dead of night after she had left the library late on Sunday, it meant he had lied about his movements. Being a liar didn't necessarily make you a killer, but it didn't make you *not* a killer either. He could easily have gone back to Dr. Dave's rooms much later that night, long after Ms. Brookethorpe had gone home, and killed India himself. Why else would Wychwood's towel be there, stained with his blood and India's?

"Wenty, I can't help you unless you are truthful with me," Ursula said.

"Can you stop sounding like some kind of righteous headmistress, Flowerbutton? I *am* telling the truth. I didn't kill India."

"Why did you lie about Sunday night?" she said firmly. She didn't care if Wenty thought she sounded like a headmistress if it was a way to get to the truth.

"What do you mean, lie?"

"Wenty, you didn't go back to your room after going to Dr. Dave's staircase."

"Of course I did."

"Someone saw you leaving college. On your bicycle. Around two a.m."

"Who?!" he demanded.

"It doesn't matter who. Wenty, just be honest with me. Did you sleep in your own room that night, or were you somewhere else?"

There was silence at the other end of the line. Finally Wenty spoke. He sounded mortified.

"Well. Look . . . okay, I slept somewhere else."

"Where?"

"That's not important."

"Yes, it is, you twit." Ursula was losing patience.

"Did you just call me a twit?"

"Yes. If you lied about your movements on the night of a murder, it does nothing except make you look like a deeply suspicious twit."

"I am not a twit! Look, I can't say where I was."

"I can't help you if you don't."

"Flowerbutton, you're starting to sound like my mother. It's not very appealing."

"Wenty, I'll take that as a compliment. I'm sure your mother's wonderful. Now, why didn't you tell me you'd left college that night?"

A long groan echoed down the phone. "I was . . . embarrassed."

"About what?"

"Look, after I heard India and Dr. Dave *at it*, so to speak, from the bottom of the staircase . . ."

Ursula decided not to tell Wenty yet that he had actually heard Otto and Claire Potter "at it." She didn't want to interrupt his flow, now he seemed prepared to talk.

". . . I was jealous. Furious, actually. So I went off Hildebeest hunting."

"What sort of a sport is Hildebeest hunting, Wenty?"

"You scramble over that garden wall at St. Hilda's,* then go knocking on doors until a really top Hildebeest answers, and if you're lucky you end up in bed with it."

"You cannot go round calling female students 'beasts'! That's horrible."

---

* Founded in 1893 as a hall for women, St. Hilda's finally accepted men in 2008.

"It's an in-joke," he protested.

"Well, it's about the unfunniest, most sexist joke I've heard in my entire life."

"Sorry." Wenty actually sounded apologetic. For once.

"Anyway, did you end up in bed with a St. Hilda's girl?"

"*Of course*," he said, sounding faintly insulted at the suggestion that he might not have been successful. "Geraldine Something-or-Other. Can't remember her surname."

"Wenty!" Ursula gasped. "If you were a character in a P. G. Wodehouse novel, you would have been labeled a hollow cad by now."

"I know it makes me look awful. You can see why I didn't want anyone to know. Least of all a saintly prude like you, Flowerbutton."

"I am not a saintly prude."

"We'll agree to disagree on that. I mean, God, you know, there I was off with dear little Geraldine Something-or-Other the night my girlfriend was killed. If that gets into Dempster,* I'll never be accepted at White's."†

"Who cares about White's?" Ursula admonished him.

"*I* do. And everyone I know, and everyone my parents know. Please don't mention Geraldine Something-or-Other in your *Cherwell* article."

"Can you stop worrying about yourself and focus on India? Just tell me anything else that happened that night."

"Okay. Well, I must have left Geraldine's room at around six a.m. I suppose. That's the usual sort of time I escape those kind of, well . . . *scenarios*. I cycled back to college, left my bike at the gates, and went straight to my staircase and up to my rooms. I was in bed fast asleep by six forty-five. Didn't get up till midday."

---

* The *Daily Mail*'s Nigel Dempster was the most influential diarist of the 1980s and was nicknamed "the Snake" for his love of gossip. London Zoo named a poisonous specimen after Dempster, much to his delight.

† White's = oldest, grandest gentlemen's club in London. Only woman ever allowed in was the Queen. Wait list is *at least* seven years long.

"Did anyone see you coming into college? Did you see anyone when you came in about six? Someone who could vouch for you?"

"God, er, can't remember really. I didn't have to ring. The gate was already unlocked. I suppose the night porter could have seen me."

"If he happened to be looking out from the porter's lodge into the gate tower at the very moment you came back, maybe. I can ask him tonight. And I could always interview Geraldine Something-or-Other. She'll vouch for you, won't she?"

"I'd rather you left Geraldine Thingamabob well alone, Flower-button."

"Why?"

"Don't want to, you know, *encourage* her . . . in *any* way. Some of these girls they . . . they get the wrong idea, you know. They think they want a boyfriend, a 'relationship,' all that messy rubbish."

"She might be able to give you a solid alibi."

"But then I'd have to actually properly go out with her," said Wenty reluctantly.

"Have you told the police all of this?" Ursula asked.

There were a few pip-pip-pip sounds while Wenty inserted money at the other end.

". . . Running out of ten-ps . . . I've told the police everything now. It's been so embarrassing. But they're refusing to believe a word of it. They're insisting that the towel proves I was in the room at the time of India's death because my blood is on it as well as hers."

"Have you told them about cutting your hand washing up?"

"Of course. But they're trying to get me to confess to India's murder. Flowerbutton, do you believe me?"

Ursula reflected that, logically speaking, if one were to invent a story about one's movements on a particular night, it would be unlikely to be one that painted as shabby a picture of one's moral character as Wenty's tale did. On that basis, she had to assume his story was true.

"I do."

"So you'll help?"

Wenty might be a Hollow Cad of a cucumber sandwich, Ursula thought to herself, but he was very possibly innocent. However insufferable his treatment of that poor St. Hilda's girl was, it didn't make him a girlfriend killer.

"Yes," she replied. "I'll try and help you."

"Thank you, Flowerbutton. I'm worried that now the police have got me, they're going to stop looking for the real culprit. You've got to find the murderer before they bang me up for good."

"I must go," said Ursula. She was freezing cold in her damp towel.

"Okay. Just make sure to go to the funeral tomorrow. I can't believe I'll be stuck in here when my poor India is buried. God," Wenty said, sounding terribly saddened about his girlfriend. "That was my last ten-p. Try and get in to see me here if you can and—"

Pip-pip-pip. Pip-pip.

"And?" cried Ursula.

But she didn't hear Wenty finish his sentence. The line had gone dead.

Chapter 30

The humble red brick workman's cottage on the corner of Cranham Terrace and Jericho Street, festooned with now-yellowing autumnal wisteria, looked like the kind of place Mrs. Tiggy-Winkle might have lived. It had a pretty sash window looking onto the street, covered on the inside with a fine antique lace curtain, and the white-painted porch was shrouded in tumbling ivy.

"This has gotta be it," said Nancy. "Talk about a love nest."

The girls leaned their bicycles against an iron railing and made their way up through the tiny front garden along a moss-covered path.

"I just hope *he* doesn't answer the door," Ursula said, realizing she had no idea what she'd do if Dr. Dave turned out to be at home. Nervously, she banged the brass knocker three times.

"*Pronto!*" came a singsong Italian voice from inside the house.

The door opened to reveal a petite girl, barefoot and dressed in a lilac silk kimono edged with gold embroidery. Her hair was wrapped in a navy-blue towel, and her enormous dark eyes were framed by ludicrously long eyelashes. She had tan, gleaming skin, and the delicious scent of tuberose perfume emanated from her. No wonder Dr. Dave wanted to marry this enchanting creature, thought Ursula, spotting an engagement ring on her left hand. The girl smiled curiously at them.

"Can I 'elp you?" she asked.

"We're students, from Christminster," said Ursula.

"You looking for Davide? 'E not here. Am sorry," the girl said, shaking her head. She started to close the door.

"Wait," said Nancy, stepping towards the threshold. "We're looking for you, we think. Are you Fiammetta?"

She nodded.

"I'm writing a story for *Cherwell*," explained Ursula. "I wondered if you may be able to help . . . with background stuff. Have you got a few minutes to talk?"

"Sure. Come in."

Fiammetta led the girls along a narrow passage towards the back of the house. They had to squeeze past a pile of suitcases with luggage tags attached, topped by a violin case.

"I'm sorry. I been traveling. Am in chaos!" she laughed. "I 'ave not an idea even what day is."

The threesome had now arrived in the modest yellow-painted kitchen, whose French doors led out to a stretch of rambling cottage garden. Piles of sheet music, books, and magazines covered most of the work surfaces.

"So, you writing about music?" asked Fiammetta, unfurling her turban to reveal her almost waist-length, damp, dark hair, and gesturing for them to sit at the small café table in the middle of the room.

"Not *exactly*," said Ursula.

"We're investigating a student's murder," said Nancy boldly.

"In Oxford?! 'Ow awful," exclaimed Fiammetta. She pronounced "awful" *ow-full*. "What 'appened?"

"You haven't heard yet?" said Nancy, sounding astonished.

"'Aven't 'eard what?"

"Lady India Brattenbury was murdered on Sunday night in Christminster College," Nancy told her gravely.

"She was *studentessa* at Christminster?"

"Yes," said Ursula.

Fiammetta looked appalled. "That is *orribile* story. But I don't know 'ow I can 'elp. I've never met 'er. Or 'eard of 'er."

Was she lying, wondered Ursula, or was she really as naive about her new fiancé as she claimed? There was no doubt that Dr. Dave would have wanted to keep tales of his previous affairs with students from his future wife. But not to tell her about a murder in his own rooms—that was not just odd; it was, Ursula decided, deeply suspicious. Still, she didn't fancy being the one to break the news to Fiammetta that the most beautiful girl in Oxford had been found dead on her future husband's chaise longue.

"I've only really got one question, Fiammetta," Ursula said, her tone deathly serious.

"Yes?" replied the girl, now seeming jittery.

"Did your fiancé spend the night here on Sunday?"

"Please-mother-of-God, do not tell me you are suspecting 'im of this?!"

"Of course not," Ursula reassured her. "We're just trying to figure out everyone's movements in college that night."

"Oh, okay," said Fiammetta, sounding slightly less alarmed. "I was in Salzburg on Sunday night. We were playing Mozart's Violin Concerto No. 5 in A. I was soloist."

"Wow," said Nancy.

"Thank you." Fiammetta smiled graciously. "Then, another concert on Monday evening. I fly back yesterday, Tuesday evening. Is why we in chaos."

"So, any idea where Dr. Dave was on Sunday night?" Nancy persisted.

"I know for sure 'e wasn't 'ere," replied Fiammetta decisively. "'E would have stayed in college. 'Ates it 'ere when I am gone."

Why had Dr. Dave lied about where he spent the night on Sunday? If he hadn't spent it at home, as he'd said, the only logical place to stay would have been in his rooms. But Ursula had seen him arrive at the threshold the next morning well past nine a.m., and after she had discovered India's body. Where on earth, she wondered, *had* he spent the night if he wasn't either at home or in his rooms? And why was he being so deceitful? Was he, she wondered, aware of rather more about the murder than he was letting on? Had he, in fact, been in his rooms much of the night? Perhaps, frustrated by India's refusal to stop harassing him, he had killed her himself, and "arrived" late for Ursula's tutorial to make it appear as though he had not been in the room overnight.

"You're *sure* he wasn't here?" Nancy asked Fiammetta.

"I suppose 'e *could* 'ave come 'ome on Sunday night. After all, I wasn't 'ere, but—*non*. It would be very unlike 'im." The Italian girl shook her head. "'E likes company."

"Thank you, Fiammetta," said Ursula. "You've been really helpful."

"You're welcome. She wasn't 'Istory student, this India, was she?" asked Fiammetta while showing the girls out.

"No," said Nancy, shaking her head. "English Literature."

Fiammetta opened the front door, gasping with surprise as she did so. There on the front step stood two policemen.

"May we come in?" one of them asked.

"Well, I suppose," she said resignedly, showing them in.

"Good-bye," said Fiammetta as Nancy and Ursula stepped onto the path. "Good luck with your article." Then she added, as though to herself, "I suppose that's why Davide didn't mention it to me. 'E probably didn't know 'er."

"Probably not," agreed Ursula.

•

"WE'RE GONNA HAVE to go back to Dr. Dave," Nancy said as soon as she and Ursula were out of earshot of the house.

"I know," Ursula agreed, clambering onto her bike. "But how do you accuse your own tutor of being a liar without being Sent Down?"

As soon as they were back in college, the girls zipped into the porter's lodge. Ursula found a handwritten note in her pigeonhole that read:

Darling Ursula,
Your Cherwell editors look forward to reading your copy on
Sunday—have you discovered whodunit yet?

No, I jolly well haven't discovered whodunit, she said to herself, and scanned the rest of the note.

If you and Nancy-Doodle-Dandy would like a lift to the funeral
on Thursday, I can pick you up outside college in my car at 7 a.m.
Perhaps catch up at the Gridiron party tonight?

Mwah Mwah,
Horatio

Ursula showed the note to her friend. "Should we go to the funeral?"

"Sure we should. How else are we going to figure out 'whodunit'?" replied Nancy.

"But we haven't been invited," protested Ursula.

"Horatio's invited us," Nancy reasoned. "And didn't you say Wenty said you must go when he spoke to you on the phone this morning?"

"True."

"And India invited me to her shooting party. There's no way she would have invited me to that and not wanted me at her funeral."

"Okay," agreed Ursula. "We'll tell Horatio tonight at the party."

Just then Deddington beckoned the girls over to his station.

"Good morning," he said in an unusually quiet voice.

"Hey, Deddy," chirped Nancy.

"Hi," said Ursula.

"I've been hearing rumors about you, Flowerbutton," Deddington said. "Rumors that you are writing about Lady India's death for *Cherwell*."

"Yes. Can you help?"

"I'm not sure. But if you were to spend a few moments in the gallery of the Long Room, you may find it very informative. I just saw that police bloke go in there."

"You think there's a clue?" asked Nancy excitedly.

"Hush!" Deddington tried to calm her down. "Go through the small attic door at the top of the staircase, two floors above the library. It's unlocked."

"Thank you," said Ursula. "Oh, and one other thing, Deddington. Where were you on Sunday night?"

"Eagle and Child, the pub on St. Giles. Can't take that awful *Dallas* Linda insists on watching. Much prefer a pint or two of ale."

•

"GOOD AFTERNOON, GENTLEMEN," High Provost Scrope was saying. "Thank you very much for coming to this *postponed*—and now emergency—meeting of the Christminster College Fund-Raising Committee. I know how busy you all are, so I'd like to get to the main business right away."

Having clambered up the cramped, winding staircase to the attic door, Ursula and Nancy now found themselves crouching on a galleried landing. The Long Room beneath them was almost as large as the library one floor below. The walls were hung with ornate tapestries, and the windows looking onto Great Quad allowed a shaft of sunlight to illuminate the highly polished mahogany table in the center of the room, which was groaning under the weight of the college silver arranged on top of it.

Ursula counted at least twenty men around the table, most of them wearing suits. The absolute youngest was in late middle age, and they were in general so prosperously corpulent they looked as though they might burst. DI Trott, she noticed, was indiscreetly installed in an enormous tapestried throne at the farthest end of the room. White-gloved college servants were sloshing claret into the men's glasses, and while Scrope addressed them, the fund-raising committee was becoming rather merrier than he seemed to realize.

". . . the main business to be discussed today is the Brattenbury family legacy to the college endowment. As you may know, Lord Brattenbury, who was a student here in the 1950s and went on to make a fortune in Africa—gold and diamond mining—has most generously already given almost a million pounds to the college, but now, with the death of his daughter—the *tragic, untimely* death of his daughter India, who was an undergraduate here, and was the sole heir to the Brattenbury fortunes—there is no longer an immediate heir to the Brattenbury estate. Which means there may be the possibility of a much larger donation forthcoming to this college . . ."

Ursula could see that Trott's eyebrows were raised so high they were almost in liftoff mode, and Nancy whispered, "How about if Scrope killed India for her inheritance?"

"Wouldn't it be too obvious?" replied Ursula.

". . . funds which could secure the future of Christminster for the next hundred years or so. The key is to find a way to lobby Lord Brattenbury to rewrite his will in favor of Christminster College. If the matter is *delicately* handled with His Lordship, I imagine we could be extremely successful. Although he is only in his late forties, I have heard that the death of his only child has put his somewhat precarious health at risk. Time is of the essence."

"Okay, perhaps we *should* add Scrope to our list of suspects," said Ursula, amazed at Scrope's blatant desire for India's fortune.

There was a hubbub while the committee members chatted among themselves. Then Scrope called out to the group, "You are all distinguished alumni of the college. But is there anyone here who was an undergraduate with Brattenbury?"

A middle-aged gentleman dressed in a tweed suit raised his hand. In the upper-crust tones of the country squire Ursula assumed he was, he said, "I seem to recall that I played a bit of rugger with 'im. Knocked 'im out cold once."

"Marvelous!" squawked Scrope. "The college would be most grateful if you could approach him about rewriting his will."

"Certainly not," replied the other man. "I only knew Brattenbury well enough to knock 'im out, not discuss money with 'im! Scrope, you'll have to get 'im to change 'is will yourself. Then knock 'im out and you'll get the money quicker."

A chuckle ricocheted around the table but stopped dead with Scrope, who was not amused. His lips were puckered and white with frustration.

"Right, let's put the matter to a vote. Those in favor of me pursuing the Brattenbury fortune on behalf of the college, please raise your hand."

Everyone at the table, except for the gent who had knocked out Lord Brattenbury in his youth, put up their hand.

"Right, that's settled. The next item on the agenda: funding for a fellowship in Slavonic Linguistics . . ."

·

"ARE YOU THINKING what I'm thinking?" asked Nancy as the girls snuck back down towards the porter's lodge.

"I don't know what you're thinking, Nancy. So I don't know if I'm thinking what you're thinking."

"I'm thinking that Deddington sent us up there this morning because he suspects that our dear high provost cut India's throat himself to steal her inheritance for Christminster. I mean, Scrope would have been in college that night."

"Or," said Ursula, "Deddington sent us up there because he wants *us* to think that *he* thinks that Scrope had a motive to kill India."

"You're not saying that Deddington killed India and is trying to frame Scrope? What possible motive would our nice porter have?"

"I don't know. But I feel as if there are a squillion sides to this," Ursula concluded. "There's a surfeit of suspects, each with a motive to kill."

"Let's go back to Dr. Dave right now," said Nancy. "We need to find out what he was *really* up to on Sunday night."

Chapter 31

When the girls reached Dr. Dave's rooms that Wednesday afternoon, they found the tutor hard at work at his desk. With the great argus finally reinstated, the don, in a state of inspired excitement, was typing ferociously with one finger at a brand-spanking-new dark green Monica typewriter.

"Chocolate bourbon, girls? I was just about to take a break. Now that Panoptes is back, the words are flowing faster than the Euphrates." He got up and handed the girls an open packet of bourbon biscuits from his desk.

"Delicious, thank you," said Ursula, munching away.

"Great," said Nancy before taking a bite of hers. "Eeooow!" she erupted. Her face crumpled with displeasure while she forced down the dry biscuit. "Is it just me or do all British cookies taste like sidewalk?"

"I'm sorry our food isn't up to American standards, Miss Feingold. Dreadful business about the Wychwood towel, isn't it?" he said, plopping into an armchair and sipping at a cup of tea. "God knows why he'd want to dispose of his own girlfriend. He adored her."

"I'm confused about something," Nancy declared.

"Who isn't, my dear?" chuckled Dr. Dave. "Didn't the *Dictionary of the Older Scottish Tongue* clear things up for you?"

"I'm not talking about the essay," she replied. "It's about Sunday night."

"Oh," said Dr. Dave. The don's ebullience seemed to ebb rapidly away.

"You see, you said that you were at home that night. At your house in Cranham Terrace."

"Indeed. That is where I was," he agreed.

"But your fiancée says you weren't there."

Dr. Dave's face whitened, and he spluttered, "Now look here, you two, you've got no right to go snooping around my fiancée for the sake of some article in a student rag."

Ursula decided to step in before things got out of hand. "We didn't tell her anything about India being found in your rooms."

Dr. Dave pulled a silk handkerchief from his top pocket and mopped his suddenly clammy brow.

"Nor should you have," he retorted. "There is no need for Fiammetta to know anything about the details of poor India's death. She doesn't know whether or not I was at home on Sunday night because she wasn't there. She was in Salzburg. Usually I never go home when she is away, but on this occasion I did."

He smiled, looking relieved. Ursula realized she was going to have to get to the nub of the matter in a less direct fashion.

"May I ask you something else?"

"If you *must*."

"Is the librarian Ms. Brookethorpe prone to telling fibs?"

"Not as far as I know," he replied. "What a peculiar question."

"I think she's told a terrible lie," said Ursula. She felt guilty as she spoke—she'd promised the librarian anonymity—but she had no choice if she were to get at the truth.

"It's about you," added Nancy perkily.

"Well, that's absurd." Dr. Dave jumped up from his armchair and went and stared angrily out the window.

"I don't know why," said Ursula as innocently as she could, "but she told me that she saw you walking along Great Quad towards Monks' Cottages after midnight on the night of India's murder."

Dr. Dave spun around and looked at the girls. "That woman is a complete fantasist. Admittedly she was attractive, in an unsophisticated sort of a way . . . a couple of years ago . . . but no, with Olive—I mean Ms. Brookethorpe—you can't believe a word she says. Particularly about men."

"I thought you said she wasn't the lying type," Ursula reminded him.

"Did I?" asked Dr. Dave. "Then I was mistaken. The truth is, Brookethorpe has been obsessed with me since I was a junior fellow. We had a brief dalliance a couple of years ago. Meaningless fling-ette, that sort of thing. After I dropped her, well, she's spread vile rumors about me ever since. She wants me out . . . Anyway, even if she *had* seen someone out on Great Quad at half past midnight, how could she possibly have known it was me, in the dark?"

"It was a full moon," Ursula pointed out. "She mentioned the 'swoop' of your hair as being particularly noticeable."

"She did always have a thing about my hair. But this story is utter rubbish. She's a bitter, envious, lying old trout."

"But someone else says they saw you there—a female Fresher," said Ursula. She didn't want to reveal Claire Potter's identity to the don if she could avoid it. "She said she saw you out there on Great Quad at *exactly* the same time. She was holding an event in the JCR, across the landing. No one showed up and she was staring out the window, looking for guests."

"Bloody hell," Dr. Dave growled, looking astonished. He glared at both girls, then collapsed back in his armchair. "Oh, all right, you've got me," he conceded. "I'll tell you where I was that night. I was in Monks' Cottages."

"Why?" asked Nancy.

"I was doing my laundry," he replied innocently. "There, now that you know I wasn't at home, or here in my rooms, can we please end this uncomfortable interlude?"

"It took the *whole* night to do your laundry?" asked Ursula.

Dr. Dave groaned with irritation.

"Does it really matter? The important thing is that you can estab-lish with utter certainty that I wasn't at home the night India died and I wasn't in my rooms when she came up here. Isn't that enough?"

The girls both looked at him, eyebrows raised. Finally, an expres-sion of defeat came over his face.

"Look, none of this can get back to Fiammetta," he insisted.

The girls assured him that it wouldn't.

"Or into your *Cherwell* article, Flowerbutton."

"I promise," said Ursula.

"If it does you will *both* be Sent Down for . . . I don't know . . . for dabbling in crime writing.

"What transpired that night," Dr. Dave told the girls, "was rather . . . sordid. I was planning to spend the night here on Sunday because Fiammetta was going to be away for a few days. I didn't want to be in the house without her cooking—and her, of course. I was do-ing some work, pretty late, here at my desk, when I heard this bloody great row from outside. I looked out of the window onto Great Quad, and there were India and Wenty screaming at each other. The night porter eventually broke it up, and then I saw India run towards my staircase. I didn't want another scene, so I slipped out before she got to my landing."

"But surely she saw you on the stairs?" said Ursula.

"Ah. Yes. I should explain."

Dr. Dave beckoned to the girls to follow him, opened the door to his bedroom, and strode in ahead of them.

"Come in," he said.

"Hey," Nancy stated firmly, "we are not interested in some kind of weird threesome with you, Dr. Dave."

He smiled at her coolly. "And, believe me, nor I with you. I am simply showing you the back stairs to my bedroom, down which I fled on Sunday night."

With that, the tutor pulled back the curtain on the far wall, revealing a small wooden door. He lifted the latch, ducked his head, and went out through the low doorway. Nancy and Ursula followed and found themselves descending a winding, cobweb-ridden spiral staircase that led out to the southwest corner of the Kitchen Quad.

"So you see," said Dr. Dave, after leading the girls back up the stairs to his rooms, "while India was climbing the JCR staircase to my rooms, I skedaddled down here. I do wonder, if I hadn't been so keen on skedaddling, would she still be alive now?"

"Where did you skedaddle to for the night?" asked Ursula, sitting back down on Dr. Dave's tartan-covered Chesterfield.

"As I said, I spent the night in Monks' Cottages."

"Where did you sleep? In a laundry basket?" queried Nancy in highly skeptical tones. Ursula could tell she wasn't going to let Dr. Dave get away with this.

The don looked decidedly sheepish. "Well, I was rather at a loose end. I couldn't go back to my rooms, knowing India was most likely in there, and the keys to the Cranham Terrace house were in there too. So I, er . . . looked in . . . on . . . um . . . Isobel Floyd. Her room's above the laundry."

"Did you 'look in' for the whole night?" said Ursula, trying to phrase it as politely as possible.

"The looking-in, yes, it took . . . erm . . . all night." Dr. Dave grimaced, self-conscious. "And that's why, Ursula, I was a few minutes late for our tutorial."

Nancy, who appeared to be far less concerned with maintaining British standards of politeness, just looked at the don and shrieked, "Gross!"

Chapter 32

What do you think?"

Nancy appeared in Ursula's room that evening dressed in a completely see-through pair of Fiorucci "jeans" fabricated from what looked like clear plastic. Beneath them, Nancy's athletic legs and a pair of silver, sequined hot pants were clearly visible, and she had finished the look with a one-shouldered purple Lycra top and high heels.

"Really trendy," said Ursula, looking up from her desk, where she'd been making notes about their meeting with Dr. Dave. His behavior perplexed her: She couldn't understand how someone could cheat so blatantly on his fiancée, let alone one as divine as Fiammetta.

"Hey, why aren't you ready?" asked Nancy, regarding Ursula's mini kilt and sweater.

"I can't go to the Gridiron party tonight. I haven't done *any* work on my essay. I think I need to spend the evening in the library instead."

"What?!" howled Nancy. "You can't let me down last-minute like this. I can't go by myself. I might get murdered on the way. Imagine how bad you'd feel if that happened."

Was there really any getting out of tonight, knowing Nancy's persistence when it came to social events? With a long sigh, Ursula signaled her willingness to give in. "I just need to finish up here."

She added a final thought:

—No wonder Isobel Floyd said that Dr. Dave didn't do it. She was being "dropped in on" by him when India was murdered.

Ursula left her article notes on the desk and hurriedly changed into Vain Granny's ball gown—again. She couldn't help but feel slightly envious of her friend's endless supply of outrageous party dresses and New York clubbing outfits. As much as Ursula loved the lilac dress, it wasn't exactly of-the-moment. But it would have to do. There was no time to play dress up in Nancy's room tonight.

·

THE GRIDIRON CLUB dinner was a small, cliquey, and mostly male affair. Ursula and Nancy arrived at the Golden Cross, a medieval, cobbled courtyard off Cornmarket Street, just before eight o'clock. They were directed past a Pizza Express restaurant on the ground floor and up a steep set of back stairs towards an attic dining room. As the girls reached the landing outside it, Ursula recognized the long sweep of a dark overcoat and saw Neil Thistleton trying to talk his way into the dinner.

"Look, mate," one of the black-tied Gridiron members was saying to him in supremely polite tones while very effectively blocking the doorway, "I'd love to help, really, but it's members only tonight. *Terrifically* sorry and all that."

Neil Thistleton turned and stared indignantly at the girls. Ursula looked at the floor, praying Thistleton wouldn't spot her.

"Members?" he said, turning back to the boy. "Isn't this one of those snotty all-*male* dining clubs?"

"We allow women as guests of members. No one else is allowed in, I'm afraid."

"Sexist tosser," said Neil Thistleton. He slunk reluctantly back down the stairs.

Beamed and whitewashed, the attic room that served as the headquarters of the secret society resembled a medieval refectory.

A long table had been laid for dinner with starched white linens and pewter platters. There were about twenty members, mostly in black tie, in the room, and no more than seven or eight ravishingly pretty girls. Good, thought Ursula, spotting Isobel Floyd surrounded by an ever-adoring group of boys, I'll wait until she's tipsy before I mention Dr. Dave. She spotted Eg standing by the bar, chatting with friends, looking as suave as ever in his tux, and wondered what they would say to each other after the peculiar end to their date last night.

"Ah, welcome!" Horatio Bentley greeted Ursula and Nancy, waddling towards them bearing two pewter goblets. "Nancy, you look just like a disco ball."

"Thank you," she said, flattered by Horatio's attention and accepting a goblet.

"Huge apols in advance, sweetie. The Gridiron's wine doesn't quite live up to its pewterware," he chuckled. "It came out of a wine box. If you drink enough, eventually you'll stop noticing the burning in your gut."

Horatio led the girls to a trio of buttoned leather chairs where he settled down, saying, "I can't believe Wenty's been arrested. Dreadful news. You *are* both going to come to the funeral tomorrow, aren't you?"

"Absolutely," said Ursula.

"Good. You're bound to get some more material there," said Horatio. Then, noticing a girl heading towards them, he said, "Ciao, Tiggy-Wiggy."

Ursula recognized the Princess Diana wannabe whom she'd seen in the gate tower on her first day at Christminster. Tiggy was now dressed in a navy silk dress with a high, pleated, stand-up collar, over which she wore a gold choker. Her fluffy, streaky blond bangs grazed her enormous blue eyes but didn't conceal the determined look on her face.

"Sorry to interrupt, yar. Look, I'm up for librarian-elect at the Union. Are you two Freshers members yet?" she asked the girls.

"I'm thinking of joining," said Nancy.

"You should," replied Tiggy. "It's a wonderful institution. As soon as you join, do register to vote in elections. Yar? *Great.*"

"By the way, Tiggy," said Horatio, "I voted in a Union election once."

"Did you?" She looked suddenly excited by the prospect of another potential supporter.

"Yup. Can't remember who for, though."

Deflated, Tiggy rushed off to canvass another group.

As soon as she was out of earshot Horatio said, "Tiggy—ugh! She's one of those gauche, pushy Pony Club types. I hate to admit it, but that utterly talentless homuncule will most likely be president of the Onion one day."

"Onion?" repeated Nancy.

"That's what the *Cherwell* hacks call the Union because the group of twats who run it are so bitter—always making each other cry. Anyway, where were we before she interrupted us?"

"Wenty," Ursula reminded him. "He telephoned me this morning—"

"Hang on," Horatio interrupted her. "Wenty phoned *you*, Ursula, from jail?"

"Yes, why?" replied Ursula.

"Nothing," Horatio said with a coy grin. "Nothing *at all.*"

"Look," she went on, ignoring his innuendo, "Wenty swears he didn't kill India. He's got an alibi for Sunday night that I need to check. He says he was at St. Hilda's with a girl named Geraldine. Do you know her, by any chance, Horatio?"

"Geraldine who?"

"Something-or-Other."

"Something-or-Other?" Horatio frowned.

"Wenty couldn't remember her last name. It sounded like he had a drunken one-night stand."

"Oh! Wenty! So many girls to remember, so many names to forget!" laughed Horatio. "There is *one* Geraldine at St. Hilda's. Geraldine

Ormsby-Leigh. But it wouldn't be her. She's madly in love with her boy-friend, Hugo Pym. He's at Trinity."

"Maybe she cheated on him," suggested Nancy. "I mean, it's not like everyone else isn't cheating on everyone else round here."

"Let's ask her," said Horatio suddenly. He waved across the room. "Geraldine! Pumpkin! Over here!"

"No, wait—" Ursula tried to stop him, but it was too late.

The particular Geraldine in question swept over to Horatio and kissed him twice on each cheek. She certainly looked like she might be Wenty's type, thought Ursula to herself. Tall and slim with blond locks almost to her waist, the girl was dressed in gold pedal pushers, a sparkly green tube top, and lilac suede stilettos. Her bare shoulders gleamed with a dusting of golden glitter that also covered her cheek-bones and eyelids, and her lips were slicked with an iridescent gloss.

Ursula examined this disco angel with some awe. Would her gran-nies ever approve of a garment as gorgeously minute as Geraldine's tube top? Ursula was wondering to herself when she suddenly heard Horatio saying, "Go on, Ursula, ask her about Sunday night."

"What about Sunday night?" interjected Geraldine.

"Well, I was just wondering . . ." Ursula trailed off, embarrassed. There just wasn't a straightforward way to ask someone you'd just met about her love life. She muddled along, purposefully vague. ". . . if, yes . . . that's it, if you happened to, erm . . . *see* Wenty on Sun-day night?"

"Wenty?" said Geraldine.

"You know, Wentworth Wychwood. Toff rower," added Horatio. "Why?"

"He says he—maybe—saw you," said Ursula cautiously.

"Well, he can't have. I was on the sleeper train from Edinburgh. Coming back from a stalking weekend in Scotland with Hugo."

"Oh, right," said Ursula, as Geraldine drifted back to the bar.

"So, sounds like Wenty's got some explaining to do," remarked Horatio as soon as she was out of earshot. "Geraldine definitely wasn't with him on Sunday."

Ursula felt exasperated. How did Wenty think he could get away with endless lies? And why had he lied about being with Geraldine? Did he think Ursula—or the police for that matter—wasn't going to bother to check his alibi? Could she trust what anyone said in Oxford?

"It looks pretty bad for Wenty," said Nancy. "I mean, his towel was found at the crime scene covered in his and India's blood. He was jealous of her relationship with Dr. Dave. He didn't spend the night in his own room, and he didn't spend it with Geraldine Whatever-Her-Name-Is either. If he wasn't at St. Hilda's, maybe he *did* follow India up to Dr. Dave's rooms. Maybe Ms. Brookethorpe saw him leaving college on his bicycle *after* he'd killed her?"

"Or maybe it wasn't Wenty she saw at all. Maybe it was someone else," suggested Ursula. "Maybe Wenty was in Dr. Dave's rooms all night and didn't leave until the early hours of the morning."

"But how does anyone prove that?" asked Horatio.

Ursula was at a loss as to how to answer him. Why was it so impossible to find out what Wenty had really been up to that night?

Soon a rather ruddy-cheeked boy announced, "Dinner is served!" The crowd found their place cards and sat down along the table while various tuxedoed members of the Gridiron Club distributed a white cardboard box onto each medieval platter. The logo across the top of the boxes read "Pizza Express."

"This is literally the poshest takeout ever," laughed Nancy, opening her box. She was sitting next to Horatio, and Ursula was seated on his other side, with Eg opposite her across the table.

He smiled shyly at her, saying, "You've got that lovely dress on—"

"—again, sadly," joked Ursula.

"No, you look so . . . pretty. Just like the first time I saw you."

Ursula suddenly found herself being poked in the ribs. "Heavens above," Horatio whispered in her ear, "the monk has fallen for the convent girl."

"I am *not* a convent girl," Ursula whispered back.

"All right, the virgin," he said.

Ursula rolled her eyes. She had nothing to say. After all, she was a virgin, like it or not. Meanwhile, Horatio slid an enormous slice of Margherita pizza into his mouth and downed it at a gulp. Just then, Ursula noticed Isobel Floyd getting up from the table a few seats down from her.

"Just going to powder my nose, darling," Isobel announced to the boy sitting next to her.

"I need to do a follow-up interview," Ursula told her friends, getting up from her seat. "Back in a moment."

Isobel was retrieving a weighty golden YSL tube from her handbag when Ursula came upon her in the powder room a few moments later. She twisted it to reveal a dark purple lipstick, which she rolled expertly on her lips. She flashed a smile at Ursula.

"Very goth, no?" she asked.

"It's lovely," said Ursula, secretly asking herself why this exquisitely attractive girl wanted to look like Adam Ant.*

"I'm trying out looks for the play. My Hamlet's going to be a New Romantic."†

"How are rehearsals going?" Ursula ventured, wondering how on earth she was going to change the subject to Dr. Dave's nighttime college rovings.

"*Really* great, thanks. But then Dom's a genius. I think he'll run the National Theatre one day. Why don't you come to a rehearsal? You could preview the play. Write it up for *Cherwell*."

"I'm still quite busy with my article about India," said Ursula. "Actually, funnily enough, I wanted to ask you one more question."

"Oh?" said Isobel, looking at Ursula out of one eye in the mirror as she dabbed emerald green shadow onto her left eyelid.

---

* Before Johnny Depp popularized pirate style, pop star Adam Ant (born plain Stuart Leslie Goddard) had the look down, only with way more makeup.

† A group of anti-punk London clubbers, the New Romantics dressed in Regency frills, vintage military jackets, and highwayman garb. John Galliano's 1984 graduate show *Les Incroyables*, a direct reflection of the scene, was heavy on bows, pantaloons, and tricorn hats.

"It was just, on Sunday night . . . you went back to your room after the argument—"

"I already told you that," Isobel snapped.

"Yes. Did you by any chance forget to tell me that someone came to your room a little later that night?"

There was a clattering as Isobel's eye shadow palette dropped from her hands and landed in the sink.

"Who told you?" The hue on Isobel's face was rapidly becoming rather similar to her purple lipstick.

"He did," said Ursula.

Isobel sat down slowly on a tufted armchair and lit a cigarette.

"This can't get out. No one can know. Ever."

Ursula nodded.

"At the time, it felt like revenge."

"Revenge?" repeated Ursula.

"I wanted to get India back. Best friend! Ha! She took my part, my boyfriend—it was only fair for me to have a pop at Dr. Dave."

"But their affair was over months ago," Ursula pointed out.

"She was still obsessed with him. Saw him as her property. Anyway, he was in my room all night. We overslept. It seemed funny, at the time, when he dashed off saying he was late for a tutorial."

"It was my tutorial," said Ursula.

"And then, when I found out India was dead—God! I regretted what I had done so much. I couldn't tell a soul. I told the police what I told you—that I was alone all night. They didn't suspect I was lying for one minute," Isobel said. Then she added with a smile, "You see, I'm a pretty amazing actress when I need to be. Have you got any idea who killed India?"

"No," admitted Ursula. "But now I feel pretty sure it wasn't you or Dr. Dave."

"Good." Isobel put her eye shadow and lipstick back in her purse, and she and Ursula returned to the dinner party.

Back at the table, Ursula found Nancy in midflow: "I just don't get why they don't have sororities here. If you can have an all-male dining club, why not at all-female one?"

"None of the girls in Oxford would want to go to an all-female club," a girl declared sharply from across the table. "It was bad enough being at a girls' boarding school. Oxford's a release from that hell."

"But what about feminism?" said Nancy. "We're all equal now."

"Saying you're a feminist," said the girl across the table, "is like saying you're a vegetarian or something—*weird*."

Nancy rolled her eyes in despair as Ursula slipped back into her seat. She noticed, to her delight, that Eg was looking adoringly at her. As did Horatio. Like quicksilver, he whispered in her ear, "He seems pretty glad Wenty's locked up. Eg was asking *all* about you while you were gone."

Ursula brushed him off, saying, "Horatio, Eg's far too nice to be glad Wenty's in jail."

Still, she couldn't help blushing slightly. Perhaps Eg *did* really like her, despite the end to their evening. But other matters were more pressing. Ursula turned to Nancy. "Do you mind if we go soon?"

"Why? I'm having a surprisingly good time at this anti-feminist dinner. It's like I'm witnessing some kind of anthropological experiment—from Victorian times."

"Look, I've realized there's someone we've forgotten to speak to. He could be the key to India's death."

•

IT WAS ALMOST eleven p.m. by the time the girls got back to college. The gate tower was dark and silent, but a warm light shone from inside the porter's lodge.

"Come on," said Ursula, beckoning Nancy into the little room.

Deddington Jr. sat at the porter's station, head buried in a pile of books, as usual. He looked up when he heard the girls enter.

"Evening, ladies," he said.

"Hey, sweetie," said Nancy. She plonked her elbows on the counter, rested her chin on her hands, and just stared at the boy. She seemed unable to resist flirting with him. "Want me to go grab you a drink from the bar?"

"No, no, thank you," responded Nick. "I don't drink when I'm on duty."

"You must be lonely here all alone all night . . . I could hang here with you, if you like . . ."

"Thank you, I can cope on my own," he replied.

"Okay, be like that," said Nancy, exhaling a long sigh.

"Nick, may I ask you something about your job?" said Ursula.

Deddington Jr. put down his pen and smiled at her. "Sure."

"Okay. What time are you here until in the mornings?"

"My dad takes over around seven. That is, unless it's his day off."

"And what time do you start at night?"

"Usually seven p.m., unless it's my day off."

"Did your father take over from you at seven a.m. this past Monday morning?"

Nick thought for a brief moment, then said, "That was the day they found the girl dead, wasn't it? Yes. Everything was as usual that morning. I mean, usual except for the awful murder."

"Did you see anyone coming in earlier than your father?"

"Only the scouts," he replied. "They all start between five and six in the morning. Mum always brings me a cuppa when she gets here. She brought me toast that morning. I remember because she'd spread it with her homemade marmalade. Real treat."

"Cute," said Nancy.

"You don't remember seeing anyone else come in very early that morning, do you?" asked Ursula.

"Let me see." Nick pursed his lips as he thought. "Yes—yes, there was one other person I noticed."

"Who?!" asked Ursula, brimming with anticipation.

"The milkman. Always comes around six."

"I see," she said. "Did you notice any undergraduates?"

"I don't think so, no . . . but I suppose someone could have slipped in without me noticing, if I was sorting mail or something. Why?"

"Nothing," said Ursula regretfully.

Wenty was starting to look more and more guilty. Why didn't he ever seem able to tell the truth?

Chapter 33

I feel like I'm in the 'Thriller' video," said Nancy as they headed out the next morning at seven to meet Horatio. Oxford was shrouded in a fog so dense that the girls could barely see their way out of the gate tower.

Suddenly, from somewhere in the icy mist beyond, a voice called out, "Wooo-oooo-hooooo!"

As they edged closer to the sound, they could finally see that Horatio Bentley, the source of it, was parked up on the apron in front of Christminster College, as promised. He waved at them from the window of a grubby, dented Reliant Robin whose engine was running. Ursula suspected the vehicle might, possibly, be green under the layer of grime covering it.

"Bentley by name, *not* by nature!" Horatio declared. Despite the prospect of India's funeral ahead, his tone was as jovial as ever.

"Why does this thing only have three wheels?" asked Nancy, regarding the triangular-shaped car with a petrified expression on her face.

"I haven't got a driving license," he explained. "But this is classed as a motorbike, so I'm allowed to drive it."

Nancy whitened.

"Stop dithering and get in," he ordered.

Horatio, dressed in a black suit with a lilac bow tie and matching handkerchief, heaved himself out of the car and let Ursula clamber into the backseat, where she made a space for herself among the piles of old newspapers, chip packets, and grimy piles of clothes. As she didn't own a black dress, she was wearing her homemade maroon velvet one under a duffel coat and her college scarf.

Nancy's funeral look was so elaborate that it took her some time to edge herself into the spare front seat. She had chosen a tiny, skin-tight black "bandage" dress, sheer black tights, high pumps, and a thigh-length black velvet swing coat with enormous puffed sleeves, a frilled collar, and gold buttons down the front. Her blond hair had been fluffed into the puffiest bun Ursula had ever seen.

"Darling," said Horatio, "you look just like Ivana Trump."

"Oh my God, that is so cute of you to say," said Nancy. "She's my style icon."

The fog in the car was almost as thick as outside. A Marlboro Red was smoldering in the ashtray—Horatio took a long drag and then said, "Let's get going before the engine stalls. Might never start again. I call it my Unreliant Robin."

He put his foot on the accelerator and jerked the car awkwardly into the road. Nancy clutched the dashboard and screamed with every lurch. The tiny vehicle felt, thought Ursula, no more substantial than a lawnmower on wheels.

"How far away is Brattenbury Tower?" Nancy gulped as they turned onto Broad Street.

"We'll be there in masses of time," Horatio told her. "Meanwhile, there's hard-boiled eggs and a thermos of tea to keep us going. Made it all myself last night. Nancy, open that lunchbox at your feet and pass me an egg, please. I'm starving."

The stench of eggs that filled the car when Nancy removed the lid from the plastic lunchbox took Ursula straight back to the revolting school meals she had suffered for so many years at St. Swerford's.

"Here," said Nancy, holding the egg as far from her nose as she possibly could.

"Help yourself," said Horatio, swallowing his egg in two gulps.

"I'm not quite ready for one yet," replied Nancy, trying to be polite.

Four hours and forty cigarettes later, Horatio's vehicle put-putted off the motorway and past a sign reading "Derbyshire Dales." The journey had taken well over an hour longer than it should have after Horatio had insisted on stopping at a greasy Little Chef in a motorway service station for a leisurely elevenses* of fish and chips.

"Brattenbury's only a few miles away now," he said, taking a turn onto a tiny, stony track-like road that wound down into a steep valley. The hills were streaked with the autumnal hues of dying bracken and lilac heather. Dry-stone walls divided the pastureland into rough fields on which wild-looking sheep were grazing.

"There's nothing, like, *here*," declared Nancy bleakly, gazing out of the window at the stark landscape.

"In certain English circles—Sloaney ones—it's considered the height of glamour to live in the middle of absolutely bloody nowhere," Horatio informed her.

A few minutes later, as they eventually motored through the tiny village of Brattenbury, Nancy's attitude abruptly changed. The village—which consisted of two or three stone-built farmsteads, a schoolhouse, a row of simple laborers' cottages, a village hall, a minuscule shop, and a pub named The Brattenbury Arms—was simply charming. As they drove past a picturesque Norman church looming from the mist, Nancy cried excitedly, "Oh my God, it's *so* cute here. I wanna move in!"

The lane out of the village climbed steeply, becoming narrower and narrower as it wound around two or three sharp bends. About half a mile farther on the party of three finally arrived at a huge pair of gray stone gateposts topped with vast, intricately carved pineapples. An ornate lodge house guarded the driveway, and miles of immaculately restored stone walling disappeared away from it in both directions. The property was clearly part of a huge estate, thought

---

* "Elevenses" = old-fashioned British meal, usually consisting of tea or coffee, biscuits and cake, eaten at eleven in the morning.

Ursula. Horatio pulled up—taking care to leave the car's engine running—and a few seconds later an elderly man appeared from the lodge house.

Horatio leaned out of the window to speak to him. "Good morning, sir. We're here for the funeral."

The old man looked at his watch. "T' all went int' chapel half hour gone." He had a strong Derbyshire accent. "Go straight up t' drive, chapel's on t' right o' big 'ouse. Chop-chop, you're late."

"I thought you said we'd have masses of time," complained Nancy.

"We did," retorted Horatio, pressing his foot down on the accelerator as hard as it would go. The car swayed precariously from side to side as they whizzed up the graveled carriage drive.

Brattenbury Tower, which soon loomed into view, lived up to its name. Ursula had never seen such a romantic-looking house. An Elizabethan dream, the house had a stone facade so delicate that it reminded her of an etching. Ancient stone mullioned windows soared up, four storys high. At least twenty chimneys peeked above the balustraded roofline. A semicircular flight of stone steps led up towards the impressive entrance. In front of the house the gravel drive swept around a circular lawn where various very smart cars, including a flashy gold Porsche, a Rolls-Royce, and a couple of Range Rovers, were parked.

"This is *so much* cooler than Disneyland," exclaimed Nancy, wide-eyed, as she drank in the sight. "Can't you just imagine Rapunzel letting down her hair from up there?" she added, gazing upwards. "And look! I can't believe the Brattenburys even have their *own flag* on their house . . . Hmmm, I wonder if Next Duke has one too."

"Nancy darling, duke types have flags flying absolutely everywhere they can. Gives them a sense of identity," Horatio explained.

"How . . . *sexy*," sighed Nancy wistfully.

Ursula, meanwhile, noted sadly that the Brattenbury flag, decorated with the family coat of arms, was fluttering at half-mast. Horatio pulled up next to the Porsche, and the three undergraduates alighted from their humble vehicle. There was no one in sight, but

Ursula thought she heard the sound of an organ and the faint echo of voices singing.

"I think it must be that way," said Ursula, pointing towards the east wing of the house.

The trio headed along a sheltered path beside the house before eventually coming round the corner of the building and spotting an ancient lych-gate at the far end of a vast lawn. Ursula, Nancy, and Horatio dashed towards it, passed under the little archway, and soon found themselves heading along a mossy path through a tunnel of yews leading to the Brattenbury family chapel. Horatio heaved open a heavy oak door and Nancy and Ursula slipped into the back of the chapel, with Horatio following, as quietly as they could.

Every pew of the tiny chapel was full, and the area behind the pews was crammed with standing guests. There was only room for them to squeeze in directly in front of the door they had just come through. A lone choirboy, dressed in a frilled white collar and a red robe, stood in front of the altar singing the poignant verses of Psalm 23:

> . . . *Yea, though I walk in death's dark vale,*
> *Yet will I fear no ill:*
> *For thou art with me, and thy rod*
> *And staff me comfort still . . .*

"I wanna take that little skylark home," whispered Nancy as the boy's voice soared and echoed around the chapel.

As the last verses were sung, Ursula watched sorrowfully while India's coffin, beautifully adorned with heather, snowberries, and wild brambles, was carried down the aisle. She found herself brushing a few tears from her cheek. Although she hadn't really known India, that didn't matter. When someone died so young, it was desperately sad. Her tears were not just for India—Ursula couldn't help thinking of her own mother and father, taken so early.

She took a deep breath and gathered herself. She remained standing with Nancy and Horatio at the back of the church, watching closely as the mourners who had been sitting at the front of the church followed India's coffin from the chapel. The women—clad in enormous black hats, shoulder-padded power suits with flashy gold buttons, coats of mink or sable, reams of pearls, and generous sprinklings of diamonds—were accompanied by smart-looking husbands and boyfriends dressed in Savile Row suits and silk ties. These must, Ursula assumed, be the grander Brattenbury family relations and close friends. This group was followed at a respectful distance by a few humbler-looking types whom Ursula imagined must be estate workers or tenants. Finally, India's crowd of Oxford friends filed out of the chapel, the Yar girls striking in their black dresses and hats.

Ursula observed India's inner circle of friends intently as they passed in front of her. There were Dom and Isobel, holding hands, both looking suitably heartbroken. Eg and Otto followed behind them, Otto's imperial red-and-white sash standing out among the sea of black. He gestured to Ursula, Nancy, and Horatio to join them.

"I can't believe Wenty's not here," said Eg miserably when he saw Ursula.

Once outside, she noticed Dr. Dave and Fiammetta, fingers entwined, drifting along with the crowd of mourners making their way across the small family graveyard to the spot where India's coffin would be buried, beneath a huge old oak. Olive Brookethorpe walked behind them, chatting to Mr. and Mrs. Deddington, who were flanked by Alice the scout, who was wearing a veiled hat. Ursula soon spotted High Provost Scrope and his secretary, Mrs. Gifford-Pennant, talking with the grand-looking relations. Detective Inspector Trott and a constable were standing on the far side of the graveyard. The mourners watched, grimly silent, as India's coffin was lowered into the ground.

"That's peculiar," said Horatio under his breath, glancing around.

"What is?" asked Ursula.

"Lord Brattenbury's not here."

"You're right, I can't see him anywhere," said Nancy, unable to

spot India's father. "Why would a dad not come to his own kid's funeral?" She paused, then added, "Unless . . ."

"What?" asked Ursula.

"Unless he killed his own daughter."

Ursula stared at her, disbelieving.

"Be sensible, Nancy," scolded Horatio. "Why would Lord Brattenbury want to dispose of his only heir? Now's not the moment to kill
off his daughter and reveal a love child in Australia."

"I guess," said Nancy.

Just then Ursula saw the elderly gentleman from the lodge house
closing up the chapel doors. "Excuse me," she said politely, "but where
is Lord Brattenbury?"

"Got t' malaria back."

"You can get malaria *here*?!" Nancy shrank away from the old man.

"Don' worry y'self. Lord B got t'sickness int' Africa. The fever
comes back now and again. 'E's a'bed."

"Horatio, we'll see you later," said Ursula, turning on her heel.
"Come on, Nancy. We haven't got long."

•

THE GREAT HALL of Brattenbury Tower resembled an ancestral hunting lodge. Every spare inch of wall was decorated with old trophies—
foxes' tails, stuffed game birds, and huge sets of antlers were hung
among decorative swords, ancient shields, and elaborate daggers.

"Forget Rapunzel, this is totally *The Jungle Book*," Nancy quipped.

But Ursula's mind was already elsewhere, her attention focused
on the dramatic staircase sweeping upstairs ahead of them. She and
Nancy could easily sneak up there now and find Lord Brattenbury's
bedroom, before the funeral party reached the house. Ursula glanced
around the great hall—there was no one else about. "Quick," she said,
beckoning Nancy to follow her upstairs.

The girls had only leapt up a couple of steps when a voice rang
out behind them. They turned to find a severe-looking housekeeper
dressed in black standing in the hall, trailed by several uniformed

maids and butlers carrying silver trays laden with platters of food. The woman looked startled.

"Goodness, we're not ready for the wake yet," she said, regarding her watch with a worried frown. "I thought we had another half hour yet. Oh Lordy!"

"Actually, everyone's still outside the church," said Ursula, thinking on her feet. "We were just . . . erm . . . looking for the loo."

The housekeeper sighed, relieved, and smoothed her dress down. "Go up to the first landing, turn left onto the main corridor upstairs, past the late Lady Brattenbury's old bedroom on the right, and you'll find a bathroom up there. Do keep your voices down as poor Lord Brattenbury is trying to rest up there. Now, if you'll excuse us, we'd better get the buffet laid out."

"Oh my God, this is a Colefax and Fowler dream," said Nancy, gazing admiringly at the décor as they headed along the second-floor corridor. "Mom would *die* to decorate like this."

The corridor was painted a sunny yellow, and a frieze of bows and leaves had been hand-stenciled in crisp white beneath the cornicing. At each window, swagged chintz curtains bulged onto the cream silk carpet, which had a yellow Greek key pattern embroidered on it. The look was, Ursula noted, extravagant, luxurious, and of-the-moment.

"We're going to have to try every one," said Ursula, looking along the vast corridor with doors all the way down it.

"Okay," said Nancy, poking her head into an empty room on her right.

Suddenly Ursula noticed a door opening at the far end of the corridor. The girls froze for an instant, then silently sneaked behind one of the huge swagged curtains. From a tiny gap, they watched as a woman dressed in a green-and-white-striped nurse's uniform and an apron and cap walked past them towards the grand staircase.

"She must be Lord Brattenbury's nurse. He's got to be in that room," whispered Ursula, closing the gap in the curtain so they couldn't be seen.

They heard the nurse's footsteps fade away. With the coast now clear, they tiptoed along until they reached the far end of the corridor.

The door to Lord Brattenbury's room was slightly ajar. With her heart thudding, Ursula pushed the door open a little more and took in the scene. The room was plain and masculine in style, the half-drawn curtains making for a gloomy atmosphere. The navy linen that upholstered the walls was barely visible, covered as it was with numerous black-and-white sporting prints. A faded Aubusson rug covered the floor. A writing table had been taken over by a heap of tablet boxes, medicine bottles, thermometers, syringes, and a pile of garish knitting. A mahogany-ended bed, flanked by two large side tables, was positioned in the middle of the far wall. The girls could see the outline of the sleeping Lord Brattenbury in it, hidden under mounds of blankets.

They walked as close as they dared to the bed, and Ursula noticed a glamorous black-and-white photograph on one side table. It showed a man dressed in white standing on the deck of a sailing yacht. He looked gorgeously raffish and tan, his thick hair ruffled by the wind, the sun catching his sharp cheekbones; he was holding a young child in his arms.

"That must be Lord B. when he was young, with India. How sad," whispered Nancy, pointing at it. "But boy, was he handsome. How come all these English guys look like JFK?"

"We just do, my dear," said a thin voice suddenly.

There was a rustling among the bedcovers. Lord Brattenbury emerged from the layers of blankets and wearily propped himself up against the pillows. Despite the film of perspiration over his face, he still looked remarkably attractive, an older version of the astonishingly handsome man from the photograph. That thick head of hair, only slightly graying, was unmistakable, and his sharp cheekbones were instantly recognizable, if a little too prominent in his drawn face. He picked up a small hand towel from the other side table and patted down his forehead and cheeks.

Nancy and Ursula peered at him curiously. He managed a smile.

"You couldn't open a window, could you?" His voice was a rasp, almost gone. Lord Brattenbury sounded very, very sick. "That dreadful Nurse Ramsbottom is trying to kill me. All these blankets and heating! Feels hotter than hell in here."

"Of course," said Ursula, pushing back a curtain and opening a window.

"Thank you. Air," he said weakly. Then he asked, "India's friends?" The girls nodded.

"How lovely," he said croakily, and asked for their names, which they gave.

"I remember," said Lord Brattenbury, ever the gentleman, even as he sweated and sweated. "Miss Feingold . . . I recall India had invited you to her shooting party. She did love Americans. Quite right. Did you go to the service?"

"Yes, it was really moving," said Nancy.

"Poor, poor darling India. My heart's broken, you know. To lose a child before you die is the greatest punishment life can inflict on a mother or father . . ."

The girls watched as a tear left the corner of Lord Brattenbury's left eye and settled on his cheek. Suddenly, he started shivering violently. "Sorry," he stuttered. "Can that window be shut now? Got the shaking chills again. My dear girl's death has brought the malaria back. I don't think I'm going to recover this time."

"Don't say that!" exclaimed Ursula, closing the window.

Lord Brattenbury drew his blankets right up to his chin and lay back on his pillows. His teeth were chattering now, and it seemed he was weakening a little more with every word he spoke.

"The illegit," he mumbled shakily. "Can you find him?"

"The what?" asked Ursula.

"My son. The illegitimate boy . . . Mary. She was called Mary. Mary Crimshaw."

"Who's Mary?" said Nancy.

"The girl. Her mother still lives in the village. Runs the shop—"

There was a light tap at the door. To their surprise, Nancy and

Ursula suddenly found themselves face-to-face with High Provost Scrope and his secretary.

"Feingold? Flowerbutton? What on earth—?" demanded the high provost.

"We were just . . . er . . . chatting," said Ursula with an innocent smile.

"Look, jolly sorry to interrupt the chat and all that, but I'm afraid I must speak to Lord Brattenbury urgently. Alone," said Scrope.

"I think he's gone back to sleep," said Nancy quietly. "He seemed really sick."

Lord Brattenbury was, indeed, lying on his pillows, eyes now closed.

"This is most inconvenient. I *suppose* we'll have to wait until later. Mrs. Gifford-Pennant, remind me to return here in an hour." With that, Scrope and his secretary reluctantly exited the room.

The door closed, and Nancy and Ursula were left with the sleeping man.

"I can't believe what Lord Brattenbury just said," whispered Ursula.

"There's another heir?" Nancy asked.

"I think so."

Lord Brattenbury opened one eye and squinted at them both.

"Now get a move on," he said, "and find that boy before I croak!"

Chapter 34

By the time Ursula and Nancy got back down to the great hall, it had already filled with mourners. As the guests sipped more and more glasses of Lord Brattenbury's finest vintage champagne, served by an army of house staff, the funereal atmosphere was gradually replaced by that of a fabulous cocktail party. The girls soon located Horatio, who was, naturally, hogging the buffet, enthusiastically consuming large quantities of food and drink.

"Horatio, you gotta drive us down to the village," said Nancy breathlessly.

"But I'm having a roaring time," he protested, gulping down another forkful of coronation chicken. "This is a funeral of bacchanalian indulgence. I can't leave until I've tried absolutely everything."

Horatio whipped a devil-on-horseback from the sideboard. He polished it off in one bite. This was swiftly followed by a slice of fruitcake, a scone loaded with strawberry jam and clotted cream, and another glass of champagne.

"Mmmmmm!" Horatio groaned with pleasure. "*Surely* we don't need to leave yet."

"Actually, we do. There's a new suspect in the case," said Ursula.

Horatio's interest was piqued. "Oh, who?"

"I don't know, exactly," said Ursula. "But I'm *sure* there is. Come on."

"All right," agreed Horatio, sneaking some homemade shortbread into his pocket and following the girls outside.

By the time the three of them had made it back to the car, Ursula was starting to have serious doubts about Horatio's ability to drive. He had swayed his way out of the house, tripped over nothing at all on the graveled drive, and been unable to operate the handle of the driver's door to get into the car. When he eventually got into it, he had wrestled his way over the top of the front seat, collapsed onto the mess in the backseat, and promptly passed out. His thumb soon found its way to his lips, and he proceeded to make a noise like a blocked drain as he sucked it vigorously.

"*Now* what are we going to do?" said Ursula, looking at the lumpen form asleep in the backseat.

Nancy stretched an arm into the back of the car, rifled through Horatio's pockets, and found the car keys, which she dangled in front of Ursula.

"No self-respecting American high schooler hits seventeen without getting her license."

A hair-raising twenty minutes later, during which Ursula tried to explain to her American friend the logic of driving on the left-hand side, Nancy parked the car opposite the village shop. The girls left Horatio snoring in the backseat.

A sign above the doorway of the shop read "Brattenbury Stores." The tiny window contained various parish notices and a few ancient-looking packets of crisps. As Ursula opened the door, a bell tinkled. Nancy tottered behind her on her high heels and followed her inside.

The small store was sparsely stocked with the kind of provisions that would last at least four or five years in a larder—or during a war. There were tinned peaches, baked beans, cans of corned beef, and packets of "squashed fly" biscuits. There was a confectionery shelf meagerly supplied with a few Walnut Whips, Caramac bars, Flumps, Black Jacks, and foam bananas. Food-wise, the residents of Brattenbury were not exactly indulged.

Ursula spotted a neat pile of newspapers on the counter, on the top of which was the *Daily Mail*. She gulped when she saw the headline: WHO KILLED THE IT GIRL? Splashed under the words was a grainy black-and-white photograph of India dressed in a mini puff-ball dress at an Oxford ball.

"Nancy, look," said Ursula. The girls read the article, which was of course by Neil Thistleton.

Brainy society beauty Lady India Brattenbury, only daughter of mining tycoon Lord Arthur Brattenbury, will be buried today at the lavish family estate in Derbyshire. Her body was discovered on Monday morning in the room of an Oxford don. Lady India was last seen alive late on Sunday night. She had been partying at a wild bash with members of the so-called Champagne Set in the rooms of her boyfriend, aristocratic rowing Blue and fellow Oxford student the Earl of Wychwood. Police sources told the *Daily Mail*, "We have a young male suspect in custody," but would not be drawn on the identity of the suspect. However the *Daily Mail* has learned that Wentworth Wychwood was arrested late on Tuesday night.

"You know, I never thought I'd say this, but I actually feel sorry for Wenty," Ursula said, returning the newspaper to the counter.

"Me too," said Nancy.

There was no sign of anyone running the shop, but Ursula could see the door behind the counter was just ajar.

"Hello!" she called out, hoping there was someone inside.

"Two ticks!" came a locally accented voice from within.

Moments later an immaculately coiffed, overly made-up woman appeared. She was dressed in a cream-collared, neatly tailored bright red wool dress that strained over her ample bust. Her brightly dyed auburn hair had telltale gray streaks at the temples.

"Wow!" exclaimed Nancy when she saw her. "You look like you should be running the cosmetics counter at Bloomingdale's."

"Come again, love?" said the woman, looking confused. "Right. What can I get you?"

"I'm starving," said Nancy, picking up a Milkybar and putting it on the counter. Ursula filled a paper bag with Flumps.

"Thirty pence please."

As Ursula handed over the coins, she said, "Do you know where we could find Mrs. Crimshaw?"

"You're looking at her," replied the woman. "Why?"

Ursula and Nancy regarded her nervously.

"What is it?" asked Mrs. Crimshaw.

"Actually, we were wondering if you could tell us where your daughter Mary is?" said Nancy, unwrapping her Milkybar. "We need to speak to her. It's super-urgent."

A melancholy expression crossed the shopkeeper's face.

"She passed away," said Mrs. Crimshaw, in a desolate tone of voice. "Died in childbirth. Twenty-two years ago now."

"I'm so sorry," said Nancy.

"Thank you," said Mrs. Crimshaw. Ursula noticed the woman's eyes welling up as she produced a handkerchief from her pocket and dabbed at her face. "Dear me. Always get like this about poor Mary. Despite the trouble she caused when she was with us."

Mrs. Crimshaw took out a compact from a drawer beneath the counter and pressed powder as thickly as she could beneath her teary eyes.

"What kind of trouble?" said Ursula.

"So-fetching-she-was-pregnant-at-fourteen kind of trouble, that's what," said Mrs. Crimshaw.

"Fourteen?!" exclaimed Nancy. "Oh my God. She was a child."

"Unfortunately, she didn't look like one." Mrs. Crimshaw shook her head. "She was always sneakin' off with boys. Got with one o' those lads in the village and that was it, she was pregnant."

Clearly, thought Ursula, Mrs. Crimshaw had absolutely no idea who the real father of Mary's baby was.

The woman went on, "Poor lass. Poor bairn."

"Barn?" Nancy looked puzzled.

"The baby. We have a saying in our family: 'Those as thinks a bairn's a baby call a sprog a child and a lass a lady.' Mary's baby was a little boy. That's all I ever knew about it, really. I would have kept him, looked after him here even with the shame of it in the village, but Ian—that was Mary's father, my late husband—well, he'd arranged for the child to be adopted even before he was born. Said it wouldn't be fair ont' baby to be brought up with everyone knowing he was illegitimate, but . . ." Mrs. Crimshaw couldn't go on. Her face had clouded with regret.

"Do you have any idea who adopted Mary's baby?" asked Ursula, as gently as she could.

"Well, what a strange question," said Mrs. Crimshaw. "Why come here asking that now, after all this time?"

"I'm trying to solve Lady India's murder," said Ursula. "I think the whereabouts of your grandchild could help us figure out who killed her."

Mrs. Crimshaw looked doubtfully at Ursula, then Nancy, then back at Ursula again.

"You don't look much like policewomen," she said.

"I'm a student reporter," explained Ursula, trying to sound as grown-up and professional as she could. "For *Cherwell*. It's just a university newspaper. We really need your help."

"All right then."

Mrs. Crimshaw walked to the door of the shop and turned the sign around so that "Closed" faced outwards, then returned to the counter and rested her ample bottom against it while she talked.

"As soon as Mary started showing, Ian packed her off to the Catholic Crusade of Rescue. Miles away, it was in Leeds somewhere. It was a home for unmarried mums and babies. If the mothers didn't have anywhere to go—and Ian wouldn't think about having Mary back home—the babies were adopted. When Ian told me that Mary had passed on and that the adoption was going ahead . . . well, there was nothing I could do."

"It's a terrible story," said Nancy.

"There's not a day goes by I don't regret not going and getting that bairn. But round here, it wouldn't be accepted. Not then, not now."

"Do you think your husband had any idea who adopted the baby?" asked Ursula.

"He always said to me he didn't. But . . ." Mrs. Crimshaw looked wistful. "Sometimes I wondered."

"Why?"

"He used to go fishing for a day or two, a couple of times a year, with Brian Wood, the blacksmith, but there was this one time when he said he'd gone fishing and I saw Brian shoeing horses at the stables. I found an address in Ian's diary written next to that date."

"Did you ever ask your husband why he had that address?"

"No . . . at the time I wondered if, you know, he was up to something, an affair . . . it seemed better to leave it alone. But looking back now, knowing Ian—he wouldn't have been up to anything. I think he went that day and saw where Mary's child lived."

"Can you remember the address?" asked Nancy.

"Oh, yes. I'll never forget it," said Mrs. Crimshaw, "because at the time I remember thinking it was so odd that Ian would go all that way down south to Oxford without telling me. We didn't know anyone who lived there. But what has all this got to do with poor Lady India?"

Chapter 35

No. 4 Penny Farthing Place—the address that Mrs. Crimshaw had scribbled on a piece of notepaper for the girls—was a twee two-up, two-down cottage located midway along a tiny cobbled alley that ran along the back of St. Ebbe's Street. A Victorian streetlamp just outside the dwelling lit the narrow pavement.

It was dark, almost eight o'clock that night, by the time Nancy had parked the Reliant Robin opposite the house. While Horatio snored away in the backseat, she and Ursula sat, watching the little house, waiting. What for, they weren't quite sure. But they were absolutely, definitely waiting for something.

"You really think a ruthless throat-slashing killer would have such a cute house?" whispered Nancy, peering at the cottage.

"Where am I?" whined a distressed voice from the backseat.

"Ssshhhhh, Horatio," ordered Nancy from the driver's seat. "We don't want the murderer to know we're out here."

"Murderer?!" he whimpered, sounding petrified. "What are you talking about?"

Ursula explained the state of play. The adoptive parents of Lord Brattenbury's illegitimate heir had, possibly, once lived in No. 4 Penny Farthing Place. She was hoping against hope that they still did, perhaps with the adopted baby, who would now be twenty-two years old.

"Oh my God, someone's coming out," Nancy said. "Quick, hide."

The three of them shrank as low as they possibly could in the car while still managing to see out.

"It can't be!" gasped Ursula.

"That is insane!" chimed in Nancy.

"Surely not," added Horatio.

The trio watched, mouths agape, as the Christminster night porter, Nick, and his mother, Mrs. Deddington, spoke briefly on the doorstep of the house. He soon left and she retreated back indoors.

Ursula whispered, astonished, "Look, Mrs. Deddington's still in her funeral clothes. They must have just got back."

Horatio was completely flabbergasted. "Am I to understand that you are saying, Ursula, that the Christminster College night porter is the illegitimate son of Lord Brattenbury? That Nicholas Deddington is the missing heir to the Brattenbury estates? Forty farms, two villages, ten thousand acres, and a garden square in Chelsea? Are you *sure*, Ursula?"

"Well—" she began.

"It's *definitely* him," Nancy interrupted her, an indisputable certainty to her tone.

"How can you be so certain?" asked Horatio.

"Oh, that's super-easy," she said confidently. "It's all about hotness."

"What?" guffawed Horatio.

"Look, the minute I met the night porter, I said he was literally as hot as JFK Jr. Remember, Ursula?"

"What on earth," asked Horatio skeptically, "has the undisputed hotness of JFK Jr. got to do with all this?"

Nancy continued, "Lord Brattenbury had this photo by his bed probably from when he was in his twenties. He was on a boat, all breezy and tan. He looked *exactly* like JFK when he was young. I even said it out loud today. Lord B. and Deddington Jr. are *literally* identical when you really think about it. They've got the same sexy cheekbones, same thick Kennedy-ish hair. Gorgeous."

"It's true," said Ursula. "Deddington Jr. does look incredibly similar to the handsome young Lord Brattenbury in that photograph."

"So . . . are you saying you think the night porter killed India?" asked Horatio. "What a delicious twist that would be."

"He certainly had motive—a huge inheritance, a grand title," Ursula replied, "and opportunity. Nick Deddington claims he was in college all night on Sunday, working. It's the perfect alibi."

"It's true that if he was prowling around the grounds at the dead of night, no one would have suspected anything," agreed Horatio. "It's his job, after all."

"But wait," interjected Nancy. "If he'd killed India, what would he have done with his bloody clothes when he had to go back to the lodge?"

"Easy enough to get rid of them," said Ursula, "if someone was helping him."

"You mean . . ." Nancy's eyes drifted over to the Deddingtons' house.

"Maybe," replied Ursula.

"Sounds like Wenty's off the hook," said Horatio.

"I think it's a little more complicated than that," said Ursula. "He's still got an awful lot of explaining to do. Geraldine Ormsby-Leigh insists he wasn't with her. We still don't know exactly where he was that night."

"Maybe we never will," said Horatio. "Wenty probably doesn't even know where he was that night. He's too drunk to know where he is most nights, after all."

"Come on, Ursula," said Nancy. "Mrs. Deddington's at home. Let's seize the moment."

Before Ursula could do a thing about it, Nancy had sprung out of the car and was knocking on the door of No. 4 Penny Farthing Place.

"Go with her, Ursula," said Horatio. "This could be the key to the story. I'll keep a lookout."

Ursula joined her friend on the Deddingtons' doorstep. Nancy knocked, and a few moments later, Mrs. Deddington opened the door. She was in stockinged feet and looked tired, her black funeral dress only exacerbating the shadows beneath her eyes. When she saw the pair of them, she looked thoroughly spooked.

"What are you doing here, girls, in the dark?" she asked, her voice wavering.

"May we come in?" Nancy asked.

"Well, all right . . . but I've only just arrived back from the funeral."

Frowning anxiously, Mrs. Deddington ushered the girls inside. They squeezed along a narrow corridor and into a small, neat sitting room. There was a bulky TV set in one corner, and the room was furnished with a matching three-piece suite upholstered in cheap flowery fabric. Ursula noticed various framed pictures of the family on the mantelpiece. There were snaps of Mr. and Mrs. Deddington with their son as a baby. There was Nicholas, smiling, gap-toothed, in school uniform. As a teenager, he was athletic-looking in football gear, his handsome features now apparent. The fact was, he didn't look the slightest bit like either of his parents, thought Ursula. There was no denying it. He *did* have those Brattenbury cheekbones.

"I'm sorry to disturb you so late tonight, Mrs. Deddington," she said apologetically. "But I want to talk to you about India."

"I already told the police. I wasn't in college on Sunday night," replied Mrs. Deddington. Ursula thought she detected a guilty look come over the woman's face as she added, "I was here all evening. *Dynasty** was on."

Dynasty? Hadn't Mrs. Deddington said that she was watching *Dallas*, not *Dynasty*, when they were having Marmite on toast in the scouts' mess? And when Deddington had said he'd spent Sunday night at the Eagle and Child, hadn't he said it was because he hated *Dallas*? Ursula would have to check her notebooks when she got home tonight.

* The Carringtons, the fictional family around which TV show *Dynasty* (1981–1989) revolved, were the Kardashians of the '80s. The whole world tuned in for the on-screen catfights between Alexis Carrington (Joan Collins) and Krystle Carrington (Linda Evans).

"It's not about you, Mrs. Deddington," Ursula told her.

"You might have said so," she answered, looking suddenly relieved.

"It's about your son."

"Nicholas? What's he got to do with any of this?"

"How old is Nick?"

"Twenty-two. Why?"

What an awkward thing to have to ask, Ursula thought to herself. She took a deep breath, then said, "Does Nick know who his . . . It's just, I was sort of wondering . . . does he know who his real mother and father are?"

Mrs. Deddington paled. She sank down onto the arm of one of the chairs.

"How do you know my boy is adopted?" she asked sharply.

"Long story . . ." said Nancy.

"*He* doesn't even know he's adopted," said Mrs. Deddington.

"Really?" asked Nancy.

"We decided right from the start he'd never know. No point in complicating life for a young lad, is there?"

"Is there any way he could have found out?" asked Ursula.

Mrs. Deddington paused for a long moment. Finally, she said, "No one in our families ever knew. I lost my own baby, and Nicholas was . . ." She trailed off, sadly. "He came to us at the right moment. No one knew he wasn't mine. But if Nicholas had somehow discovered he was adopted, he'd have told us, I'm sure of it. We're a close family. But I can't think how he'd ever have found out. No. It's impossible, really."

"So you don't think he's ever known who his real parents were?" asked Ursula.

"No. How could he? *We* don't even know who they were. We weren't allowed any information about them when we adopted him. Now, what has this all got to do with poor Lady India, anyway?"

"I'm not sure," said Ursula. "I think I've made a mistake. I'm sorry we bothered you tonight."

"So am I," huffed Mrs. Deddington angrily. "Remember, Nicholas must never know about any of this. Ever."

•

"IF DEDDINGTON JR. doesn't know that Lord Brattenbury is his real father, how could he have a serious motive for killing India?" asked Nancy.

They were sitting cross-legged on the floor of Ursula's room later that night, drinking tea and trying to warm up by the electric fire. Ursula had taken her notes about the murder from her folder and spread them out on the floor. Occasionally she wrote down a new thought.

"Maybe he does know," she said.

"How?"

"I don't know . . . Or maybe Mrs. Deddington does. Maybe *she's* lying."

"I can't see it," said Nancy. "She wasn't even here on Sunday night, we know that."

"The thing is, I'm starting to wonder about Mrs. Deddington's story about Sunday night," said Ursula.

"Why?"

"When we first spoke to her about the night of the murder, she said she was at home that evening watching *Dallas*. Just now, she said she was watching *Dynasty*. *Dynasty*'s not even on TV on Sunday nights."

"That's weird," Nancy agreed. "I mean, how could anyone confuse *Dallas* and *Dynasty*? The clothes are *completely* different."

"Exactly."

"So, are you saying," said Nancy slowly, "that you think that Mrs. Deddington is lying about Sunday night? That she wasn't home after all? You think she *does* know who Nicholas's parents were? That *she* killed India?"

Just then, there was a rap on Ursula's door.

"Come in!" she called.

Both girls were startled to see Deddington Jr. pop his head around the door. Ursula covered her notes with her arm as subtly as she could.

"Evening, Miss Flowerbutton," he said, smiling at her. "Actually, I'm looking for you, Miss Feingold—thought I might find you in here. There's a telegram for you." He handed a brown envelope to Nancy.

"That's very kind of you," she said.

"Good night, ladies," he said.

The girls listened in silence as his footsteps faded away down the stairs.

"That was *really* weird," said Nancy. "Do you think he could have heard what we were saying about his mom? Ugh. Spooky."

"I know. Who's the telegram from?" asked Ursula.

"Hopefully it's Frank replying to mine," Nancy said, tearing open the envelope.

She read the missive, then handed it to Ursula. The telegram contained just two words:

RUBBER GLOVE

"I don't get it," said Ursula.

"The sodium dimethyl-whatty," replied Nancy. "Frank's saying it's something to do with a rubber glove."

"May I keep this?" said Ursula. Her mind was whirring. "I think it might be useful."

"Sure."

She tucked it inside her folder. "I think we need to get in to see Wenty tomorrow. We can't properly rule him out unless we get the real truth from him about where he was late on Sunday night."

"Do you think Detective Trott will let us see him?" said Nancy.

"I don't know, but it's worth a try."

"It's already nearly eleven," said Nancy, getting up to go to her room. "I need to get some rest."

After her friend had gone to bed, Ursula added to her notes, writing:

—Is Mrs. D. lying to cover up for her son? Or her husband? Was Mr. D. really at Eagle and Child on Sunday night? Deddington Snr. would, potentially, have had just as much motive as his wife to dispose of India.

—And, as if I am not confused enough already, what on earth is significance of "rubber glove"?

Chapter 36

Wentworth Wychwood managed a tired smile when Nancy and Ursula walked into the interview room to which he had been brought that morning. Having spent the last couple of days in a cell in Oxford police station, he was unshaven and looked disheveled. The girls sat down on two uncomfortable plastic chairs at a table opposite Wenty while a constable remained by the door.

"Flowerbutton," Wenty said gratefully to Ursula, "I *knew* you'd sort everything out."

Ursula shook her head sorrowfully. "I have *not* sorted everything out. Your story about Geraldine doesn't stand up."

"What!" exclaimed Wenty. "But—"

"Wenty, Trott's only allowing us twenty minutes with you," Ursula interrupted. "We need to go over the details of your story again, as quickly as possible." Then she dropped her voice, hoping the constable couldn't hear. "There's another lead."

"What kind of lead?" asked Wenty.

"There's an illegitimate heir to the Brattenbury fortune," Nancy explained. "Lord Brattenbury told us when we were up in Derbyshire yesterday at the funeral. He called him 'the illegit.' Which I thought was really mean, by the way."

"Are you saying that an illegitimate heir to Lord Brattenbury killed

India so that he could inherit?" Wenty seemed dumbfounded.

"I wish it were that simple," said Ursula.

"Trouble is," added Nancy, "the illegitimate heir doesn't know he's the illegitimate heir. Or at least we don't think he knows. Which means he wouldn't have a motive for removing India."

"So India had a brother?"

"Half brother. Before he married India's mother, Lord Brattenbury got a local girl pregnant. Her name was Mary Crimshaw. She was the daughter of the village shopkeeper. But she died in childbirth and her baby boy was adopted. India never knew him," explained Ursula.

"Actually," pointed out Nancy, "that's not *quite* true. India did know her half brother, but she didn't know that she knew her half brother. In other words she had no idea that the guy who was her half brother was her half brother."

Wenty looked exasperated. "You've lost me. Let me get this right. You're saying that the illegitimate heir didn't know he was the illegitimate heir, and that India knew the illegitimate heir but that she had no idea he was the illegitimate heir?"

"Exactly," said Ursula.

Wenty shook his head. "I don't see how I'm going to be any help in proving this theory of yours."

"Let's just go over what happened on the night of the party," said Ursula.

"If I must," he sighed.

"Wenty, you haven't been telling the complete truth," Ursula said.

"What do you mean? I've told you *everything*, even the embarrassing stuff," he pleaded.

"You lied about Geraldine Ormsby-Leigh. She was on the sleeper from Edinburgh on Sunday night," Ursula continued.

"Geraldine. Geraldine Ormsby-Leigh?! I didn't say Geraldine, I said *Gwen*doline. Gwendoline Something-or-Other," said Wenty. "Yes. That was it. Gwendoline Orr-Little. They all sound the same."

"I'm *sure* it was a Geraldine you mentioned," insisted Ursula.

Wenty looked sheepish. "Look, Geraldine and I—Okay. I *think* we did it once. But not on Sunday. Sunday was Gwendoline. I swear to God I didn't spend that night in college, murdering my girlfriend."

Nancy and Ursula looked at each other doubtfully.

"Wenty, if this turns out not to be true . . ." warned Ursula. She paused for a moment, allowing her words to sink in. She couldn't help Wenty unless she knew he was telling the truth. "I think we need to go over the towel incident. I mean, the police are using it as their main piece of evidence against you, right?"

Wenty ran his hands through his hair. He looked frustrated.

"They're saying that I killed India, in a fit of jealousy, with a champagne glass from my own party; that I then returned to my rooms, collected a towel *with my initial on it*, went back up to Dr. Dave's rooms—without another soul seeing me, incidentally—where I mopped up the blood from India's neck and then stuffed the towel up the chimney, hoping it would be burned the next time Dr. Dave lit his fire. I did explain to the police that, having been brought up in a freezing-cold country house heated *only* by open fires and a pathetic broken Aga, I am well aware that if you want to burn something you put it *on* the fire, not up the bloody chimney, where it has not a chance of burning to ash."

"How did they take that?" asked Nancy.

"They said I was a fibbing toff," he said despairingly. "But if I was going to kill my girlfriend, why would I do the deed and then go all the way back to my rooms—presumably covered in blood—to fetch a towel that identifies me? Someone put that towel there. Someone's trying to frame me."

"Let's go back to the start of the party," suggested Ursula, checking the clock. "We've only got a few minutes left."

Wenty sighed. "Well, as you know, by the time you two arrived, at around nine p.m., we'd started running out of champagne saucers. I met you two at the door of the Old Drawing Room, and asked you to come and help me get some more glasses from the bathroom."

"True," said Nancy. "I remember being a little upset that my first experience of an Oxford ball was doing the dishes—"

"It wasn't a ball!" exclaimed Wenty. "It was an Opening Jaunt. It's a completely different thing. Anyway, I remember that we three were in the bathroom, and I ended up trying to wash a champagne saucer in the sink because there were no clean ones and—"

"May I interrupt?" Ursula asked. "Why were there no clean glasses?"

"The washer-uppers had disappeared," replied Wenty. "I think they must have been worried about being reported to the high provost for moonlighting. They came back later, at around eleven."

"Who were the washer-uppers?" asked Nancy.

"Just a couple of scouts. Anyway, while I was washing up the champagne glass, I cut my hand. So I used one of the monogrammed Wychwood hand towels to clean myself up. It was a nasty cut, lots of blood. But I was so pissed I barely noticed any pain."

"Remind me where you put the towel," said Ursula.

"I think I just chucked it on the floor," Wenty recalled.

"Where anyone could have found it," Nancy said.

"Not exactly *anyone*," said Ursula. "Only those who went into the bathroom that night."

"Can you remember seeing anyone unusual in your bathroom?" asked Nancy.

"Not really," Wenty replied. "Masses of people must have gone in and out that night."

"But wait! What about anyone who was *not* unusual?" said Ursula, suddenly excited.

"There's no way Eg killed India," protested Wenty.

"I'm not talking about Eg," she insisted. "I'm talking about the washer-uppers. It wouldn't have been unusual, or particularly remarked upon, for them to have been in and out of the bathroom all night."

"Except when I really needed them," said Wenty.

"Which scouts were they?" asked Nancy.

"I managed to persuade Alice and Mrs. Deddington to help out that night . . . Come to think of it, I still owe them a fiver each. Ursula, what are you doing?"

She was grabbing her notebook off the table.

"No wonder Mrs. Deddington didn't know whether she watched *Dallas* or *Dynasty* on Sunday night. She didn't watch either of them. She wasn't home. Come on, Nancy, we need to go," she said.

Nancy sprang out of her seat.

"But what about going over the details of Sunday night?" Wenty looked confused.

"Don't worry. I think we've got enough," Ursula replied. "You'll be out of here soon, I promise."

As Ursula and Nancy rushed from the interview room, Wenty called, "Try and get me out by Saturday night. I really want to go to Christian's night at the Playpen. It's such a brilliant nightclub—"

"Wenty, I cannot believe you are worrying about your social life right now." His priorities were, thought Ursula, amazingly superficial.

"Just trying to be positive about everything," said Wenty. "Oh, and if you see Alice or Mrs. Deddington, tell them I haven't forgotten about their fivers!"

Chapter 37

Mrs. Deddington was finishing off her morning tea break alone in the scouts' mess when Ursula and Nancy came upon her. She seemed jumpy.

"What is it now?" asked the scout, nervously putting her cup of tea aside.

"It's about Sunday night," said Ursula.

"I told you. I was home. *Dallas* was on. I told the police the same thing." Mrs. Deddington checked her watch. "Now, I really must get on with the high provost's ironing."

She started gathering up a pile of shirts.

"The thing is, Wenty Wychwood says you were washing up at his party on Sunday night," Nancy said, adding, "He said to tell you he hasn't forgotten that he still owes you a fiver."

Mrs. Deddington turned a shade of crimson usually reserved for those unfortunate enough to have contracted scarlet fever.

"Girls, please, you *mustn't* tell anyone I was working for an undergraduate," she implored them. "I could lose my job if anyone knows I've taken money from a student here."

"Don't worry," Nancy reassured her. "We're not going to tell anyone. We just want to find out if you saw anything suspicious during the party."

Mrs. Deddington glanced anxiously around her. "The other scouts will be in here soon for their break. I'll have to be quick."

"Do you remember finding a bloodstained towel in the bathroom opposite the Old Drawing Room that night?" asked Ursula.

"The one with the *W* embroidered on it?" asked Mrs. Deddington.

"So you did see it then?" Nancy said.

"Yes. Alice and I, we'd come down here for a bit—didn't want to get caught moonlighting. When we came back to carry on washing up, it must have been just after eleven, I saw the towel on the bathroom floor. I picked it up—of course I did, I like things spick-and-span."

"What did you do with it?" asked Ursula.

Mrs. Deddington looked surprised to be asked such a simple question.

"Put it in the laundry basket, of course. As I said, I do like things spick-and-span."

At that moment the door to the mess opened and a couple of scouts appeared for their break.

"Cup of tea?" asked Mrs. Deddington, filling the kettle again, before saying, rather louder than necessary, "Thank you for letting me know about the hot water breaking down, girls. Someone will be up to fix it today."

•

URSULA WAS NOT quite sure what to do next. She had a nonnegotiable deadline for her history essay that coming Monday, and had made few inroads into the apocalyptic—or not—vision of the Scottish Covenanters, but the deadline for her article was sooner.

How on earth was she going to solve the riddle of India's murder and write it up before Sunday morning? After all, Mrs. Deddington's story seemed to explain far less about the case than she had hoped. The only thing Ursula had ascertained from the brief interview with the scout was that she had lied about her whereabouts on Sunday night for fear of losing her job. The mystery of exactly how the bloody

towel had made its way from Wenty's laundry basket, thence to India's garroted neck, and finally into Dr. Dave's chimney breast was no
nearer to being solved.

Ursula climbed the stairs to her room. Even if she didn't have the
ending of her article yet, she had the grim beginning. She could at the
very least add to the notes she'd started writing up last night. Maybe
there was a crucial clue or fact she had overlooked that would be revealed while she was writing.

The door to her room was ajar when she arrived, and Ursula entered to find Alice beavering away, polishing the desk. Perhaps she
could shed some light on the mysterious movements of the bloody
towel.

"Hello, love," said Alice. "Am I all right to carry on?"

"Of course," Ursula replied. "I just need my desk."

"I've just got to do your bed and then I'll be gone."

Alice bustled over to the bed and started making it. Ursula sat
down at her desk, where her work had been arranged in a neat pile,
with the red folder containing her story notes on the top. She opened
it and read the last note she had written on her pad:

. . . what on earth is significance of "rubber glove"?

"Alice, can you help me with something?" said Ursula.

"I very much doubt I can help with your essay, but go on, give me
a try," the scout chuckled.

"Actually it's about Sunday night."

Alice stood stock-still, a blanket in her hand. She turned slowly
towards Ursula.

"Look, I know you were working at Wenty's party that night—"

"Miss Flowerbutton, please don't mention that to anyone," Alice
begged, sounding just as desperate as Mrs. Deddington had. "We
tried to stay out of sight. The extra money's just so helpful."

"Don't worry, no one's going to say anything. But I'm curious
about something—"

A tap on the door, followed by Nancy's arrival in Ursula's room, interrupted them.

"Hey, Alice," Nancy called to the scout. She was holding a blue airmail envelope in her hand. "Mind if I hang out and read my mail here, Ursula?"

"Of course not," she replied.

As Nancy sat in the armchair and started opening her letter, Ursula turned back to Alice, and said, "Anyway, I was curious about a towel that was left on the floor of Wenty's bathroom on Sunday night. It was one of his monogrammed hand towels."

"I know the ones," said Alice, arranging the blanket neatly on top of Ursula's bed. "Very nice. But that one had a nasty stain on it." She then addressed Nancy, saying, in worried tones, "Miss Feingold, you won't say anything about me washing up on Sunday night, will you?"

"No way," said Nancy, scanning her letter.

"So, I was just wondering," Ursula continued slowly, "did you see Mrs. Deddington put the hand towel into the laundry basket?"

"No." Alice shook her head. "She put it into the pocket of her apron."

Ursula noticed Nancy stiffen in her chair. A startled look appeared on her face.

"Mrs. Deddington took it?" Nancy reiterated. "You're sure?"

"Yes. We'd gone off for a break to the scouts' mess. When we came back later, there it was on the floor. She picked it up and said she was going to wash it herself," replied Alice, starting to gather up her cleaning things now the bed was made. "She wanted to get the stain out before it marked."

"Oh, right," said Ursula, trying to remain cool as she noted Alice's words in her book.

"Righty, I'm off, girls," said the scout, picking up her bucket.

Just as Alice was about to leave, Nancy suddenly emitted a long cooing sound. She was holding something in her hand.

"Oooooooh! Mom's sent the *cutest* photograph!" she exclaimed, jumping up and holding out a photograph of a wrinkled newborn baby dressed in a smocked, frilled romper suit for them to admire. "My cousin has had her first kid. Winston. He's so adorable."

"Sweet," said Ursula, getting up from her desk to take a closer look.

"Lovely," chimed in Alice, looking at the picture. "Beautiful bairn."

Suddenly, Nancy froze. What on earth was wrong with her? wondered Ursula.

"Did you say *'barn'*?" Nancy asked the scout.

"It means 'baby,'" replied Alice. "That's what we say up where I come from. Now, I'll leave you ladies to it."

The minute Alice had departed, Nancy shut the door to Ursula's room firmly, leaning against it as though to bar entry to any interlopers.

"Did you hear that?" she whispered dramatically.

"Hear what?" asked Ursula.

"She said *'barn.'*"

"It means a baby."

"I know. She used the *exact* same word for baby as Mrs. Crimshaw did . . ." Nancy continued.

Suddenly Ursula twigged.

"Oh my God! Mrs. Crimshaw said 'bairn' yesterday when she was talking about the illegitimate baby. Nancy, are you saying that you think Mary Crimshaw might not be dead?"

"I'm saying I think she was standing right here two seconds ago. She uses the same local slang as Mrs. Crimshaw. She could easily have been raised in Brattenbury."

Ursula dashed back to her desk and turned to a fresh page in her notebook.

"Right, brainstorming time," she said, hurriedly scribbling lines as she thought out loud. "If Alice, who was in college on Sunday night, is in fact Mary Crimshaw, who is in fact the birth mother of Nicholas Deddington, who is in fact the illegitimate heir to Lord Brattenbury . . . then she had the motive *and* the opportunity to murder India."

Nancy nodded enthusiastically as she rifled around in her purse for a packet of cigarettes. She then retreated back to the armchair, lit her cigarette, and puffed madly on it while Ursula went on, "But—hang on—how would Mary Crimshaw have found out where her son went when he was adopted?"

"Minor detail," insisted Nancy between smoke rings. "It probably wasn't that difficult to trace him. Perhaps her father secretly helped her. He knew where the baby had been taken."

"But why would Mary's father have told his wife that their daughter was dead if she wasn't?" asked Ursula, halting her writing for a moment to ponder so many new twists.

"Look, we all know that you British are pathetically uptight—"

"What?" Ursula protested.

"A pregnant, unmarried teenage daughter would have brought shame on Mary's family. Maybe her father forbade her from ever coming home. Maybe it was easiest to say she'd died," Nancy suggested.

"Perhaps that's why Alice was wearing a veil at the funeral . . . she didn't want any of the locals to recognize her," Ursula surmised. Suddenly, an extraordinary thought came to her: "Do you think she just lied to us about seeing Mrs. Deddington taking the towel?"

"That's it, Ursula!" Nancy sprang up from her chair. She was so excited she didn't notice the blizzard of ash falling from her cigarette to the floor as she did so. She came and perched on the corner of Ursula's desk. "What if *Alice* took the towel from the laundry basket after Mrs. Deddington had put it in there? What if *she* did everything that she's claiming Mrs. Deddington did?"

How on earth could that be proven? Ursula wondered, opening the top drawer of her desk and retrieving the bar of Kendal Mint Cake that Plain Granny had sent her. She broke off a large chunk and offered it to Nancy.

"You want me to eat Kryptonite now?" she said, shaking her head at the sight of the alien white bar.

"All the more for me," Ursula declared happily, crunching on the sweet mint cake. It tasted sublime, and reenergized her to continue. "Let's go back to the scene in the bathroom. Wenty said that after the row in Great Quad, he and Otto chatted in there—where, we now know, Alice and Mrs. Deddington were washing up—"

"Wait! Washing up! That's it!" cried Nancy. "It's what Frank said in that telegram. 'Rubber glove.' He meant a washing-up glove. You never see Alice without her yellow gloves. She must have been wearing them to hold the shard of glass when she killed India so she didn't leave her fingerprints. That's why Doc found that trace of sodium diamithy-whatty on the tiny glass fragment that was found in India's neck."

Ursula looked at Nancy with admiration. Her powers of deduction were razor-sharp. But there was a possible flaw in her theory.

"Lots of the other scouts wear washing-up gloves," Ursula pointed out. "Including Linda Deddington."

"True." Nancy looked deflated. She walked over to Ursula's sink, ran her cigarette stub under the cold tap, and chucked it in the trash.

"But, still, let's run with this hypothesis that Alice is the murderer," Ursula went on.

"Okay," said Nancy, taking a Milkybar from her purse. She sat cross-legged on the floor, munching chocolate.

"Alice, washing up in the bathroom at midnight, would have overheard Wenty asking Otto to go and get India back from Dr. Dave's rooms."

"Meaning she knew where India was that night," added Nancy.

"Exactly. Now, I don't know why, but at some point that night Alice decided to go up there. No one would have suspected anything peculiar if they'd seen a scout go into Dr. Dave's rooms at any time of the day or night, would they?"

"I guess not," agreed Nancy.

"She had Wenty's bloody towel in her apron pocket, which she had taken from the laundry basket sometime that evening. She found India alone. Here was her chance to dispose of India, remove the obstacle to her son's possible inheritance, and cast suspicion initially on Wenty by planting his bloody towel in Dr. Dave's chimney. By later saying she'd seen Mrs. Deddington take the towel, Alice could make it look as if Mrs. Deddington had planted it in Dr. Dave's chimney to frame Wenty, thereby making her the prime suspect."

Ursula looked at Nancy questioningly, as if to say, *Tell me if I'm completely mad.*

"You've left something out," Nancy said.

"What?"

"The flaw in Alice's plan: Mrs. Deddington. If she doesn't know her adopted son is the offspring of Lord Brattenbury, then she had no motive to murder India. Mrs. Deddington only lied about her whereabouts on Sunday night for fear of losing her job, not because she had killed someone."

"The only problem now," said Ursula, "is that we don't know for sure that Mary Crimshaw isn't dead."

•

URSULA PUT A ten-pence coin in the slot in the pay phone at the bottom of the staircase and dialed a Leeds number as fast as her fingers would allow. The line seemed to ring and ring forever before someone answered.

"Leeds Register Office," a man's voice answered.

"Hello. I'm wondering if you can help me locate a death certificate," said Ursula.

"I just need the name of the deceased and the year that they died."

"Her name was Mary Crimshaw, and I think she died some time in 1963 or 1964."

"Right. You'll need to send a postal order for two pounds, fifty pence, made payable to Leeds Register Office. When we receive your payment, we'll send you a copy of the death certificate."

That was going to take weeks, thought Ursula.

"Can I ring back later to see if you've found it?" she begged. "You see, this is really very urgent."

"It's always 'urgent,'" came the deadpan reply.

"Oh." There was nothing else for it. Ursula was going to have to tell a terrible lie if she was going to get anywhere. She crossed her fingers and said, in as sad a tone as she could, "You see, the thing is, the dead woman . . . she was my mother."

"Well . . . I suppose . . ." said the man, his tone softening, "in exceptional cases, I can elevate requests to 'officially urgent.'"

"That would be so kind," she said, sniffing as loudly and sadly as she could.

"All right. Don't worry, love. Someone can try and find the certificate today. If you give me a telephone number, we'll ring you back later."

Chapter 38

The scene at Vincent's Club* that night was, declared Nancy, "blazer heaven." The sight of the "Vinny's boys," the university's most elite sportsmen, lounging around on comfy-looking leather chesterfield sofas and swigging cocktails, dressed in the white-trimmed navy blazers and navy ties of the Oxford Blues, was, she concluded, "better than a Ralph Lauren ad." Thank goodness, Ursula thought to herself, she'd dressed up properly for the club's first cocktail party of the term: Nancy had lent her a ruched, fitted shocking-pink taffeta minidress that only just covered her thighs. It wasn't exactly her style, but it was fun to wear. Nancy, meanwhile, was dressed in a frothy off-the-shoulder dress that consisted of tumbling layers of pale yellow organdy frills held in place by tiny bows.

"Oh my God, Horatio?!" Ursula exclaimed, suddenly spotting her friend across the room. This was the last place she'd expected to see him, especially wearing the navy blazer of the Full Blues.

"He's not exactly a jock," observed Nancy.

Horatio saw the girls and beckoned them to join him.

"Horatio, I'm intrigued," said Nancy. "What sport did you get your Blue for?"

---

* Membership to Vincent's Club on King Edward Street (started in 1863) requires possession of a Full or Half Blue, as well as intellectual and social standing to match. Women members were, finally, accepted in 2016. (No, that's not a typo.)

"Tennis," he said, a contented smile on his face.

"*Really?*" Ursula couldn't help but sound amazed.

"If you are implying, dearest Ursula, as you seem to be, that I am far too rotund a personage to dash around a tennis court with any effectiveness—"

"No, no, I didn't mean that at all," said Ursula, hoping she hadn't been rude. "I wasn't saying—"

"—that I'm too fat to play tennis? Well, you're completely right. I'm far too pudgy. I got my Blue for sitting. On the umpire's chair. It's simply lovely up there, bossing everyone about. Everyone comes to my matches. Apparently I'm more entertaining than John McEnroe."

Horatio ordered snowball cocktails for the girls and then went on, "Anyway, Ursula, I don't know what you're doing out enjoying yourself so close to your story deadline."

"Actually, I said I'd meet Jago here for a drink—"

"Woooooh! Do be careful, Ursula. He can be dreadfully lecherous."

"No, honestly, it's all fine," she insisted. "It's an official no-strings-attached drink."

"That old cliché," chuckled Horatio.

"Really, I'm only staying for a bit tonight. I've got to get back to work on the story. I've got tons of notes to go through."

Just then, Jago sauntered up to them. He was wearing the stripy jacket of the Half Blues.

"Ah, my star reporter!" he said, pecking Ursula on the cheek, throwing an arm around her shoulders, and squeezing her into his chest. Horatio whispered in her ear, "*No strings attached.* Ha!"

"Solved the case yet?" said Jago. He sounded as though he was half joking.

"Almost," replied Ursula, removing his arm.

"You think you know who did it?" he said, suddenly serious. "*Who?*"

Ursula looked around at the room, which was now bulging with guests. She didn't intend to go into the details of India's murder with so many people within earshot.

"I can't say yet."

"You know how to drive a man crazy, don't you, Ursula?" said Jago, looking at her lasciviously.

Ursula said nothing. She just looked coolly at the boy. She didn't want him getting any ideas about attaching any strings whatsoever to her. Finally, Jago said awkwardly, "Anyway, yeah, I'm looking forward to reading your copy on Sunday morning. Do come and use the typewriters in the *Cherwell* offices, won't you?"

"Sure," she said noncommittally.

Secretly, Ursula was not convinced she would be anywhere near the *Cherwell* typewriters by tomorrow afternoon. The final, crucial question in the mystery of India's death—whether or not Mary Crimshaw had died in childbirth—still remained unanswered. She had stopped by the porter's lodge every half hour that afternoon, hoping that the Register Office in Leeds had called back and left a message—but there was nothing.

"Good," said Jago. "I do like a reporter who keeps to their deadline. Right, I'll go get another round."

Jago set off towards the bar, and Ursula turned back to her friends, who were in the midst of an important conversation.

"Hey, what should I wear for my date tomorrow morning, with Next Duke?" Nancy was asking Horatio.

"It might be very cold. A tweed suit would be ideal," he suggested helpfully.

"Oh God, that sounds *so* old-school classy. Next Duke would like that, right? But where do I get one at this time in the evening?"

"I can lend you my old tweed hacking jacket," offered Ursula. "It's in my room."

"Okay. That sounds totally authentic. What about the pants?"

"Sorry, I don't have tweed trousers. But I've got a pair of jodhies you can borrow."

"Jodhies? What are those? They sound ugly," Nancy declared.

"You know, jodhpurs . . . riding breeches. I've got Plain Granny's old ones, from when she was a girl. They look like wool pantaloons. They're beautiful."

"Okay, I'll take your word for it," said Nancy.

"The main thing is, you'll be warm. You just need some boots as well," added Ursula.

"I'm good for boots. Can you leave the clothes in my room to-night?"

"Sure," said Ursula. "I'm going back now to write. Horatio will walk me, won't you?"

When Horatio dropped Ursula back at the porter's lodge about thirty minutes later, Deddington Jr. was at his station. Nancy was right, Ursula thought to herself; he did look uncannily similar to the photograph of Lord Brattenbury as a young man that they had seen by his bedside yesterday. Ursula wondered what would happen when he discovered his true identity. She felt uneasy, knowing something so crucial about him that he didn't.

"Evening, Miss Flowerbutton," he said when she entered. "Some-one telephoned, about half an hour ago. Said it was urgent."

He handed her a note, which read:

No certificate found. No need to send postal order. Leeds Register Office.

She stared at it, then read the words over again: "No certificate found." No death certificate meant no death. Mary Crimshaw was not dead.

Ursula suddenly felt fearful, excited, and nervous all at once. Had she discovered who the murderer was? *Was* it Alice? Was a murderous scout, Ursula wondered as she walked hesitantly towards the Gothic Buildings, lurking somewhere between the lodge and Ursula's room, hiding in the shadows, waiting to kill again?

Perhaps, thought Ursula, she should tell Trott her suspicions and let him deal with it. The situation was dangerous. But . . . could Alice *really* be a cold-blooded killer? Alice seemed so nice, with her kind words, cozy cups of tea, and jolly aprons. She'd been so friendly with India. If Ursula told Trott the latest developments and it turned out that Alice was innocent, she could be landing her helpful scout in undeserved trouble.

In any case, there was nothing Ursula could do at this hour. She decided the best course of action would be to ask Alice some leading questions when she came to clean tomorrow morning after the six a.m. rowing session. Perhaps the scout would say something incriminating. Or else clear herself of suspicion completely.

In the meantime, back in her room, Ursula jotted down the new clues in her notebook, trying to prepare for writing the article on Saturday afternoon.

—Mary Crimshaw is not dead. True.

—Mary Crimshaw is real mother of Nicholas Deddington. True.

—Is Alice Blythe Mary Crimshaw? Maybe.

—Nicholas Deddington is illegitimate heir to Lord B.? Very likely.

—If Mary Crimshaw wanted her biological son to inherit, she had motive to kill India. Possible.

—Am I wrong about it all? Possible. After all, how could someone who dusts with such dedication be a murderess?

By ten o'clock, Ursula was done for the night. She put her notes carefully into the folder on her desk. It was only then that she noticed a brown paper bag sitting on her bed. What on earth was that, she wondered, and who had left it there? Ursula approached the bag with caution, picked it up, and opened it. Inside, something was glistening. India's tiara! She reached her hand inside the bag and pulled out the jeweled headpiece. There was a note with it, from Claire Potter. It read:

Knicker drawer no longer as safe as previously thought. CP.

No way. Did Claire Potter have a boyfriend? *Already?* Ursula examined the tiara curiously. Inside, she noticed a stamp. This must be the hallmark, she thought, trying to read the tiny letters. She made out the words "Butler & Wilson." Butler and Wilson! Ursula couldn't help but laugh. She had heard of Butler & Wilson, an ultra-trendy costume jewelry shop in London where Chelsea girls shopped for gigantic diamanté earrings, golden chokers, and glittery bangles. Claire needn't have worried about stealing a family heirloom. India had fooled everyone with her fake tiara. Ursula would hand it into the police as soon as she could. She'd just say it had mysteriously appeared in her room, which was, after all, completely true.

Before bed, Ursula put out her old riding outfit for Nancy. The hacking jacket—dark brown tweed with a pale blue windowpane check—looked perfect. The jodhpurs, on the other hand, had an old grass stain on the left knee. She'd have to go wash and tumble dry them in Monks' Cottages before she went to bed. Nancy wasn't the sort of girl to be seen on a first date in grubby clothing.

Twenty minutes later, as Ursula sat in the laundry awaiting the jodhpurs, doubts crept into her mind. What if Alice wasn't Mary Crimshaw? Ursula and Nancy had no real, concrete proof that she was, except for her Derby accent and the fact that she used the word "bairn" for baby. Her rubber gloves *could* place her at the scene of the murder, but no more so than any of the scouts in college. Maybe the sodium dimethyldithiocarbamate hadn't come from the killer at all. Maybe it had been on the glass before the killer touched it, transmitted when the glass had been washed or dried up before Wenty's party.

Perhaps this whole journalism thing, the *Cherwell* article, the dream of being a writer one day—well, maybe it wasn't going to happen. If Ursula didn't know the identity of India's murderer, she didn't have a story, and that was that. She consoled herself with the gruesome thought that maybe there'd be other murders while she was studying in Oxford with which she'd have better luck.

Ursula didn't get back to the Gothic Buildings with the dry jodhies until close to midnight. Just as she was about to walk from the stone passage across the courtyard, she saw someone coming out of the archway of her staircase. Alarmed, Ursula scurried into the shadows of Staircase A and hid, watching.

There was no mistaking those yellow rubber gloves or that flowery apron. It was Alice. But what on earth was she doing in college at close to midnight, with her rubber gloves on? Surely it was much too late for cleaning, even for the most enthusiastic scout? Alice swiftly exited Staircase C, looking behind her as though to check no one had seen her. She then hurried straight past Staircase A, without seeing Ursula, and along the passage back towards Great Quad. She'd looked nervous, thought Ursula, who had never seen the usually jolly-faced scout in a fluster until now. Maybe she *was* Mary Crimshaw.

Once upstairs, Ursula left the clean jodhies, tweed jacket, and a plaid shirt in Nancy's room, hoping her friend's sunrise breakfast would be as romantic as Nancy dreamed, before going back to her own quarters. As she walked into her room she noticed that two pages of her *Cherwell* story notes had fallen onto the floor beneath her desk. She was sure she hadn't left them like that. She picked them up and put them back in the folder, carefully closing the cover.

Before she went to bed, she checked—several times—that she had locked the door to her bedroom. She was properly scared. As she lay in bed, fretting, fearful, Ursula started to wonder if the idea of confronting Alice alone tomorrow was a sensible one. She resolved to ring Trott from the pay phone downstairs the minute she woke up. In the end, the only thing that got her off to sleep was thinking about rowing practice. Counting oars, Ursula soon discovered, was as good a cure for sleeplessness as counting sheep.

Chapter 39

Ursula was having some kind of nightmare. She couldn't wake up from it. "Uuughh-ggghhh!" she yelped. "Uggrrrrhhhh." She couldn't breathe in her dream. Air—there was no air! If only she could wake up, she could breathe. She wriggled. Struggled. But still she couldn't wake up. A pillow was being pressed over her face. Someone was suffocating her. She thought she heard an alarm clock ringing. But she still couldn't wake up. She was still in the nightmare. Not breathing. Choking.

Maybe Ursula had passed out for a few seconds. Maybe she'd dreamed that she'd fainted. Someone was banging on her door in her nightmare—*rap-rap-rap*!

"Ursula! You're late for rowing!"

But Ursula couldn't answer. She couldn't move her head. She realized she wasn't dreaming. She was in fact awake, and she was being smothered. Someone really did have a pillow over her face. Someone was trying to kill her. She tried to move her arms, to hit her attacker, but they were pinned to her chest by someone's body.

Suddenly there was a loud cracking sound. The attacker's grip loosened. A body collapsed like lead on top of her, and Ursula could finally move her head. Gasping for breath, she pushed the body off of her. It thudded to the ground. Ursula looked up. There, looming above her, oar in hand, was Moo.

"Didn't quite mean to, Ursula," said Moo, "but I think I've just bumped off our scout." She sounded about as apologetic as a Girl Guide who'd just caught a mouse in a trap. "I came in to wake you up for rowing and found Alice trying to suffocate you. So I decided to go for a massive bonk on the head."

Ursula struggled up in bed and looked at the floor next to her. There lay Alice, slumped unconscious. Her head was oozing blood. Ursula couldn't help noticing the bright yellow rubber gloves on her hands.

"I can't believe she tried to kill me," Ursula croaked, her voice almost gone after the shock of the attack.

"But why would Alice want to kill *you*?!" gasped Moo.

Everything made sense to Ursula now. But in her dazed state, her thoughts came out in a jumbled garble.

"That's why she was always tidying my desk," Ursula told Moo. "She was secretly reading everything I wrote down about India's murder."

"What are you talking about?" Moo looked concerned.

"I saw Alice coming out of our staircase late last night. She must have been in here, reading my notes. I found two pages on the floor—I never would have left them there."

"Are you sure you're not concussed?" Moo asked.

"No, I'm fine. Once Alice knew that I knew she was actually Mary Crimshaw, the mother of the illegitimate heir to the Brattenbury estates, she had to get rid of me."

"Why would someone called Mary Crimshaw pretend she was Alice?" asked Moo. She looked completely and utterly confused.

"No, Alice was pretending she *wasn't* Mary Crimshaw," Ursula corrected her. "She murdered India and tried to frame Mrs. Deddington."

Suddenly the scout stirred and gingerly lifted her bloodied head. "I only wanted to get my son what was rightfully his," she whimpered before flopping to the floor again.

Moo then offered, "I'm jolly good at boating knots. Do you have a belt?"

Without waiting for a response, Moo rifled in Ursula's closet, dug out a couple of Ursula's belts, and cheerfully tied them around Alice's hands and feet.

"Someone better call the police," she said. "Deddington Jr.'s in the porter's lodge. He can do it."

"No. I'll ring from the pay phone downstairs," said Ursula.

Knowing what she did, she didn't think it was fair to ask Deddington Jr. to turn in the woman who would soon be revealed as his birth mother to the police for murder. Ursula threw on her dressing gown. Just as she stepped on to the threshold of the landing, a loud scream came from Nancy's room. The door flew open and Nancy appeared, wearing Ursula's riding gear, which she had imaginatively teamed with a pair of very impractical high-heeled yellow suede boots. She looked absolutely terrified.

"Ursula!" shrieked Nancy. "I've made a terrible mistake. Alice isn't the killer at all."

"What?!" cried Ursula.

"This weird street person showed up in my room at six o'clock this morning carrying champagne glasses and a bottle of Dom Pérignon, claiming to be the next Duke of Dudley. But it's not him. It's an impostor. I think he wanted to kill me, just like he killed India, with the champagne saucer."

"Where is he?" said Moo, rushing out of Ursula's room and into Nancy's, brandishing her bloodied oar.

Nancy pointed at the wardrobe. "I shut him in there and locked it."

A hammering came from the inside of the wardrobe.

"Could someone please let me out? I promise I am the next Duke of Dudley, and I have no interest in murdering the lovely American girl I met at Wenty's party," wailed a muffled voice.

"What does he look like?" asked Ursula. She suddenly remembered the moment at Wenty's party when Nancy had spilled champagne over Next Duke and Otto had laughed mischievously.

"His clothes are full of holes and he's got hardly any hair," Nancy told her.

"Sounds just like a duke-in-waiting to me," said Ursula, unlocking the door to the wardrobe.

"What are you doing?" screeched Nancy.

"He didn't kill India," said Ursula as a scruffy-looking boy stumbled out, glasses and champagne bottle in hand. "You were right about Alice. She *is* Mary Crimshaw. She tried to suffocate me this morning."

"No!" gasped Nancy.

"Don't worry," said Moo. "I saved the day. That's the whole point of being head girl."

Ursula recognized the boy from the wardrobe immediately. He was the rather country-bumpkinish young man who'd been standing by the fireplace when Nancy had been flirting with the tall, dark, handsome undergrad she'd assumed was the next Duke of Dudley. Ursula had wondered at the time whether the handsome guy had been a little too good to be true—no one was that good-looking *and* the heir to a dukedom. How devilish of Otto to allow Nancy to carry on thinking he was!

"Hello," said the scruffy boy. Horatio was right. Next Duke did have a Paddington Bear quality about him.

"Hi," said Ursula. "Are you okay?"

"I was expecting the next Duke of Dudley," said Nancy.

"Well, I *am* the next Duke of Dudley," replied the boy. "Who did you think I was?"

Slowly, the truth started to dawn on Nancy.

"I'm so . . . sorry," she stuttered, completely mortified. "There's been a terrible mistake. I thought the next Duke of Dudley was someone else."

Next Duke looked bereft.

"I thought you were . . . *you*," he said, downcast.

Nancy smiled at him, charmed. "But your idea for a sunrise date in a meadow was *very* cute."

"It's going to be a beautiful dawn," said Next Duke. "Awful shame to miss it."

Ursula saw Nancy flush a little.

"Yes . . ." she said.

"Would you like to see it . . . with—with me?" he mumbled.

"Actually, I would," she replied, a dreamy smile coming over her face.

Next Duke looked overjoyed by Nancy's response. Then he said, taking in her equestrian look, "I'm afraid we'll be walking. We could ride another time."

"I'm psyched!" said Nancy. Then she turned to Ursula and added, "You will remember to make an excuse for me when you get to the river, won't you?"

"Actually, I need someone to make an excuse for me," said Ursula, who now looked pleadingly at Moo.

"Just this once," she agreed. "I suppose being attacked by a blood-thirsty scout is an acceptable excuse for getting off games."

"No, it's not that, I'm not hurt," Ursula insisted.

"What is it then?" asked Moo.

"I've got an article to write. I've barely started it and I've got to hand it in first thing tomorrow. Everyone, will you guard Alice in my room while I go to the pay phone? I need to call the police."

As Ursula rushed down the stairs, she thought about India's tragic end. Murdered for nothing more than money. Killed for being a Yar. How sad that no one would ever see her perform Shakespeare. What were those famous words the ghost of Hamlet's father had said? "Murder most foul." Indeed, thought Ursula as she dialed 999, India's murder was most foul. The phone rang only once before someone picked up.

"Hello," said Ursula, "I'd like to report the capture of a murderess."

THE END

(ALMOST . . .)

Champagne Set Murder

cont. from Page 1

BY URSULA FLOWERBUTTON

After I telephoned the police on Saturday morning, I returned to my room, where Algernon Dalkeith, aka the next Duke of Dudley, and Nancy Feingold (now holding hands), as well as Felicia Evenlode-Sackville were guarding Alice Blythe. The scout, whose real name is Mary Crimshaw, claimed that she had never intended to commit murder. Her plan had been to blackmail India Brattenbury.

She said, "I was going to tell India about Nicholas. I'd threaten to tell the college authorities about her affair with a famous don if she didn't promise to cut him into her inheritance."

Crimshaw thought her moment had arrived on Sunday night. After overhearing Wentworth Wychwood commiserating to Otto Schuffenecker that India had gone to the aforementioned don's rooms, the scout realized that if she caught India and the don together she could put her blackmailing plan into effect.

Having cleaned up Wychwood's party and bidden Mrs. Deddington good-bye, Crimshaw removed Wychwood's bloody towel from his laundry basket and put it in her apron pocket. (She claims she was planning to wash it at home to prevent staining.)

Around three a.m., Crimshaw snuck into the don's rooms, where she found India alone, passed out on the chaise longue. Noticing a broken champagne saucer in the girl's left hand, she went to clear it up. As she picked up the sharp, broken piece of the saucer, she was convulsed by a terrible thought.

Crimshaw says, "I thought, wouldn't it be simpler for Nicholas if India was gone altogether?"

Wearing her rubber gloves, Crimshaw cut the girl's throat with the shard of glass. She claims that India was so drunk that she didn't stir, despite the violence of the injury inflicted upon her.

Crimshaw then dabbed Wychwood's towel in the blood on India's neck and concealed it in the chimney, believing she could use it later to frame fellow scout Mrs. Linda Deddington. When the towel was found, suspicion would initially fall on Wychwood. But Crimshaw would tell the police that Mrs. Deddington was the last person seen with the towel, thereby placing her at the scene of the crime. As the adoptive mother of the illegitimate heir to the Brattenbury fortune, Mrs. Deddington would appear to have motive and opportunity. Crimshaw planned to plant the piece of broken glass that she had used as the murder weapon among Mrs. Deddington's effects, but never found the opportunity.

"Nicholas would have inherited one day. He'd never have known what really happened," insisted Crimshaw. "I would have disappeared. Just like I had when I was fourteen. I was 'dead' then. I could be dead again."

Moments later, DI Trott and a constable arrived and arrested the scout.

As Crimshaw was led away by police, Nancy Feingold said tearfully, "So sad. I'm really gonna miss Alice. Those hospital corners she did on our beds were totally awesome."

JOHN EVELYN'S DIARY
by Horatio Bentley

Freshers—Where did they come from? Why didn't they stay there? I am usually unsympathetic to Oxford's scarf-wearing, kettle-wielding newbies. But after an eventful 1st Week in which the University was shaken by the murder of Christminster beauty **Lady India Brattenbury**, I can reveal that the delightful pair of Freshettes who unraveled the identity of the murderess have turned heads.

The crime-busting duo are as beautiful as they are brainy. American student **Nancy Feingold** (affectionately known to her (new) friends as "Lawnmower" — her cash comes from her parents' gardening-tools empire) was spotted dressed in saucy riding kit on Saturday morning, cuddling up to Algernon Dalkeith on a mossy knoll in Port Meadow. He is said to be infatuated with the New Jersey native, who has changed his nickname from "Paddington" to plain old "Next Duke."

Nancy Feingold's bestie, **Ursula Flowerbutton**, author of the riveting article on the preceding pages, also found time to dabble in romance on Saturday night. Despite the attempt made on her life earlier that day, this diarist noticed Miss Flowerbutton boogying enthusiastically to the romantic twang of "The Love Cats" at the Playpen, the Saturday evening nightclub favored by the **Champagne Set**. She started the night dancing with Christminster disco diva **Eghosa Kolokoli**, but *Cherwell* editor **Jago Summers** cut in, stealing her away as soon as was politely possible.

When **Lord Wentworth Wychwood** arrived at the club, just after being released from Oxford police station, he was overheard asking Ursula to dance. Flowerbutton refused the dishy earl, saying she had to leave. When he asked her why, Ursula only answered, mysteriously, "To write my essay."[*]

---

[*] Ursula *did* finish her essay on "The Apocalyptic Vision of the Early Covenanters" in time for her tutorial on the Monday morning of 2nd Week. Dr. Dave's only comment on her effort: "This isn't high school, Miss Flowerbutton." Devastated (until now she had been a straight-A student), Ursula promised herself that she really would—honestly, absolutely, definitely, cross her heart hope to die, stick a needle in her eye—spend 2nd Week in the library working much harder on her next essay.[†]

[†] Unless someone else was murdered.

ACKNOWLEDGMENTS

Thank you so much to everyone who has helped me research, write, edit, and publish this novel. I would like to thank especially: Detective Chief Inspector Gareth Bevan; John Smith, chief executive officer of police and crime commissioner at Avon and Somerset; Tom Bailey; Tara Lawrence; Lisa Wheden; Miranda Elvidge; Caitlyn Rainey; Miles Guilford; Dr. Hugh White, retired forensic pathologist; Professor Peter Frankopan; Romain Reglade; Roberto Wheedon; the staff of the Oxford Union Library and the Codrington Library; Professor Marcus du Sautoy; Max Long; all at *Cherwell Newspaper*; Katie Bond; Christine Knight-Maunder; Kara Baker; Jonathan Burnham; Emily Griffin; Alexandra Pringle; Rebecca Carter; Luke Janklow; Jonathan Bate, Paula Byrne, and all at Worcester College Oxford; Eve MacSweeney; Crispin Jameson; Zac Posen; Jo Allinson; my brothers and sisters, Lucy, Fred, Alice, Josh, and Tom; my early readers, Victoria Elvidge, Catherine Ostler, my husband, Toby Rowland; our daughters, Ursula and Tess; and my mother, Valerie.

A very special thanks to my great aunt Rosey Goad, who was the great P. D. James's editor. When I asked her advice about writing crime, she told me: "Plum, don't have more than two bodies—it will confuse the reader. And never have more than one secret staircase."

ABOUT THE AUTHOR

Plum Sykes is a novelist and fashion journalist who frequently contributes to American *Vogue*. She studied modern history at Worcester College, Oxford, which inspired her memoir *Oxford Girl*, and is the author of the *New York Times* bestsellers *Bergdorf Blondes* and *The Debutante Divorcée*. She lives in London with her husband and two daughters.